Cynthia R Mid-
Glamorgan d in
Porthcawl, s the
setting for her novels. She has been a teacher and a journalist, contributing to a variety of magazines and newspapers and also to radio. She has written two previous novels, *The Running Tide* and *Upon Stormy Downs*, and is at present working on the fourth in this series about Welsh village life.

Also by Cynthia S. Roberts

The Running Tide
Upon Stormy Downs

A Wind from the Sea

Cynthia S. Roberts

KNIGHT

First published in 1989
by HEADLINE BOOK PUBLISHING PLC

First published in paperback in 1989
by HEADLINE BOOK PUBLISHING PLC

This edition published 2000 by
Knight an imprint of Caxton Publishing Group

10 9 8 7 6 5 4 3 2 1

ISBN 1 84067 265 X

Typeset by
Colset Private Limited, Singapore

Printed and bound in Great Britain by
J. H. Haynes & Co. Ltd., Sparkford, Somerset

Caxton Publishing Group
20 Bloomsbury Street
London
WC1B 3QA

To William E. Lloyd Rees,
Consultant Ophthalmic Surgeon,
with my gratitude and admiration
this book is dedicated.

Chapter One

All day the sky had been bruised and menacing, the keen edge to the wind honed to a cutting sharpness. Joshua Stradling, feeling it scythe through the thickness of his caped coat, urged his horse onwards, anxious to reach home before nightfall. His fingers upon the reins were numbed and unfeeling, but the grey, intelligent and perceptive, responded to the merest touch, sparing no effort.

The windswept heights of Stormy Downs were scarcely a place to linger. A bleak haunt for foxes and birds of prey; desolate and unfriendly to hunter and hunted.

The young constable saw again the starkness of the quarry face, walls rising sheer, and the man he had pursued flung awkwardly as a child's toy in a rage to its rocky floor. Yet, it had been flesh and blood that he turned to the sky: mutilated, grotesque, the eyes wide and sightless. Joshua shivered, less from the cold than from memory. His hands must have tightened involuntarily on the reins, for the mare, sensitive to his mood, hesitated, stumbling awkwardly upon the rough track.

With a word of reassurance, the grey was calmed; he could have wished his own fears as swiftly eased. The dead man had been an ungodly wretch: murderer and wrecker, a worthless husk. God alone knew what violence he had wrought. It was from the family of one of his victims that Joshua now rode, having foolishly ventured abroad with a gift for the boy Dafydd's birthday. Joshua had been glad to see the child's face alight with innocent pleasure at the gift, a fishing rod, skilfully fashioned by Dafydd's friend and mentor, the old fisherman Jeremiah Fleet. With the widow Crocutt smiling, and the babe and infants clutching their sweetmeats, and Dafydd's glowing pleasure as he examined his prize, it had been a happy family scene. Yet, even as he watched, Joshua was seeing the awful desolation of the great barn, with Jem Crocutt's body skewered upon an upright by the tines of a hayfork, and the boy's face anguished and bloodless as the dead man's own. They were hard and evil times, Joshua reflected, when an eight-year-old boy was forced to assume the mantle of a man and become provider. Yet, Dafydd had done so, unwilling to see the smallholding, which had been wrested from the rocky land, reverting to wildness, or the family set apart in poorhouse and orphanage.

The first flakes of snow had begun to fall now, soft and gentle, and with their falling the iciness of the wind had mellowed. By the time the mare, firm-footed and calm, had reached Dan-y-Graig Hill, the snow had formed a carpet, silencing her hooves, and horse and rider were isolated in an unfamiliar landscape, without sight or sound.

It was with relief that Joshua turned the mare under the archway to the Crown Inn, and into the cobbled yard.

Ossie, the little bowed ostler, hurried out of the stables to take the grey, shadowed as through a veil, snowflakes settling upon his eyelashes and hair, and in the weathered creases of his skin.

'You have cut it fine, Joshua! I feared the mare might

wander from the path and stumble into some bog or quarry.' His face was pinched, anxious.

'I thank you for your concern, my friend,' said Joshua gently, 'but the mare is dependable. I would stake my life on her.'

'As you have, many times!' agreed Ossie, smiling. Yet his eyes remained curiously perturbed and his hands tightened nervously upon the reins as Joshua dismounted, stamping the snow from his boots.

'Come!' commanded Joshua. 'Tell me what ails you. I may hope that it is not my safe return which sets you in such a flux?'

Ossie hesitated, then blurted, 'You will think me a stupid, ignorant fellow . . . a prey to maidenish fancies.'

'Never!' Joshua declared, disturbed by the little ostler's agitation. 'You know how I value your advice and opinion.'

'The stage . . .' confessed Ossie, 'I have fears for the coach.'

'It is overdue?'

'Yes, by an hour and more. And Doonan and his bride, Rosa, upon it, returning from their visit to his family in Ireland . . . Rebecca's wedding gift to them.'

Joshua thought fleetingly of the dark face and remarkable blue eyes of Rebecca de Breos, the girl he was pledged to marry, before saying reassuringly, 'The storm will prove no danger, I swear. The coachman needs but to seek shelter. There are so many inns and posting houses upon the way, they will bed down in some hostelry or farm and, like as not, be monstrously overcharged for a straw mattress amidst the hogs!'

Ossie shook his head stubbornly, removing a hand from the reins to wipe the melting snow from his face. 'Last night I slept fitfully, my mind still dwelling upon a sick horse I had been tending. I was wide awake, I swear, when a bird flew against my window-pane, battering itself upon the glass again and again . . . the *Aderyn Corff*: harbinger of death.'

Joshua stared at him in silence. Ossie was the sanest, least superstitious, man he knew. 'Perhaps,' he ventured at length, 'you were alarmed by yesterday's newspaper reading upon the village green. It preyed upon your mind. I recollect your distress when you told me of that unhappy coachman who perished in the blizzard upon Dartmoor.'

Ossie shook his head saying quietly, 'It is not things natural which I fear, Joshua. The bird had neither feathers nor wings.'

It might have set Ossie's fears to rest had he but known that, at that very moment, the stage-coach of which he spoke was surmounting Three Steps Hill and approaching Tythegston Court, the manor house of the squire and justice, the Reverend Robert Knight. Moreover, every one of its passengers was, mercifully, intact. True, they were inordinately crowded, for the two young blades who had so vociferously claimed their places 'in the attic', next to the coachman, had been forced by the snow to vacate their perch and find shelter within. Consequently, the original six inside passengers, who had so far rattled and jolted in individual discomfort, were now wedged in solid suffering, unable even to bounce and cushion themselves from pot-hole and rut. Cramped and numbed by cold, they were wretchedly silent, save for an involuntary groan or cry. Their feet, under their covering of heaped straw, might have been shod in ice, and the intimacy of extra bodies gave off not warmth, but the heavy odour of unwashed flesh, ammonia, and stale victuals and liquor upon foetid breath.

The big red-headed Irishman, Doonan, had taken his bride, Rosa, upon his knee, less out of courtesy to the interlopers than from prudence. If she were forced into indecent proximity to male flesh, then he would rather it were his. Certainly, his enormous muscled body, wild eyes and raw hams of fists would have discouraged advances from any but a declared lunatic.

One of the young gentlemen, banished from the box, had so far forgotten himself as to whisper to his companion that she was 'as pretty a piece of muslin' as he had ever clapped eyes upon. Certainly, with her pale translucent skin, hair the colour of sun-bleached corn and delicacy of features, Rosa was lovely enough to turn the head of any man. Yet, incredibly, she had eyes only for Cavan Doonan, the rough, fiery quarryman who had taken her to his heart and bed. Being so securely lodged in his heart, it was her own sweet bed Rosa yearned to be lodged in now. She would not have forgone the visit to Ireland for the world, and more, and the memory of the spontaneous warmth and gaiety of her welcome would bring sunshine to many a cold winter's day. She glanced at the high window of the coach, seeing the blur of falling snow: flakes soft as curled goose feathers against the early dusk.

The dark, cadaverous gentleman seated opposite – for gentleman he indubitably was, despite the shabbiness of his clothes – stirred in his sleep and awoke with a start and a cry, only to recollect himself and glance about with a half smile and a mumbled apology. Rosa, covertly observing him, wondered what dream had made him cry aloud and why his eyes had opened wide and fearful before realisation of his circumstances came. Certainly, with his saturnine features and reserve, he was the most interesting of their fellow passengers. The two young bucks from the box were still wet behind the ears, giggling and posturing like moon-struck maidens, their skin and features as bland and unmanly. She smiled, thinking of Cavan and the unexpected gentleness of his warm, hard-muscled body, and snuggled closer to him for comfort, arms encircling his bull-like neck.

The old countrywoman, wedged uncomfortably between one of the young blades and the gentleman who had just awakened, smiled indulgently at Rosa, and settled the wooden cage containing a goose more comfortably upon her ample lap. Crabbed with age and infirmity she might be, but memory stayed sharp. It was flesh which blurred, not feelings. Why, she thought complacently, she could remember as clearly as if it were yesterday how Elias came . . .

A sudden cry from the coachman, raw and anguished, pierced her pleasurable introspection. There was a fierce confusion of sound and movement as the carriage jolted and shuddered, the horses plunging and slithering in the soft snow, harness and horseflesh tangling as the coachman battled desperately to bring them to a stop. For a moment it seemed that the startled beasts, crazed with terror, might bolt and overturn the coach. It swayed perilously and old lady and goose pitched forward to the floor with a scream and a hissing blur of feathers as the goose escaped, adding to the confusion. Rosa clung to Cavan so wildly that she all but choked the breath from his body as the carriage drew to a bone-jerking halt.

There was barely time to disentangle limbs and parcels and heave the old lady back into her seat, clutching the recaptured goose, which was, mercifully, dazed and unresisting, before the carriage door was wrenched open. There was a moment of incredulous silence as the passengers glimpsed through the thickening snow the highwayman upon a chestnut mare, a pistol held firm in his hand, as he dismounted crying, with the barest hint of amusement in his voice, 'Stand and Deliver!'

It was a monstrous hoax, the passengers thought in relief. Some local prankster seeking a tale for the ale-houses and inns.

They were soon disabused.

The eyes behind the slits in the black mask were steely, uncompromising; the voice, although muffled by the silk scarf, incisive as the highwayman commanded, 'Ladies, you will surrender your jewellery, if you please, and you, gentlemen, your valuables . . .'

His pistol lifted slightly with the tone of his voice. 'At once, I say!'

Doonan made to move threateningly, Rosa still clinging to him, but the dark gentleman leaned forward, laying a restraining hand upon the Irishman's arm, and said urgently beneath his breath, 'No, sir! I beg of you, you have too much to lose . . .'

Doonan nodded, subsiding, his face flushed with fury at his own impotence. The old lady, hampered by the goose, had somehow managed to take a canvas pouch from under the voluminous folds of her petticoats and thrust it, unopened, at the young blade sitting rigidly at her side. He took it from her wordlessly, never taking his eyes from the highwayman's pistol, face pallid and sweating.

'You, sir,' instructed the highwayman, 'gather it all together in this.' He tossed him a leather pouch. 'And be quick about it, lest you feel a bellyfull of lead.'

The young man, trembling uncontrollably, did as he was commanded, adding his own stock pin and ring to his companion's gold repeater watch. Doonan, with ill grace and not a few muttered oaths, surrendered a purse of gold half-sovereigns, and the pale etiolated clergyman beside him, and his sallow-faced wife, hurriedly divested themselves of their few meagre coins and trinkets.

'Now, sir,' the highwayman addressed the saturnine gentleman with insolent deliberation, 'I will relieve you of your valuables.'

'Then, sir,' returned the man, his mouth curving into the barest parody of a smile, 'you relieve me of my one possession.' He removed the silver watch and chain unhurriedly from his waistcoat pocket. 'I have no use for it now. Yet I could wish that the minutes and hours it measures for you bring to your future what it brought to my past . . .'

There was a tense, uncomfortable silence as he handed it to the already overburdened youth, who all but dropped it in his nervous agitation.

'I believe, ma'am,' said the highwayman, the glittering eyes behind the concealing mask turned upon Rosa, 'that you have something to offer me . . .'

Doonan's arms tightened protectively around her.

'No, sir! You are mistaken! I have nothing of interest to you . . .' Rosa had struggled free and stood amidst the straw of the carriage floor, facing him defiantly.

'Indeed, ma'am, you do yourself an injustice!' The highwayman's eyes were amused, assessing. 'You have much to interest any man.' His glance travelled with insolent slowness over her body. 'But your jewellery, if you please.'

'I do not please!' Rosa stamped her foot in vexation, sending a shower of chaff into the air, which made the passengers wheeze and choke.

'Your ring, ma'am!' the highwayman insisted implacably. 'Remove it!'

'No! Never!' Her voice was firm, with no hint of fear. 'This, sir, is my marriage bond, placed upon my finger at the altar; sacred. I will not have it defiled by a common thief!' Her chin lifted stubbornly as she stared at him in contempt.

'Have a care!' His voice was dangerously calm. 'I have been patient long enough in deference to your undoubted charms, but you begin to irk me . . . a dangerous pastime, mistress. Be warned!'

The gun was pointed, now, at her breast.

'You will remove it or I will take it by force, and you . . .'

There was a roar and an oath as Doonan sprang to his feet in blind fury, thrusting Rosa aside so violently that she fell to her knees. The passengers, transfixed in disbelief, saw the Irishman lunge forward to grasp the highwayman's wrist, before a deafening explosion sent Doonan reeling back, eyes surprised and disbelieving. He actually lifted a hand towards his breast as the dark stain disfigured his coat front, then fell awkwardly to lie partly over Rosa's fallen body and partly over the legs of the saturnine gentleman. The highwayman, seemingly unmoved by the tragedy he had wrought, grasped the leather pouch from the young man's unresisting hand, and spurred his horse back, shouting to the coachman upon the box, 'I have one more bullet, sir, to fire. You would do well to remember it!' Then, reining his horse, rode off, all sign of him obliterated swiftly by the curtain of snow.

Within the carriage, the stench of cordite lay heavy upon the air, mixing with the smell of fresh blood, and fear. Rosa was to say, afterwards, that the horror of it was so intense that she actually tasted it in her mouth and breathed it in her nostrils, as if choking in some all-pervading odious fog . . . She remembered that she did not scream. Indeed, she was unable to make a sound; she merely clung wretchedly to Cavan's inert body, willing him to life, praying silently and more desperately than she had ever prayed before.

It was the dark stranger who lifted her bodily from him, giving her into the care of the countrywoman who, in turn, thrust her struggling goose upon the clergyman's whey-faced wife without so much as a 'by your leave', and pressed Rosa to her comforting breast, soothing her like a frightened babe, until the tears flowed freely.

The doctor, for so the dark stranger proved to be, rendered what assistance he might give to the wounded man, attempting to staunch the blood and covering him in hastily gathered cloaks and travelling rugs for warmth. Meanwhile, the distraught coachman attempted to calm the horses, disentangling leaders and wheelers from twisted harness, while bemoaning that such a poor, ill-used stage-company could not afford the services and protection of a guard.

Within minutes, the two young gentlemen, now much subdued in manner and one still trembling and sobbing quietly, were dispatched to the house of the justice nearby, with the news of what had occurred, and with an urgent plea that help be sent for the shot man.

So it was that Leyshon, the Reverend Robert Knight's manservant, and the coachman arrived directly, bearing between them a makeshift stretcher of greatcoats set upon poles, and with a gardener and the justice himself bearing storm lanterns to light their way.

The rest of the passengers and the coachman, revived somewhat by liquor and victuals thoughtfully dispatched from the kitchens of the Court, continued soberly on their journey to the Crown Inn in the ill-fated coach, horses slithering and reluctant, half-blinded by snow. Their flesh ached with cold, and weariness had entered into their very bones as they took the archway into the cobbled yard, silent save for the muted sighing of breath and harness, as some ghostly equipage.

Ossie and a stable lad came forward to greet them, and make them comfortable.

'There has been a shooting!' the coachman called out agitatedly from his perch. 'A highwayman upon the road. A man has been shot!'

Ossie paused, staring up at him in fear. 'Who?'

'The man Doonan. A big Irishman.'

'He is dead?' Ossie's voice was harsh.

'I fear that it is likely. They have taken him to the house of the justice, and his young wife with him, near senseless with shock and grief.'

The stable lad took hold of the reins as Ossie began to uncouple the horses. Sickness burned in the ostler's throat, and he knew not if it was snow or tears that lay damp upon his cheeks as he painstakingly unbuckled the heavy harness. 'I had best tend to the horses,' he said quietly, 'for they are all but frozen, and in sore need of care.'

Joshua, summoned by an urgent message delivered by the justice's groom, set out at once for Tythegston Court upon the grey. It grieved him to override the mare, for she was little rested from the earlier rigours of wind and snow upon Stormy Downs. Now, with darkness already falling and the snow thickening into a blizzard, he knew that he would trust no other to carry him safely. There were horses aplenty at the livery stables, and Ossie had offered him the pick of those at the Crown, yet the ostler had understood and respected Joshua's refusal, murmuring as he saddled the beast, 'Well, my beauty, needs must when the devil drives!'

'I trust,' Joshua called back drily as he rode towards

the arch, 'that you do not speak of my horsemanship, sir!'

'Indeed, no!' shouted Ossie after him. 'For it would not be proper so to insult Beelzebub, although 'tis a rare treat to see a rider with hooves finer than his horse's!'

Joshua, whose exchanges with the little ostler invariably lightened his spirits, was grateful for Ossie's banter, knowing what effort it had cost him to appear so carefree. In truth, Doonan's shooting lay heavily upon the both of them. For all his swaggering, rumbustious ways, the big Irishman was a loyal and valued friend, and there was no one that the constable would have preferred to stand beside him in a battle for life and death. And now, Doonan battled for his own life . . . Joshua sighed, and turned his attention to the road ahead and the swirling, all-enveloping snow. He had resisted Ossie's urging to take a lanthorn upon the way, pleading that both hands and wits were needed merely to stay upon the mare. Already the wind from the sea had swept inland, violent and raw, driving the snow against walls and hedges, flaying his skin until he could believe his face encased in ice. The mare moved more slowly now, hooves sinking into the soft snow, every step and breath a determined effort. They moved blindly in a shrouded world, Joshua knowing only by the fierce gradient and the mare's struggles that they were nearing the summit of Dan-y-Graig hill. With Joshua's urging, and the grey's spirit, a final thrust took them clear, with mount and rider trembling and exultant upon a level with Stormy Downs. Joshua's praise came haltingly through lips stiffened by cold, and he could not be sure that in the wind and deadened silence he even spoke the words aloud. Yet, there was between man and horse such trust and closeness that he felt the exhilaration in her blood as surely as in his own.

Now, all that was needed was the strength and will to

follow the highway until they reached the Court. He could only hope that Dr Mansel had a mount as brave, for with the wind rising and drifting the snow abreast of the hedges, there was no hope of venturing abroad in a carriage. Of one thing Joshua was sure, Mansel would fight to ride through, or perish in the attempt. He had a sudden picture of the plump, little beetle of a man, with his pink and white face, boiled-gooseberry eyes, and pale flyaway hair, and felt the hint of a smile upon his lips. Then, ahead of him, he saw the entrance to Tythegston Court, lanthorns upon its snow-drifted walls reflecting the stone faces of the griffons atop the pillars. Then he felt the aching pleasure of being helped from the saddle, and half led, half carried into the warmth within.

As the wounded Doonan and the bleak little group from the coach had been shepherded into the justice's house, the Reverend Robert Knight had feared that it might already be too late to offer final words of comfort to the dying man. Yet, still the Irishman clung stubbornly to life, seemingly unable to see or hear the feverish activity about him, yet reluctant to leave its clamour. Rosa, still holding his hand as if her own warm blood might force life into his own, thought the cruellest thing of all was to see him so passive, all his brave wildness gone to waste.

Fight, Cavan! she cried silently. For God's sake, and my own, fight! I beg you. You are all of my life. There is nothing without you . . .

The justice, seeing her pale set face and dry eyes, said gently, 'Perhaps, my dear, it would be better if you could rest awhile. I will have a bed prepared for you nearby, where you can be called if –' He broke off awkwardly, his protuberant brown eyes hurt and anxious. 'You will need to conserve your strength.'

'I thank you, sir, but I will neither rest nor sleep. As for strength, I believe that God will give me as much as I shall need to see this night through.'

The Reverend Robert Knight did not insist, moved by the quiet dignity and courage of the young woman who had so lately stood as a bride before the altar of his own church. There was little of that cool, composed delicacy in the woman before him: her eyes dark now with pain, the bodice of her soft grey dress stiffened with Doonan's dark blood, from cradling him to her, and smeared upon her face with the ravages of old tears.

Dear God, he thought humbly, show me the way to tell these people of my caring. I pity them with all my heart, and love them, yet I cannot find the words to bridge the gulf that divides my world and theirs . . . He turned at a light touch upon his arm, his eyes, without the habitual gold-rimmed lenses, soft and unfocussing. 'I fear I have neglected you, sir,' he said, recalling himself, and bowing stiffly to the gaunt-featured stranger who stood waiting beside him, 'I have offered you neither rest nor refreshment, fearing to interrupt the urgency of your ministrations.'

The doctor raised a hand dismissively. 'It is of no account, sir, although,' he smiled fleetingly, 'I confess that I am relieved that he still has need of my ministrations, rather than yours.'

The justice nodded. 'It was provident, sir, that you were upon the coach and able to offer your services, for I fear that your patient is much weakened by shock and loss of blood. But forgive me, doctor, the gravity of the situation has robbed me of the barest of courtesies . . . I confess that I do not even know your name. As for mine –'

'I know your name, sir,' the stranger replied quietly, 'and your occupations as justice and priest. I think that you might well be familiar with mine.' He offered his hand. 'My name is Burrell.'

The justice stared at him for some time in silence, forgetting even the civility of accepting his hand in his surprise and confusion. Then he took it firmly in his own, saying earnestly, 'There are no words, Dr Burrell, that can obliterate, or even salve, the evil that was done to you in this place, for I fear that you were hunted here as ruthlessly as an animal, and upon my orders.'

'You believed me, sir, to be guilty of a murder and acted accordingly, but it is not of that I wish to speak. There are more pressing matters.' He inclined his head towards Doonan, lying inert and barely breathing upon the bed beyond, with Rosa seated watchfully beside him. 'There is need for the bullet to be removed without further delay, if the wound is not to become festering and corrupt. Yet I have no instruments, you understand? With poor makeshift ones, he has but the barest chance of survival, yet, without them, none at all.'

'You ask me to decide?' the justice's voice was bleak, uncertain.

'No. It is already decided. I ask, sir, for your co-operation, and for the help of any in your household.'

The justice nodded, his face troubled. 'Tell me, Dr Burrell, what you require. I shall see that it is provided. But, first, a confession.'

Burrell looked startled, a flush staining his sallow features, as he admitted, 'I thought, sir, for a moment . . .'

Robert Knight smiled in understanding, 'No. We speak at odds. The confession I have in mind is my own.' He hesitated. 'Unwittingly, for I could not have known . . . I ask you to believe that, Dr Burrell –' he broke off uncertainly, at a loss for words.

Burrell waited patiently for him to continue, but there was some unexpected commotion at the main door, followed by the hurried entry of the manservant, Leyshon, who spoke briefly to his master, glancing anxiously in Dr Burrell's direction from time to time.

'It is as I feared,' said Robert Knight nervously. 'I had hoped to spare you this – I had sent word to the Home Office pathologist and surgeon, seeking his help, but believing the storm might prevent him – he is here, sir . . . Mansel. He whose wife perjured her testimony at your trial.'

There was silence between them, with each man's thoughts dwelling upon the woman, now dead, who had committed Burrell to almost a quarter of a century of incarceration under the meanest and most vile of conditions . . . a living death. Burrell had, the justice knew, barely survived with his life and sanity. Small comfort now that Madeleine Mansel had been branded liar and thief: a woman dependent upon laudanum, and so corrupted by its evil that she would murder and sell her body to possess it . . . Indeed, Robert Knight reflected now, grimly, she would even sell her soul.

Burrell was staring at the justice intently, not speaking, when Mansel entered, his plump face aglow with cold, still clutching his silk hat and surgical bag, and stamping the snow from his boots.

He glanced towards Burrell, then stood motionless.

Burrell hesitated only briefly and walked resolutely towards him, hand outstretched, saying, 'There is work to be done, sir. A man is in need of our help. The present is of more relevance than the past.'

Rosa, who had been seated beside her husband, so still that she might have been lifeless, rose to her feet and came towards them. She glanced down, seeing for the first time the blood congealed upon her hands and darkening the bodice of her dress.

'I will go now and make myself clean,' she said quietly, 'for Cavan would want to see me so, when he awakens.'

'Yes,' said Mansel, his eyes fixed not upon Rosa's face but Burrell's, 'one must do what one can . . .'

Chapter Two

Upon the justice's express instructions, a small ante-room had hurriedly been prepared as a rudimentary operating theatre. The kitchen staff were instructed to keep a constant supply of water bubbling upon open fires and stove, and to bring it, upon an instant, with a ready supply of clean boiled cloths and cotton sheets. Leyshon, the justice's manservant, had taken unchallenged command, mobilising the household and staff into a well-drilled army, unobtrusive and efficient. Robert Knight stood by to assist the two surgeons and, beside him, his head gamekeeper and water bailiff, whom he considered to be 'quick to respond to orders, physically strong, and not squeamish' – attributes which, considering the bloodiness of the operation, its urgency, and Doonan's vast strength and fury should he recover consciousness too soon, were essential.

With commendable self-abnegation, the justice had sacrificed a small cask of brandy from his cellar to clean the wound, and to pour hastily down the Irishman's throat, should it be needed. He could have been excused for hoping that it might be spared for more appreciative palates after the operation. In the event, Doonan remained as innocent and unaware as a sleeping babe, to the great relief of those in range of his massive fists and legs. Despite the strength of the bonds which secured him to the table, it seemed likely that he would have snapped them as effortlessly as a spider's thread.

If there had been any awkwardness or reserve between the two doctors, it was soon lost in the delicacy and concentration of their task, and, with the bullet cleanly extracted, and the wound cleaned and padded, there was a sense of relief and camaraderie within the room.

Rosa had been closeted in the small bedroom apportioned to her by the justice, who had sternly forbidden her to leave it until sent word to do so. Dimly aware of the noises and activity below, she wandered restlessly from place to place, occasionally lifting and replacing small trinkets, or smoothing non-existent creases from the bedcover and drapings, in an effort to calm the trembling of her hands and inner agitation. Joshua, accompanied by the justice's housekeeper, came upon her seated upon the dressing stool and staring, unseeing, into the looking glass, her eyes filled with a hurt and desolation which raked him with pity.

'Rosa,' he called softly.

She turned and stared at him silently for a while, then cried, 'Joshua . . . Oh, Joshua, I have been so afraid,' and ran to him, flinging her arms about his neck gratefully, and weeping unrestrainedly. He smoothed her pale hair, whispering words of comfort and holding her close, feeling the wetness of her tears.

'It will be all right, my dear,' he consoled her, stroking her face gently. 'It will be all right, I promise. Cavan is strong, and will fight. He has you to fight for.'

He dried her eyes gently with his kerchief. 'No more tears, for you are a brave and lovely girl, and it would grieve him to see you so.'

'Sir?'

Rosa and Joshua turned as one, to see Leyshon standing

beside the housekeeper in the doorway, his face impassive.

Joshua made to stride towards him, but Rosa cried out sharply. 'No! What is to be said concerns me. I will hear it now.'

'It is over, mistress. The bullet is extracted.' Leyshon's gaunt, lugubrious face widened into a smile. 'There will be harsh days ahead, and need of constant nursing and care . . . but he survives. Thanks be to God, he survives.'

'Thanks be to God!' echoed Joshua fervently, and Rosa, the tears of relief spilling through her fingers and on to her bloodstained bodice, nodded her head.

Robert Knight, when he had offered his services as a surgical assistant to Burrell and Mansel, had done so fully aware that it was his services as priest which might be demanded. It was with relief, tinged, to his shame, with a degree of nausea, that he saw the operation completed. Having first given thanks to God, then, on a more mundane level, to his household staff, he was intent upon restoring himself, the two doctors and Joshua upon the remains of the brandy, and discussing the events of the day.

'You believe, Burrell, that this highwayman lived hereabouts? That he was familiar with this area?'

Burrell's gaunt face was puzzled, reflective. 'That, sir, I cannot say. I know only that from his voice and clothing he was a putative gentleman.'

'Putative?' repeated the justice sharply.

'I mean, sir, that his demeanour was not that of a true gentleman. His treatment of the young lady, Mistress Doonan, was brash to the point of insolence. Her husband was deliberately provoked into attacking him, in order to defend his wife . . . of that, I am sure. The rogue's offensiveness was studied, calculated.'

'Indeed?' Robert Knight's voice was cold. 'A most bloody and distasteful episode. The sooner the man is apprehended, Stradling, the better!'

Joshua muttered agreement.

'There is one disturbing element,' continued Burrell, 'and one which alarms me more than I can say.'

'Its violence?' supplied the justice, nodding.

'More. His complete detachment. He showed no remorse, nor even interest, in Doonan's fate. There was an iciness about him which chilled me –' He broke off awkwardly. 'I have been going over and over it in my own mind, and cannot make sense of it.'

'The shooting?' asked Mansel, who had been listening intently.

'That, and what persuaded him to stop a small provincial stage with poor, undistinguished passengers . . . countryfolk, who could hardly be expected to yield a rich return.'

'And your conclusions?' persisted Mansel quietly.

'That it was executed for pleasure, not gain. That he actually enjoyed the danger, the thrill of possible capture. Even the bloodshed,' he finished helplessly.

There was a moment of tense silence before the justice turned to Joshua, demanding irascibly, 'Well, Stradling? How do you intend to pursue the matter?'

'I fear, sir, that it will not be easy. The blizzard will already have obliterated his tracks, and secured his escape. I have demanded that the coachman holds himself ready to be questioned as soon as I return, and the passengers, too. The coachman will, perhaps, be able to give me a more considered description of the man and his mount, and place the direction in which he rode off. One of the passengers might, conceivably, have stored some piece of knowledge, however trivial, which might be of use.' He was aware that it sounded implausible.

'And afterwards?' asked the justice brusquely.

'One can only assume that in this blizzard he will not ride far, sir. Both he and his mount will soon be exhausted, travelling blindly. I shall call at the inns, farms and livery stables, seeking news of any stranger who has sought an exchange of horse.'

Robert Knight nodded, unimpressed, and turned to Burrell, pressing more brandy upon him, and declaring, 'Since the blizzard shows little sign of abating, it would give me pleasure to accommodate you within my house, sir.' As Burrell hesitated, he continued, 'You would do me a service, for my life here is remote, and I welcome the prospect of congenial company.'

Burrell smiled, saying, 'I accept most willingly, for, in addition, it will give me the opportunity to observe the progress of our patient.'

'Then it is agreed,' said the justice delightedly.

Despite Robert Knight's warm entreaties, both Mansel and Joshua insisted upon returning to Newton, declaring that they were warmly clad and their horses knew every inch of the highway. They would travel together for company and safety. So it was resolved, but not before they had been prevailed upon to dine at the justice's table, their agreement seeing him scurrying to the cellar with his manservant to discuss the choice of wines demanded, while Dr Mansel excused himself to view his patient.

'I believe, sir, that I am to congratulate you,' said Burrell to Joshua when they were alone.

Joshua looked at him perplexed.

'Your engagement, sir. It is for that reason I return, upon the invitation of your fiancée, Miss Rebecca de Breos. You were aware, perhaps, that we have been corresponding over the past months?'

'Yes, sir,' said Joshua uncomfortably, adding stiffly, 'and that she helped you by secreting you in the disused shepherd's hut upon Stormy Downs, against my express wishes.'

'I am relieved that you did not say orders, sir, for I think Miss de Breos is not a young lady who takes kindly to orders, or commands of any kind.'

Burrell's mouth twitched into a smile, and Joshua's in response as he admitted, 'If I have appeared to treat you with reserve, sir, it is because I was not, at that time, aware of your innocence, and feared that her recklessness would lead her into danger.'

Burrell nodded, saying, 'It is proper that you should be concerned for her, sir. She is a truly remarkable woman, Stradling. I owe her my life,' he said simply. 'More, I owe her what I am today. For so great was my fury and bitterness, I would certainly have killed both Mansel and his wife.'

Joshua, returning the intensity of his gaze, knew that the man spoke but the truth.

Burrell continued, 'You know, perhaps, that my work has been in London of late?'

'Yes, Rebecca told me of your commitment to the cholera victims . . . the epidemic.' Joshua hesitated. 'It was brave of you, sir.'

'Not brave. Expedient. There is no courage required if you have nothing to lose.' Burrell's voice was dry, toneless. Then he asked, more gently, 'Are you aware that Rebecca sent money to provide care and shelter for those most desperately in need? The dying and the homeless?'

'No,' Joshua confessed, adding carefully, 'it does not surprise me, for she has set up a fund here, in the three hamlets, to help paupers and the lunatic parishioners wrenched from families who are too poor to support and care for them. She has known the anguish of poverty herself, sir, although her condition has, mercifully, changed.'

'Yes,' agreed Burrell, 'it is a far cry from being Rebecca, the simple cockle-gatherer, to being the granddaughter of Sir Matthew de Breos of Southerndown Court, and a great lady.'

'She was always that,' exclaimed Joshua with more heat than he had intended, making Burrell look at him in curiosity, and chide, 'We must both be grateful that she has not changed, Stradling.'

'I think there is no fear of that,' said Joshua stiffly. 'And you, sir? You will return to London?

'No. My work there is done. The cholera epidemic is over, thank God. I worked there at every menial and degrading occupation, for the need was so great that none enquired my name or credentials. The fear of death is a remorseless leveller, Stradling.' His tone was amused, without bitterness. 'As remorseless as "the grim reaper" himself.'

Joshua, regarding Burrell with compassion, thought that with his gaunt figure and dark, cadaverous face, he was not unlike a death's head himself. Yet he could not bring himself to forgive this man for involving Rebecca in his dangerous bid for revenge, so forcing her to deceive those who loved and trusted her. Joshua was painfully aware that the deficiency lay in him rather than in Burrell, and the knowledge brought him scant comfort.

'But now, sir,' he said briskly, 'you are pardoned and your good name restored. The future . . .'

'Has more relevance than the past, as I reminded Mansel,' finished Burrell, with a wry smile. 'I thank you, Stradling, for reminding me!'

'And your plans, sir?'

'To attend your engagement festivities at Southerndown Court, as the guest of Sir Matthew, and to renew my acquaintance with Rebecca and Jeremiah Fleet.'

'That will bring them great pleasure,' Joshua said formally. 'Jeremiah is well aware that you saved his life, sir, by attending him in his fever, and risking your own by doing so. He is indebted to you.'

Burrell looked at him quizzically. 'There are no debts between friends, Stradling. True friends. For the privilege is in helping, as much as in receiving help – as you, in your vocation, must well know.' He placed an arm upon Joshua's shoulder saying quietly, 'I am aware that you are unable to like me, or accept me as a friend, and I regret it, for I believe that you are a shrewd and honest man whom I should be grateful to count as friend . . . Perhaps, one day?'

Joshua was spared the discomfort of replying by the return of the justice, in rare good humour, declaring that he had chosen the wine and sent a firkin of ale to the kitchen that the household might share in the general pleasure at Doonan's survival . . . a circumstance upon which they were all agreed.

Mansel, feeling some awkwardness at being in Burrell's company after their enforced intimacy at the operating table was broken, had gratefully made the excuse of needing to see his patient.

Doonan still lay unconscious of the day's violence and the events around him, while Rosa, resisting all efforts to prise her from his side, kept quiet vigil. She had courteously, but firmly, refused the justice's invitation to dine with the gentlemen, and a tray of refreshments lay, untasted, upon a small table beside her husband's bed. She watched silently as Mansel ministered to him, her face pale and remote. Mansel saw that she had changed from the blood-sodden dress into a pretty fresh one of aquamarine silk with a delicate lace collar, no doubt brought from the coach by some lackey, and her hair was carefully brushed and rearranged. Yet, there was no disguising the bruised shadows beneath her eyes, or the exhaustion in every line of her young body.

'He has improved, sir, I am sure of it.' Her voice was questioning, uncertain.

Mansel turned, blinking his pale eyes, plump face concerned. 'It is a very grave wound, my dear, and he will need much care. It will be many days before we know if . . .' He did not complete the sentence, and the unspoken words lay heavily between them.

'But he is no worse, sir?'

'No, my dear. I believe that his breathing is less shallow, and he grows restless, fighting to break through to consciousness. He will be glad that you are here beside him.' He patted her shoulder lightly. 'You are a good, loyal girl, Mistress Doonan, and a loving wife. He has every reason to be proud of you.' He cleared his throat noisily, colouring in embarrassment at his unlikely outburst, then hurried away.

Rosa, left alone, began to weep silently at the irony of Mansel's words. No! She was not a loyal, loving wife: she was a stubborn, headstrong girl, selfish and wilful. Her stupid pride had brought her dear Cavan to the edge of death, and she would know, and grieve for it, all the rest of her life. If he died . . .? She began to weep noisily, without restraint, burying her head upon the coverlet.

There was a light, almost imperceptible, touch upon her hair.

'Rosa . . .?'

She looked up into Cavan's soft, unfocusing eyes and, sensing his pain and seeing the pallor of his face, wept anew.

'He did not hurt you?' The words were almost inaudible, and she had to bend towards him.

'No. He did not hurt me, Cavan.'

He nodded, satisfied, and closed his eyes, as if the effort of trying to think had drained him, as the wound had drained him of blood.

'Oh, Cavan! Forgive me, forgive me!' she cried wretchedly.

'Forgive you?' His eyes were wider now, filled with inexpressible love and warmth. 'Why, Rosa my love, when you refused to take off your wedding band, and stood there defiant as a little fighting cock . . .' His voice faltered. 'My heart near burst with pride. You are all I ever wanted in a wife . . .' His eyes closed, and she leaned over gently to touch his broad cheek with her lips.

I will fight so hard to deserve you! she vowed silently.

For the justice and his three guests, their lives so strangely interwoven by past events, their enforced intimacy at the dinner table might have proved restricting and an embarrassment. There was no doubt that Burrell's sudden reappearance affected them all; Mansel, perhaps, most deeply. His mind was filled with thoughts of his dead wife, Madeleine: always, the picture of her dying, because he had failed her, even at the end, lacerated his mind. There was the added pain of remorse for what she, deliberately, and he, unknowingly, had done to Burrell.

Robert Knight, too, initially, had been consumed with guilt for his part in the affair. Legally, he had carried out his duties with exactitude. None could fault him in the role of justice. Yet, as a priest, he knew he had prejudged Burrell, believing him guilty, and sparing no thought for his suffering, or prayer for his redemption.

Joshua was angry with himself. He was ashamed of his

pettiness, for Burrell had offered him friendship and he had turned away, grateful for the justice's intervention. He did not know, even now, what he would have replied. He looked up, alerted, perhaps, by the silence, to see the three men staring at him expectantly. He realised, embarrassed, that he had been meant to reply to some question and, seeing the justice's finger-tapping, a sure sign of his irritability, muttered an apology.

'I was asking about the description of this villain . . . the highwayman we seek, Stradling,' Robert Knight explained tersely.

'I have briefly discussed the question with Dr Burrell and Rosa . . . Mistress Doonan,' Joshua corrected himself, 'but I fear, sir, that the mask he wore, and the silk kerchief which covered his mouth, will prove a hindrance to our enquiries.' He did not add that Burrell had described the man as having 'cold, alert eyes with clear dark irises', whereas Rosa had offered, more vividly, that his eyes were 'somehow pale, yet brilliant . . . watchful, like a snake's', adding, with a rush of colour beneath her pale skin, 'then they seemed to grow moister, softer as he looked at me . . . like Cavan's when . . .' She had broken off in confusion, busying herself with Cavan's coverlet, and Joshua had not attempted to question her further. 'I will, of course, sir, question the coachman; Doonan, when he has recovered sufficiently; and the rest of the passengers upon the coach.'

The justice nodded curtly.

Joshua had no doubt that he would have as many different responses as there were flowers in a hedgerow. Yet, whether the clinical detachment of Dr Burrell would prove more reliable than Rosa's more intimate, subjective assessment of the man's character was academic for the moment. Whether viewed with repelled fascination, analytically, or not at all, upon one thing they were all agreed: the highwayman must be caught, and soon!

Well wined and dined, the quartet of gentlemen grew steadily more relaxed and expansive as their topics of conversation became less insular. Burrell was a stimulating companion, amusing and provocative by turn, and soon they were chaffing each other and arguing companionably, with no evidence of reserve. Finally, having lingered too long over the port, Mansel and Joshua took their leave, with every show of reluctance and gratitude, first saying their farewells to Rosa and the wounded man.

Rosa had clung to Joshua's hand tearfully, bidding him tell her mother, Widow Howarth, and their friends, of Cavan's plight, and her determination to see him restored to health and well-being.

Doonan, himself, had rallied sufficiently to take Joshua's fingers in his great fist, his grasp unnaturally cold and lacking strength. The big Irishman had awkwardly thanked Dr Mansel for his services, but to Joshua he merely bade him, 'Have a care, my friend', his eyes blurred with tears of pain and weakness.

Joshua nodded in return, feeling unutterably depressed. It was, he thought, like seeing a great, shambling bear at some fair or inn, legs shackled, jaw muzzled and held by a chain . . . forced to lose all freedom and dignity before others.

For Mansel and the constable, the journey home was scarcely less hazardous than their excursion to Tythegston Court and, although each was conscious of the presence of the other and grateful for it, barely a word was spoken between them. Exhaustion, and the rigours of the blizzard and events, rendered them uncommunicative until their final words of parting at Dr

Mansel's gates. Then Joshua set the grey down the snow-drifted slope to the Crown Inn.

As horse and rider came, almost silently, into the white landscape of the yard, Ossie hurried out of the stables bearing a lantern, his face strained and anxious in its glow. Joshua wondered for how many hours he had been waiting there, alone, for his return.

The ostler helped him to dismount. 'There is news of Doonan, Joshua?' His voice was raw with concern.

'Yes, thank God! He has been operated upon, and the bullet cut out.'

Ossie's little wizened face broke into a smile of pure joy, lantern beams catching the glimmer of tears. 'Praise be to God!' he exclaimed fervently, 'that Dr Mansel rode through . . . I had almost despaired of it. The storm is so fierce.'

'Mansel and Burrell,' said Joshua carefully. 'For Dr Burrell was a passenger upon the coach.'

'He has returned? Why?' asked Ossie, perplexed. 'There are too many reminders here of what he has suffered. I pity him, Joshua, yet I doubt the wisdom of it. Reliving old pain may sometimes ease the wound, seem to cleanse it . . . but, more often, deeper hurts fester unseen.'

'I think you are right, my friend,' agreed Joshua gravely, 'the past should be the haunt of ghosts, and not the living.'

As Ossie took the mare to be rubbed down and bedded in the stable, Joshua walked reflectively through the bandaged landscape, village green and church padded and creased with snow, his boots sinking deep in its softness.

Within his bleak, thick-walled room at the cottage, and his narrow bed, his thoughts turned first to

Rebecca de Breos, and his longing for her was so intense it was a physical ache within his breast. Then he thought of Rosa, and her quiet sleepless vigil over the wounded Irishman. Sleep was slow in coming, for he was cold and bitterly exhausted. With the shudder and fall of snow from the eaves, and its swift white passage past the small-paned window, he could have fancied, like Ossie, that it was the flight of the *Ederyn Corff* he saw - wingless, but with feathers of snow.

Quickly, he thrust the thought from him.

Chapter Three

After a restless night of tangled dreams, pierced by the sighing of the wind from the sea, and his own sighs, Joshua was awakened by the light. There was a clear radiance about it, a luminosity which heightened the starkness of the small cell with its sparse furnishings. Lying there, eyelids heavy with sleep, the white beams of light falling through the high window, he was reminded of the carved-oak bible box at his childhood home, the farm . . . his unformed hands tracing the grave faces of the saints, eyes turned piously to the shafts of holy light.

He smiled wrily. There was scant reflection of the warmth and comfort of the past in his present circumstances. He climbed out of bed, bare feet recoiling from the coldness of the boards, and braced himself against the sting of the icy water upon his skin from the washbowl. Shaving was a penance, made harsher by winter. But, this painstakingly completed, Joshua negotiated the steep stone stairs to his living-room, to exchange his nightshirt for the uniform which had been left drying before the last vestiges of the wood and turf fire that, despite his tiredness, he had banked the night before.

At the farm in the Vale, the servants would be abroad early, and the farm labourers, bailiff, grooms and those who tended the animals already returning from their tasks. In Southerndown Court, Rebecca and her companion, Elizabeth Crandle, would be at their lessons with Dr Handel Peate, or breakfasting with Sir Matthew: the two young ladies, doubtless, with their minds less upon French verbs than their dresses for the party planned for Rebecca's friends from the three hamlets to celebrate her betrothal to Joshua. He hoped that the weather would not worsen, and glanced apprehensively through the snow-drifted window panes into his bleak yard. The imprints of the wild birds' claws already upon the sill lay like small splayed twigs. Their tracks across the virgin snow patterned with the delicacy of the veining of a leaf. He thought instinctively of Rosa: her pale transparent skin showing the blue of the veins beneath, and of Doonan's dark blood, pumping through the wound in his flesh and staining Rosa's bodice . . .

He had promised her, most faithfully, that he would tell her mother, Widow Howarth, and their friends, of the tragedy . . . for tragedy it undoubtedly was. He would go this very morning to the small lodging house in the Port, to bring the widow what little comfort he could. It would surely please her that the Reverend Robert Knight had taken them into his house, and that Cavan would have the sole, devoted care of Dr Burrell: a privilege rarely afforded, even to the rich. Cavan was a proud man, with never an idle bone in his huge body, used to working long and hard hours at the quarry face. Yet, industrious as he was, the few coppers a week he paid into the quarry's medical fund would barely have bought the services of a doctor to attend him at an accident at his work. The big Irishman would not have appealed to the guardians of the fund for The Medical and Surgical Relief of the Poor, of that Joshua was quite certain. It humiliated even the out paupers seeking its charity, for it was doled out with a parsimony and public show which laid raw their spirits, with their wounds.

The previous eve, at the justice's house, Joshua, soundlessly approaching the door of the room where Doonan lay, had overheard Rosa tentatively broaching the payment of Mansel's bill, and her promise that 'every penny will be paid, sir, in full, and with a grateful heart'. Mansel had paused only fractionally before replying, 'There will be no bill presented, ma'am, I do assure you. What little I have done has been done from common humanity, and out of respect for your courage. It would grieve and offend me to have it otherwise.' Joshua had stood aside to let him pass, seeing his face flushed and the pale opaque eyes blinking nervously beneath the fiercely overhanging brows. He had nodded curtly, absently smoothing the circle of flyaway hair that surrounded the pinkness of his scalp as he went. Not a word was spoken of the conversation by Rosa, but Joshua knew that she had been unable to thank Mansel because her voice, and heart, had been too full with treacherous tears.

He suspected that Rosa's approaches to Dr Burrell would reap the same return. Rebecca spoke of John Burrell seldom, sensing Joshua's reserve and lack of interest in his well-being and concerns. It was from his friend, the old fisherman, Jeremiah Fleet, that the constable gleaned the little he knew. Although Jeremiah, like most of the cottagers, was unable to read or write, he had promised Dr Burrell, upon his recovery from the fever which had assailed him, that, unschooled as he was, he would ask that 'his thoughts and wishes be set down upon paper for the good doctor, that he might not forget the folk of the three hamlets'. Emily Randall had willingly acted as amanuensis. She had once been a governess, and wrote sedulously and without alteration, all that Jeremiah confided in her. In return, Burrell sent vivid, unemotional accounts of his daily life among the cholera victims of the London slum dwellings. Jeremiah had said that Mistress Randall's eyes were sometimes filled with tears, and she had to pause in her reading, so upset was she by the reality of it, for Burrell lived with the stricken, sleeping and eating in the stinking dens and putrid hovels where they lived, and all too often died, claiming that 'after his prison cell, such places held no terror for him'.

Joshua, his mind still set upon Doonan and Rosa, made a simple breakfast of oatcakes, ale and cold bacon from the farm and, donning his boots and helmet and greatcoat, set some turf smouldering upon the kindling of the fire. Finally, securing the door of his cottage, he walked out thoughtfully into the snow.

The morning sun was pale and veiled in misted cloud, as if the storm of the night had leached it of all warmth and brightness. Joshua welcomed the cold crispness of the air, the snow crusted with a glittering rime, sharp as hoarfrost.

The sea wind had sculpted the snow into curves, drifting it against barriers of stone and hedgerow, leaving small pockets of bare grass upon the village green, like giant footprints. There were other tracks recognisably human and animal, for the cottage labourers would already be about their work at farm, quarry, brewhouse and brickyard, and the few stray curs intent upon ceaseless scavenging.

Joshua glanced towards the clock upon the church tower, and saw, with some amusement, that it showed twelve o' the hour, midnight: its hands impotent 'neath the burden of snow, as impotent as he to proceed with the business of the day! Already, he had decided that it would be folly to take out the mare, for there would be deep, impassable drifts upon the lanes and byways, and he would not unnecessarily drive her into danger. He had no hope of following the highwayman's tracks, for they would early have been obliterated and, wherever he was holed up like a restless fox, he could not venture out. Perhaps, thought Joshua, he had perished in some snow-drift upon Stormy Downs or the acres of sand dunes, riding until exhausted, then dying where he lay . . . Despite the man's callousness and Doonan's wound, the thought gave Joshua no pleasure. He had best return to the Crown, he thought, dispiritedly, and see what little he could glean from the coachman and passengers.

Ossie seemed to Joshua a little more bent and old as he came into the snow-covered yard to greet him, the lines of his creased walnut face deepened by exhaustion.

'You look tired, my friend!' said Joshua, adding penitently, 'I fear my late return last night must bear some blame.'

'No!' exploded Ossie. ' 'Tis that confounded goose!'

'Goose?' echoed Joshua, bewildered.

'Certainly! You know what a goose is, surely? Were you not born and bred upon a farm? 'Tis a hissing, spitting, pecking, venomous bird, fit only for the Christmas table! Stuffed and lifeless!'

Joshua stared at him, astonished. 'This goose, Ossie . . .' he said carefully, 'I do not understand, for you love and respect all of God's dumb creatures.'

' 'Tis not dumb!' cried Ossie impassionedly, 'nor, I vow, did God create it. More like it was the Devil's work! Never have I seen a more vicious, cantankerous bird. No! I swear! Not in all of my life! See!' He showed Joshua his bruised and bleeding hands. 'That is what the varmint gave me for my trouble!'

Joshua was hard pressed to restrain a smile. 'This hellish creature,' he asked, 'belongs to the landlord?'

'No indeed! Some poor old countrywoman upon the coach, who bade me care for it as carefully as a babe, declaring it to be "sensitive and of a delicate disposition". As delicate as a polecat!' he said in disgust. 'She swears that the bump upon its head, when she fell upon it in the coach, deranged the creature! 'Tis my opinion that she is the one deranged!'

'Come, now,' chided Joshua, fighting to retain his gravity, 'I know you have never let a horse master you yet, whether rogue or wild.'

'That is a different matter,' replied Ossie stiffly. 'The horse is an animal of sense and dignity, as you well know, and amenable to reason. I would as soon tame a wild herd as that fiend in feathers!'

'What will you do?' probed Joshua.

'Do? I have already done it, although sore tempted to wring its scrawny neck!'

'Well . . .?'

' 'Tis firmly caged in the kitchen treadmill, working off its spleen by turning the spit and doing something useful with its idle carcass!'

Joshua could no longer control his mirth and broke into peals of unrestrained laughter, which had him wiping his streaming eyes; the sound so infectious that Ossie was soon laughing with him. When the constable entered the inn, to approach the landlord, Tom Butler, for some quiet corner in which to conduct his interviews with the passengers, he saw the goose plodding irascibly upon its appointed task. The lean cur usually employed was stretched exaltedly before the blazing hearth, a look of divine revelation upon its scarred and grizzled face. Not all the goose's hissed imprecations could rouse it.

Tom Butler, brawny and well-muscled, strode to greet Joshua warmly, his usually jovial face serious as he enquired as to Doonan's progress. 'It is the very devil!' he said wrathfully. 'For I had thought such violence upon the road all but ended. I can scarce credit the man's infernal callousness!' He shook his head despairingly.

'You would do me the favour of allowing me a quiet place to interview your guests?' asked Joshua, presently.

'Guests, indeed!' exclaimed Butler drily. 'The highwayman took all their coins and valuables, and they have not a farthing to bless themselves with, much less me!'

'You will lodge them nevertheless?'

'Of course . . . I could scarce toss them back into the blizzard!' His ruddy face broke into a smile as he admitted, 'They are all, save the coachman, destined for farms and houses hereabouts, come to celebrate the New Year. I shall send word to the families when the snow has abated, for I know the bills will be paid and promptly. It is a rash villager who would default and imperil his supply of ale!'

He led Joshua into the small private parlour where Mrs Butler was engaged upon some stitching, wearing her plain cotton gown and house bonnet of lace. She stood up eagerly, spilling her scissors and thread in her anxiousness to enquire about Doonan and Rosa.

'She is a dear, kind girl, as we learnt at the Wassail party at her small cottage: as welcoming as she is pretty. As for Cavan Doonan,' she shook her head, smiling indulgently, 'he is nothing but a great, overgrown babe, all noise and wind, yet needing a firm but tender hand . . . and I truly believe that in Mistress Doonan, he has found it.'

'Indeed,' agreed Joshua, 'and to his credit, he is aware of it, ma'am, and swift to declare it. Yet I fancy she will need more tenderness than firmness in her fight to save him, for he is gravely wounded.'

Mrs Butler's eyes filled with ready tears as she waved aside Joshua's protestations about driving her from her own parlour. 'It is a small enough service . . .' she said with dignity. 'I would willingly relieve Rosa at her task, if I could, as would every woman in the three hamlets . . . I pray that you bring this rogue to justice, Constable Stradling, for if the men hereabouts reach him first, I fear their justice will be rough indeed.'

Joshua, seated at the fireside, a table bearing his journal and the quill and ink which Butler had supplied, motioned the coachman to the vacant chair opposite.

'Now, sir, you will, perhaps, give me a description of this highwayman, and any other details which you consider relevant?'

The coachman, still clutching a pot of ale, looked at him in alarm, stuttering and blinking nervously in his effort to be of help.

Joshua, seeing the strain in his eyes, and the fragment of straw upon his tiered coat, which spoke of a night spent uncomfortably in the stables, said gently, 'It was a cruel and bitter experience for you, sir. I bid you take your time and finish your ale before you begin, and if there are any victuals which you require, I shall ask the landlord to supply them, upon the instant.'

The fellow thanked him profusely, but declined, saying that Ossie had seen him well supplied and, although he relaxed visibly, his round, wind-burned face growing loose-jowled, there was little he could offer in the way of information. Joshua established that the highwayman had indeed been riding a fine chestnut mare and had ridden off in the general direction of Newton or Stormy Downs.

'I did not see him, sir, when I continued my journey to the inn, but that need not signify, for he could have sheltered in some byway, only to retrace his steps, knowing there was none to pursue him.'

Joshua agreed that it might well be so. 'There is, perhaps, some physical characteristic that remains in your mind, sir?' he persisted. 'Some scar or abnormality, some peculiarity of voice, or movement, even?'

'Indeed, Constable, I wish that I could recall one, or anything of use to you . . . I remember only that he was of average height and build, sir. His voice might have been that of a gentleman, but with the wind and the snow deadening sound, and the protection of his mask and scarf, and his greatcoat, and that beaver hat hiding his hair . . .' He shrugged helplessly. 'Besides which, I saw him through a veil of snow-flakes, for the blizzard was unceasing.' He looked up at Joshua, hesitated, then said resolutely, 'I do not mind admitting to you, sir, that when he pointed his pistol at me, with ill-mannered threats, I could scarce see at all for the sweat pouring into my eyes, for all I was cold and frosted . . . and my breeches, sir, were wet, and, I confess, not with the snow alone . . .'

Joshua thanked him gravely, rewarding him with a shilling to buy ale for Ossie and himself, for he had learned that the coachman had thrown down his meagre purse when first accosted, and keenly felt his lack of means to repay the ostler's kindness.

The old lady who owned the recalcitrant goose could offer little more, although she enquired most kindly about Rosa and the wounded Doonan. Joshua had replied that Mistress Doonan had spoken generously, and with gratitude, of her ready help and comfort, for she had been sorely in need of a warm and sympathetic friend.

'At least I deceived that odious villain, the

highwayman,' she exclaimed with satisfaction, 'for all his airs and graces!' She lifted her skirts unashamedly to show her plump legs, sturdy in knitted woollen stockings. 'Some I know travel with bankers' notes and credits cut in half, sending one half upon the mail coach, to attend them upon their arrival. I, Constable, took the precaution of carrying two purses!' She cackled delightedly, triumphantly producing her coin-filled pouch. 'I had pinned it securely to my drawers, sir, knowing that if he were a gentleman, he would not search me, and even if he were not . . .' She cackled louder, her withered russet face wrinkling with delight. 'Then he would feel no temptation to accost me!'

In the face of her unashamed glee, Joshua could not but laugh with her.

'What is more,' she continued, with satisfaction, 'I got the better of that ostler in the yard.'

'How so, ma'am?'

'I bade him care for my goose, claiming, with tears in my eyes, that it was a dear and loving pet, gentle in spirit, the very light of my life . . . In truth, I carted it for a neighbour to my cousin's farm, to provision their New Year's revelling. Had I known it was such a fierce, ungodly bird, vicious and ungrateful, I would have sat harder upon its head, I swear, and knocked it senseless. Still, it will provide a tender succulent meal.'

'Indeed, I hope that you are right, ma'am,' said Joshua civilly, bowing and accompanying her to the door, 'although, perhaps, if asked, it might be wiser to choose a slice of breast, for legs are sometimes inclined to be tough and stringy!'

After a fruitless half hour spent in questioning the two young gentlemen from the box, both self-confident and vociferous, and claiming to have acted with the greatest of courage, and then the clergyman and his whey-faced wife, who confessed truthfully that they had displayed none, Joshua bade the landlord 'Good day' and walked back into the snowy yard. He must trudge his way through to the Port and Widow Howarth's lodging house, as he had promised Rosa. It was not a prospect he viewed with equanimity. Yet, like his hunt for the highwayman, it could not be avoided.

Joshua's mile-long journey across the normally sandy wastes of Picket's Lease to the Port, was strange indeed. The snow had drifted over its rills and hollows, making it an arctic landscape, desolate and eerie, with only the sounds of waves and gulls, and the fresh salt tang of the sea to remind him that there was life beyond its unfamiliar bleakness.

He saw no one upon his way, although he glimpsed the distant masts of ships in the dock basin, gaunt as bare trees, and must have, somewhere, crossed the tramlines of the horse-drawn tramroad buried deep under the snow. He supposed that the valleys beyond were cut off by the blizzard, cupped in the mountains which spilled snow from the torn clouds. By tomorrow, most of the snow which lay upon the sea's edges would be eaten away by the salt-laden air and, inland, the labourers would already be shovelling it aside, tunnelling white-walled gullies that the beasts might start their coal-laden, twelve-hour journey to the shore.

It was with relief, mixed with natural hesitancy, that Joshua came in sight of the small row of Lias cottages, where Rosa's mother lived, and the yard and livery stables beyond.

Doonan had lodged here once, in his fierce, hell-raising bachelor days, when the Widow Howarth had looked upon his unlikely courtship of her only child with misgivings. Yet, she too had grown to love the wild Irishman for his loyalty and generosity, and for his tender protectiveness towards Rosa. Now, it was Joshua's unhappy duty to tell her that Cavan might well die.

The Widow Howarth opened the front door with difficulty, for the snow had drifted deep against it, crumbling and falling into the narrow passageway where she stood. She smiled with delight at seeing the constable, then grew nervous, apprehensive. Joshua thought, not for the first time, how strange it was that such a plump-bosomed brown bird of a woman could have produced anyone as ethereally lovely as Rosa . . . almost as if a hedge sparrow had inexplicably given birth to a delicate, iridescent hummingbird.

She was staring at him in concern, saying awkwardly, 'I am forgetting my manners, sir, leaving you standing upon the doorstep. Please come in, and welcome. You must be tired and frozen through. I will warm you some ale, to take the chill from your bones.'

Joshua laid a gentle restraining hand upon her arm, and she looked up at him, saying tonelessly, 'You have come about Rosa. Something has happened to Rosa . . .'

'Cavan, ma'am. There has been an accident . . . a shooting upon the coach. He was hurt defending Rosa.'

'You must drink something warm,' she urged as if she had not heard him, 'or you will take a chill.' Then her face twisted, ugly and pained, as she began to weep, and Joshua cradled her awkwardly against the dampness of his greatcoat.

'Forgive me, ma'am,' he said, 'for I am a clumsy, useless fool. I should not have blurted it so. But there was no way to soften the hurt of it . . .' He led her wordlessly into the small parlour, scoured and shining as a new pin, and smelling of wood ash and lavender.

When she was recovered, and the sequence of the whole affair told, to renewed tears from the Widow Howarth at Cavan's bravery, and the generosity of the justice, and the two doctors, she insisted upon fetching Joshua's ale. He sipped it gratefully, its warmth stinging his veins, as if it melted all that was frozen within him. As if in need of the comfort of everyday things, their talk turned to news of Rebecca, and their friends in the three hamlets, then the rigours of the blizzard, and its effects upon the fisherfolk, and those upon the remote, outlying farms. Joshua knew that his father's farm in the fertile Vale of Glamorgan would be well-manned, and the beasts fed and rescued from snowdrifts, the cattle and horses led into shelter of byre and stable. Yet, what of the poor farms and small holdings like the child Dafydd's, remote and ill-equipped? There would be losses, certainly, and some would lose their livelihood, and be dragged into the relentless whirlpool of paupery, unable to struggle out.

'I declare, sir, that I was surprised to see you abroad,' Mistress Howarth was saying, 'I swear that apart from you, and the little crippled hayward, Illtyd, none has ventured out.'

'Illtyd?' Joshua's voice was sharp. 'You are sure, ma'am?'

'Indeed!' She was emphatic. 'For he passed close by, as I stared from my window, the small piebald all but swallowed up in the snow . . .'

'You will excuse me, ma'am?' Joshua hastily scrambled to his feet. 'I did not think that Illtyd would venture out in such a climate. Yet I should have thought . . .' he chided himself, 'for he is conscientious and thoughtful for the animals in his care.'

'You will search for him?'

Joshua nodded. 'I will hire a beast from the livery

stables, if they will let me have one, for my own mare is exhausted. I thank you, ma'am, for your hospitality, and beg you to believe that I shall return upon the instant I receive news of Rosa and Doonan.'

Their leave-taking completed, Mistress Howarth stood upon the doorstep to see him safely upon his way: a plump, speckled bird upon frail legs which hardly seemed fashioned to support her. Then, with a final brave tilt of her head she turned and secured the door.

The livery stables were small, with that thick clotted odour which pervades all such places: a mingling of straw, leather, steaming ordure and animal sweat, overlaid with the sharp pungency of equine urine.

The owner, for it was served only by him and a young stableboy, was grooming a big, dark gelding and paused in his labour, astonished to see Joshua abroad in such weather.

'I may be of service to you, Constable?' he asked, abandoning his task, and bidding the lad continue with it.

'I had intention of hiring a mount.'

'I fear, sir, that we have none as fine as your own grey, for we are in a small way of business, as you can well see. I have but the five horses. Four have come to me by way of the carriage trade: already broken down, and winded by age and ill use. Yet the gelding is a good animal, strong and reliable. You would do well to take him.'

Joshua nodded and, terms being agreed to their mutual satisfaction, asked casually, 'You do not own a chestnut mare?'

'No, sir, nor am I like to, for business is slow in the wintertime and, with the inclement weather, all but non-existent! The lad is my own son, for I could ill afford to employ another. People do not venture far afield when winter comes, preferring to hug their own hearths. And who can blame them?'

'Who indeed?' agreed Joshua.

The boy, who had finished grooming the gelding and saddling him, handed the beast to Joshua, who thanked him, smiling, and offering him a sixpence for his trouble, adding, good humouredly, 'It is weather fit only for fools and villains, I swear! Though, perhaps, 'tis better to be a fool in search of a villain than a villain in search of a fool,' at which father and son laughed in agreement, and bade him good-day.

Joshua, comfortably astride the big gelding, had little difficulty in picking up the small piebald's tracks – its miniature metal shoes scattering deep sunken crescents across the white landscape.

It seemed that Illtyd had taken the way to the common lands which bordered the seashore: a wild place thick with gorse and bracken, where the villagers' flocks and herds might roam freely, under his care.

Yet Joshua was filled with unease. He doubted only the strength of the tiny horse and rider to weather the drifts and cold, for their courage and ability could never be faulted.

Illtyd held a special place in Joshua's affections, as he did with all who lived in the three hamlets. Crippled and hunchbacked from birth, the young man was none the less brave and filled with gentle humour. His work in caring for their animals, and protecting them from predatory birds and foxes, or human marauders, was a local legend. Oftimes the hayward's life itself had been put in peril.

Joshua, thinking of Illtyd's large ungainly head set awkwardly upon the wry neck, and his clear intelligent eyes, knew that he must not demean the little man. He must come upon him as if by accident, hiding his concern and true purpose.

He only prayed that Illtyd had not ridden out to Stormy Downs to seek those sheep buried there beneath snowdrifts. The hidden marshes and gullies, and old quarries overhung with growth, were treacherous, even in summer. In winter they might easily provide a tomb.

Chapter Four

Rebecca de Breos, granddaughter of Sir Matthew de Breos of Southerndown Court, was seated in the old schoolroom of the great house, dark head bent sedulously over her lesson books. Her friend Elizabeth Crandle was equally intent upon her learning, her hair, only a degree or so lighter than Rebecca's raven-black tresses, forming wings about her gentle composed features.

Their tutor, Dr Handel Peate, had given them a poem about the dying year to translate from the French, and was gratified and enchanted by their understanding, not merely of its vocabulary but of the subtle depths of its meaning. The profound melancholy of autumn seemed far removed from this innocent, pastoral setting and the two pretty young ladies in their elegant morning gowns. Sere winter outside, he thought, smiling fleetingly, yet all of spring and loveliness before me. He recalled himself guiltily, rebuking himself for such ill-judged romanticism. It ill became an elderly pedant, bachelor and man of the cloth to degenerate into sentimentality!

Yet, he admitted honestly, his years of teaching Classics at Cowbridge Grammar School and tutoring growing boys, had not prepared him for such unfeigned and exquisite delight as the two girls found in poetry, young and unworldly as they were. No, he corrected himself, unworldly was not the adjective to apply to either of them. Rebecca, orphaned and forced to work at a harsh, pleasureless occupation merely to survive; and Elizabeth . . . glancing covertly at her serene expression, it seemed hard to believe that she had known the horror of her brother murdering her childhood friend, and her father's disgrace, bankruptcy and imprisonment, taking the responsibility which her mother should have borne upon her own slender shoulders; visiting him, even now, where he lay silent and withdrawn into a world of his own making, not recognising her, or even knowing that she came.

He shook his head regretfully, seeing his hands upon the pages of the book he held against his knees thin and fleshless, parchment skin dappled with age. If he could slough it off as a snake sheds useless skin, the flesh beneath firm and young again . . . Would he then choose this dry pedantic life or, like young Joshua Stradling, forgo the cloistered calm of Oxford for a new experience, pulsing with vital, quickening life . . .? Living through his own actions rather than through other men's thoughts . . .? He recalled himself guiltily, realising that Elizabeth was staring at him anxiously, expectantly.

'You were saying, my dear?' he asked mildly, his keen blue eyes alert in the ascetic face.

'That the man who wrote these lines, Dr Peate, about the sadness of the violins of autumn, their melody . . .' She hesitated, flushing.

'Yes, Elizabeth?'

'He must have known grief, sir. Loss. For he has captured the feel of it: the anguish, the rage, the feeling of . . . desolation. He could not have lived it only in his imagination.'

'Yes. I am sure that you are right,' he said compassionately, 'there is a sadness in the falling of a leaf . . . and an ending. Yet, as Christians, we must believe, Elizabeth, that there is renewal of life, that nothing is wasted: not a dead leaf, nor past experience, whatever its hurt. It falls to earth to feed and renew, there is a rebirth, a resurrection . . .'

'But the leaf does not know it,' she said unexpectedly, 'for it no longer feels the warmth of the sun, or the tug of the wind, or the rain upon its face. It has returned to earth . . .' He saw the shimmer of tears upon her lashes, and did not know if they were for her dead brother, the girl he had killed, or the dried husk of a man, her father.

He was saved the difficult burden of replying by an urgent knock upon the schoolroom door and, in response to his call of 'Come', the immediate entrance of a footman.

'I beg your pardon, sir, for the interruption,' he apologised to Dr Peate, 'but Sir Matthew wishes to speak to Miss de Breos in the library, upon a matter of some urgency.'

The two girls exchanged glances of surprise and apprehension at such an unprecedented disruption of their lessons and, upon Dr Peate's excusing her, Rebecca went swiftly to attend her grandfather.

'My dear, you had best be seated,' he said gently, 'for what I have to tell you will distress you . . .'

'Joshua?' her voice was alarmed.

'No, Rebecca, nor yet your friend, Jeremiah Fleet.' He paused, his fine eyes unusually hesitant in the strong-boned, imperious face. 'I have received a letter from my fellow justice, Robert Knight. It concerns your friends, Rosa and Cavan Doonan.'

'But they are in Ireland, sir, with his parents. The extended honeymoon . . .' she broke off, warned by the gravity of his face.

'No, my dear. He lies at the justice's house, gravely wounded by a highwayman's bullet. There is fear that he might not live . . .'

'Oh, Grandfather!' She ran to him instinctively and buried her face in his waistcoat jacket, and he held her to him, stroking her loose dark hair, and murmuring words of comfort.

'Now, my dear,' he said finally, holding her away, and wiping her tears tenderly with his silk kerchief. 'The time for crying is past. Rosa has need of you, your strength and your courage. You must go to her, without delay. There is not a moment to be lost . . .'

'But, sir, the roads? They are blocked with snow. Impassable.'

'The messenger has ridden through, taking the main roads and, although the way is treacherous,' he smiled, tilting her chin to look into her vivid, blue eyes, 'remember you are a de Breos!' His voice was warm with affectionate amusement. 'To a de Breos, nothing is impassable, nothing impossible!'

'Oh, Grandfather,' she cried, hugging him impulsively, 'what would I do without you?'

'Survive, Rebecca, as you survived all those years without me . . .' he answered soberly.

'I am glad that it is no longer necessary.'

'And I, for you have changed my life, my dear,' he said simply. Then, becoming the austere, well-disciplined campaigner again, 'I have given instructions that the smaller coach be made ready for you at once, with a pair of dependable horses. The coachman will see that a spare pair is tethered behind the carriage lest the leaders grow fatigued. It will slow your progress, my dear, but ensure your safety, which is what I care about most . . .'

Rebecca gravely nodded her understanding.

'The carriageway to the house has already been cleared by the estate workers, and they are labouring at the moment upon the approaches to the main highway, knowing of the urgency of their task. I have ordered your maid and the housekeeper to pack whatever is needed for your comfort: clothing, and refreshment. You will take Elizabeth, of course, as companion and chaperone.' It was a statement, rather than a question.

'No, sir. I would not put her to the inconvenience, although she would accompany me willingly. Tomorrow she visits her father, declaring it both obligation and pleasure, although I fear it brings her no pleasure.'

'Yet perhaps some to him, although he is unable to express it?' Sir Matthew rebuked gently. 'Then you must take Mrs Crandle or your maid, my dear, for I will not have you travel alone.'

'My maid, sir, for I fear the haste and perils of the journey, and its ending, might incommode Elizabeth's mother. She has had too much of sadness and death.'

So it was arranged.

Rebecca, dressed in a warm shoulder-caped travelling coat and matching velvet bonnet of holly berry red, sat rigidly upon the leather-buttoned seat within the de Breos coach, crest emblazoned on its side, her maid facing her. Her thoughts were upon Rosa and the wounded Doonan. Yet, beyond her sadness, stirred the faint unacknowledged hope that she might see Joshua, whom she loved so dearly. Yet, even as it surfaced, she thrust it from her, ashamed at such selfish indulgence in the face of Rosa's all-consuming grief.

The housekeeper had set a warmed brick, wrapped in flannel, at Rebecca's feet, and she held a pewter flask of hot water within her gloved hands, beneath the muff suspended by a silver chain about her neck. Yet, already, she grew cold, the thick travelling rug seeming to give no comfort.

Her grandfather had kissed her affectionately, bidding her have a care for herself, and to send word by one of the justice's grooms upon her safe arrival, and if she should find need of anything which Southerndown Court might provide. His pleas were reinforced by Mrs Crandle, all faded prettiness and concern, as she bade her farewell, with Elizabeth beside her.

'You must eat well, Rebecca,' she adjured, 'dress warmly, take plenty of sleep, but moderate exercise . . . not spend too much time in the sickroom, for you might grow depressed and lose your health and youthful bloom. You must behave circumspectly, as befits a young lady with no proper chaperone . . .' Rebecca kissed her delicately scented cheek, her eyes sparkling mischievously at Elizabeth's, while promising gravely to obey.

The small coach seemed to be one of the very few which had braved the snowdrifts, moving slowly but steadily over the compacted highway, its slenderness and good springing making its progress tolerable.

Sir Matthew had positioned a workman with a shovel to hand upon the luggage seat at the rear of the coach, where he stayed, perched precariously, lest it became necessary to make a way, or extract them all from danger. Sir Matthew had taken the further precaution of arming the gamekeeper with pistols and blunderbuss, setting him as guard beside the old coachman upon the box, lest the highwayman reappear, bidding him, 'Shoot only in the most dire of circumstances, and to defend Mistress de Breos'. Mrs Crandle had become so agitated upon hearing this that Elizabeth was forced to remove her indoors and revive her with a strong inhalation of sal volatile; an occurrence which strengthened Rebecca's belief that she had been right to eschew her company.

The journey proceeded irritatingly slowly, for they were hampered both by conditions and the tethered horses following the coach. Mixed with Rebecca's concern lest their halting progress make Rosa despair of their coming, was the biting discomfort of cold and the tedium.

Effie, the young pauper girl whom Rebecca had chosen to train as her maid, was diligent and willing, but still cowed from her days in the poorhouse. She was overawed by her surroundings and by Rebecca herself, whom she considered a very great lady who had delivered her from a life of drudgery. Although her gratitude was touching, Rebecca would have been more thankful for Elizabeth's wry humour and cultivated conversation.

With the paucity of other carriages and wildlife limiting even such puerile games as 'Spot the Magpie' or 'How many Grey Horses?', pastimes further blighted by Effie's irritating determination to defer to her, Rebecca would have penned a letter to Joshua upon the lid of her rosewood coaching box, which contained a writing compendium. Having tried, and failed, to produce anything legible, because of the roughness of the track, she took up an improving book furnished by Mrs Crandle, who was ever eager to fill the idle hour and encourage the polite arts. It proved so unreadable that it had the unexpected benefit of lulling Rebecca into sleep.

Joshua, unaware of Rebecca's progress towards Tythegston Court in the de Breos' coach, was intent upon following the distinctive tracks of Illtyd's miniature piebald, Faith – a name which, given the treacherous conditions, the hayward's disabilities and the difficulty of his quest, struck Joshua as ludicrously apt.

Having scoured the bleak expanse of the common lands to no avail, the constable veered towards Nottage, hoping that pony and rider might have returned to the warmth and safety of the cottage and stables beside the blacksmith's forge. Illtyd's mother, the Widow Cleat, confirmed that he had indeed done so, merely to snatch a hasty breakfast and, despite her entreaties and warnings, ride at once to Stormy Downs to see to the safety of the flocks.

'Indeed, Joshua,' she confided, her plump pretty face drawn into anxious lines, 'I begged him not to go, most earnestly, but I might more usefully have saved my breath to cool my porridge! He would rather vex me than see a beast hurt or distressed. It is the way he is, and there is an end to it!'

Ben Clatworthy, the blacksmith, was busy at his anvil, despite the lack of horses in need of his services, confessing, with a shamefaced smile, that he was grateful for an opportunity to work upon farm implements overlong in need of repair. The forge was cocooned in white-hot heat from the fire, furiously fanned by the small apprentice who seemed barely as high as the bellows he wielded; each breath the bellows exhaled as laboured as the boy's own.

Joshua had to discipline himself not to linger and to ride out upon the gelding into the cold air, which seemed to meet him as a real physical barrier. Then, thoughts of Illtyd's safety brushing all aside, he embarked upon the cold, perilous journey to Stormy Downs.

When he finally saw Illtyd ahead, the piebald making tortuous progress and all but swallowed up in the landscape of snow, he cried out urgently. Illtyd stopped, half turning in the saddle the better to look back.

'Joshua,' he called out sharply as the gelding approached. 'You have come to seek me?' His gaze was intent, questioning.

'No. I seek less welcome company! The highwayman who wounded Doonan . . . You have heard of it?'

Illtyd nodded, his intelligent blue eyes filled with concern. 'Yes. I happened upon Tom Butler from the Crown. It is a cruel blow for Rosa. I pray God that he survives, for he has been friend and champion to me.' Their conversation and commiserations over Doonan continued as Joshua skilfully, and unnoticed by Illtyd, pushed the gelding ahead to make a way.

There was a fierce cry of alarm as Illtyd, seeing the awkwardly humped snow in the lee of the hedge and the telltale breathing holes, leapt from the piebald, floundering breast high in the drift as he scrabbled with his bare hands to free the interred sheep. Joshua as swiftly dismounted and went to his aid. The terrified creature, fleece matted with crusted ice, fought as they made to release it from its snowy tomb, protuberant eyes rolling with terror, spindle legs raking its captors. Then, with a cry, it was away to safety upon the trail their mounts had made.

Again and again, as they rode, they halted to repeat their task, not feeling the cold in the exhilaration of delivering the beasts. Their wet clothing clung to them rawly, and their hands grew numb and mottled as brawn as they worked. Yet they felt nothing but that deep glow within that flamed their cheeks and eyes with colour.

Then, exhausted but secure in their closeness as friends, they made to part: Joshua to ride to Tythegston House to seek news of Doonan and Illtyd to retrace his way to Nottage along the trail that Joshua's gelding had blazed.

'I thank you for your timely appearance and help,' Illtyd said, remounting. 'I hope your search for the highwayman yields as rich a reward.'

'I would sooner see him buried than those poor ewes!' replied Joshua feelingly. 'Yet, like them, he seems to have been swallowed unseen into the snow!'

'How will I know him should I stumble upon him unawares?' asked Illtyd.

'He rides a fine chestnut and, from enquiries at the Crown and the livery stables, it is not recognised hereabouts. You know of it?'

Illtyd shook his head regretfully. 'No, and I know and recognise most mounts and riders hereabouts. Try the itinerant horse-dealer, Joshua. He has some part in most transactions where horse flesh is involved. He is a coarse loutish fellow, and would steal a crust from his own mother's mouth were she starving. Yet he might help, for Doonan's sake, or money!'

'Where can I find this paragon?'

'Upon the first of every month, he is to be found in the yard of the Prince of Wales Inn at Kenfig. It is where the freemen of the borough meet over a pint of ale, and near enough to the great Pool to water his beasts. I swear if he sold them by weight, he would make them drink it dry! You will have but a few days to wait for his coming.'

'A pleasure, indeed,' muttered Joshua.

With a smile, and renewed hopes for Doonan's recovery, the little hayward set out upon his way, trusting that the farmers upon Stormy Downs would already have tended their flocks, for upon such care were their futures founded. He had done what he could and was content.

Rebecca was jerked from her shallow sleep by a frenzied

shouting and the rocking of the coach as the coachman first whipped up the horses, then brought them to a shuddering halt, the animals blundering and plunging into the snow, and the reserve pair stumbling into the rear of the coach, to the terrified cries of the man atop the luggage. She tried to marshall her senses and to quieten Effie who was screaming, hysterically, that they would all be murdered, kidnapped, or worse. Rebecca struggled to the window to enquire of the coachman what was amiss, believing that they might have met with some obstacle upon the highway or stopped to aid stranded travellers in distress. What she saw so surprised her that she could but stare in open-mouthed astonishment, soon to be replaced by a cold shaking rage. A highwayman sat astride a chestnut mare, face masked and screened by a silken kerchief, cocked pistol trained upon the coachman and guard.

'Stand and deliver!'

The words came to her clearly, so banal and ridiculous that, for a moment, forgetting Doonan, she was tempted to leap down from the coach and box his stupid ears! The guard must have made a sudden movement then, for there was a swift explosion from the highwayman's pistol and a fierce thud as his bullet found the structure of the coach; the horses reared and neighed in alarm, saved from bolting only by the shouted command and close reining of the old coachman.

The highwayman stared with insolent coolness at the window of the coach, seeing Rebecca's flushed and handsome face, eyes furious, and filled with contempt.

'Your servant, Mistress de Breos,' he said languidly, and there was no mistaking his amusement. 'I wager that there is no jewel you carry to equal you, ma'am, but you will surrender them none the less.'

The air was ripped by a shattering noise, and the

highwayman seemed to be thrown back in the saddle, dropping the pistol from his left hand as, with a shout, he spurred his mare and made off down the snow-filled lane to Merthyr Mawr and the old stone-dipping bridge which straddled the river. The gamekeeper leapt from the box, the pistol he had discharged swiftly discarded, his loaded blunderbuss clutched threateningly. He gave chase on foot but, though he fired wildly after the highwayman, he knew that he was powerless to follow.

The safety of the passengers assured, the terrified wretch upon the luggage box who had fallen off in the commotion, and all but been trampled senseless by the spare horses, was restored to his perch. The old coachman, having disentangled the reins and inspected the four horses, declared them to be frightened and bruised but otherwise unharmed. Despite the pleading of the gamekeeper, he declined to uncouple and change them, insisting that it was but a short journey to Tythegston Court, and he would not risk the highwayman's returning to find them at a disadvantage. Sir Matthew had placed Mistress de Breos in his care, and her safety was his only thought. Rebecca sat, quietly composed, her mind so firmly upon the highwayman that she was unconscious of Effie's pinched face and her subdued snivelling. There was something about him which she seemed to recognise. His voice, perhaps, or merely the arrogant assurance of a gentleman used to being obeyed? Of one thing she was sure, although the gamekeeper had stood deliberately to hide it as he picked up the highwayman's pistol, there had been blood upon the snow.

The highwayman had been wounded.

Joshua, within sight of the justice's house, was astounded to see the de Breos' coach negotiating its griffon-topped entrance, an armed guard beside the coachman and a man at the rear, with two tethered horses following.

He thought, at first, that fatigue and cold had made him imagine it, but the jangling of harness, and the clatter of hoof and wheels, and the human cries were all too real as he drove the gelding forward to investigate. He was fleetingly aware of his dishevelled state, and what a poor ungentlemanly figure he cut, before the coachman had pulled down the steps, flung open the door and Rebecca had descended. Her eyes alighting upon the dark gelding, she half turned away without sign of recognition before halting to stare at Joshua. Then, a smile of joyous incredulity so illumined her pretty face that he could only gaze at her, unmoving, startled by her radiance. Without a thought for her host, the justice, or the servants gathered, she all but flew through the snow of the yard and flung her arms about him, knocking her bonnet askew upon its ribbons, dark hair cascading about his face, as she kissed him with a most unladylike display of passion, exclaiming, when she could take breath, 'Oh, Joshua, my love! My dear! I have so longed to see you.' A sentiment which occasioned a discreet cough from the waiting justice, and would most certainly have brought a scandalised rebuke from Mrs Crandle had she the wit to speak before resorting to her vinaigrette. 'Such a commotion upon the way! That wretched highwayman accosted us and actually fired a shot!' There was a moment of incredulous silence before Rebecca cried despairingly, 'Rosa! Oh, I must go at once to Rosa. How could I have forgotten, even for a moment?' Her voice was raw with compassion and shame, and the justice, seeing her fatigue and the glint of tears upon her lashes, put his hand comfortingly on her shoulder.

'You shall go at once, my dear. My housekeeper, Mrs Blayney, will take care of you. You will excuse the discourtesy of your host, I know, for it is imperative that I speak with young Stradling and the guard upon your coach.'

'Cavan, sir. His condition . . .?' Her voice was so low as to be barely audible.

'Grave, I fear. He has developed a fever, some inflammation upon the site of the wound, but Dr Burrell attends him devotedly.'

'Dr Burrell, sir?' she exclaimed, bewildered. 'But Grandfather told me nothing of his presence . . .' She looked at Joshua for enlightenment.

'He was upon the coach, by chance, and gave what assistance he could afford.'

At a nod from the justice, the housekeeper, a strong-featured chatelaine with the firm yet gentle persuasiveness of a child's nurse, came forward to shepherd Rebecca within.

'Now, sirs, to our business!' instructed the justice briskly, first commanding his grooms to remove the carriage and horses to the coach house, and Joshua's gelding to the stables for rest and fodder. 'You will return with two fresh mounts,' he added, 'that are both reliable and swift, for the constable will need to ride out at once, and Sir Matthew's guard with him.' He turned to Joshua saying irritably, 'The damned impudence of it! To actually strike twice, and almost upon my very doorstep!'

Joshua quickly suppressed a smile.

'There is something you find amusing in the situation, sir?' The justice's voice was dangerously level.

'No, sir. I find no humour in having a friend lying mortally wounded by the creature, and my fiancée's life imperilled,' Joshua replied truthfully.

'Quite so, Stradling,' the justice approved, mollified. 'This wretch must be apprehended at once! I could wish him already dangling from a gibbet upon Stalling Down, his skull a haunt for carrion, and his fate a warning to others of his profession!'

Joshua, remembering their first encounter when the justice had remarked, coldly, that judgement was the prerogative of the jury and God, smiled involuntarily, remarking blandly, 'I am sure, sir, that were he to appear before you he could expect judgement to be both merciful, and savagely appropriate, as befits a clergyman and magistrate.'

The justice glanced at him suspiciously, taking his gold-rimmed lenses from his pocket and clipping them over his fleshy ears, the better to examine him. Seeing the constable's expression to be sober and guileless, he merely grunted, stroking his dark jowls, then demanding, 'Now, guard, where did you encounter this villain?'

'At that byway which leads to the sheep-dipping bridge over the Ogmore river, sir, near Merthyr Mawr.'

'Hmmm . . .'

'I have his pistol here, sir, for he dropped it in his eagerness to escape.'

'The devil you have!' The justice inspected it gravely. 'It is no ordinary pistol, Constable,' he declared to Joshua. 'This is a gentleman's pistol, as you may witness by the silver wire inlay upon the barrel, and by its craftsmanship. One of a pair of holster pistols, I have no doubt.' He examined it more closely. 'The barrel and lock are signed, "Delany of London" and I declare the touchholes to be of gold! It bears some crest, yet I cannot quite make it out, for it is too well worn. A family piece, perhaps? What do you make of it, Stradling?'

Joshua took the gun and studied it carefully. 'Indeed,

sir, a fine pistol, with the refinement of a safety catch fitted behind the cock. Therefore his firing has been coldly deliberate. Yet, does it prove him a gentleman? Might it not be part of his spoils?'

The justice looked downcast. 'Yes. I confess that it is likely. But, if he retains its partner . . .? He recalled himself with an effort, removing the pistol from Joshua's hands, and saying, 'I will study the crest with my eye-glass, to see if I can identify it, sir. I fancy it to be an heirloom, for it has been well cared for, for a century or more, as befits its quality. Should it be necessary, I shall establish its provenance and history with its makers.'

'I believe, sir,' volunteered the guard diffidently, 'that I grazed the man with my pistol, a flesh wound at worst. Yet I saw traces of blood upon the snow.'

'Then you had both best be gone!' declared the justice, 'Before the trail grows cold, and he makes good his escape.' Upon seeing Joshua's hesitation as the groom brought forward their mounts, saddled and ready, 'What is it, Stradling?' he demanded, irascibly.

'I had hoped to see Doonan, sir.'

'When you return,' the justice stated implacably. 'It will bring him greater pleasure to know his assailant is caught.'

'Yes, sir,' agreed Joshua, mounting obediently.

'I declare, sir,' Robert Knight observed testily, 'your appearance as constable does you small credit. You appear to have been thrown into a pool, then dragged through a thicket.'

Joshua offered no explanation.

'In view of your engagement to Miss de Breos,' he continued grudgingly, 'and Sir Matthew's expressed approval, you may return to dine this evening, in your capacity as gentleman rather than your official role as constable.'

'I thank you, sir,' said Joshua, raising his helmet courteously, 'and I accept most gratefully. As for my roles as constable and gentleman, I confess that there is little confusion, for I try, at all times, to remember that I am both.'

The gamekeeper who awaited him turned away to hide a smile, thinking, Well said, young Stradling, sir! Then he heard a strange, grumbling noise that grew in volume and, glancing back, saw that Robert Knight was fighting to control himself, his plump jowls trembling, and his whole body shaking with mirth.

Chapter Five

Rebecca, despite her fatigue and the unexpected rigours of the journey, had insisted upon going at once to Rosa, declining all offers of rest and refreshment. She vowed that she would not waste a moment more in delay, even to wash away the grime of travel, although all had been most scrupulously prepared and set out for her in her dressing-room. Thankfully surrendering the care of the distraught Effie to the competent Mrs Blayney, and being reassured as to the well-being of Hughes, the old coachman, already ensconced and being comfortably fed in the servants' hall, she was shown to Doonan's sick-room.

The footman having been dismissed, she hesitated outside the door, reluctant to lay her hand upon the door knob and, by turning it, to enter a world of grief and disorder. Then, with an effort, she forced herself to enter, seeing the little tableau before her with the clarity of a painting, frozen and unreal: Doonan's flushed and fevered face; Rosa's paleness; and Dr Burrell's dark intensity as he stood bowed over his patient, narrow fingers upon Cavan's wrist.

Then the painting, blurred with her own tears, grew real, and Rosa was in her arms, and she in Rosa's, smiling and crying their relief, as if each might take comfort from the other's warm flesh. Dr Burrell had released his patient's wrist, setting it gently upon the coverlet, and in that small, expressive gesture, Rebecca fancied she saw a relinquishing of his task, an acknowledgement. Yet the massiveness of Cavan's hand, the rough fleshiness of its palm and fingers, calloused by toil, spoke only of life. He could not go so gently, unresistingly, away. Burrell came hesitantly towards her, his dark, cadaverous face shadowed and unreadable. He held out his thin hands, grasping hers in greeting. In answer to her unspoken query, he said gently, 'Rebecca, I am glad that you have come. Rosa has need of your friendship, as deeply as I once needed it . . .'

The man in the bed stirred massively, crying out in terror from some dark, unreachable place, and Rosa was at once beside him wiping the sweat from his flushed face with a cloth, lying across his body to stifle the harsh tremors which shook him. Then she wrenched herself upright, gripping his shoulders hard.

'Fight, Cavan!' she raged at him fiercely. 'Fight! Don't go away from me! Stay, I beg of you . . .' Then her voice grew quieter as she entreated despairingly, 'Oh, God! Don't let him die. I have had him so short a time . . . Don't take him from me. It would be too cruel. I will never ask you for anything else as long as I live, I promise, just give me this one thing. Take what you will from me afterwards. I will never complain, I swear it! Only give him back to me!' Her voice was raw, anguished. Burrell, gripping Rebecca's hands more tightly, wondered how many times before he had heard the same despairing cry.

Whether the pain of Rosa's grief broke through to him, no one in that room could know, but Cavan's hand reached out blindly to touch his wife's upon the coverlet.

'I am here, my love,' said Rosa gently. 'I am here . . .'

Rebecca would have gone to her then, but the pressure

of Burrell's hands increased, drawing her back, as he helplessly shook his head.

Joshua and Sir Matthew's gamekeeper were finding the way over Three Steps Hill still bleak and treacherous with drifted snow, their mounts restive and sometimes unwilling to proceed. They were grateful that the de Breos' coach had carved out tracks for them, and these they followed until they reached the main highway, where the going became easier and their horses gradually more responsive. When they reached the lane where the highwayman had appeared, the constable dismounted first, and together they examined the trampled snow, still bearing the darkly brown traces of the highwayman's blood.

'It is as well, sir, that I have you with me,' said Joshua appreciatively, 'for you will be an expert upon tracking, of that I am sure . . .'

'I could wish the trail warm, sir,' responded his companion, 'for I fear that it has by now grown cold, and that the fox, for that is what he is, vicious and cunning, will have used all his wiles to elude us. There is no doubt that, but for my bullet finding his flesh, he would have done Mistress de Breos harm.'

'Then I am in your debt, sir, and gratefully acknowledge it.'

The gamekeeper brushed his thanks aside, saying, 'I think it was not the prospect of gold alone which drew him, if you will forgive the impertinence, sir . . .' The man's lean face was awkward, embarrassed. 'I have said nothing to Mistress de Breos, or any other, but it troubled me that he called her by name.'

'He recognised the crest, you think?'

'No, sir, that he knew who she was. He addressed her

without hesitation, and,' he paused, 'in an insolent and over-familiar manner, sir, begging your pardon. I believe it was that which stirred me into letting fly with my pistol, against Sir Matthew's express advice.'

'I am sure that Sir Matthew would approve your actions, sir,' observed Joshua warmly. 'You may have no fears on that score.'

The gamekeeper nodded. 'I should have killed him, sir,' he said regretfully. 'One does not leave a wounded fox. The scent of blood, whether his own or others', stirs in him a kind of madness. Blood lust, spurring him on to wilder, more cruel excesses . . .'

'Then we had best make haste and catch him!'

They carefully followed his tracks along the dry-walled lane, bare skeletons of trees rising darkly on either side, branches stark against the winter sky. At the approach to the hump-backed dipping bridge, the snow had been trampled into a blur of hoof prints and fresh sheep droppings that told of a flock's entrance into a nearby field, their tracks leading across the bridge and far beyond.

Careful scrutiny on the far side revealing nothing, they retraced their steps, taking the river bank, riding for some time in silence.

'It seems,' said the gamekeeper, 'that our fox took to the river, sir, to throw us off his track.' He pointed. 'There, upon the far side, is evidence of his scrambling out and fresh blood . . .'

Crossing the river, they followed resolutely through a small copse of beeches and over a riverside meadow, its ploughed surface uneven beneath the snow. Then the tracks reached down once more into the river. Each went his separate way back into its icy waters, deepened and made swift by the fallen snow. But, at last, they had to admit defeat. It was with anger and disappointment that they rode dispiritedly back to Tythegston Court.

The justice, interviewing Joshua in the library, an austerely masculine retreat, air permeated with the smell of ink, leather and that musty dankness peculiar to such places, was not best pleased.

'It seems to me inconceivable, Stradling, that, given the benefit of the rogue's clear tracks in the snow, you were unable to follow and apprehend him . . .'

'He used the safety of the river, sir, to confuse us,' mumbled Joshua.

'Confuse you!' Robert Knight's dark eyebrows rose warningly. 'It is not your business to be confused, sir. Your business is to catch him! What sort of a fool does it make me look, unable to apprehend a villain upon my own doorstep? What sort of fool?'

Joshua declined to comment.

'I shall be the laughing-stock of the neighbourhood, sir! Two of those under my very roof attacked and threatened by this man. It will not do, Stradling! It will not do at all!' He smashed his fist savagely upon the desk, sending inkwells, quills and all else upon its surface leaping and trembling with agitation. 'I take it that you have some plan of action in mind? Some positive steps to pursue . . .? At the moment you seem to be stumbling blindly, merely floundering deeper and deeper into the mire.'

'There is the clue of the pistol, sir, the crest, and I have hopes, too, of tracing his mount through an itinerant horse-trader.'

'Indeed?' the justice's voice was cold, unimpressed, as were the protuberant brown eyes behind his lenses. 'You are to be congratulated, Stradling, upon your drive and perspicacity! A formidable catalogue. I wonder that you will have the energy to pursue it all!' Joshua shifted uncomfortably under his scrutiny, as he continued scathingly, 'I shall expect results, sir! Either the highwayman's head on a platter - or your own.'

'As befits the rector of the parish church, St John the Baptist.' The words had risen, unbidden, to Joshua's lips.

The justice stared at him unblinkingly for a moment, then his lips twitched involuntarily as he strove to regain his composure. 'Impertinence does nothing to strengthen your case, Stradling!'

'No, sir. I apologise. A thoughtless aberration.'

'As, indeed, is this whole operation,' countered Robert Knight severely. 'I take it, sir, that you will be dining here tonight?' he added with an abrupt change of mood.

'Yes, sir. I had planned to visit Doonan, briefly, if you and Dr Burrell will allow it, then to ride home and make myself presentable.'

'I am relieved to hear it,' said the justice drily, 'and that you consider a change of clothes will perform the miracle. I should have suggested an entire change of attitude and manner, sir!' His eyes twinkled, 'Well, have you no pertinent answer, Stradling? Come, you are not usually at a loss for words!'

'Only that "Manners Makyth Man", sir.'

'Precisely what I said,' observed the justice with some satisfaction.

After visiting Doonan, and giving news of her mother and friends to the seemingly indefatigable Rosa, who still refused to leave her husband's bedside, Joshua embraced her with the greatest gentleness and affection, vowing to return that evening. Should she wish him to take over the care of the invalid, by day or night, he promised, she had but to say the word. He would keep himself ever at their service.

He made no attempt to see Rebecca, although he would dearly have loved to take her in his arms and demonstrate, with loving words and actions, how gravely he had missed her. Already, Joshua reasoned, Robert Knight had reservations about his claims to being styled 'gentleman'. Perhaps it was safer to meet Rebecca discreetly, and in the company of others, for if Joshua saw her alone the justice might well be proved right.

Rebecca had no heart for the formality of the justice's dinner table, but Rosa's insistent pleas that she attend, and the expected presence of Joshua, finally persuaded her. She dressed with the greatest of care, in a dinner gown of the deepest rose pink, with the neckline fashionably low to show her fine shoulders. About Rebecca's neck, with many exclamations of excited admiration, Effie had fastened the de Breos' necklace of sapphires and diamonds, and upon her slender wrist, the matching bracelet which, Joshua had insisted, paled insignificantly before the beauty of her fine eyes. The memory of that encounter, in the orangery, brought a warm glow to her cheeks, which Effie's romantic little soul was quick to observe and approve. She was surprised that her young mistress fastened at her waist that simple, almost valueless, brooch, which the old fisherman, Jeremiah Fleet, had given to her in the days when she was but a poor cockle-gatherer upon the shore. If she, Effie, were a great lady, she would throw away all such drab reminders of her former life and wear diamonds and rubies every hour of the day and night, even when asleep . . . She sniffed, for her nose was always sore and raw-tipped, and haughtily lifted her narrow chin. Rebecca, feeling the tug of Effie's chilblained fingers as she applied the comb to her mistress's wayward black hair, thought that she would never make a lady's maid out of Effie, however patiently she instructed her! No, you could not make a silk purse out of a sow's ear! Catching sight of her own elegant reflection in the looking glass upon the dressing table, she thought in amusement, and yet, that miracle was somehow worked upon me! And Effie, seeing Rebecca's mouth curve into unexplained laughter, obligingly laughed too.

Rebecca, thus prepared for her grand entrance into the company of Robert Knight's dinner guests, first made ready to visit Rosa, to display her finery, as she had promised, yet feeling an awkward reluctance to do so, because of the cruel difference in their circumstances.

As she approached the sick-room, Dr Burrell came out, his face tense. So withdrawn and preoccupied was he, indeed, that he passed her without a word.

'Is it your patient, sir, who so engages your thoughts?' Rebecca asked tentatively.

'Oh, Rebecca!' He came to himself with a start. 'I beg your pardon, most humbly. Yes, they were indeed engrossing thoughts which could divert my mind, even for a moment, from a vision of such elegance.' He bowed gallantly. 'But, no, it was not with my patient I was concerned, for I fancy there is the slightest improvement in his condition.'

'You think he will recover, sir?' Her voice was low.

'I do not know, Rebecca,' he admitted honestly, 'there are too many imponderables. Had you asked me but a few hours ago, I would have answered, unhesitatingly, no, I fear that he is dying. Yet, who am I to discount the illimitable power of love? And Rosa has that in abundance.' He hesitated. 'I have known the terrifying power of hatred,' he continued soberly, 'and I must believe that it is exceeded by the power of love, or I have learnt nothing.'

'I have not vexed you, sir, in some way?'

'No, my dear child.' He took her hand, clasping it affectionately between his stronger ones, saying, 'I well remember when this hand, now so soft, was roughened with work for me, Rebecca, in the disused shepherd's hut upon Stormy Downs.'

'Our fortunes have changed much since then, Dr Burrell.'

'Indeed. And mine, as yours, might well do so again, if I will allow it.'

'You speak in riddles, sir,' Rebecca admitted, puzzled.

'I have received a letter from Mansel,' he confided, 'delivered by his groom not ten minutes since. He begs me take up a position as his partner, claiming there is much sickness and work to be done in the three hamlets.'

'Yet you hesitate, sir? Perhaps you feel that you will not be happy here? You would prefer to return to some great hospital . . .?'

'No. My work with cholera victims is over. And as for returning to the harsh, impersonal world of the hospital ward, my time spent in prison has made me solitary, ill-fitted for such a gregarious life . . .' He smiled and added drily, 'Even had I still the youth and strength.'

'What is it that really prevents you, sir?' she asked gravely.

'I fear, Rebecca, that Mansel merely wishes to make amends, that it is an empty gesture, to salve his wounds and mine. I will not accept his pity!'

'Perhaps he asks you because he feels that you are a good doctor, sir, as he has proved himself to be. Loyal, and not self-seeking.'

'Do you rebuke me, Rebecca?' he asked, smiling.

'I ask you, sir, merely to speak to him, face to face, for his sake and for your own. The past is dead, sir, and should not imperil the living.'

'Old sins cast long shadows, Rebecca,' said Burrell helplessly.

'But they are shadows, sir, and not reality, unless we choose to make them so.'

He nodded. 'You are wise, Rebecca, and compassionate, and beautiful. I hope that young Stradling is aware of his good fortune,' he said gently.

'As aware as Rosa is of hers, sir, in having known Cavan, whatever the future may bring. We must live for the day, cherishing every moment . . .'

'Yes,' he said soberly. 'It is as well to do that.'

To Rebecca's disappointment, the small intimate dinner party envisaged by the justice had grown in numbers and, consequently, formality.

Robert Knight, most elegantly attired, yet, despite his careful preparations, still managing to look ill-shaven because of his darkly shadowed jowls, introduced his three unsolicited guests with a lack of cordiality which he made no effort to disguise, explaining stiffly, 'My nephew, Charles Doddridge, and his travelling companions, Mr Humphrey Edmonds and Sir Peter Antrobus were journeying to Swansea, and thence to Ireland. The snow most regrettably marooned their coach, and with admirable ingenuity they took a horse apiece from the carriage, leaving a fourth to the coachman to carry him to the nearest inn.'

'It was felicitous, sir, that I remembered that you lived nearby,' interposed his nephew, a dark-haired, slender counterfeit of his uncle. 'And that I knew we would be assured of a warm and gratifying welcome.'

'Felicitous, indeed!' agreed the justice without enthusiasm.

'You will forgive the wretchedness of our attire, ma'am,' volunteered Sir Peter Antrobus, a pale, effeminate youth who affected an eye glass upon a riband. 'But we could not anticipate meeting a member of the *haut ton* in such a dull provincial backwater.'

'How fortunate then,' Rebecca rejoined immediately, 'that I was confident of meeting three gentlemen as my fellow guests.' She paused. 'For Mr Knight had advised me of the presence of Dr Burrell, Dr Mansel and Mr Joshua Stradling . . .'

Burrell, who had entered the room to hear the end of the conversation, smiled, saying ironically, 'I am grateful, ma'am, that you number me in the glorious company of gentlemen, for I am aware that it is an accolade which needs to be earned, not conferred by birth.' He turned to Robert Knight. 'As, indeed, sir, do your titles as priest and justice . . .'

'And your own, sir, as physician,' supplied the delighted justice, amused by this turn in the conversation.

Hitherto, Mr Humphrey Edmonds, a most unprepossessing young gentleman of middle height, with sharply moulded features and eyes and hair of the same indeterminate brown, had not spoken, save to acknowledge the justice's introductions. Now he came forward, to claim, surprisingly, 'I believe, Miss de Breos, that we will be much in each other's company in future.'

'How so?' replied Rebecca coldly. 'Since, to my knowledge, sir, we have no previous acquaintanceship.'

'It is my intense pleasure and good fortune, ma'am, to have recently been appointed by your grandfather, Sir Matthew de Breos, to be drawing master to you, and to

Miss Crandle, the young lady who shares your lessons. The position relied upon the recommendation of the Nicholl family of Merthyr Mawr House: a family to whom I have the honour to be distantly related.'

'Then I am sure, sir, that your credentials are impeccable, as is your pedigree. If you will now excuse me.' She crossed the room to where Joshua and Dr Mansel were entering, divested of their outer coats, faces glowing pink from their ride in the frosty night air. Mansel, despite his corpulence and the tufted flyaway hair, looked unusually distinguished, in his formal, black Albert coat. And Joshua, with flesh-hugging trousers, commonly called unmentionables, flaring above his boots at the foot, and with his frilled shirt and elaborate neckcloth beneath his brocade waistcoat, looked every inch of his six feet and more the fashionable gentleman. Their greetings were, of necessity, formal, but as she entered the dining-room upon the arm of her host, Rebecca's eyes, that deep incredible blue of the sapphires upon her throat, strayed mischieviously to Joshua's, holding a promise more delightful than any words.

Rebecca found the dinner-table conversation both stilted and boring, for the three young men bound for Ireland seemed to have no interest in anything beyond horseflesh, gaming, and the fashionable watering places, with occasional outbursts about the ruinous bills presented by their tailors and bookmakers, 'driving them', as Doddridge complained languidly, 'to the very edge of beggary'.

'It should be enough,' Sir Peter Antrobus declared petulantly, 'that such people enjoy the patronage of their betters, without demanding to be paid for the privilege.' A witticism which had Joshua replying evenly, 'I do not doubt, sir, that fine feathers make fine birds, and those who provide the plumage must oft be entertained by those poor-plucked carcasses beneath.' Antrobus regarded him quizzically through his eye glass as Joshua continued, unabashed, 'Such rare amusement would be payment enough, I'll warrant, to cancel any debt!'

'I understand, Stradling,' said the judge's nephew, 'that you are a low constable . . . I use the term, of course, merely to distinguish it from the rank of high constable.' His manner was mocking, insolent. 'You consider it to be the occupation of a gentleman?'

The justice gave a gasp of outrage at such effrontery. But, before he could remonstrate, Joshua replied, unruffled, 'Any occupation well done, sir, brings no discredit to a gentleman. As for its designation, it is irrelevant. As irrelevant and cheap as any jibe I might make about your own occupation with being a low gentleman. I use the term, of course, merely to distinguish it from the rank of true gentleman.'

There was a bellow of laughter from Robert Knight, quickly swollen by more general laughter, in which all but the unfortunate Doddridge joined. Dr Mansel tried gallantly to guide the conversation into other less contentious channels, which might be of interest to Rebecca, but his efforts were thwarted by the boorish behaviour of Doddridge and his friends, who drank too much wine, with too little appreciation for the justice's fine cellar. It was with relief that Rebecca at last withdrew to Doonan's room, and left them to their port. But not before she had heard the justice castigating his nephew for his 'loutish behaviour which ill befits a kinsman, and a guest under my roof, sir!' insisting finally, 'You will apologise to Miss de Breos, before you leave'.

Rosa and Rebecca sat with the quiet restfulness of good friends, watching over the wounded Irishman.

There was no doubt in either of their minds that he was rested and breathing more normally, and the feverish anguish had left his skin. It was thus that Joshua found them and, after expressing his delight that his friend Cavan had smiled at Rosa with true recognition and spoken a few gentle words to her, Joshua bade Rebecca accompany him into the garden, that they might have a moment alone.

The night air was chill, and Rosa placed her own cloak upon Rebecca's bare shoulders, bidding her, 'Have a care, for I could not do without you'.

'Nor I,' confessed Joshua as, under protection of the yew hedge, he drew her unresisting into his arms, and kissed her with a fervour and longing which brought the blood coursing through her veins.

'You are not cold?' he fussed anxiously.

'No, sir, nor like to be. For I'll wager such kisses would melt an icicle!'

'And you are not that, Miss de Breos.'

'No, Mr Stradling, I am not that!' she said demurely, as he swept her into his arms again, feeling her soft body warm against his chest, eagerly unfastening her cape that he might shower kisses upon the exposed flesh of her shoulders, the pulse of her throat, her eyelids and her dark fall of hair, before finding her mouth with his own, his lips hard against hers.

'A cold night, Dr Mansel,' came the justice's harsh stentorian voice from the open doorway, where a hung lanthorn shed a pale silvery gleam upon the snow, and Rebecca's and Joshua's interwoven footprints. 'Not a night to linger, however hot and young the blood! My own, I confess, grows cold and sluggish. Yet, despite my lenses, I pride myself upon my impeccable eyesight. I swear, sir, my night vision is so remarkably acute, I could see clean through the densest bush or thicket, or, indeed, any excuses!'

Mansel's reply was inaudible as the door closed upon them, but Joshua could not ignore the justice's implied warning.

Damnation to the old tyrant! he thought, amused against his will. Well, I will set him a poser to confound his fine eyes!

He swung Rebecca effortlessly into his arms and, pausing only to kiss her soundly, made a fresh single track in the virgin snow, carrying her triumphantly within.

Chapter Six

The following morning Rebecca was awakened early by the unexpected sound of rain spattering in flung gusts upon the casement, then settling into a steady relentless downpour. She ran to see, peering through the snail trail of droplets and out on to the grounds. Already the snow had thinned into soiled craters, edges transparent as melting ice, trees and shrubs dripping remorselessly over all.

At least, she thought, creeping back between the cold sheets to lie shivering, Cavan is improving by the hour, and soon I shall be able to travel to Newton to see Joshua, Jeremiah and all my dear friends in the three hamlets. With the highway cleared of snow, Rosa's mother will be able to visit and take charge of the invalid, bullying and cosseting, and organising his recovery like a battlefield campaign. A capable commander, marshalling the justice, Dr Burrell and the household staff into disciplined unmutinous obedience . . . She smiled at the thought of the redoubtable Mrs Howarth arriving by carrier's cart, baskets piled high with 'good nourishing food, unlike that high falutin pap' which the cottagers were sure made milk sops of the gentry.

Rebecca imagined the good lady's arrival and meeting with Sir Peter Antrobus and his expression of horrified fascination as he surveyed her through his ubiquitous glass . . . At least the rain would see an end to his visit and that of his companions! They were ill-mannered boors, with no thoughts in their idle heads other than drinking, gaming and, she was prepared to concede, wenching at the whorehouses and gin dens. She thanked God that her former life had allowed her to meet a man with the strength and character of Joshua, who had given up a life of ease as a gentleman to become a constable, dwelling amongst, and caring for, those in the community who were least able to protect themselves. A low constable, the justice's nephew had called him, and his insulting condescension still rankled within her! Doddridge was nothing but a feckless, posturing gadabout! Even to give thought to such a worthless fellow was to unnecessarily dignify an irrelevance! She would waste no more time upon him! So resolving, Rebecca fell into a deep untroubled sleep, where her mind was better occupied with persistent dreams of being pursued by an unremitting young constable from whom she had not the slightest desire to escape.

The leave-taking of the three young men, bound for Ireland, was brief, and parting with his kinsman, Rebecca was amused to see, caused the justice no grief at all. The trio had eaten a hearty breakfast, and consumed more of the local brew of ale than was good for them, and stood ready in the hallway awaiting the arrival of the grooms with their horses. Robert Knight had particularly asked Rebecca to accompany him and, seeing the justice's curt nod and the relentlessness of his gaze, Doddridge came forward with ill grace to say, without conviction, 'I believe, ma'am, I should apologise for any . . . inconvenience or embarrassment our high spirits at the dinner table might have caused you.'

'Then I accept your apology, sir,' replied Rebecca,

'although the inconvenience was minimal, as I had the pleasure of the good company and conversation of Mr Knight and his other guests to divert me. As to embarrassment, you caused me none, as I had no reason to feel any such emotion.' She removed her hand from his, conscious that he had held it for a fraction too long for politeness, and that his eyes were frankly admiring.

Sir Peter Antrobus, surveying the scene foppishly through his eyeglass, came forward to bid her farewell, his hand limp and soft as if it were boneless, and murmuring some well-rehearsed pleasantry. Of the three, it was Edmonds whom she disliked most, although she could not have explained why, for he had done nothing to offend the proscribed rules of behaviour. Yet, even as he took her hand to bow formally, she was conscious of a distaste for him, an involuntary recoil which she hoped was not evident to others.

'A pleasure and a privilege, Miss de Breos. I do not bid you "Goodbye ma'am", for our parting is but brief. I shall presently be attending you at Southerndown Court, where I shall hope to foster your talent for art and, dare I hope? for friendship.'

The justice, who considered him presumptuous, said coldly, 'I think, sir, that your duties, and status, will be most stringently defined by Sir Matthew, as with all his household servants. Now, I believe the grooms have arrived with your mounts. I wish you a safe and uneventful journey, with the hope that you will not be harassed by snowstorms, should you again find yourselves in this,' he paused, 'Godforsaken, rural backwater.'

He held out his arm formally to support Rebecca's hand and, bowing icily to the young men, led her away.

'My dear Rebecca,' he said, as they walked with dignity

across the hall, 'I know that it is graceless, and lacking in tact, to declare that I dislike my own nephew, unchristian, too, yet I cannot deny it! He is quite intolerable! A fool whom I do not suffer gladly . . . In fact, I am ill equipped to suffer him at all! His mother has indulged him ruinously, and his father all but disinherited him, so shameful and vexing is his behaviour. His friends, and lifestyle, are gross and idle.' He removed his eyeglasses which had become quite misted up with the heat of his eloquence, and polished the lenses with his silk kerchief. 'But I must not bore you with my prejudices and rambling. I shall escort you to Mr Doonan's room, for I believe that Dr Burrell and Rosa will be there, in attendance.' He smiled, replacing his lenses. With his squat figure and large protruding eyes, he seemed for all the world like a benevolent frog.

'I confess, my dear,' he said, with his hand above the doorknob of the sick-room, 'that it is when I see devotion such as Rosa's and Dr Burrell's that I realise that for every selfish rogue, like my nephew, there are a thousand others who practise what I so readily and impertinently preach.'

'No, sir. It is pertinent,' declared Rebecca gently. 'Else from where would their inspiration come?'

'You are a joy and a treasure, Rebecca,' said Robert Knight, smiling broadly, 'and an enigma, too . . .'

'How so, sir?'

'I would have been pondering late into the night, how there was a set of your footprints and young Joshua Stradling's leading into the shrubbery, yet his, alone, returning . . .'

'And you solved the riddle, sir?'

'By the merest chance, for I glimpsed, through the library door, your somewhat unconventional return.'

Rebecca found herself blushing as Robert Knight continued, eyes twinkling, 'But I think, my dear, that must be our little secret. We will let our mutual friend, "the low constable", believe that the rain washed out his little jest, or he will be getting altogether too "high" for his boots!'

Joshua, awakened by the sound of rain upon the deep window high in the eaves of his little cottage, overlooking the village green, gave a sigh of relief. The salt-laden air would, doubtless, have eaten the snow away before many days had passed, but the early coming of the rain might mean the difference between survival and paupery to many upon hill farms, and wresting a scant living from the sea.

He would go this very morning to see his old friend Jeremiah Fleet, who must have been vexed indeed that the snow had prevented his hand-trawling upon the shore, and his weekly excursion, taking fresh-caught fish to the produce market at Bridgend, in his primitive cart. The little Welsh cob which drew it would be in sore need of exercise, for it was plump already from the old man's overindulgence, and Charity, the bull terrier, with his blunt wedge of a face and pink-rimmed eyes, would be fairly dancing with impatience to be away upon sand dune and bay.

Yes, he would go early, Joshua decided, with news of Doonan, Rosa and Rebecca, whom the old man loved as dearly as a daughter, for she had nursed him lovingly through a long and bitter illness, and forced him to survive, as Rosa now willed Doonan to life.

Jeremiah Fleet had also heard the rain and the wind from the sea rattling the window panes of his low, white-washed cottage on the edge of the burrows. The dog, sleeping at his feet upon the narrow iron-framed bed, had grown alert at once upon Jeremiah's movement and cocked an enquiring head, slanting eyes staring into the old man's faded blue ones.

'Yes, we will go to the beach today,' said Jeremiah solemnly, 'for I fancy the gulls have been missing your hue and cry, and the bounty of my fish-leavings. They will give us a welcome, of that I am sure.'

There was a companionship between the pair which was remarkable, uncanny, as if, even without speech, the dog heard and understood Jeremiah's every thought. Sometimes, he admitted, it was as if the creature was aware of his intentions even before they formed in his own mind . . . It was as well that Sophie and her son, Illtyd, were as besotted with the dog as he, otherwise, when he and the Widow Cleat were wed, it would have been a poor look-out for Charity! Much as Jeremiah loved his pretty, good-natured bride-to-be, it would have grieved him to see the animal banished, forced to bed down with the cob in the outhouse, or lie unprotected in the yard. But then, he would not have chosen to wed a woman so lacking in warmth and generosity of spirit! No, it was all down to Jeremiah's own good sense and discrimination, and he hoped that the cur was cognisant of the debt it owed him.

Joshua, having returned the hired gelding to the livery stables, and told Rosa's mother of the justice's insistence that she visit the newlyweds at Tythegston Court, walked back to the Crown Inn through greying rivers of melting snow, grateful for his high leather boots, waxed with dubbin. His mother had made him a handsome gift of two pairs, skilfully fitted upon him and crafted by a master bootmaker in Cardiff, their supple skins offering protection and comfort. It was as well that she was shamelessly extravagant, he thought smiling, or, like the drovers who called at their farmhouse to buy, or merely drive their flocks to London, he would have been forced to use makeshift leggings of Bristol Brown paper, tied with thongs, and waterproofed with soap. No doubt, a spectacle which would have offered Sir Peter Antrobus the keenest of amusements.

Ossie, having saddled the grey for him, and heard Joshua's good news of Doonan and Rebecca, watched him ride out under the arch, the mare's hooves clattering upon the rain-swept cobbles of the yard, and along the track to Jeremiah's cottage at the edge of the dunes.

The old fisherman greeted the constable with undisguised affection, clasping Joshua's hand warmly in his great gnarled fists, eyes sparkling in the weather-beaten face. With the powerful frame honed by work to a spareness of flesh, and his thick grey beard and hair, Joshua thought that Jeremiah looked, more than ever, like some Old Testament visionary: commanding and proud. A far cry indeed from the defeated old man he had once seemed. 'Lamentations Fish' the cottagers had called him then: a lonely figure upon the shore. Trailing his sack of bloodied fish heads for the gulls, he had forsaken human company, having lost the only company he sought, that of his wife and new-born son . . . He had carried his grisly pack like a burden, clasping it tight, never relinquishing it, as if it held the memory of them and he was loath to let it go.

'Doonan?' Jeremiah was demanding, forcing Joshua back to the present. 'Come, my boy, tell me! What news? Glory be to God for His great mercy,' he exclaimed devoutly when Doonan's condition had been discussed. But upon hearing of Rebecca's trials, his face grew troubled. 'I do not like it, Joshua. I do not like it at all. There is something here that speaks of deliberation, some calculated evil, personal and obscene. Rebecca is aware of it?'

'No,' admitted Joshua. 'I think that so great was her rage and indignation at the highwayman's presumption that it was an aspect of the affair she missed.'

'You do not think he would do her physical harm?'

'I do not know, my friend.' Joshua's voice was expressionless. 'Yet how can she be protected? She is a free and independent spirit, from her days upon the shore, as well you know.'

Jeremiah nodded agreement.

'If I warn her,' continued Joshua tensely, 'it will serve no purpose, save to alarm her and destroy her peace of mind. There is no way upon this earth that she can be protected both night and day. And I am useless, unable even to track him down. Yet, I shall tell Sir Matthew, in confidence, of what I fear, and let him make what plans he may for her safety.'

'It seems,' offered Jeremiah reflectively, 'that this highwayman is a bold and arrogant fellow, to halt two coaches within so short a space of time, in such a climate, and with so much violence.'

'Yes, there is some madness in him, some contempt for human flesh and feeling, and without remorse . . . I do not think our search is for some poor scoundrel fallen upon evil times, and desperate to survive, as Dr Burrell testified.'

'Burrell?' cried Jeremiah, astonished. 'He is here?'

Their talk turned to his patient care of Jeremiah in his sickness, the doctor's past, and his part in treating the cholera victims, then to lighter, less disturbing matters.

'Dafydd was pleased as a magpie with the fishing rod you fashioned as his birthday gift,' recalled Joshua, smiling at the memory. 'Strutting and showing off alarmingly, declaring you to be the finest fisherman, not only in the three hamlets, but in all of the world! He also insisted that you are generous, good-natured, and brave as any lion ever born. I wonder your ears did not burn with it, and burst into flame!'

'Why?' asked Jeremiah, ' 'tis but the simple truth, for he is a boy of more than average intelligence and discrimination. I fancy he deserves a birthday treat, some special outing, perhaps, upon the cob and cart, with Charity.'

The bull terrier, who had been snuffling noisily on the hearth, picked up his ears at the mention of his name, body trembling at the prospect of such a rare treat, and came and lay his head upon Jeremiah's knee, almond eyes questioning.

'Yes, you shall come,' promised Jeremiah, patting the broad head and hearing the responsive thump of his tail upon the bare flagstones.

'Do you know,' he demanded of Joshua wrathfully, 'that the landlord of the Ancient Briton asked me if Charity was a Llantrisant White, bred specially for bull baiting? A barbarous sport! Thank God it has been all but ended by law. To teach one of God's creatures to bait another, and hang upon its tongue – what amusement is in that, save for fools and madmen?'

'What did you reply, Jeremiah?'

'I said, "No, I put him to better use . . . savaging the backsides of any damn fool innkeeper crass enough to pose such stupid questions"!'

'And did he believe you?'

'No, for the shameless cur licked his hand for the price of an overripe veal pie.' He shook his head sadly. 'It is a harsh world indeed when your best friend will betray you for his belly!'

And Joshua, laughing indulgently, could not but agree.

Later, Joshua, grateful for the scourging power of the rain which made all but the bleakest tracks and byways to the hill farms and outlying cottages passable, set out upon the grey. Now that the downpour had ceased, there seemed to be, once more, a chill feel to the air, giving a promise of night frost. It would not please the farmers, he knew, for their small plantings of winter root crops, grown to supplement their main harvestings of wool, butter and grain, would lie useless in the ground, unfitted for marketing, or their own use. Frustrated first by snow, then by the rain which stirred their fields into a slough of stinking mud, in turn to be frozen into a barrier of ice. It was small wonder they both loved and cursed the land, as though it were a person of flesh and blood, obtuse, and difficult to live with – or without.

Wherever Joshua rode, to the meanest cot, small holding or farm, he was greeted with courtesy and respect, and begged to 'please warm yourself' at the blazing fire of kindling and turf. More often than not, a kettle hung from a chain above the flames, at a constant boil, or an iron pot of 'cawl', a broth of vegetables and barley, and mutton when it could be spared, simmered from a spithook. Had he sampled but a portion of the refreshment offered, he would have been ill-equipped to remount his mare, much less pursue his enquiries about the highwayman . . .

'No, he has not been seen here, sir,' was the invariable answer, 'for had he come, in the storm, we would not have turned him away, but made him welcome at our poor fireside, as we would any stranger, or lost beast . . .'

Joshua, seeing the half-dead lambs, finger fed and warming to life in fireside oven or hearth, could not doubt it. Even the poorest of those he met pressed upon him some small gift: a single brown hen's egg; a few dried herbs; or the last of the autumn's apples, desiccated and wrinkled as an ancient's skin. These he accepted with the grace and dignity with which they were given, for it would have been insulting to refuse such kindness.

Yet, even at the local inns and ale-houses, his quest for the highwayman, and his search for knowledge of the elusive chestnut mare, fared little better. One such chestnut mare, he was told gravely, belonged to the justice; another to Ossie, the bent ostler at the Crown, although it was a poor beast he had rescued from ill treatment from a stage-coach, and it was doubted if the highwayman could have made use of such a wreck, for it was longer in the tooth than Ossie himself, although the ostler had but few, and the poor horse was as winded as Ben Clatworthy's old bellows, and could scarce stand without being propped up at all four corners!

The few livery stables he visited, before it grew dark, yielding no better result, Joshua dispiritedly turned the mare for home. The wind had turned around and blew now from the south-east, bringing the feel of ice to his face, stiffening the skin. Unlike the justice, he did not wish to see the highwayman dangling from a gibbet upon Stalling Down, the prey of rat and carrion crow . . . It was a sight he had witnessed but once, and recalled with horror. Yet, having seen Doonan's punishment for protecting Rosa, and fearful of what might have befallen Rebecca, Joshua was forced to admit that were the highwayman to be strung aloft by the revenge of another, he might hesitate to stay the man's hand.

That eve, the dirt of the day sloughed off in the icy water of the well in his small bailey, Joshua rode out again, but with a lighter heart. He was to dine, once more, at Tythegston Court, upon the firmly declared whim of the justice. It seemed that Robert Knight, angered and humiliated by the boorish behaviour of his nephew and his two companions, sought to make amends. The ill-fated dinner party was to be resurrected, as originally planned. The prospect of seeing Rebecca and Doonan, and enjoying a well-produced meal, with civilised wines and conversation, pleased Joshua immensely. He actually sang a few bars of *Greensleeves* in a reasonably mellifluous baritone as he took the hill to the Clevis, to the delight of an old lady securing her chickens in their hen-coop by lantern light. In the encircling darkness, the unseen rider, with the rhythm of his horse's hooves upon the highway, and the sweet nostalgia of the refrain, brought unexpected tears to her eyes. Yet, she could not explain, even to herself, what moved her . . .

Joshua rode on, the darkness and cold enveloping him like a cloak, the evening ahead filled with promise. He might not have been so sanguine had he known that a conscientious servant in the justice's house had, that very morning, performed an act of kindness for her master, Robert Knight. Knowing of his wrath for his nephew and his roistering companions and seeking to spare the good priest more, she had removed the blood-soaked bandage from whence it had been quickly bundled within a spoiled shirt and set it secretly upon the laundry-room fire. The glow from it was only equalled by her glow of virtue. It would have served no good purpose to have angered the justice, she reasoned. When the last sparks had died into ash, she returned to strip the linen from the beds of the other two young gentlemen, with all evidences of their sojourn. It was a bewilderment to her that those who should know better could revel in a filth and squalor which no self-respecting pig in a sty would tolerate.

The ritual of the evening meal, with its table set with pristine white napery, and the glow of silver and sparkling crystal, beneath the candle-lit chandelier, set the small party in the best of spirits. Rebecca, Joshua thought, had never looked more lovely, the soft flesh of her shoulders gleaming above the frilled bodice of her dress of pale silvery green, the colour of downy chestnut buds in early spring. Around her throat was clasped a string of milky pearls and, as always, at her waist, Jeremiah's simple gift. It pleased Joshua that Rebecca had not changed, save superficially in beauty and dress. There had always been about her a natural arrogance and style, an inner radiance, which poverty and ill-use had been unable to dim. Yet, it was her real love and understanding of the simple folk like Jeremiah and Illtyd, and her appreciation of their true worth, which Joshua most valued in her.

She was smiling at him now, her fine blue eyes bright and luminous above the silver candelabrum, its candles flickering shadows across the curves and hollows of her face as she held aloft a glass of wine.

'To the partnership and good fortune of Dr Mansel and Dr Burrell,' the justice was proposing. 'May they long share increasing friendship and prosperity.'

Joshua raised his glass, guiltily realising that his study of Rebecca had made him remiss, and that he had taken no part in the preceding conversation. He hastily joined in the toast, seeing the wine within their glasses gleaming blood-red, luminous as beads upon a string . . . and for a moment they did, indeed, seem linked together in closeness and goodwill, an unbroken circle of friendship.

'I shall be sorry to see you leave, sir,' the justice was telling Dr Burrell, and there was no doubting his real regret. 'Yet, as you say, your patient Doonan is recovered enough to demand but one visit from you a day, and it will be more convenient for you to share Dr Mansel's practice, and his house.'

'Yes,' agreed Mansel warmly. 'It pleases me that he will accept.'

'At least,' continued the justice, 'I may enjoy the company of Rebecca for a little while longer. She has plans to visit her friends in the three hamlets, and Sir Matthew is agreeable to her request.' His bulbous brown eyes gleamed wickedly behind his lenses as he said directly to Joshua, 'I fear, sir, that my duties as priest and justice take up much of my time. I hope that if I instructed you, in your capacity as constable, to squire and protect the young lady in my absence, that it will not be too arduous a burden, in addition to your other duties?'

'No, sir,' replied Joshua with mock gravity. 'I assure you that my duties will be carried out with a zeal and ardour which will astound you.'

'Indeed, Stradling,' observed the justice, 'being *in loco parentis*, I am at pains to decide whether such eagerness delights or confounds me!' His ebullient laughter was echoed, good naturedly, by the whole company.

Joshua visited Rosa and Doonan, who greeted him with some of the old vigour, his rough, unlovely face bright with pleasure, and then returned to pay his respects to the justice.

Having apprised Robert Knight of his searches, and his concern for Rebecca, the justice agreed to keep a manservant inconspicuously upon watch at night, before the door to her room, and to send a message to her grandfather, the very next morning.

'You may have a word with her, sir, in private, in the library,' he conceded, 'since you are affianced, and a man of honour and dependability.'

Joshua repressed a smile at the implied warning, thanking him with every evidence of gravity.

Once summoned to the library, Rebecca ran to Joshua with flattering haste, throwing her arms about him affectionately, and kissing him with a fervour completely lacking in modesty. Mrs Crandle would indubitably have cautioned her for behaving in a most unseemly manner, adding that, 'Ladies, my dear Rebecca, do not demean themselves with carnal matters. It is the property of women of ill repute, and the beasts of stable and field'.

It is doubtful if such strictures would have deterred Rebecca, for she was finding these few snatched moments of amorous encounter with Joshua increasingly more pleasurable. As she made to unbutton his shirtfront and slip her soft hand against the hardness of his breast, caressing him the while, Joshua was sore pressed to remember that he was a gentleman, and not to respond in kind.

Damn Robert Knight to little wild pieces! he thought as he regretfully resisted her advances. He has set me upon my honour! Indeed, it is as if he is in this very room, peering at me unnervingly through those confounded lenses!

To Rebecca's disappointment, it was but a few minutes before, with many protestations of affection, he rode away.

The justice, hearing Joshua ride off, smiled as he poured himself a generous measure of cognac.

Ah, young Stradling, he thought, as the liquid warmed and quickened his blood, you think I caution you because I forget what it is to be young. You are wrong, sir. It is because I remember . . .

[illegible]

[illegible]

[illegible]

[illegible]

[illegible]

[illegible]

[illegible]

Chapter Seven

Early next morning, before his usual hour for rising, the justice was at his desk penning a letter to his friend Sir Matthew begging him to send a messenger upon the next day with a letter containing some pretext for Rebecca's early recall. 'She is, indeed, the most accomplished of young gentlewomen, sir, in all the polite arts, and her conversation is as stimulating as her company is amusing. I shall miss her sorely,' he wrote. 'Yet, I would not allow her into danger through my own selfish needs. I cannot guarantee her safety when she leaves this house for her visits to the three hamlets, although I shall see that here she is guarded well and, beyond these walls, put in the care of young Joshua Stradling, who is devoted to her well-being.'

Adding the usual courteous wishes for Sir Matthew's health and fortunes, he signed his name, sanded the letter and placed it in an envelope which he fastened with warm wax, making the clean impact of his seal. He still awaited news from London of the provenance of the pistol, he recalled, and had not yet identified the worn crest upon its elegant butt.

Having summoned a servant to see that his communication to Sir Matthew was dispatched at once by reliable messenger, he sighed and turned his attention to the letter which had newly arrived upon the mail-coach.

His sister, Clara, wrote despairingly that she was:

> 'at my wits' end, sir, with worry and grief. That incorrigible boy, your nephew, has been absent these two months with never a word of his whereabouts, or fortune. He might well be lying sick and wasted somewhere, or suffering from a memory loss, and unable to utter a word . . .'

The justice snorted loudly, remembering how easily he might disabuse her.

> 'He left, sir, in the greatest of ill humours, his father having refused to guarantee the most trifling of debts, for tailoring, I suspect, or some small wager. I gave him every penny which I could rightfully spare, only to find that he had taken the few guineas set aside for those small purchases which a lady prefers to make for herself, sir . . . I also seem to have mislaid a small citrine and diamond brooch, and the pearls which our dear papa gave me upon my marriage to Roderick. I declare, Robert, that the boy must be beside himself with despair, for he would not otherwise have behaved so. He is not a wicked boy, as well you know, simply weak and easily led by those of baser disposition . . .
>
> 'Will you not offer me some comfort and seek him out, for your contacts are wide and discreet, sir? As you would undoubtedly beg me to do, I have freely forgiven my son's venial lapse, and care only for his safety, and swift return to his loving mother. For I cannot declare, in truth, that his father is in the same mind as
>
> 'Your affectionate sister,
>
> 'Clara.'

Robert Knight sat for a long time cogitating as to how he should proceed. If Clara had written but a day sooner, he would have taken the young jackanapes to task, delivering him to the firm hand of his brother-in-law, Roderick, to deal with harshly, as he deserved! What was needed was to put the fear of God . . . the rector corrected himself apologetically, the fear of the Devil into the young reprobate! It was all very well Clara preaching love and forgiveness, but the Bible spoke of real repentance, Robert Knight thought irritably, and he had seen little save arrogance and self-satisfaction in that accursed boy!

Well, at least the episode had yielded an unlooked-for advantage – his text for Sunday's sermon. He would eschew the New Testament for a roll of Old Testament thunder, and perhaps a lightning flash or two of rhetoric and invective. He polished his lenses absent-mindedly. Should it be 'Honour thy father and mother' or 'Spare the rod and spoil the child'?

In the early dawn, Jeremiah Fleet, having taken the cob and cart across the sandy wastes of Pickett's Lease to the sea, paused atop the cobbled ramp to the bay to breathe gulps of clear, iodine-smelling air into his lungs. Ah, he thought with satisfaction, there is nothing on God's own earth its equal . . . I would not exchange it. No, not for wealth, nor food, nor, even, the love of a good woman! He chided himself guiltily with the thought of Sophie, who loved him, and soon would be taken to his bed. Well, he amended generously, perhaps for Sophie, Illtyd, Charity and the cob together, although, mercifully, he need not sacrifice the one for the other . . . Yes, it was a miracle, indeed, when Providence decreed that a man of Jeremiah's advanced years could retain his strength and vigour with a lust for life, and his occupation.

The cob took the cobbled ramp to the bay, the fish frails rattling upon the cart, and Charity bouncing impotently, shrill barks of excitement and fear rising above the scrape of slithering hooves and the jangle of harness.

The bull terrier sped across the tide's edge as Jeremiah set about his task, leaving the fat-rumped cob to its contemplation of the rock pools.

When all was done, the cob ambled unbidden to where its master stood, its reward a piece of carrot which Jeremiah scrupulously divided with his fish knife, delivering a portion to the eager dog. Charity, when the woven frails had been returned to the cart with their heapings of sandy cockles from the nearby beds, and limp iridescent fish, had all but to be lifted upon the cart floor. The dog set himself well out of reach of the importunate claws of the lobsters and crabs, for they were not above settling a nip upon his exposed backside, a lesson he had early learnt. As they looked back across the curved sickle of the sandy bay, held between two scarred arms of curving rock, Charity could see his own petalled footprints along the sea's white-foamed edge, and the gulls which he had chased with such wild abandon, circling above. Jeremiah lifted his sack of guttings and fish heads, scattering them in a timeless ritual across the wet sand. The gulls screamed and wheeled overhead, cries ripping the air, as their beaks and talons ripped at their spoils, bloodying the sand. The air was filled with the beat of their wings and Charity's staccato barks until, with Jeremiah safely returned, the cart moved off. When they were distanced from the grisly feast the dog's threats died to a low growl, then a whimper as he crept to join his master, laying his broad-boned head upon Jeremiah's arm, eyes begging approval.

'You told them!' Jeremiah agreed. 'You had the measure of them, my lad! They knew how far they could go . . .'

The pink-rimmed eyes stayed unblinking, but Charity's tail ecstatically thumped the cart floor.

'You won't change them . . . it's their nature. Red in tooth and claw. They know no better, for they have not your intelligence, nor your breeding.'

With a sigh of sheer contentment, Charity sank down upon the empty sack, bracing himself as, with a clatter of wheels and of hooves, the fat cob took the ramp for the dunes.

Once the cob had been unharnessed, returned to the outhouse and fed and watered, Jeremiah's hard work began. He slit the iridescent bellies of the fish, setting aside the livers to grow rancid for lamp oil; washed the cockles free of sand and boiled them upon the round brick oven in the yard, then bearded the blue-shelled mussels he had wrenched from the rims of the rock pools. When all was to his satisfaction, he reharnessed the cob, now rested and refreshed for several hours, and eager to be upon its way. With the yard thickly clotted with the damp pervasive smell of boiled shellfish and offal, and Charity happily ensconced beside him, Jeremiah took the track to Newton village to deliver the shellfish, fresh crabs, lobsters and wet fish to his customers at cottages, farms and inns. His baskets were but part full, for the snow had robbed him of his livelihood, and he had garnered what little he could before the encroachment of the tide. Yet some, he knew, must be disappointed. Tonight he would return to set his nightlines once again, and perhaps take the boy Dafydd to help him at his cockle-gathering, if the child could be spared from the farm.

Tomorrow was New Year's Eve, and there would be plenty of merriment in the three hamlets, not all of it to the rector's taste, Jeremiah well knew . . . There would be the last of the wren hunts begun on St Stephen's day, with the captive bird set into the little house of wood and carried from dwelling to dwelling upon four crossed poles. It was an old tradition, yet dying now, and no one seemed aware of its origins, or meaning . . . Once there had been a song chanted by the men who bore it aloft, but its words had long been forgotten, and it had become but an excuse to line the men's pockets with coppers, to squander upon ale at the taverns. Jeremiah was soft-hearted, and often the last call they made was to his cottage near the dunes, for it was well known that he would give with a reckless generosity to pay for the poor trapped creature's release. Although the darkness hid its flight, Jeremiah had sometimes glimpsed the bird briefly in the light of the beams from the men's lanterns and felt his own heart lifted, with its wings, to freedom.

Doubtless there would be wassail parties, with spiced apple cake and the company sharing too much ale from the vast twelve-handled bowls. Gifts of apples and nuts would be pressed upon the first stranger met to ensure good fortune. And, upon New Year's Day itself, the children would collect the 'callenig', the New Year's gift of a shining new coin, or sweetmeat, from those they visited. Jeremiah had thoughtfully set aside four little bundles for Dafydd and his three young siblings in cotton kerchiefs, of sweetings, dried cob nuts and an apple set upon four twigs, and crowned with a circlet of herbs and oats.

What did it symbolise? Jeremiah never knew, but

thought that the children would welcome the gifts for what they were: a sign of affection and hope for the year ahead.

These were harsh times for a family without a grown man to protect and support them and, pagan or otherwise, the little family, like many another in the three hamlets, would need all the good fortune they could garner to face the year ahead.

Jeremiah vowed then that, forsaking all, he would go at once to Sophie's and Illtyd's little cottage alongside the forge, taking them a gift of the finest lobster on his cart and a crock of his plumpest, most delectable cockles. He flicked up the cob and, with Charity's excited barks heralding their arrival, saw Sophie's pretty face, warm and pink with smiles, as she ran to greet him. Charity was there before him, leaping into her arms to be fondled as she bent low, but her eyes were for Jeremiah as she straightened up, and the love and joy in them stirred in his breast with a long-forgotten sweetness.

'I have brought you a New Year's gift, my dear,' he said, embracing her awkwardly, 'to offer you good fortune in the coming year.'

'You are all of my good fortune, Jeremiah,' she said gently, 'all I shall ever need or want. And I shall be loving you, and thanking God for it until the day I die . . .'

Jeremiah tried to smile, but he could not control the tell-tale trembling of his mouth, so he turned to bring her gifts from the cart, but Sophie had already seen the tears upon his lashes.

Joshua, riding out from the Crown to visit the livery stables and inns farther afield in his quest for the highwayman and his elusive mount, saw a small procession of youths in the distance, searching the bare hedgerows, one carrying a makeshift cage, roughly lashed together from twigs. He smiled involuntarily, thinking that their chances of so heavy-handedly trapping so spry a bird were as unlikely as his own of tracking down his quarry . . .

Joshua purposefully skirted Tythegston Court, although sorely tempted to linger and pass a pleasant hour with Rebecca, and Doonan and Rosa. There had been no invitation to dine that night from Robert Knight, and the constable supposed that the justice's own conviviality and laxity towards him had melted as inevitably as the snows, and that he would be expected to be sedulously about his lawful duties.

Had he but known it, Robert Knight was engrossed in his role as cleric, rather than justice. The traditions of Winter's Eve, which seemed so harmless and mystifying to Jeremiah and his friends, were clear to him. They were pagan and corrupt; the more so since their perpetrators practised them in innocence, unaware of what evils might be conjured up.

He would go, this New Year's Eve, to the church of St John the Baptist, and keep a solitary all-night vigil at the altar, praying and asking God for His help. He had vowed, upon his ordination, that he would never close the doors of the church, for there were many in his flock who would need the benefit of God's presence in adversity or affliction, and it would be a sin to deny it to them.

Yet, he was aware that the old evils lingered. Had he not seen, with his own eyes, the burning of candles in that awesome silent procession around the church, as the villagers tried secretly to call up spirits to foretell, by the flickering of the candle flame, who would grow sick or die within the coming year? He had banished the ill-doers, startled and shamefaced, as zealously as Christ himself had scourged the money lenders from His temple.

He shook his head sadly. They were poor, ill-educated people, who did not know what demons they set loose. There would be no listening within the church porch for raised voices of the dead that night, he would make sure of it! If he could not always deliver them from their sins, he thought wrily, at least he could deliver them from evil!

With the vanishing of the snow, and the coming of the rain, the gypsies had returned to the three hamlets, to the open hostility of the farmers, and the delight of the cottage children. They came on foot, or upon simple wooden carts drawn by small donkeys with delicate hooves, their moth-eaten hides the softly blurred shades of newly turned earth. The carts were piled high with cloth-fastened bundles and faggots of wood, and hung about with the clutter of work and living. Iron cooking pots, blankets and the myriad jangling vessels to be bartered or repaired, for many plied their trade as travelling tinkers.

Wherever there was room, and often where there was not, the high-piled bundles bore an old woman, too frail to walk, or a child too young. The ancients smoked clay pipes, like the menfolk, their faces wrinkled and walnut-dyed under mats of coarse hair. The children were quite extravagantly beautiful, with dark solemn eyes and wide-boned faces. Their skin, burnished by sun and wind, glowed like comb-honey, their soft bee-sting lips opening over strong, luminous teeth. They seemed to be always smiling, shouting, scrapping among themselves, like the lean curs which followed the carts and, with them, the raggle-taggle ponies, hollow-backed and winded, pied and plain.

There was something exuberant about the procession, despite the poverty and hardship of the living: some inexpressible, joyful arrogance, a relic, perhaps, of some unknown ancestry, its genesis a warm sun-filled land where they were princes, not outcasts.

Ossie, seeing them pass the archway of the Crown and hearing the crashing and jangling of the pots and pans, the uproar of carts, and children, ponies and barking dogs, could not help but smile as they passed by, the younger women barefooted and lissom, the men dark and arrogant in their tattered clothing. They bowed to him extravagantly as they passed by, dancing to the sounds of a fiddle, and Ossie returned their salute with an aristocratic sweep which all but pitched him to the cobbles.

With their laughter ringing in his ears, he waved them upon their way to some resting place, perhaps in the sheltered hollow of the dunes, a plain where small underground streams surfaced upon the bay below; or else some wayside patch aside a brook or pool, where they might water themselves and their beasts. The bolder children of the hamlets postured behind them, shouting and calling them names, excited and terrified by the tales of children stolen, never to be returned.

The farmers would keep a watchful eye upon their flocks and fields, lest they augment their clay-baked hedgehogs with some richer stew, Ossie thought, amused. Whatever they were called, Romanies, travellers, didicoys, they were outcasts, homeless, doomed to wander restlessly. Not for the first time, as he set about his work, Ossie sent up a private prayer to God for his home above the stables.

Late in that afternoon, when sweeping the yard free of horse muck from the mounts of some ale drinkers within the Crown, Ossie was surprised to glance up and see two strangers hurrying through the church gates of St John the Baptist. At least, he supposed them to be strangers, for he could see little of them, save for their all-enveloping cloaks and beavers, high collars and brims hiding their faces. Although his task was first halted, then afterwards prolonged by the unexpected arrival of a private coach, he did not see the two men return. Then, berating himself for 'a nosey old besom', he turned aside to the stables. At dusk, when he was lighting the lantern to be hung from the archway of the yard, he heard the sound of approaching hooves upon the highway and hastily stepped back, lest some gentleman be in so great a stir for his mead that he trample him underfoot.

The rider he saw from the glow cast by the archway lantern and the one which the man held to light his way, was Robert Knight. He was mounted upon a black horse, its polished hide gleaming bright as the jewels of Whitby jet, which ladies of quality upon the coaches wore to signify their mourning.

The ostler wondered what had drawn him to the church at so late an hour upon New Year's Eve, and alone. Then, supposing it might be some delicate matter of business with the verger, or in response to an urgent cry from a parishioner seeking his help, Ossie took himself to the stable to tend a sickly mare whose weakness, he thought angrily, sprang from neglect and starvation at the hands of some feckless coach proprietor, one of the many who would sacrifice the well-being of a mare for profits, working them even when blind until they died in harness. So fierce was his anger that he dismissed the rector and his affairs from his mind, eager only to bring the poor animal what comfort and solace he might.

Robert Knight, leaving his mare tethered at an iron ring set into a stout beam, lay down his lantern, opening, with difficulty, the great oak doors to the church porch. The lantern beams flickered over the rough stone walls and benches, and he surveyed it with pride, grateful that it could once again serve its original purpose – as a place to provide rest, shelter and spiritual refreshment.

It had long irritated him that it had been appropriated as a meeting place for the local council of vestrymen! It was certainly not built to house thirteen stout yeomen! Some of them, he conceded, very stout indeed! He smiled involuntarily. It was for this reason that they had conveniently voted to permanently remove themselves and their affairs to the Farmers' Arms at Nottage. Well, now, they might rest more agreeably upon wooden benches, and refresh themselves more liberally, if less spiritually, upon the landlord's ale!

Still smiling, he opened the inner doors to the church, holding the lantern aloft that he might illumine the edges of the pews flanking the aisle. He would not light the oil lamps upon the great chains which hung suspended from the carved saddle-back roof. No, he would light the altar candles and kneel here, alone, in silent communion with God. There was no fear in him, no sense of aloneness, as his lantern lit the flagged aisle to the altar steps. He was, after all, in the preserve of a dear and real friend . . .

It was only when the candles were glowing softly in their sconces, making circles of haloed, rainbow-edged light, that he became aware of some movement in the darkness from the pews which lay beneath the stone pulpit built into the wall.

With anguish, he cried out, 'Whoever you are, show yourselves. You are in God's house. If it is help you need, or forgiveness, you have but to speak.'

There was a movement towards him in the darkness, and the sound of running feet upon the flagstones, but what he saw in the lantern glow and the flickering of the candles made his blood congeal. Two silent figures, black-draped, and upon their faces hideous, obscene masks of some animal he had never seen.

'If it is some prank,' he said, aware of the hoarseness of his voice in the echoing church, 'I bid you go in peace. You defile the house of God.'

No word was spoken, but one of the creatures, for he could not call them men, stepped forward to take his lantern, and before Robert Knight could stumble his way through the gloom to the altar steps, he was thrown heavily to the floor, struggling and crying aloud, to no avail. Silently they were bundling some sort of sack about him and binding him so tightly that he was only aware of the intensity of pain as the cords cut into his flesh. Unable to move, or even breathe without effort, he lay trussed and helpless upon the stone floor, a kerchief gagging his mouth and nose.

Dear God, he prayed desperately, do not let Your holy place be violated, desecrated . . .

Then he saw in the lantern light the snuffing of the altar candles, and heard the metallic striking of the jewelled cross, the altar sticks and plate, as they were hurriedly thrown into a sack.

Suddenly, incredibly, there was a deafening explosion of sound at the church door as it was thrown back upon its hinges and, in a burst of light, Robert Knight heard the voice of Joshua Stradling, and the clamour of men behind him, as the constable cried commandingly, 'I am armed! I warn you! Surrender, for I will not hesitate to shoot . . .'

His ringing voice seemed to fill the small church, reverberating from stone walls and floor, and high carved rafters, authoritative and unyielding. There were a few muttered oaths from the two villains who had thus far been silent, and the rector acknowledged, with relief, that the oppressors were not of his own flock of the three hamlets.

Then, as Robert Knight was urgently relieved of his bonds by sympathetic hands, the thugs were secured with their own cords, and roughly manhandled into the night by Ossie and the villagers. The rector's cramped fingers were rubbed abrasively into life, and even more agonising feeling, by Joshua, who half led, half carried him to the safety of a pew, so numbed were the priest's feet and limbs that he would have stumbled and fallen.

When he was sufficiently restored, Robert Knight, with Joshua holding the lantern, took the altar vessels from the sack upon the floor, and reverently replaced them, kneeling awkwardly and with some discomfort before the altar to give thanks. Joshua placed the lantern gently upon the flagged floor, that the rector might know the peace and privacy of communion with God. Then he, too, knelt in gratitude, first for the safety of the rector and the church treasures, but also for the warm concern of good men like Ossie, and those who had come unhesitatingly from the inn, not knowing what dangers they faced.

With Robert Knight safely conveyed homeward in the landlord's carriage, and Dr Mansel called upon to attend him, notwithstanding his protestations of being unharmed, Joshua returned to question the would-be thieves. Despite the hostile villagers who surrounded them in the kitchens of the Crown, threatening them with staves, and doling out occasional sly kicks and blows, their prisoners would not answer, save to spit contemptuously and mouth obscenities. Finally, the crowd became so enraged and restive that Joshua ordered the landlord, Tom Butler, to bid Ossie make ready the gaol-coach which the vestrymen had converted for the purpose of conveying offenders to the cells at Pyle. He would not secure them overnight in the small cell above the coach-house, but remove them that instant, lest the mob grow violent, provoked by the villains' surly manners and their ill-handling of the priest and the church treasures.

With Ossie at the reins, and Joshua and vestryman Tom Butler, armed within, to guard the captives, the fortified coach moved upon its errand, to the accompaniment of rained blows and imprecations from the villagers. Joshua's patient questioning upon the way eliciting no more information as to whom they were and from whence they had come, he delivered them into the hands of the gaoler, a coarse and brutish-looking fellow, bidding him, 'See that they are well guarded! They will be swiftly brought to account, for not only have they assaulted a priest and committed sacrilege, but chosen to wreak havoc upon the local magistrate!'

It was only upon hearing this that the two prisoners began feuding and fighting, one with the other, but even then they would disclose nothing, their fear of outside vengeance greater than their fear of the law.

Leaving them in the none-too-gentle hands of their gaoler, Joshua, Butler and Ossie returned to Newton over Stormy Downs, seeing in the darkness beyond the poor light of the whale-oil carriage lamps, the dying flames of the fires of the itinerants' encampment, and hearing the harsh challenging barking of the curs as they strained at their restricting chains.

Ossie's horny palms tightened upon the reins as he suggested, with seeming inconsequence, 'In such a place, if well protected and well disguised, both men and horses might lose themselves with ease. Do you not agree, Joshua?'

'I do, Ossie,' answered Joshua, smiling, 'although it would need a man of rare courage and resourcefulness to enter the encampment.'

'And a man of greater intelligence and wisdom to have thought of it,' replied Ossie blandly.

The next morning, well before the break of dawn, Joshua was dressed and had saddled his grey and set out for Stormy Downs, bearing a horn lantern to light his way in the enfolding darkness. He was gratified, as always, for the sure-footedness of his mare, and her intelligence and responsiveness.

When he arrived at the camp, fearful that the travellers might have moved on, and only the filth of their animals and the ashes of their fires remaining, he was greeted by such a fury of barking, braying, and other animal and human cries that even the grey trembled and halted. Joshua dismounted, deliberately placing a hand upon the pistol in its holster as he did so. A tall, well-muscled man of below middle-age arose from his fireside as Joshua came forward, and as a young boy snatched a burning brand from the fire, bade him fiercely to 'let it lie!'. The youth reluctantly consigned it to the flames.

'I do not come to harass you, or to move you to some other place, but to seek your aid,' said Joshua truthfully. 'You have horses here, the ostler has told me, to barter or sell . . .'

Their leader nodded, indicating where the beasts were to be found in a makeshift enclosure . . .

It was, thought Joshua, as he moved forward, as if the eyes of each living creature grew watchful, and fastened upon his every step, waiting for some signal to be given.

He did not hesitate, but with more calmness than he felt, lifted his lantern high. In its beams, the patient prick-eared donkeys stared solemnly back, together with the ragged ponies and two nervous-eyed horses, one a sleek dark-brown, and the other a magnificent chestnut mare, its forearm, breast and knee recently stained to black.

Chapter Eight

Upon relating his adventure to Ossie, Joshua freely admitted that, for a moment, his wits had deserted him, and he had half expected to be set upon by all the company and beaten near to death, and the grey stolen.

'So what did you do, my friend?' Ossie asked, face clenched with concern.

'I spoke directly to the man who was their leader, saying: "I have no quarrel with you, sir, nor with your people. I respect your independence and your customs, indeed, I would fight to maintain them for you".'

'And his answer?'

'He merely nodded, holding up a hand to silence those about him who would speak, and waited for me to continue. "I do not ask you how you came by the two horses, for that is not my affair, sir. Nor, indeed, the purpose you have in mind for them. I ask you simply to tell me what you know of their former owners. They are the grossest villains, and have desecrated a holy place, and assaulted a priest, which, I know, is not your way. The men have already been taken to the gaolhouse at Pyle to await their trial".'

'He helped you, then?' observed Ossie. 'Else you would not now be here, intact in body and spirit.'

'He could tell me little,' replied Joshua, 'save that the wretches approached him demanding that they be allowed to return to the settlement by night, to be disguised and set amongst the company. They would move with them upon the following day, and depart when it was safe to do so, leaving their horses as payment.'

'A clever plot,' approved Ossie, 'simple and bold, and yet, of value to both parties. Yet I fancy you do not think either of the men to be the highwayman you seek?'

'No. I am convinced of it. They are poor, ill-spoken creatures, coarse and lacking both intelligence and refinement, in no wise matching the descriptions I have been given of him. I fancy theirs was a small, accidental part and the robbery of the church their own plan. It was as well, Ossie, that you grew suspicious of them and, after listening at the window, warned me . . .' praised Joshua warmly.

Ossie flushing with pleasure, asked quickly, 'And the gypsies, Joshua? What of them?'

'I told them that despite their willingness to help, I could not promise to forgo my report to the justice, but my duties were onerous and it might be some time before I felt able to inform him . . .'

'Indeed,' said Ossie admiringly, 'a blessed deliverance from all your afflictions!'

'But not from the justice,' corrected Joshua wrily.

'He castigated you?'

'I enquired most earnestly after his health, but he brushed it aside, having seemingly forgotten his gratitude of last night, and declaring irritably, "It was foolhardy of you, Stradling, to have ventured into that encampment alone!" I protested that it would have been more foolhardy to have gone with others and that I had achieved what I set out to do without bloodshed.'

'What did he reply to that?' demanded Ossie, intrigued.

'He asked why I had not appropriated the chestnut

mare, since it was quite clearly evidence.'

'He was right,' said the ostler doubtfully. 'So how did you answer?'

'That, as he had so sensibly pointed out, being wiser and altogether more experienced, I too became aware of the peril I had placed myself into by going alone . . . Alas, by the time I rode back with assistance, their fires and trail were already cold.'

'But not the justice's wrath, I'll wager!' cried Ossie, delighted.

'There is no merit in gambling on a certainty!' said Joshua.

Overnight the promise of the north-east wind was fulfilled, bringing in a New Year that was crisp with frost. It came so suddenly that the villagers were ill-prepared, rising in the night to heap more turf or kindling upon their fires and clothing upon their beds. Those denied the luxury of a bed simply settled themselves deeper into the vermin-infested straw of loft or barn, grateful for the warm breath and animal bodies about them, and a roof above their heads. Those denied even these small comforts crept unnoticed into pig-sty, the shelter of a wall, or some hollow.

'But the Son of Man had nowhere to lay His head . . .' the rector had read in his deep melodious voice a few days earlier, at the celebration of the Christmas Eve watch night service.

The good folk of the three hamlets were genuinely saddened by the age-old tragedy of the Christ child, as tragedy it assuredly was, and many had tears in their eyes which blurred the flickering candlelight.

Jeremiah Fleet, whose own son had lived so brief a

time, felt Sophie's warm hand slip comfortingly into his own, and gripped it hard to show her he understood. He could not tell even Sophie, whom he loved, that his thought had been that the real tragedy of Bethlehem was that so little had changed, even after eighteen hundred years. Jeremiah was a simple man, with no book learning, and was ashamed that he was unable to control his restless thoughts.

But now, as he drove the cob and cart over Stormy Downs, and towards the Crocutts' little farm at Grove, he was a happy man. He sang cheerfully and loudly as he went, and Charity, sharing his pleasure, lifted his wedge-shaped head to the sky and stridently joined in a chorus, howling so dismally that Jeremiah could scarce hold the reins for his laughter. The cob had pulled down its ears and quickened its pace, in an effort to escape the pursuing sound, but the cur, encouraged by Jeremiah's mirth, only sucked in his cheeks and, with throat muscles vibrating tremulously and muzzle raised high, howled even louder, his solo ending in a frenzy of barks and acrobatics which seemed set to tip the animal into a ditch.

'Well done!' exclaimed Jeremiah aloud, still laughing helplessly, 'the performance of a true artist, sir, showing both skill and enthusiasm! Such an act deserves a wider public.'

The cob snorted delicately, its breath a cloud upon the frosted air.

'And a more appreciative one!' chided Jeremiah. 'It is a sad thing when one's talent goes unrecognised.'

The cob raised its coarse black tail, leaving a heap of steaming green-brown ordure upon the way.

' 'Tis best,' advised Jeremiah, 'to ignore one's critics, and behave always with more dignity than they.'

As they entered the cobbled yard to the farm, scattering a blur of hens, ducks and a defiant menacing rooster, Dafydd, unable to contain his excitement, ran from the open doorway of the house to greet him. Charity leapt impulsively from the cart to be clasped in the boy's outstretched arms, hind legs and rounded pink stomach dangling absurdly as the dog raked the boy's face with abrasive wet kisses.

Inside, the farmhouse was warmly comforting, the fire of logs blazing in the huge ingle-nook, crackling, smelling faintly of applewood, and sending out swift showers of sparks. Dafydd's mother, the Widow Crocutt, welcomed Jeremiah most cordially, her plump cheeks and darkly expressive eyes absurdly echoing those of the babe crawling upon the floor. Marged, with Huw the other young child, ran forward to greet Jeremiah, thrusting a hand shyly into his cavernous one, then clinging to his thigh, face upturned to be kissed, laughing and protesting delightedly at the tickling of his fine grey beard.

Their New Year's gifts received with ecstatic cries and most flattering pleasure, Jeremiah gave them a polished new penny apiece, which produced yet more gratitude, although the baby's coin had to be appropriated by the widow, for it was in danger of being swallowed with the sweetmeats. While the baby screamed her deprivation, the widow pressed Jeremiah to take some mulled ale or some 'shot', a comforting drink of baked oatcakes, crushed and covered with buttermilk. Jeremiah would have liked to have rested a while and eaten some of the light cakes, still warm from the iron bakestone, but Dafydd's anxiety to be gone was so acute that Jeremiah could not disappoint him by tarrying – so the widow wrapped a small bundle of them into the kerchief from Dafydd's callenig gift, and bade Jeremiah sample them upon the cart, at which Charity's tail thumped agreement.

'You will behave with respect to Mr Fleet,' Dafydd's mother adjured the boy quietly, when Jeremiah was occupied with the cart. 'Not becoming a nuisance by pestering him with questions, or setting yourself forever in his path. Remember, do not eat like a hog at the trough or speak with your mouth full, for he will think you have no more manners than your Tamworth pigs, and will not like you. Wipe your nose upon the kerchief wrapped around the light cakes. No! not now, boy! When they are eaten,' she said in exasperation. 'Now, take care that you do not do anything wilful or dangerous. Don't play with Mr Fleet's fishing hooks, or take liberties with the sea . . .'

'I will take good care of him, ma'am,' promised Jeremiah gently, for he knew how the violence of her husband's death had grieved and unsettled her. 'You need have no fears.'

'And I am grateful to you, sir. It is sometimes hard to be a man when you have never had the opportunity to be a child.'

Jeremiah nodded.

But Dafydd was already seated upon the cart, clutching his new fishing rod, with Charity by his side, broad head resting upon his lap; in imagination they were already running across the wet sand, joyously, the wind from the sea fresh; the caressing west wind that the old people called in their ancient musical language 'The breath from the ox's nostrils'.

Mrs Crocutt, Marged, Huw and even the babe waved gaily to Dafydd, but he only gripped his fishing rod tighter and nodded back in acknowledgement, dignified and aloof, as befitted the man of the house. No one could have told that his bare toes were curling painfully with excitement and, under the cut-down jacket that had once been Jem Crocutt's, his heart was beating as wildly as a New Year's wren against the bars of its cage with the thought of his freedom.

Rebecca, browsing appreciatively through the justice's library at Tythegston, was troubled to receive a communication from her grandfather, delivered by messenger from Southerndown Court.

He bade her return upon the morrow, claiming that there was some private matter of business concerning the estate, which he would have her discuss with him, adding, 'I shall be grateful for your opinion, my dear, and for the sight of your face'.

It was true that, apart from her visits to their tenants, the cottagers, and acting as Sir Matthew's hostess upon more formal occasions, Rebecca was now deeply involved in all matters relating to the smooth running of the estate for, as Sir Matthew gently reminded her, it would, one day, be hers and Joshua's. Yet, there seemed an urgency about the summons which was out of character and filled her with alarm. Perhaps he was sick and unwilling for her to be told of the gravity of his condition, choosing instead to ensure her return upon some less distressing pretext. He was certainly an old man, yet she had never thought of him as such, or considered the imminence of his death, for he was possessed of such great physical and mental energy and joy in living. Had she been so selfishly wrapped in her own concerns, her love for Joshua, the preparations for their betrothal party for their friends of the three hamlets, that she had neglected him? Rebecca asked herself, stricken: how could she have been so thankless and obtuse, when his every thought and action was for her well-being?

She would have gone at once to Robert Knight, to beg his opinion of the letter and tell him her fears, but he was away visiting a family in Nottage who had suffered a bereavement. Bidding Effie pack all of those clothes which would not be needed either at dinner, or for her travels upon the morrow, Rebecca summoned Leyshon. The old man, harassed with pain from a diseased spine, sometimes moved slowly and seemed taciturn and uncommunicative, his lugubrious expression setting him apart. Yet, the justice had no finer or more loyal retainer. Upon hearing Rebecca's request that the de Breos' carriage be prepared for a visit to friends in the three hamlets, he became agitated and clumsy, not knowing how best to act in the justice's absence. He could not betray his master's confidences by telling her of what he knew of the danger which threatened her, nor could he reasonably refuse her request, inventing some excuse, for she was Robert Knight's guest, and a lady of quality in her own right.

'I will see that it is done, Mistress de Breos,' he said, adding courteously, 'would you, perhaps, care to take the guard who travelled with you, ma'am, as well as your coachman? The way is icy, and there are robbers and footpads, as well you know . . .' He broke off, flustered, fearing he had overreached himself in offering advice.

'No, I thank you, Leyshon,' Rebecca smiled gently, for she was fond of the old man and aware of his affliction, as Joshua had told her of it. 'I will go alone, leaving Effie, my maid, for she has work to do.'

'But, ma'am,' Leyshon blurted desperately, 'is it wise to travel unchaperoned and unprotected, begging your pardon, ma'am, for the impertinence,' he recalled himself sharply. 'I think but of your safety and the justice's concern for it.'

'I thank you for your kindness, Leyshon,' returned Rebecca gravely, 'and know it is out of protectiveness that you speak. But,' she added firmly, 'there is not a soul in the whole of the three hamlets who would harm me, or wish me ill. I would not insult them by allowing them to believe I have any fears upon that score.'

So Leyshon, admiring her courage and loyalty, nodded his head and, bowing stiffly, did as Rebecca bade him.

Joshua, meanwhile, had taken the grey and was riding out to the Prince of Wales Inn at Kenfig, the solitary stone tavern set in acre upon acre of sand-drifted dunes, their surfaces tufted with silvery marram grass and pitted with coney warrens.

It was a desolate place, with but a few simple cottages, the tiny square-towered Norman church nearby set upon a stone-walled hill. The people were poor, for the soil was sandy and infertile, and earned their living upon the sea shore, or as labourers upon the richer, more productive farms inland.

The way was little better than a roughened cart track, its many craters and ruts now rain-filled and frozen, making it treacherous. The mare trod warily, but Joshua was aware that the coldness and the cracking of ice beneath her hooves unnerved her, making her restless.

Upon leaving the fertile greenness of the farms at Nottage, the landscape became bleak, barren, with little vegetation other than the struggling, windswept gorse, bracken and an occasional thorn tree, black bark sheathed in ice. On the flatter stretches between the dunes, Joshua could glimpse the crumpled greyness of the sea, its surface merging into the iron-coloured sky.

It was with relief that he came to the Prince of Wales Inn, a small, solid building of rough-hewn stone. From the stables where Joshua left the grey to the care of an ancient but obliging ostler, the view was so breathtaking in its beauty that he could only marvel at its unexpectedness. As far as the eye could see, spread out before him, were the pale golden dunes, flowing in waves to the sea beyond. In the midst of them, set like a dark opaque jewel, the vast Pool, a lone ruined building of grey stone rising from its depths. It was said to be the bell tower of some long-submerged church, part of a village buried deep in the encroaching sand. When the wind from the sea ruffled its sleeping waters, the church bell was stirred into life, its plaintive, muffled sound echoing the wind's sadness.

Joshua's mood was broken by the coming of the landlord, a squat, cheerful fellow, whose solid fleshiness was undeniably real. He ushered Joshua within with much ceremony, declaring that it was a crisp, cold day to be abroad, and one which merited a warmed ale. Having settled Joshua at the fireside, he returned with a pewter pot filled with the spiced liquid, thrusting into it a red hot poker from the fire, which hissed and steamed agreeably. With its aromatic smell tantalising his nostrils, Joshua drank, feeling warmth spreading through his flesh, comforting and soporific.

'There is a horse-dealer, I believe, sir, who frequents this inn?'

The landlord nodded.

'He is expected here, today?'

'Unless something untoward befalls him.' He hesitated. 'If you will forgive me, sir, for I do not mean to pry . . .' His face grew flushed, and his manner awkward, as he blurted, 'But I see you are a gentleman, and he is not!'

'I take your warning, landlord,' said Joshua, 'and I thank you for it.'

The landlord shook his head, plump chin all but scraping his chest, for he seemed to be deprived of neck, his head resting squarely upon his shoulders. 'If it is horseflesh you seek, sir, it would be wise to look elsewhere.'

'No. It is not trading but information I seek.'

'Then take even that, Constable, with a peck of salt rather than a pinch!' advised the landlord, smiling. 'For he is as much a stranger to the truth as to honest dealing! A plausible rogue, and an entertaining one, as, indeed, so many scoundrels are. But keep as tight a rein upon your purse, and your credulity, as he does upon his horses. Like them, he is easily led: ready to be sold to the highest bidder!'

Joshua thanked him, begging him to share an ale, which the landlord did willingly, saying that in an hour or so, when the horse sales began, he would be hard pressed to breathe even!

With honest pride, he showed Joshua the room above, which housed the fine silver mace, the charters and regalia of the ancient borough, saying it had been a fortified township and part of the lands of the Lords of Glamorgan since the twelfth century.

'But the sand was no respecter of lords, or Norman earls,' he added sombrely, 'for Nature was ever more powerful than men, and more destructive. The sand drifted in remorselessly, covering all in its path, until the great sandstorm of the sixteenth century overwhelmed the borough, castle and church, holding them, for ever, in its fierce, choking grip . . .'

As Joshua rode out to the vast Pool, two miles in circumference, where the landlord had told him that the horse-dealer and his men would first halt to water their stock, he pondered upon what lay beneath the mare's galloping hooves: houses, farms, churches, the bones of those who died? Their warm flesh excoriated by the harsh, invasive grains of sand . . . He was filled with a depression which not even the greenness of the distant rolling hills and the wide sweep of coastline beyond the curve of Swansea Bay could diminish. He could not but think of the terror of it, and the violence . . . as if Jeremiah upon the bay, Rebecca, and Illtyd about his haywardship upon the Downs, were to be cruelly, and without warning, engulfed and buried alive.

He turned the mare to the far side of the Pool, where a scattered herd of horses drank from the clear, ever-changing waters, their keepers at hand, having cudgelled the thin crust of ice from the outer fringes. The man he sought came forward reluctantly, Joshua's uniform as constable making him anxious.

'You seek me, sir?'

'No, merely your advice.'

The horse-dealer relaxed perceptibly. There was about him, Joshua thought amused, not only the smell of horseflesh and sweat, but a look of the animal in his restless eyes and narrow long-boned face with its flared nostrils.

'My advice I give you free, for, unlike horseflesh, I cannot gauge what it will be worth.'

'A gold half-sovereign if it buys me the result I seek.' It was more than Joshua had intended to offer, and he wondered if the man's cupidity would cause him to lie. 'You have sold a fine mare in the past week, or earlier?'

'All my mares are fine, sir, and of known pedigree.'

'No doubt,' agreed Joshua drily, 'but this is a special beast: a fine chestnut. Has it been sold by you, or offered to you?'

'My stock is constantly changing,' the dealer prevaricated.

'Then I am sorry I have wasted your time,' said Joshua, nodding and making to ride off.

'Wait!' the man wetted his lips, long bony face intent as he strove to balance the value of discretion against gain. 'It was after the snow, when the blizzard had eased. We, that is, my two partners and I, were encamped near the Stepping Stones across the river Ogmore at Candleston, beyond Merthyr Mawr – all but marooned with our beasts, with only the shelter of the ruined walls of the old castle –'

'And?' persisted Joshua, dismounting. 'Well? The rest of it . . .?'

The man stared pointedly at the gold coin in Joshua's hand, but since the constable made no move to offer it, the dealer continued, 'This stranger, he made towards us upon this fine chestnut mare, of which you speak. Thinking him to be lost and seeking shelter, I offered him the warmth of our fire within the ruined walls to thaw his bones . . .'

'He accepted?' asked Joshua sharply.

'No. He asked merely that we exchange his mare, which was bitterly exhausted, for one of our own. I hesitated, for I knew we had nothing as fine to offer . . .'

'But you did not hesitate overlong?' hazarded Joshua.

'No. In truth, I am a trader. I do not enquire too closely into other men's business, being more concerned with bettering my own!'

'So . . .?' prompted Joshua. 'You offered him a horse?'

'Indeed, feeling that the good Lord was on my side in sending me a fool, or a lunatic . . . But, being a gift horse . . .'

'You did not look it in the mouth,' finished Joshua.

'Exactly. It would have been insulting to do so, and

unnecessary, Constable, since I was fully aware of its worth already.'

'This stranger, he did not mention his business, whence he came, or to where he was travelling?'

'No, save to say that he had but a short way to go and that the beast would serve him very well, since he would soon have the pick of many.'

'You can describe him? His features? Build?' Joshua held the gold coin between his fingers, waiting.

'I have told you of the conditions, the weather. He was muffled by cloak and beaver, his face covered with a kerchief to ward off the cold and snow. There was nothing about him to remember, sir, or to deliberately forget . . .' he observed pointedly. 'He was, perhaps, a gentleman. Beyond that, I know nothing, I swear it upon all that I hold sacred and dear.'

Which, being itemised, would certainly resolve itself into money! Joshua thought sceptically, but persisted, 'The horse, then? Surely your experience of horseflesh and your . . . business acumen did not desert you, nor the snow completely blind you to her appearance and worth! You have said only that the mare is chestnut-coloured. Are there no markings? Nothing to distinguish her?'

'Well . . .' The man hesitated, face surly, eyes fixed anxiously upon the coin, then wetted his dry lips, 'I recall, sir, that there were white flashes . . . patches upon her breast, and from forearm to knee.'

'I must congratulate you on your convenient return of memory,' Joshua said drily. 'One further question, sir.'

The horse-dealer sighed, looking resigned, then nodded wearily.

'To whom did you sell the mare?'

'To two strangers . . .' He looked apologetic. 'There

is no law which says I have to recognise my clients, sir. Yet these two, I would certainly know again. Shrewd, hard-bargaining devils, rude in manner, surly and foul spoken.'

'You did not get the better of them, then?'

The horse-dealer smiled. 'It seems that is a question I should be asking you, Constable,' he said slyly, 'since you are so anxiously seeking their whereabouts.'

'You mistake me, sir,' corrected Joshua. 'I know where they are: safely incarcerated in the gaol cells at Pyle, with many another such villain.'

'Then it is as well that most of us are honest, sir.' The dealer pocketed the half-sovereign with satisfaction, lips curling back over long equine teeth. 'You know, perhaps, where the chestnut mare is now, Constable?' he demanded, 'I would drive a good bargain . . .'

'No doubt,' said Joshua, smiling, 'but I fancy its new owner might prove your equal in shrewdness and guile.'

When he returned to his cottage, leaving the grey briefly tethered to the iron ring set into its walls, Joshua bent to retrieve a small carved box from the doorstep, marvelling at the delicate tracery of flowers and symbols vividly painted upon its lid. There was no note accompanying it, and no indication as to its use. Opening it gingerly, he saw within an exquisitely hand-carved miniature of a mare, perfect in scale and detail – even to its chestnut-coloured hide, and the black-stained forearm, knee and breast, skilfully concealing all tell-tale flashes of white.

Chapter Nine

Dafydd and Jeremiah and Charity, returning from the shore upon the cart, were in perfect agreement. It had been a wonderful day. There was no reason to speak the words aloud, for they shared the closeness of friends: that rare understanding when silence itself communicates. Dafydd's face was whipped raw with colour and his hands, still clutching the precious rod, lashed blue by the iciness of the sea, and the north-east wind. If he had thought about it, he might have reflected that the soft breath from the ox's nostrils veered more towards a cold blast from the raging white horses upon the tide. He did not notice the keen edge to the wind, the gusting sand, or the frozen edges to the rock pools. A man does not notice such things. Today he was a man in the presence of a man. He viewed his catch of two small pouting, a crab, and the lobster which Jeremiah had told him was to be his own, 'for I have placed that lobster pot particularly for you, and you may have whatever it contains'. A sigh of pure bliss escaped him, unbidden, and Jeremiah turned his head and nodded, understanding. It was strange, the fisherman thought, this affinity between young and old; the stripping away of inessentials. The young saw with a perfect clarity. To them, everything was fresh and new. Perhaps the old, with their faded vision, saw in the same way, recognising only the things that mattered, all else blurred and softened.

'You have been invited upon a visit,' he told Dafydd.

'Oh?' Dafydd's tone was anxious, abrupt.

'You are to take tea with Mistress Randall, who lives in the coach loft at the Crown Inn. Is not that a rare treat and a privilege?'

Dafydd nodded, biting his lip, and demanding, 'Will you be there, Mr Fleet, sir?'

'No, my boy. I have all my work to do with the wet fish, gutting them, seeing to the boiling of the cockles. I have to earn my living!'

'I could help, Mr Fleet!' the boy offered eagerly. 'I am good at boiling, sir.'

'No!' said Jeremiah firmly. 'It is all arranged. I will come later to collect you upon the cart.' He softened, 'But if you like, I will leave Charity with you for company, for Mistress Randall's cookery will be a fine treat for the dog.'

Dafydd nodded slowly, even the pleasure of the bull terrier's company failing to lift his spirits.

'You will not be alone,' chided Jeremiah. 'There will be a friend for company. Someone your own age.'

'A boy? Do I know him, Mr Fleet?'

'No. A girl.'

'A girl, sir!' Dafydd lay his rod dispiritedly upon the floor of the cart, the bright promise of the day tarnished. 'But, I have three of them at home: my mother, Marged and the babe, Sîan. I would rather be in the company of men, Mr Fleet,' he said seriously, 'for that is what my father said I must learn to be.'

Jeremiah, seeing the boy's earnest face, all but relented, but said, more sharply than he intended, 'It is not enough to be a man! You must strive to be a gentleman, too!'

Dafydd, his first lesson in the art reluctantly learnt,

merely answered obediently, 'Yes, Mr Fleet.' And Jeremiah, watching the boy pick up the rod, gripping it so fiercely that the knuckles showed white, turned his head away to hide a smile.

Rebecca, arriving at Jeremiah's cottage breasting the dunes, in the de Breos' coach, had descended and was about to knock upon his front door, when she heard the unmistakable sound of his cob and cart. When they came into view, she ran to meet him, careless of her pretty clothes trailing the sandy track, face radiant with affection and excitement. She went to soothe the cob's rough mane, kissing the tip of its moist nose. It whinnied and snorted its pleasure, trembling, and pawing the ground.

'You see!' she cried to Jeremiah, 'He remembers me! I have not been forgotten.'

He had climbed down and was regarding her gravely. 'No. You have not been forgotten.' Then, despite his protests about spoiling her fine clothes, she was in his arms, laughing and crying, burying her face in the rough cloth of his coat with its smell of salt and the tide, and all the small creatures of rock pool and shore that had been part of her life.

'I have come home, Jeremiah,' she said simply.

'Yes,' he replied. But there was, nevertheless, a hurt in him that could not be quenched. A loss. Even the warm reality of her flesh could not dispel it.

'Come inside, my maid,' he said gently, 'and the gentleman upon the coach, for it is a cold day, and the wind is chill.'

The old coachman hesitated a little, upon his dignity, until Jeremiah said, 'The door to my house is always open, sir. There is none in the three hamlets who would not be welcome to enter at any time, even in my absence, for what I have it is my pleasure to share. I bid you enter. It would give me joy, I do assure you.'

The old coachman nodded, thanking him courteously and, stepping down from the box, tethered each of the two horses securely to a stout tree that they might graze beneath.

As Jeremiah drove the cob and cart to the shelter of the yard, the coachman, Hughes, removed his tricorn, hair straggling about face and neck, and held its brim in fingers made awkward by age. Rebecca, her hand upon the door knob, turned to bid him follow and, seeing behind him the starkness of the tree with its gnarled twigs and swollen boles, thought how cruel were age and winter.

No, thought Jeremiah, as he unharnessed the cob, Rebecca has not come home. She has already moved on to another life, another country, where I can no longer follow. We cannot wipe out the past, for it is what we are, and what has made us. I must thank God that I was part of her growing, for a brief while, and let her go . . .

When he returned into the long, whitewashed room of the cottage, with its low-beamed ceiling, he saw Rebecca touching things gently, smoothing them as she had smoothed the cob: as if they were alive, as if by tracing them, she might retain the memory of them in her finger tips . . .

Hughes was seated in Jeremiah's wheelbacked chair at the fireside, hands outstretched to the flames which Rebecca had raked into life with the curved iron poker, and newly heaped with driftwood from the shore. There was a warm comforting feel in his bones and, with a mulled ale at his side, and another within him, he was soon dozing, his head upon his chest, wisps of grey hair tufting his bald pate. For all the world, Rebecca thought, like a dandelion clock, with most of its seeds blown away by the wind.

All Jeremiah's pleading with Rebecca to take some refreshment having failed, for she insisted that her only hunger and thirst was for news of him and their friends of the three hamlets, he settled himself beside her in one of the shieldback chairs.

'The news of Doonan is good, Joshua tells me,' he began.

'Yes,' she smiled, 'they are to return to Newton tomorrow, in the justice's own coach, no less! Rosa's mother was intent upon getting the carrier, her brother, to take them upon his open cart, but the justice would not hear of it.'

'I am glad that someone shows an inkling of good sense!' exclaimed Jeremiah forcibly. 'Doonan might look like a great ox of a creature but, from all accounts, the wound has weakened him sorely. In this climate, the carrier's cart might well prove his funeral cart!'

'Which would not grieve Ezra the Box one jot!' said Rebecca of the odious little village undertaker with the sly, ferrety smile and unctuous ways. 'If he were not such a pathetic, craven little specimen,' declared Jeremiah, who detested him, 'I would suspect him to be the highwayman, for I would not put it beyond him to provide his own clients, when trade is slow . . .'

Rebecca laughed delightedly, and they fell to discussing Joshua and the highwayman, the attempt to rob the church, and the fortunes and misfortunes of their friends, with passionate concern, and, as with Hannah the wheelwright's wife, a little affectionate amusement.

'And does she still keep her sow in sunbonnets to ward off sunstroke, Jeremiah?'

'She does indeed, although in weather such as this, 'tis

more like to perish of frostbite!' he said, shaking his grey head indulgently. 'Daniel says she is besotted with the animal and thinks it human, declaring that if he did not curb her, she would dress it in petticoats and pantalongs, and carry it about in a shawl, like a greedy fat babe! She calls it Jemima, if you please, claiming the creature responds to its name . . . although, I have a fancy it trots to her more in answer to the clanging of the bucket upon its trough!'

'She would not eat it, then?' asked Rebecca anxiously, 'for I know that the villagers oft rear a bacon for a Christmas treat.'

'She would sooner eat Daniel!' said Jeremiah, 'and to tell you the truth, I would be hard pressed to choose which would prove the tougher, or more indigestible! Daniel is abrasive enough in all conscience, and sometimes downright curmudgeonly but, compared with that old sow, he has the disposition of a saint and martyr!'

They laughed companionably, for both held a warm regard for Hannah, who was generous and loving in all her ways.

'I should like to see her, for I shall be leaving upon the morrow, Jeremiah.'

'So soon!' He had not meant his voice to sound so bleak.

'My grandfather has need of me. Some business venture . . .'

He nodded his understanding. 'Well, it will not be many days before we meet again, my dear, at your betrothal party to Joshua,' he consoled himself. 'Sophie is in a positive lather of excitement at the prospect, and is having a new gown made by the local seamstress! Such grandeur! She has changed her mind a hundred times and more about the colour and style, to my certain knowledge, and still is undecided . . .' He shook his head. 'Sophie swears that every woman in the three hamlets is fighting for the dressmaker's services. That poor woman's fingers must be as pricked with needles as a hedgehog's back!' Jeremiah's laughter died away as he asked, 'You remember, Rebecca, how you had your first new dress stitched for you, to visit Joshua's farm? It was so pretty a blue,' he said fondly, 'to match your eyes. Yet it could not match them for loveliness or joy.'

'I remember, Jeremiah,' Rebecca's voice was very low, 'and how you fastened this brooch at my throat, saying, "I pinned it upon my young wife at the birth of our son. I pin it now upon you, my daughter, for that is how I think of you".' Her fingers stayed upon the delicate tracery of hearts and pearls and, when she looked up, he saw that her eyes were brimming with tears. Jeremiah watched helplessly as they overflowed, and spilled through her lashes. She made no attempt to brush them away, saying, 'I do not wear the brooch to remind me of you, Jeremiah, for I do not need reminding of what I owe to you, the only father I knew, for my own was never that to me.'

Jeremiah felt the burn of tears behind his own eyes as he wiped the tears gently from her cheeks with his roughened fingertips. Then he took her hand, and looked at it. 'The hand of a lady, Rebecca,' he said, his voice threatening to betray him by faltering. 'But you were always that to me, my maid, even when it was coarsened by work and the sea. Yes, you were always that to me.' He looked at her intently. 'I am not good with words, my dear, for I have no schooling or book learning. I am a simple man, and I find it hard to make words say what is within me, you understand?'

She nodded.

'I can only say that our lives are changing, Rebecca. There will be Joshua to love and care for you, as I must love and protect Sophie, and Illtyd, too, for he is not as others. Yet my love for you will not change. It is constant, and I cannot believe that even death can alter what I feel for you, my child. I do not believe that in loving another, or many, our love grows less. It is not a fixed thing, to be divided, leaving us empty of feeling. It is infinite, like the sea and sky, encompassing everything and everyone, if we will let it.'

'Oh, Jeremiah!' Rebecca flung herself into his arms, embracing him. 'You are a truly good man, and I will never forget you, or stop loving you!' She kissed him, and the old coachman at the fireside stirred and groaned as Jeremiah said, embarrassed and pleased, 'You are happy, Rebecca? Truly?'

'Yes, Jeremiah, I am happy. I have three good men in my life. You, Grandfather and Joshua. How could I be other than content?'

'How, indeed?' asked Jeremiah fondly.

'There is but one small thing, Jeremiah, that I must say. When you took my cottage, as a kindness to me, you vowed that there would always be a place for me, a home . . .'

'Yes, that is true, my dear,' he said, puzzled.

'Then I ask you to take back your vow.' As he made to protest, 'No, Jeremiah, hear me out, I beg! This is soon to be Sophie's home, and yours and Illtyd's. Then let it be hers, from the day she enters. Let there be no shadows of the past, no reservations between you. It is a new life. You have told me that your love for me will not change . . .'

'Yes, and know it to be so.'

'Then I have no need for a place of stone and mortar to bond me to you.'

'If that is your wish, my dear.'

The coachman at the fireside blew heavily through his lips, like a restless cob, startling himself awake and spilling his tricorn to the floor. He looked about him uncertainly, then gathered his wits hurriedly, and bent to retrieve his hat. Seeing the two of them staring at him, he rose to his feet awkwardly, saying, 'I beg your pardon, mistress, I am at your service. I must have closed my eyes but for an instant, with the warmth and the ale . . .'

Rebecca smiled gently. 'I am ready to go, Hughes. If you will prepare the horses.'

He thanked Jeremiah gravely for his hospitality and, with his rimmed opaque eyes still heavy with sleep, took his leave. He had heard more of their conversation than they believed, and was more than ever convinced that Rebecca de Breos was a fitting heiress to Sir Matthew, and his estates. He placed his tricorn hat upon the straggling grey locks, and carefully unfastened the horses' reins from the tree, reflecting upon the first time he had seen his young mistress, here at this very cottage. He had delivered Sir Matthew's message to her, bidding her attend him, for he believed her to be his granddaughter. She had demanded if Sir Matthew were crippled or suffering from some sickness, or other infirmity. When he had replied to the contrary, she had said, simply, 'Then bid him, sir, attend me!' Hughes chuckled aloud at the memory of it. A poor cockle-gatherer with the spirit and manner of a high-born lady. And so she was, but her gentleness and respect for the old fisherman showed that she still possessed the common touch. Humanity. Yes, Sir Matthew had every reason to be proud of her, he reflected with satisfaction. It augured well for the servants and villagers of Southerndown.

Rebecca's visits to her old and valued friends began at the cottage aside the forge at Nottage with a call upon

Sophie and Illtyd, who were beside themselves with pleasure at her unheralded arrival, plying her with refreshment, and demanding news of Elizabeth Crandle, Rosa's and Doonan's plans, and Rebecca's own. In return, they apprised her of the few local events which Jeremiah had omitted, and of the voyage to Valparaiso of Roland Devereaux, newly commissioned master of the clipper, *Pride of Glamorgan*. The young sailor and Illtyd were the firmest friends, and kept up a varied and exacting correspondence, with the little hayward tracing the clipper's route upon the way, his reading augmented by Devereaux's vivid accounts of the voyage.

'It is to be hoped,' Sophie whispered when Illtyd had slipped away to fetch his charts and letters, 'that there will be news of an engagement between Mr Devereaux and your friend, Elizabeth, for he mentions her constantly, with warm affection.'

'Yes,' agreed Rebecca, 'I believe that the friendship might well develop into something deeper and more lasting.'

'Then I am glad,' said Sophie fervently, 'for they have both suffered grievously by the death of his sister. Who could have foretold that such a tragedy could end in love? For I believe Elizabeth must have been all but killed by the horror of discovering that her own brother had so cruelly murdered her dearest friend. And her father, he is recovered now?' Her voice was compassionate.

'No, and it is feared that he never will. He is little more than a helpless babe, without memory or reason.'

'Perhaps,' said Sophie wisely, 'it is better so, Rebecca. The memory of his son's crime, and of his own wickedness, might give him no peace, gnawing and feeding upon his mind constantly. Perhaps forgetfulness is

Nature's way of being kind, blotting out those things which might prove unendurable.'

'Perhaps you are right, Sophie,' agreed Rebecca gravely. 'Yet I wonder how he would survive the horror of it, should reason and understanding ever return. As for Elizabeth, she has had no such respite, but lives with it constantly, even taking upon herself his medical care, and visiting him devotedly.'

'It is the care Mrs Crandle should have taken upon herself!' declared Sophie hotly. 'And not burdened her daughter with. Every woman should have a loyalty and deep, abiding love for the man she takes as a husband, and for her child. She is a selfish, unfeeling woman!' she finished impassionedly.

Rebecca reached out and touched Sophie's hand, then held it to stop its trembling, saying gently, 'You cannot demand love, or responsibility, from those who do not possess it, Sophie. And perhaps Mrs Crandle finds salvation in forgetting; banishing it from her mind as her husband has done. That is her nature; as it is your own to be warm and compassionate. How dear a thing it is, for Jeremiah, and for Illtyd, that your love and loyalty will encompass them, whatever befalls. They are truly blessed.'

She arose, and kissed Sophie with real affection upon her soft plump cheek, and their arms were soon wrapped around each other, in understanding and friendship, with not a few tears shed.

Illtyd, returning upon the scene with his charts and letters, paused in the doorway, saying, with a smile, 'I would not have tarried so long had I known my absence would be so keenly felt! I had not expected tears and the need for consolation!' His intelligent eyes were shrewd, questioning.

'We were talking of Elizabeth,' Sophie explained, 'and the tragedy of Mary Devereaux's murder and how she has learnt to be strong, through necessity.'

'Yes,' said Illtyd quietly, his head lifting awkwardly upon the wry neck. 'I understand. The real tragedy is that it is a lesson she has learnt so young.'

Rebecca, impulsively, would have put out a hand to reach him in comfort, but she felt Sophie stiffen beside her, as she chided briskly, 'You could have ridden to Valparaiso and back twice over, Illtyd, in the time it has taken you to find those things.'

Illtyd smiled, saying without a trace of ill humour, 'I fear Faith might have found the ocean something of an obstacle, Mother, despite her stamina. She would have been as much out of her depth as I might be as a sailor! Yet it is a journey I have taken many times in my imagination, and with Roland Devereaux's letters and charts. See, Rebecca!' He spread them upon the table, face glowing with real pleasure as his fingers began to trace the clipper's route. 'Oh, it is a wonderful, absorbing life, filled with excitement and adventure! What a privilege I share!'

Rebecca, viewing above the cruelly hunched bones of his shoulder, glanced up to see Sophie's carefully expressionless face.

'You are right, Illtyd!' she said warmly. 'Come, show me where the *Pride of Glamorgan* is now, that I may tell Elizabeth.' And Sophie smiled her gratitude.

It was with reluctance that Rebecca left their little cottage, for she wished to be back at Tythegston Court before dusk fell, and the winter days were short. She bade Hughes refresh himself at the Lamb Inn, for it was but a few minutes' walk to Hannah's cottage and the messuage beside, where Daniel worked at his craft as a wheelwright. She would send Daniel's apprentice to alert the coachman when his services were required to convey her to the Crown Inn at Newton, she promised, as she could not leave without calling upon her good friends, the ostler, and Mistress Randall in the coach house.

After gravely inspecting Hannah's sow-prodigy and declaring the animal to be 'a most wondrously wise, expressive, and friendly creature', and partaking of yet more news and refreshment, Rebecca was transported to the Crown Inn, where Ossie, seeing the unexpected arrival of the de Breos' coach, grew almost incoherent in his efforts to bid Rebecca welcome. Then, with pride, he escorted her up the stone steps to Mistress Randall's small quarters above the coach house.

Emily Randall, serene and gentle as always, despite already having provided victuals and entertainment for two small children with excessively large appetites, greeted Rebecca with unfeigned pleasure. The two children, Dafydd, and the girl Haulwen, daughter of Emily's friend and former pauper, Elwyn Morris, were awkward and tongue-tied in the presence of so grand a lady, so elegantly dressed, and all her cheerful banter and easy questioning could not reassure them. It was only when Rebecca bade Ossie take them outside to view the de Breos' coach, and to allow them to sit inside and, if Hughes would countenance it, to be set upon the horses, that their excited chatter returned. It was with stern admonitions, befitting a former governess, that Emily allowed them to go, bidding them observe and act upon Ossie's every direction, and afterwards to wander no farther than the village green. Then, with no other thought save for her visitor's welcome presence, she devoted herself wholeheartedly to Rebecca.

The delights of the coach exhausted, Dafydd and

Haulwen, and Charity carefully crossed under the archway of the Crown, eyes and ears alerted for the sound of riders or carriages. Then, seeing the highway was clear, hurried over to the green. Charity, intent upon foraging, unearthed some beansticks in the long grass behind a cottage and, with a stone for a ball, the two played a spirited game of bando, without rules, until, breathless and agreeably bruised, they entered the churchyard to continue the competition, Charity barking encouragement. Their forays between headstones and tombs were eventually curtailed by the outraged verger, who boxed Dafydd's ears soundly until menaced by Charity. They drifted aimlessly about the byways, Dafydd's ear still smarting from the blows, and the humiliation and unfairness of it, and even the bull terrier's coldly sympathetic nose nuzzling at his clenched fist brought little comfort, until they came upon the opaque, ice-crusted surface of Newton Pool.

Haulwen was quickly upon it, slithering and slipping, her petticoats aflutter about her, the dog sliding awkward and splay-legged in her wake.

'We had best be getting back,' called out Dafydd nervously, 'Mr Fleet will be coming for me with his cart.'

Haulwen went on sliding, her delighted screams filling the air as the dog, seeking to emulate her, went down with a bump, limbs flailing, scrabbling helplessly, arising to look about him, dazed and disbelieving. Even Dafydd, reluctant as he was, could not help but laugh at Charity's woebegone expression, before shouting peremptorily, 'Haulwen! Come back! Come back I say! It is stupid and dangerous.'

Haulwen, turning only to give him a look of contempt, dark eyes flashing, called accusingly, 'Coward! Milksop! You are afraid. Admit it!'

'I am not!' Dafydd stood his ground, refusing to be baited, insisting, 'I am afraid only for you, the ice is thin, it might not bear your weight. Haulwen! Come back, I beg of you . . .'

Some urgency in his tone half convinced her and she paused, only to spurt away rapidly to the centre of the pool.

Dafydd called sharply to the bull terrier and, with a glance towards Haulwen, the animal came cowed and with head bent, to stand shamefacedly beside him upon the grass.

'Stay!' Dafydd commanded harshly, then stood hesitantly upon the frilled ice at the pool's edge, hearing the brittle crackling of it and seeing the water surge and splash menacingly beneath. Then he was away after Haulwen, struggling to stay upright, angry and foolish, determined to bring her back. Even as he moved, he heard the first crack of ice, loud and menacing, and the white fissure snaking across its surface. His heart began to pound in his chest, agonised and fearful, as the taste of sickness rose in his throat and the cracking noise grew fiercer and more violent. His eyes were fixed now, not upon the ice but upon Haulwen as she stretched out a hand to him, a cry breaking from her throat, her face a pale dissolving mask, as the surface shattered beneath her. He stared, horrified and impotent, as the ice descended, sucking her into the water below.

For a moment he could do nothing, so great was his shock. He seemed numb, incapable of movement. Then, seeing the darkness of the jagged hole where she had disappeared, he moved forward, the ice bending and creaking with every step. He felt the sweat wet upon his neck and trickling down the hairline, blurring his eyes as he sank to his knees. Then he lay out flat upon the surface, edging forward, inch by inch, until he plunged his hands into the icy waters, gasping and sobbing as he groped to find her. He heard his voice scream to the dog upon the shore, 'Go! Go home!' Then he too was in the icy water, its coldness forcing the air from his lungs as he gulped for breath. Then, without knowing how, he was holding Haulwen, first by her hair, and then beneath her arms as, sobbing with relief and terror, he supported her dead weight against his breast, head clear of the water. There was a red mist before his eyes as Dafydd strove to keep her afloat, pain breaking in every vein and muscle. At last, he closed his eyes, knowing that he could do no more.

Haulwen was mercifully asleep in Emily Randall's own bed, a warm brick wrapped in flannel at her feet, cold flesh tingling from being bathed in hot water from Emily's footbath. She had been rubbed soundly from neck to toes with goose-grease and a hot raw onion, and dosed with hot elderberry.

'She smells,' said Ossie, wrinkling his nose in disgust, 'like an ill-cooked dinner!' But he was grateful, beyond words, that she had been saved.

He admitted afterwards that when Charity had come back alone, whining, and darting at him, hindering him and getting under his feet, he had spoken sharply to the cur, and laughingly threatened him with a hay fork.

But the dog's alarm was so great, and his barking so agitated, that he finally saddled a mare, and followed where Charity led.

'It is as well, sir, that you did,' Haulwen's father, Elwyn Morris, said fervently, 'and that the boy held her upright for so long in that icy water. He had courage beyond the ordinary, and commonsense. If I had lost her, I do not know how I could have survived. She is all my world.'

Dafydd, wrapped like a babe in blankets while his clothes steamed damply, as puddings in their nets, before the fire, felt a delicious warmth overtake him as the hot buttermilk, laced with some of Tom Butler's finest keg brandy, raced through his veins. Charity lay beside him, sharing the fire and the heroes' plaudits with Dafydd, and with Ossie, but unaware of it, for the dog was fast asleep, lips quivering noisily with every breath expelled.

'I had best make tracks to Grove Farm to tell the boy's mother,' said Jeremiah, 'for he must stay the night, lest he take a chill. There is room for him in the cottage with me, and he will be fit to travel that short distance if wrapped up warm.'

Dafydd thought that no reward in all the world could have equalled the glory of staying for a night with Charity and Jeremiah, and his heart was too full to speak. Oh, but he had been glad when Ossie had come through the ice upon the mare, breaking it before them with a stick and dragging Haulwen from his arms, which had all but frozen into shape around her, and then laying him, too, across the saddle . . . the water surging about the mare's breast as he drove her towards the bank.

'You will tell my mother it was an accident, Mr Fleet?' he asked anxiously. 'That it was not wilfulness. That I did not offend you knowingly, or Mistress Randall.'

'I will tell her all,' promised Jeremiah, 'and that Haulwen admitted to Mistress Randall that you strove to dissuade her, and then risked your life to save her own.'

Dafydd felt a hotness flame into his cheeks which had nothing to do with the brandy's glow. 'You will take my mother the pouting, sir, and the lobster?' he asked quickly.

Jeremiah smiled. 'Yes. They are prepared ready for eating, and already upon the cart, my boy.' He looked at Dafydd steadily before promising gruffly, 'I shall tell her, too, that you behaved with real courage and intelligence. That you are a man I am proud to call friend.' He patted Dafydd awkwardly upon the shoulder, clearing his throat to hide his treacherous emotion. It would not do to show the boy how the episode had unmanned him.

'I hope that you will always be proud to call me friend, Mr Fleet,' returned Dafydd with dignity, 'as I, sir, will always be obliged to you.'

There was a silence as Ossie, Jeremiah, Elwyn Morris and Mistress Randall stared at the child's grave old-young face, seeing in him the man he might become. Ossie was so moved that the flames of the fire blurred and he was forced to blink his eyes so that the flames sprang to life again behind his eyelids.

'Well!' declared Emily Randall with deliberate briskness, 'I have good news for you, Dafydd. Before she left, Mistress de Breos promised that she would found a school here. You and Haulwen are to be among my first pupils!'

There it was, thought Dafydd, and nothing to be done about it. For every moment of pure joy, there was a price. A penalty. It was ever so, and ever would be. It seems he was to be made a gentleman whether he liked it or not.

Chapter Ten

When Joshua had with some difficulty brought a bucket of water from the well, having first to break the crusted ice from its surface, he washed away the grime and fatigue of the day, then dressed in his evening finery for a visit to Tythegston Court. The monastic austerity of his bedroom under the eaves had, of late, changed. Rebecca's yuletide gift to him had been a small plain, but undeniably handsome, Georgian mahogany dressing table with a fitted interior and toilet glass which he had now raised in order to view himself, first carefully placing the lighted chamberstick upon its slide.

Well, he thought, regarding himself with amusement in its flickering light, who, and what, are you, Joshua Stradling? Like this room you seem not to have made up your mind. Plain or elegant? Gentleman or one of the labouring masses? Have a care! In striving too hard to be both, you might end up by being acceptable to neither!

The clattering hoofbeats of a horse without, and the sounds of its rider hurriedly dismounting, took Joshua scurrying down the stone staircase, candle in hand, almost before the visitor's knocking had died away. He opened the door upon his good friend the chief exciseman, Peter Rawlings, whose broad strong-boned face broke into a ready smile.

'I beg your pardon most humbly, squire,' he said,

touching his forelock and bowing low, 'I have come to the wrong place. I sought a friend, your lordship, a humble, low constable.'

'Come inside, idiot!' cried Joshua, laughing, and dragging him within. 'Would you have me a laughing stock? Now, tell me your business with me.'

'Your elegance had quite put it out of my mind,' said Rawlings. 'It is true that I come on business, but it is not official, you understand? A matter of friendship only.'

Joshua bade him be seated and poured him some ale, while Rawlings continued, 'There is disquiet at the Port, ill-feeling and suspicion.'

'Contraband?' asked Joshua, for they had joined forces often to trap smugglers and wreckers.

'No, not to my knowledge. Smaller, pettier things which cannot be traced. Thefts from passengers' luggage, small cargo, jewellery, coins, anything which may be quickly concealed and sold.' He shrugged helplessly. 'Its value is of little account, Joshua, yet it breeds an atmosphere of unease and anger out of all proportion. I fear there might be a conflagration, violence done, even a killing, should it continue long.'

Joshua looked disturbed. 'You have someone in mind? An organiser, perhaps?'

'No, that is the damnable twist to it, that no one is beyond suspicion: my own men, the ships' crews, the labourers upon the dockside wharves, those in the companies' offices, even I might be implicated.'

'Come, you exaggerate, my friend. Who would believe that? I would stake my life and reputation upon your honesty,' declared Joshua, smiling.

'I would rather you staked them upon discovering the thieves,' said Rawlings soberly, 'much as I appreciate your testimonial, Joshua! I tell you truthfully, that the whole atmosphere has become poisoned with distrust.'

'I will begin my enquiries tomorrow,' promised Joshua, 'as soon as it is light . . . pretending to be engaged upon some other business which involves us both, some exercise upon the coast, perhaps, or my enquiries concerning the highwayman. There are men of yours whom you can trust?'

'I had thought so . . . believed it to be so,' Rawlings corrected himself. 'Yet now, that is the devil of it! I cannot be sure, even of that.'

'Well,' said Joshua lightly, 'at least we trust each other. It is a beginning! You have apprised the justice, Peter?

'No. Nor sought his permission to approach you.'

'I will seek a word with him, have no fear, for I dine with him this very night.'

'Dear soul!' exclaimed Rawlings, unable to suppress his laughter. 'So that is why you are all frilled and jaunty as a coxcomb! Rather you than me! I would prefer a bloody confrontation with the wreckers!'

'That it may well prove to be!' declared Joshua grimly. 'If I do not harness my mare and ride out at once.'

As Joshua reached hurriedly for his high silk hat, Rawlings smiled, rising to his feet and muttering, ' 'Tis well said that punctuality is the politeness of kings.'

'And serfs!' parried Joshua, opening the door. 'For justices, sir, with kings, command obedience and are swift to wrath!'

Rebecca, awaiting Joshua's arrival for dinner at Tythegston Court, was seated at her dressing table in a strangely pensive mood. She was as unaware of her reflection in the looking-glass before her as of the taper light which cast flickering shapes upon the waxed furniture and over the faded tapestries and drapery of the room. Her mind was upon the swiftly changing pattern of her own young life.

New Year's Day. A new beginning to a year, as to life itself, she thought. A time of bright promise, but a time for reflection, too, upon what was ended and could not be changed.

There had been so many changes in the past year, but, God willing, the beckoning year would bring the dearest change of all – her marriage to Joshua.

'Rebecca de Breos; Rebecca Stradling,' she spoke the words aloud and heard their echoes whispering from the carved and panelled walls.

Other voices, sights, memories came crowding now, jostling, spilling, without pattern or shape: insistent shades of her life and friends of the three hamlets and beyond. Past, present and what was yet to be. Rosa and Doonan wed, and so nearly parted by death; Jeremiah's love for Sophie; Illtyd, no longer an outcast; Dr Burrell returned; and Emily delivered from paupery; Elizabeth and Mrs Crandle sharing the promise of kinder times; Dr Peate; her grandfather, so generous in all his ways, and dearly loved.

Here, within Robert Knight's great house, the age-old traditions of New Year had no place. As a priest he could not do other than denounce them as pagan beliefs: pernicious, corrupting, best left to die unmourned. Yet a part of Rebecca cried out that they be allowed to survive. Their true meaning had long been forgotten, and they held no menace now, nor evil, in the minds of those who practised them. They were no more than links in that human chain of living and dying which shackles all. A remembrance of things past, the touch of flesh grown cold: ghostly and without power.

At Southerndown Court, the cottagers would have

come early to claim their gifts in the great hall, festive with swagged greenery, bright with ribbon bows and crimson berries. The poorest villagers might choose from the bounty provided by Sir Matthew, their squire: a bolt of warm flannel, perhaps, to ease winter's chill, or a flitch of smoked bacon to hang suspended from their ceiling beams, alongside the fire; beef, from cattle fed upon Southerndown's salt-pastures, or bales of comforting bedding.

In return, each cottager would offer an apple set upon a tripod of twigs, and prettified with oats, a sprig of herb rosemary, and the greenery of holly and mistletoe, their simple gifts cherished until the apples withered into decay.

What did such offerings signify? Who could now say? The embodiment of life and death? Certainly herb rosemary was for remembrance, and mistletoe, sacred to the druids, was said to be their amulet against all ills of flesh and spirit. And the apple? The earth itself, perhaps; and the oats a symbol of fertility and harvest, as the greenery spoke of new life and the end of darkness with the passing of the winter solstice.

Rebecca recalled how Joshua had told her of the ceremony of the plough, long cherished by farming folk. It was borne into the farmhouse kitchen on Christmas Eve, decorated and placed beneath the table of scrubbed wood which was the centre of all their yule-tide preparations. There it remained, a silent guest, to be sprinkled with ale when visitors were plied with refreshment and hospitality, lest it feel itself neglected and forgotten. With the coming of the New Year, and a return to work, it, too, was returned to the appointed place.

Upon his father's farm in the Vale, Joshua had confessed that the tradition lingered still that each cow which gave birth to its calf after the midnight hour and the death of the old year was granted a sprig of mistletoe for its stall. None remembered why.

The sound of urgent knocking upon her door startled Rebecca from her introspection and, when she opened it, Rosa came hurrying in, grasping her hand impulsively, begging her to come at once, for Joshua was already late, and had a New Year's gift to give her, a callenig, which he was eager to present. In Rosa's and Doonan's company, she was reminded, she would be suitably chaperoned, for they were already decently wed.

Joshua, face whipped to colour from his ride, eyes dancing with excitement, pressed into Rebecca's hands his gift, most elegantly wrapped and tied with bows of silken ribbon threaded through with greenery.

'You must be quick, my love,' he urged, 'make haste, for I am already late.'

'Oh, Joshua!' Her pleasure was dimmed by the knowledge that she could give him nothing in return. 'I have no callenig for you. I did not think.'

'Hush! It is of no account. I cannot believe that Mr Knight would approve my action, either in meeting you in secret, or in perpetuating so pagan a rite, but I could contain my eagerness no longer.'

'Nor I!' Rebecca's fingers were awkward in their excitement and haste as she tore aside bows and wrapping, and in her hands held a small cage of golden wire, exquisite in its delicacy. Within, upon a bough, sat a miniature bird, perfectly fashioned, even to its dainty feathers and beak.

'Oh, Joshua.' Her pleasure was swift and undisguised. 'I have never owned so pretty a thing.' She stood upon tiptoe to kiss his cheek as his hand settled gently upon hers, as he guided her fingers to turn the tiny golden key.

The sound of a blackbird's singing, mellifluous and clear, filled the sickroom as the tiny bird opened its beak and sang, turning its head as though alive and singing for sheer happiness.

Rosa had settled herself beside Cavan's bed, and had taken his brawny hand in her own small fist, and saw that her husband's eyes were wet with tears of weakness, or sudden pleasure. 'It is like a real bird's song,' he said quietly. 'A melody of joy in being alive.'

'Yes,' agreed Rosa, her fingers tightening upon his, ' 'tis a song for being alive, Cavan, my dear.' And she gave thanks with all of her soul and flesh that it was so.

Joshua, with his gaze upon Rebecca and the radiant pleasure in her face, said simply, 'I could not bring you a live wren in a cage upon Saint Stephen's Day, for it would have grieved you to see it confined and songless. I did not think it deserving of such a fate, even if the legend be true: that Saint Stephen's escape from his prison cell was defeated by the singing of a wren which aroused his gaoler from sleep.'

'If it were so, then that was punishment enough,' protested Rebecca, 'it is cruel that it should still be hunted and trapped.'

'A fate not unlike my own . . .' declared Joshua, smiling. 'For, like the bird within the cage you hold, Rebecca, I am captive for ever to your charms. Although I would ask for no release.' He took a sprig of mistletoe from the pocket of his coat, and held it above her head, kissing her soundly, and with considerable fervour.

'I'll wager,' ventured Cavan's hoarse voice from the bed, 'that should the justice find you so employed, it would not be a song of welcome he would sing.'

And Joshua, laughing his agreement, reluctantly left them.

* * *

Having arrived at Tythegston Court within a barely acceptable time, thanks to the mare's efforts and his own fierce urging, and then snatching a few precious moments with Rebecca, Joshua presented himself, breathless and lightly dishevelled, before the justice. His own condition paled before that of Robert Knight, who was suffering the backlash of his assault by the ruffians. Indeed, so swollen and bruised was the poor gentleman from head to toe that he seemed incapable of any but the most rudimentary movement, and even that, painful and awkward.

'I fear that you were very roughly manhandled by the villains, sir,' said Joshua, trying not to stare too fixedly at the bruise which engulfed the justice's right eye, and spilled across his cheekbone.

'Hmmm. A hazard of one's occupation, sir, when one seeks to bring villains to justice! I fancy my wounds will not go unnoticed in the court room.'

Or anywhere else! thought Joshua, amused. 'You will give evidence against them, sir?' he said aloud.

'Evidence? Evidence?' repeated the justice testily. 'I shall be sitting in judgement, sir.'

'Is that wise, sir?'

'Wise, Stradling? What have you in mind, sir? That my judgement might be prejudiced? Suspect?'

'How could I believe it to be so?' declared Joshua urbanely. 'It would make me a greater fool and villain than they. No, I merely feared that the prisoners, or those who instructed the wretches, might seek revenge.'

The justice appeared mollified. 'I thank you for your concern, Stradling,' he said, 'but it is misplaced. Your sympathy should be for the accused, for I warrant they will not get off lightly: a few weeks upon the treadmill; or displayed in the stocks; then, a salutary term in a house of correction.' He recalled himself swiftly, 'Always assuming that they are proved guilty. To my satisfaction.'

'To your satisfaction . . .' echoed Joshua innocently.

'You have a most irritating habit of repeating what I say, sir,' declared the justice abrasively. 'Now, where was I? Oh yes, one must do one's duty without fear or favour, Stradling, ignoring the cost! *Pro bono publico* . . .' he quoted pompously.

'For the general good,' agreed Joshua blandly.

The justice regarded him with suspicion, seeking some evidence of insolence, but, finding none, declared tartly, 'I am well aware that you were a Latin scholar, Stradling, perhaps you would be better employed directing your mind to finding the highwayman than flaunting your scholarship! You are no nearer a solution, I suppose?'

Joshua told him of his meeting with the horse-dealer, asking, 'You have learnt any more of the pistol and crest, sir?'

'I shall inform you as soon as I have established its provenance,' rebuked the justice. 'Then you may make your own enquiries as to how it came into the highwayman's keeping.'

Joshua nodded, turning to his visit from Rawlings and the unrest at the Port.

'It has grown too quickly, Stradling! The influx of newcomers has been too great; their customs and beliefs too diverse to be easily absorbed by the villagers. These thefts must be the work of some stranger.' As Joshua did not respond, he conceded grudgingly, 'Well, you had best investigate, with more success, it is to be hoped, than with the highwayman!'

Robert Knight turned awkwardly, his grimace of pain changing to a smile of quite astonishingly sheepish delight. 'Why, Rebecca, my dear, what a vision of loveliness you are.' He held out his arm to escort her in to dinner, wincing involuntarily as he did so, but continuing gallantly, 'You bring joy to this old gentleman's heart.'

For which benison, thought Joshua, may we all be grateful . . .

The conversation over dinner might have proved stilted and uncomfortable, for their host was evidently in some discomfort from his injuries. However, he seemed gratified for the distraction of their presence and set out to charm Rebecca with great good humour, his conversation cultivated and wide ranging.

'You have heard news of your nephew and his companions, sir?' enquired Rebecca. 'Since they left for Ireland?'

'No, none, I am relieved to say, although I have been reluctantly making enquiries, for his mother's sake. If he has gone to Ireland, it is doubtless in search of some bloodstock or because the gaming is better, and he hopes to escape his creditors. Yet, nothing has been reported of him!' He looked at Joshua, the gravity of his face flawed by the ridiculous bruise encompassing his eye. 'Never live beyond your means, Stradling!' he adjured. 'Squandering your money upon base, indulgent pleasure, it brings nothing but regret.'

'I am as inclined to that course, sir, as you,' returned Joshua pleasantly, 'notwithstanding the tempting generosity of my salary . . .'

The justice started to chuckle, and so infectious was his mirth that Rebecca and Joshua joined in the merriment until, clutching his bruised and aching ribs, Robert Knight begged them to desist.

'Well, Mr Stradling,' said Rebecca, when they were finally alone in the justice's drawing room, 'I must congratulate you, sir, upon your strategy.'

'To what do you refer, ma'am?' demanded Joshua. 'I confess that I am at a loss to know.'

'Indeed? I believed, foolishly, that you deliberately incapacitated our host with mirth that you might have your wicked way with me unhindered.'

'You do me too much dishonour, ma'am,' said Joshua with mock gravity. 'But I declare that now you put the hypothesis to me, I can see its advantages. However, there is a greater disadvantage! The justice has not lost the use of his pistol arm, nor his sense of propriety, ma'am.'

'Well, you had best kiss me then, before he demonstrates both!' she cried, flinging her arms about his neck.

'I declare, Mistress de Breos, you are quite incorrigible!' he said severely when he could take breath. 'A wanton, corrupting influence upon a poor wretch with none of your experience or social status. It is enough to turn a low constable's head.'

'A little more in this direction, then, that I may reach your lips the better!' instructed Rebecca, not a whit abashed.

After a few moments of passionate, and quite exquisite exploration, Joshua was reluctantly forced to draw away, exclaiming, 'Oh, Rebecca, if you only knew what your nearness, and the sweet warmth of your flesh, do to me, you would be afraid to rouse me so . . . It would be so easy to forget that I am alleged to be a gentleman.'

A resonant shout for Leyshon from the justice in the library, and the unmistakable sound of Robert Knight's footsteps tramping heavily outside, were evidently meant to remind Joshua, as was the harsh coughing, of his return journey.

' 'Tis a pity that his bell pull is out of order yet again,' declared Rebecca. 'It is a strange affliction which seems to be caused by your presence, sir.'

'Then I had best remove myself,' said Joshua, smiling, 'for he suspects our silence, yet suspects unruly sounds the more . . .'

'Perhaps,' suggested Rebecca wickedly, 'we might kiss unrestrainedly, while shifting our feet in dance upon the floor, or playing a duet upon the pianoforte?'

'I fear, ma'am, that my limited musical education did not prepare me for such virtuosity,' declared Joshua regretfully. 'And, even were I to take up the harp, my hands and feet would be fully occupied . . . I suspect we must postpone our amorous adventures until another day.'

With regret, Rebecca concurred, suggesting that their betrothal party might present just such an opportunity. Then, laughing, Joshua went to take his leave of Doonan and Rosa, whom he would attend at their own cottage upon the morrow, and to bid good-night to the justice.

'Ah, Stradling,' Robert Knight said expansively, 'I hope that my shouting did not disturb you unduly. This confounded bell rope is a curse, and my injuries have rendered me so stiff and awkward, I was compelled to call aloud for Leyshon to replenish my brandy. You will take a measure?'

As Joshua murmured his agreement, Leyshon muttered discreetly from the doorway, 'When you rang, sir, I took the opportunity of bringing another glass, anticipating your request. It is as well, sir, that the bell pull has been repaired.'

'Yes,' agreed Joshua gravely, studying the justice's bruised and rudely flushed face. 'under the present circumstances, it is more than a mere convenience. It is a necessity.'

Upon the morrow, his bedroom still filled with winter dark, Joshua arose to visit the Port, as he had promised Peter Rawlings. He planned to catch the high point of the tide, when the bustling activity at the docks was at its peak, reasoning that it was the best time to observe without being observed. His presence there was not unusual because of his liaison with the excisemen and his past investigations, and he had oft times been summoned to some sailors' brawl at the Ship Aground or the Knights Arms, or to arbitrate in a quayside dispute. Usually, his very presence and his official status served to subdue the offenders who, even in a drunken stupor, seemed to respond to the commands of a disciplined hierarchy, so ingrained in it were their lives. If pressed, Joshua could call upon the services of Doonan, Jeremiah and his friends, Daniel and Emrys, or Ben Clatworthy, the blacksmith. Their justice was swift and unstoppable, like their huge fists, and none had yet queried its fairness. Had they done so, there was always the ultimate ignominy of the gaol-coach, and the cell above the Crown Inn.

As he set out from the Crown Inn upon the grey, a lanthorn throwing a truckle of beams across the highway and the deep-windowed cottages of local limestone, Joshua thought how much at one he felt with the people of this place, living their frugal lives upon its raw, tempestuous coastline. There was a strength and ruggedness about them, a bare honesty. Like the rocks formed by the savagery of wind and tide, their own character had been honed by climate and circumstance. If they were rough and unpolished, they were also firm in body and spirit, else they could not have survived. Joshua had sometimes thought that the 'hell, fire and damnation' preaching of Robert Knight was of little solace to them. Yet, now that he knew them better, he realised that it cruelly reflected the expectations of their lives: no reward without labour; no sin without punishment. To be fed a milksop diet of compromise would have left men like Jeremiah and Illtyd unfilled and dissatisfied. Better a hunger of the body than the soul! Joshua thought with wry amusement as the mare cantered steadily across the arid loneliness of Pickett's Lease. And if they finally achieved eternal salvation and rest, he wondered, would the time lie heavily upon them? They were ill disposed towards idleness and indulgence. Perhaps, like Ruth in that strange Biblical land, they would feel it an alien place and cry out for this wild shore, with all the bleakness of the circling gulls. Impulsively he gave the mare her head, letting her gallop unchecked, finding in the salt wind from the sea and the pounding of her hooves a release from his melancholy.

The Port was absurdly small for all the hubbub and feverish activity it provoked. It seemed that so concentrated were the sights, noise and smells of its one tiny dock with its crude stone-blocked walls that they had burst out to infuse the sky above, the sea and the land, with its colour and vitality. All along the wharves, cargoes lay heaped: gleaming peaks of coal; limestone marl; minerals; resin-scented pit props jostling with the mingled fragrances of coffee beans and spices; and the sunbursts of colour from fabrics, woollen goods, farm produce and fruits. Among them moved the dwarfed scurrying figures of the men, and the occasional, bonneted fishwife: busy worker ants in a bustling ant heap.

The sweetest sight, to Joshua, was the forest of masts, austere as the shorn pit props from Scandinavian shores, rigging spread precise and delicate as spiders' webs. In dock, and lying off, he could distinguish brigs and brigantines, coasting smacks and schooners, ketches and Severn trows, those small, unlovely sailing barges peculiar to the Bristol Channel and seeming, to Joshua, to reflect the unadorned, honest character of those who sailed them.

The dock was a tidal one, raked by fierce westerly gales, which sent the Atlantic breakers pounding and shattering against the shore with a force and violence that nothing could withstand. In winter, the severity was so great and the danger from hidden rocks and currents so real that none but the smaller vessels, with crews who knew its vagaries, would attempt to enter. Joshua thought of his friend, Roland Devereaux, master of the three-masted schooner *Pride of Glamorgan*, who had but yesterday sailed from Cardiff for South America, braving the rigours of Atlantic gales and breakers, and the harsher loneliness of command. It was a way of life, like Joshua's own, which served to set one apart: testing and severe. Yet, what beauty there was in a sailing ship under full sail, canvas bellying, blunt bows thrusting the sea to foam. At moments like that, Devereaux must almost believe that it was he who held the powers of life and death over his vessel and crew rather than the elements which held them all at their mercy.

Joshua returned reluctantly to his own work. Where should he begin? The offices of the iron, coal and mineral companies? The ships' chandlers? The offices of Her Majesty's Customs and Excise? The tiny repair yard? The shore messuages which housed the craftsmen; sail-loft; ropewalk; carpenters' shed; and smithy? They sounded grand and impressive, but in reality were scarcely more than one-man businesses, sometimes employing a young apprentice, for the larger, more prosperous vessels carried craftsmen of their own as crew.

No, thought Joshua, I will start with the harbour master, for he is honest and discreet, and our conversation will go no further. The constable had no wish to provoke resentment and suspicion, for he valued his easy acceptance by those who worked at the Port, and their respect for his occupation.

The harbour master, Captain Ayde-Buchan, RN, was already well known to him: a Canadian by birth, and a cheerful, efficient administrator with the spare, weather-beaten look of a sailor, whose eyes seemed restlessly set upon far horizons. As if, one day, like those vessels purposefully drying their sails, he might cast off and sail to deeper waters.

'Well, Constable Stradling, and how may I be of service, sir?' he asked courteously. 'I may take it from your expression that this is not merely a social visit?'

Joshua explained his mission, remarking that he masked his true enquiries by declaring his search to be for the highwayman.

'You may rely upon my absolute discretion, sir,' declared the harbour master. 'I am as eager, sir, to clear up this affair as you. I like to keep a tight ship, with crew and stores. One rotten apple in a barrel quickly corrupts the others.'

Joshua nodded, repressing a smile. 'You have some idea, sir, as to whom the culprits may be?'

'No, none,' he said regretfully. 'Save that there must be several involved in the thefts for they are widespread and most skilfully planned and executed. Yet they have no recognisable pattern. I mean, they are not purely thefts from cargo, which might put suspicion firmly upon the ship's crew or cargo-loaders. There are random searches at the dock gates upon all who pass through here, saving the passengers, of course. Yet, of late, their baggage has been most scrupulously checked, with no result, save to substantiate that the losses they claim are genuine.'

'It is a damnable puzzle!' agreed Joshua. 'And one, I fear, which will not be easy to solve.'

'I have always believed the old adage that if you give a man enough rope he will hang himself,' said Ayde-

Buchan. 'As his confidence and arrogance grow, he will become contemptuous of authority, thinking himself invincible.'

'Agreed,' said Joshua dubiously. 'But it might take more time than I have to spare.'

'Added to which, the anger and hostility will grow, with every man fearing his own honesty impugned, and suspicious of others.'

Joshua nodded.

'Well, I do not know what the answer will be!' said Ayde-Buchan. 'But I have easy access to every part of the Port, and docks, and the co-operation of all the masters of the vessels which berth here. I will watch and listen most carefully, sir, and inform you at once if I learn anything of import.'

As Joshua made to thank him, he brushed it aside, saying, 'It is on my own behalf, sir, as well as yours. It reflects upon my own authority and administration here. Meanwhile, perhaps you will take a measure of brandy with me, Constable?' His eyes twinkled mischievously. 'I give you my word of honour as a sailor and a gentleman that it has been honestly obtained!'

Joshua smiled and accepted, thinking good-humouredly that they would have been better served splicing the mainbrace in rum.

His business with the harbour master concluded, and having left the mare at the stables of the Ship Aground upon arrival, Joshua continued his patient observation on foot, ostensibly questioning and seeking possible news of the highwayman from labourers and administrators. He crossed the horse-drawn tramway, upon which the wagons made five consecutive journeys a day to and from the iron and smelter works in the hinterland, and to the new collieries opened along the line of the road. He looked back at the patient horses waiting to take out their loads of iron ore to the furnaces, thinking how hard and difficult were the lives of the animals and men so employed, with each journey taking six full hours; a man and his team working twelve hours each day.

'Constable Stradling, sir?'

Joshua turned to see a labourer alongside a tram-horse, his hand upon the animal's bridle. The man was slight of build and all but unrecognisable in his frayed clothing, his face obscured by coal dust, through which sweat had traced small runnels of flesh.

'You do not recognise me, sir, and it is no wonder,' the man said. 'I do not apologise, sir, for my clothing or for the filth of my trade, for having been a pauper so long, such work is a godsend.'

'Elwyn Morris!' said Joshua at once, recognising the ex-pauper from the poorhouse at Bridgend who, although hounded and threatened with murder by the wreckers whom Joshua had once brought to justice, came forward to give evidence against those who had murdered Dafydd's father, Jem Crocutt, so cruelly. 'I am glad to see you, sir.' Joshua took his hand, regardless of the coal dust and dirt ingrained upon it. 'I am most pleased that you have found work here.'

'Yes. I thank you. It has given me back the confidence bled from me as a pauper.' He smiled. 'I have been able to make a home for my daughter, Haulwen, and me. 'Tis but a room, sir, but, oh the joy I find in it, and my freedom.'

Joshua, recalling the indignities and deprivations Morris had suffered at the hands of the workmaster at the poorhouse and when in hiding with his child, said compassionately, 'Yet you never gave up hope, of that I am convinced.'

'No, sir, for it was all I had, the hope of finding my daughter one day. That, and the struggle to keep my self-respect.'

'You were never in danger of losing that,' said Joshua warmly.

Elwyn Morris looked at him hard before replying, his voice low. 'I dare not admit, even to myself, how near I came, but I have tried to cling to it, always. If a man cannot respect himself, Mr Stradling, how can he gain respect from others? Being treated as a beast of the field does not make you one.' With a touch to his forehead, he was upon his way, leading the horse which had been waiting patiently and still beside him, grateful, Joshua suspected, for a rest from its labours. He watched them go, curiously moved by the encounter, horse and haulier swallowed up in dust, and the grinding and clanging of wheels upon the tramway.

By what unspeakable arrogance do we judge a man's worth by his work, or an accident of birth? thought Joshua. Denying such a man his right to be called 'gentleman'? Of one thing Joshua was sure, the thief he sought was not Elwyn Morris.

The return of Doonan and Rosa to their tiny cottage in Newton was an occasion which not only its villagers, but the folk of all the three hamlets would long remember.

Doonan was to be transported in the justice's own coach, as befitted the hero who had sought to defend his wife's honour even at the risk of losing his own life.

The inhabitants of the place were known to be a phlegmatic people; indeed, strangers had once described them as 'positively bovine' in their calm contemplation of life. It was true that they were not easily hurried or swayed; seemingly unimpressed by power and fortune alike. Perhaps, because they accepted the indiscriminate nature of both, believing that, as swiftly as they came, so might they vanish. Yet, for their own, they had a fierce loyalty. And Doonan and Rosa were undoubtedly their own.

As the invalid and Rosa, with the justice's liveried coachman upon the box, drove into Newton, the sight they witnessed from the carriage was droll in the extreme, yet so unexpectedly moving that Doonan, weakened by sickness and fatigue, had to knuckle the tears from his eyes with his great fists.

Every doorstep had been patiently scoured with sand, and scrubbed with rottenstone. Upon their pristine surfaces sprouted coloured patterns of roses and shamrock, fashioned like the intricate shapes which decorated the edges of their stone-flagged cottage floors. The few who could copy by rote had added their initials, or the single word 'Welcom', the original perhaps misspelt, and perpetuated, for none could read. Every door was garlanded with a wreath or spray of rosemary and rue, and women and children, and those men too old or infirm to work, were lining the streets before their dwellings, dressed in their best, and in some cases only, clothes, freshly laundered and pressed. From the tops of closed casements fluttered ancient flags, resurrected from celebrations in the wars with the French, and those who had none waved cotton kerchiefs or scraps of cloth. A small trail of them fluttered from the archway of the Crown and, below, Ossie had marshalled three of his mares, groomed within an inch of their lives, manes and tails aflutter with plaited ribbons, his gap-toothed smile wide in welcome.

Jeremiah's cart, and that of his friend Emrys, who worked with Doonan at the quarry face, were a rare sight, 'all frilled and furbelowed as a fine lady's drawers' as

Jeremiah declared, although no one had the wit to ask him how he had come by such information. Charity sat proudly upon the floor of the cart, a red bow at his neck, a model of style and fashion. Even Ezra the Box had decorated his funeral cart with purple drapings, coffin thickly heaped with greenery of holly berries and mistletoe; the little Welsh pony with a mourning plume adance upon his pretty tossing head.

' 'Tis a shame,' mumbled Emrys to Jeremiah. 'The old hypocrite merely seeks to peddle his wares. And it will do Doonan no good, I'll be bound! He was too nearly set inside it!'

'At least,' said Jeremiah, anxious to be fair, 'he has made the effort, Emrys, and 'tis all the same in the end, for we must patronise him, every last one of us, whether we want to or not!' Whereupon, Emrys broke into spontaneous laughter more suited to the joyfulness of the occasion.

The old lady's goose, now Tom Butler's pet, for he had paid handsomely to keep it, so great was its prowess upon the treadmill, was also decked out for the occasion, and held upon a sturdy rope by the potman. It stood in a clear patch of its own before the inn door, for employment had not noticeably improved its disposition and there were not a few viciously pecked shins and thighs among the onlookers. Although now it was more intent upon hissing and menacing the lean cur it had displaced in the kitchen, which, with a bright ribbon about its mangy neck, looked as the potman confided, 'Like a trollop who has squandered a sixpence upon a pedlar!'.

The villagers had thoughtfully scattered straw before Rosa's and Doonan's door that, when the invalid was bedded, he might be spared the interruption of carriage wheels and hooves. The house and, indeed, the street outside overflowed with offerings, from firkins of ale from the landlords of the inns, to baskets of eggs and butter from the farms, freshly caught fish, and hares, and home-baked bread and cakes, and sweetmeats from the cottagers, as was their way.

When the carriage breasted the corner towards the church, Rosa, peeping shyly and overcome with the unexpected warmth of it all, saw Illtyd upon his piebald, Faith, tooled saddle gleaming and, held between his hand and Sophie's, a banner reading: 'Cavan and Rosa – WELCOME HOME'.

Beside them, Hannah stood with her sow, prettily bedecked in a straw bonnet, tail tied with a pink ribbon, a circlet of flowers from some long-discarded hat set upon its plump thigh, like a garter. It looked directly at Rosa, flat nose twitching, small slit eyes brightly inquisitive.

Rosa, seeing it, set up a howl of laughter, turning to tears, which all but drowned the music of the two hired fiddlers and the dancers from the Lamb Inn at Nottage who had been awaiting some signal of the approaching carriage from the village green. There was a spontaneous burst of cheering, wave upon wave of it, breaking in ripples through the crowd, as inevitably as the sea upon the shore.

Joshua, standing with Rosa's mother upon the door-step of Doonan's house, thought fleetingly of Ossie's bird of death, and wondered whence it had flown.

Chapter Eleven

Rebecca, during her journey back to Southerndown Court in the de Breos' coach, was less concerned about the risk of meeting the highwayman than about her grandfather's health. She had grown to love the austere, dignified old gentleman dearly, recognising in him the loneliness which, for so many years, had set her apart from others.

The bond between them was more than that of common blood. They shared the same character; the same love of beauty, learning and the arts; even the same prejudices and sense of humour. It was almost, Rebecca sometimes thought, as if her own father had been a changeling: his weakness and self-pity corrupting his life, and her own. His dependence upon her, even when she was but a child, had reversed their roles. It was she who had nursed and protected him, shielding him from the cruel realities of poverty by working upon the shore at her shellfish gathering. She had laboured at a meaner task and for longer hours than many grown men, paying no heed to season or weather. Sometimes, she recalled, her hands had been chapped and bleeding from the keenness of wind and shell, her legs chafed raw by the wet hem of her dress. As she awkwardly loaded the frails of cockles upon the cart, thinking of the hours of boiling which lay ahead, she could fancy the rain, or salt-spray from the sea, burned her cheeks like an open wound or froze upon her skin. Even when she had scarce stood high enough to lift the heavy baskets to the floor of the cart, she would not admit that she cried from fatigue and hopelessness, burying her face in the cob's rough mane for comfort from a living creature. Was it her father's fecklessness, or her de Breos' blood, which had made her strong? Rebecca wondered.

'We have arrived, Mistress de Breos.' The scraping of the carriage door, and the concerned voice of Hughes, recalled her to the present. She saw how frail he looked, frame shrunken so that the thick livery hung loosely about his thin shoulders.

Stopping only to thank him dutifully for the swiftness and comfort of the journey, Rebecca left him in the company of the guard and ran impetuously to the library, that she might see her grandfather without delay.

With a single knock and not pausing for his command to enter, she flew to where he was seated at his desk, embracing him, and kissing him impulsively in the relief of seeing him hale and in no distress.

'Oh, Grandfather!' she cried, when she could take breath. 'I have been so worried about you . . . I feared you were sick!' She hugged him again. 'Oh, I am so very glad to be home!'

'My dear,' Sir Matthew's usually stern face was flushed, indulgent, his eyes bright as he chided gently, 'I think that perhaps you are forgetting yourself in your anxiety and haste. We are not alone, ma'am.'

Rebecca turned to see a gentleman standing at the far side of the desk, and facing them, a wan uncertain smile upon his lips.

'I believe, Rebecca, that you have already made the

acquaintance of your new drawing tutor, Mr Humphrey Edmonds. He has come to us sooner than expected. He was of a mind to journey to Ireland upon business with some companions, but decided that duty must take precedence over pleasure.'

'Indeed, sir,' the bleak, colourless eyes were lifted to Rebecca's as he bowed gallantly, 'you do me an injustice. Instructing the young ladies will be both pleasure and duty.'

Rebecca felt the same irrational fear and withdrawal from Edmonds as when he had taken her hand at the justice's house. It was absurd and childish, she knew, and she would not weary her grandfather with talk of it.

Emily Randall, in the simple rooms above the coach-house of the Crown, was seated upon a wheel-backed chair beside the bed, reading a story to Haulwen, who seemed remarkably recovered from her submersion in the icy waters of Newton Pool. Emily had a real affection for the child, heightened by the knowledge of her earlier suffering. For as far back as she could remember, Haulwen had worked upon the poor hill farm, tending the sick old woman who had given bleak home to a pauper child. When Elwyn Morris had fled the poorhouse and found his daughter after years of separation, he had helped the child to tend the barren land and few remaining beasts, and to give ease to the old woman until she died.

After Elwyn had risked his life to return and give evidence against the wreckers, it was to Emily he had come, for she was the only one he knew who had shared the soullessness of the workhouse, and escaped its degradation.

Emily saw in her mind's eye the pathetic spectacle of

the two of them entering the yard of the Crown, Elwyn's crudely made cart pulled by a donkey, its ribs scoring its moth-eaten skin. There had been strain and anguish upon the man's face, but the child had been wary, defiant, scrambling down to protect the scrawny beast with her own fierce body, until Ossie had taken both child and donkey into his pitying care.

Mistress Randall hugged the child now impulsively, and Haulwen smiled, begging her to continue the story of 'The little girl with the pretty hood who met a wolf in the forest'. Emily thought of Mary Devereaux, and all her other pupils through the years, secure in their privileged sheltered childhoods, who had begged for the same tale, in the same way. 'Rich or poor,' she thought, 'the minds and feelings are the same: the curious thirst for knowledge. What a blessing then that Rebecca had given her the opportunity of starting her own school here in the three hamlets. It would be a challenge, certainly, but a glorious adventure, too!' She was aware that Haulwen was impatiently clamouring for more immediate news of the adventures of *Red Riding Hood and the Wolf*. The child, wrapped in one of Emily's voluminous cambric nightgowns, with the sleeves rolled back, was watching her intently, small grave face tilted expectantly, dark eyes round with curiosity. She looked, thought Emily, stifling a desire to laugh, like a ridiculously solemn barn owl, white-plumaged and unblinking. She could restrain her bubbling mirth no longer, laughing aloud from affection and sheer good humour, Haulwen laughing with her, although she knew not why and wiping her eyes upon the hem of her nightgown.

The knock upon the door startled them into silence as Emily, smoothing her hair, went forward to open it.

Dr Burrell, upon the stone stairs, saw a lovely, serene

woman, traces of laughter still about her gentle mouth, and warm intelligent eyes. Her hair was softly drawn back to the nape of her slender neck, its brownness barely lightened by grey. There was a natural grace about her, some quality of stillness which he found restful.

'I have come to see the invalid, ma'am, the child. I believe that I have the honour of addressing Mistress Randall?'

Emily, seeing the small apothecaries' chest which he carried beneath his arm, and glimpsing Dr Mansel's carriage in the yard below, said, 'I confess that I do not know you, sir, or who has summoned you, but I bid you enter and welcome.'

Burrell followed her into the long, neatly furnished room, thinking how elegant were her movements and manner, in spite of the simplicity of her dress and surroundings.

'I had best explain, ma'am, that the constable, Mr Stradling, gives me news of those in the three hamlets in need of my services.'

Emily, knowing that Elwyn Morris could not hope to pay the sum required, said gently, 'If you will discuss the fee for your services, sir, I will make it ready for when you have finished your examination.' She turned to reach for her reticule, where she kept the little money earned at her sewing skills from the village seamstress, but Burrell put a restraining hand upon her arm, withdrawing it awkwardly, lest he cause offence.

'No, Mistress Randall,' he insisted firmly, 'there is no charge. It is a small duty I undertake, in my own time, from choice, and freely.'

'Then you have my gratitude, sir, and my admiration.' Fearing that she had been indiscreet, she flushed, and Burrell, seeing the warm colour flood her skin, said quickly, 'We are not strangers, ma'am, and it is I who should be grateful to you.'

'I do not understand, sir,' Emily confessed in bewilderment.

'My name, ma'am, is John Burrell. You have told me much of my friend, Jeremiah Fleet's life, in your letters, and, in doing so, told me much of yourself.' He set down his case upon the table and offered his hand in greeting.

She took it gravely in her own, saying with sincerity, 'I have long wished to make your acquaintance, sir.' She studied Burrell's lean cadaverous face earnestly, without embarrassment, and seeing his shadowed eyes, and the deep lines of hurt about his mouth, had a fierce urge to smooth them tenderly away.

They stared at each other, unspeaking, for a moment, in startled recognition, until Emily deliberately broke its intensity, saying, 'I admire you for what you have made of your life, Dr Burrell. Your reports of the privations and sufferings of the cholera victims oft moved me to tears at my own impotence, and the depth of their pain. I have not, sir, known the degradation of being imprisoned, unjustly, as you . . .' She hesitated painfully. 'Yet, I have known what it is to be a pauper, through no fault of my own, losing my name, my dignity, and even the will to survive, so complete was my sense of rejection.'

Dr Burrell nodded, but said nothing as Emily continued with excoriating honesty, 'The worst is being alone, forsaken of hope and human comfort. Yet, you gave them that, sir, even those who could not be saved.'

He saw the softness of tears in her eyes, and heard it in her throat as she spoke, and was so moved by her understanding that he could not reply. He turned away to the child, who had been listening carefully upon the bed, saying to her, 'What a solemn little owl it is! Well, my small fledgling, shall we see what wonders there are in this magical box of mine?'

Emily, meeting his dark eyes amidst Haulwen's quick, excited murmurings, smiled approvingly, and John Burrell, as approving, smiled back.

Joshua, returning to his cottage, was relieved to see that his cleaning woman had restored the cluttered surfaces to something resembling order, and that the washerwoman had returned his purified clothes, neatly ironed, setting them out for his use.

He picked up a white shirt, marvelling at its cleanliness and the smoothly ironed and goffered frills. Unlike his mother's washerwoman, who was permitted the indulgent luxury of soap, despite the iniquitous soap tax, his own, Joshua knew, would have used a lye of ferns gathered freely from the verges and woodside. The fronds were hung to dry, like herbs, in the open air then, when brittle, burned in an iron pot, the ashes carefully saved as washballs. Often, the clothes were washed in rock pools, the salt providing a natural bleach, or at brookside or pool, the flat pebbles and stones providing a washboard. Few had, like Jeremiah, the refinement of a boiler in the yard to heat water, and many cottagers used cold water set in wooden half-casks or troughs, bleaching white garments with stale urine or dried animal dung.

Joshua hastily replaced his shirt, not wishing to speculate any further upon its history, but looking with satisfaction at the platter of cold fat bacon from the farm, the cooled potatoes, and pickles which had been left out for him in readiness for his return.

As he was about to start upon his victuals, having poured himself some ale, there was a knocking upon his door, so timorous and indistinct that he was not sure if he had actually heard it. Puzzled, he went to investigate, opening the door upon a thin, ill-dressed stranger with a gaunt, pinched face who stepped back nervously as if to efface himself. Joshua waited for him to speak, but the man seemed to have difficulty in forming his speech, for his lips moved soundlessly, as if practising the words.

'Forgive me, sir . . .' he blurted at length, 'I bring a message from Mr Littlepage, the workmaster.'

Joshua courteously bade him enter and, after some persuasion, the messenger reluctantly did so.

'The workmaster bids you attend him, sir. I am to say –' He broke off, repeating anxiously, 'I am to say –' His face twisted in an agony of doubt as he realised that he had forgotten what he was to impart.

'It is of no consequence,' said Joshua lightly, bidding the pauper warm himself at the fire, for the man's bare hands were blue with cold and he shivered beneath his threadbare clothing. 'You have ridden here?' asked Joshua kindly, thinking the man had stabled his mount at the Crown.

'No, sir. Walked.'

'The six miles? And in this weather?' cried Joshua, outraged. 'Then Mr Littlepage cannot be in dire need of an answer, else he would have lent you one of the horses at his disposal.'

'No, sir,' the man's voice was barely audible. 'He said it would be of too much temptation for me. I might choose to ride away upon it, make my escape in order to sell it for gain.'

'The damnable impudence of the man!' cried Joshua, unable to contain his irritation. 'He has given you orders to walk back?'

'Yes, sir. I am to return directly. If I am not there

before dusk, then I am to be locked out, to sleep wherever I can find shelter.'

'You will sit here,' commanded Joshua, 'until you are recovered, and share a meal with me.' As the man protested mildly, fearing to give offence, 'No, sir, I will brook no argument, and you may safely leave Mr Littlepage to me! I swear that he will show you no wrath, else he will feel the full power of mine!'

The pauper took a chair and together they ate a hearty meal of cornbread, bacon and potatoes, with pickles and ale, followed by cheese and oatcakes. Little was said, for the fellow was engrossed in feeding himself, his eyes rarely leaving the food or his fist his mouth, as Joshua heaped liberal helpings of everything upon his plate.

'Now, sir,' said Joshua kindly, when the pauper had eaten his fill and was trying, vainly, to quell the wind which rumbled in his overloaded stomach, 'do you now recollect the message you were to deliver to me?'

The man hesitated, shaking his head unhappily, trying in vain to recapture Littlepage's instructions. 'No, sir,' he admitted shamefacedly.

'It is of no import,' consoled Joshua. 'I shall ride over directly, and he shall never know of the omission, I promise you.'

The man nodded, and then his face miraculously lightened, grew clear, as he touched Joshua's arm, saying, 'He bids you attend him upon a matter of extreme delicacy which he cannot entrust to . . . to stupid inferiors like me, being a gentleman.' The relief of dredging the message so triumphantly from his mind, dredged up an equally triumphant belch from his belly.

'Well said, sir!' encouraged Joshua, as the pauper fought to hide his confusion. 'I am sure that your pronouncement is correct in every last detail!' Having said which, he gave him a sixpence to squander at the Crown.

Joshua set off for the poorhouse at Bridgend, not in the best of humour, for the 'workmaster', as the paupers called their administrator, was one of the least likeable men whom the constable had ever the misfortune to meet. Littlepage, under any other circumstances, might even have seemed amusing, so exaggerated were his conceit, self-delusion and pomposity. The tragedy was, as Joshua well knew, that the man's insensitivity could wreck the lives of those unfortunates in his care: crushing their spirit and sense of worth.

It was surely enough, he thought, as he rode on to the highway trailing the banks of the Ewenny river, that a man was forced to lose his home, and see his family wrenched apart, without heaping further indignities upon him. He was allowed no possessions of his own; no privacy; his work oft times menial and degrading; his food poor; his clothing inadequate; the uniform of paupery setting him apart from his fellow men as surely as the lepers of old with their warning bell and cry of 'Unclean'.

The stench from the river filled Joshua's nostrils, brackish and sour, the accumulated filth of human excreta, rotting vegetables, and the occasional dead animal.

Seeing the square, forbidding shape of the poorhouse crouched ahead, he felt unutterably depressed. Why had it been made so bleak? Was it to warn those who entered that thereafter their lives would be as hard and unlovely as the austere walls which enclosed them? It seemed to offer no escape, no hope. Once set upon the treadmill of poverty, a pauper would be forced into cheap, unremitting labour upon the land, or in a factory, or kitchen. Even children must endure the damp and clamour of the local woollen mills, or, God protect them! thought Joshua pityingly, the blackness of coal mines. He dismounted, giving his mare into the care of a tall, ill-fleshed fellow, all bony angles and wrists.

At least, thought Joshua philosophically, one pauper will sleep this night well-fed and sated with a sixpence worth of ale!

Upon knocking at the door of Littlepage's room, Joshua was at first kept waiting, then bidden 'Enter!' by a harsh clipped voice. From the workmaster's flushed skin and feverish scrabbling to close the drawer of his desk, Joshua could only suppose that he had caught him at a bottle of spirits. Littlepage wiped his fingers briefly across the pink overfull lips, then arose to offer his hand, which Joshua took with little enthusiasm.

'Pray be seated,' said Littlepage, and Joshua, viewing him anew at eye level, thought how absurdly plump and cherubic he looked, with his fat pink cheeks, aureole of thinning curls, and his mouth set into a pout. 'Well, Constable,' demanded Littlepage, elbows upon the desk, finger-pads pressed closely together. 'You received my message, then? I half expected the fellow to return with the message forgotten. A witless dolt of a man, who can scarce be trusted to remember his own name.'

'Why did you send him, then?' demanded Joshua.

Littlepage looked surprised. 'Because he could be spared, and as a test of his initiative, sir.'

'I should have thought a walk of six miles and more, in bleak weather, more a test of stamina,' declared Joshua coldly. 'Why did you not send him out upon a mount? There are many in your stables.'

Littlepage looked genuinely astonished. 'He is a pauper, sir, dependent upon the generosity of others! He has no hope of ever possessing such a thing. It would merely make him dissatisfied, give him ideas above his station.'

'There seems to be some confusion about his return,' said Joshua, fighting to keep his tone reasonable.

'How so?' asked Littlepage, sniffing. 'His instructions were clear enough, even for his limited intelligence! He was to return immediately.'

'I bade him rest and refresh himself awhile,' confessed Joshua, 'but the poor wretch was afeared that he would be locked outside should he tarry overlong! "Good heavens, man!" I exclaimed. "Mr Littlepage is incapable of such a crass, ill-bred autocracy! It is but a notion of your own, a stupid fancy." And I gave him my word that he would be admitted, sir, knowing your true disposition.'

'Of course! Of course!' said Littlepage testily. 'I told you the man was a fool! But to business, sir . . .'

'Indeed, but, before I forget, I have news of some of your former charges.'

'It does not surprise me that they have fallen foul of the law,' declared Littlepage sententiously.

'On the contrary, sir, it is my pleasure to acquaint you with their advancement. They have made quite remarkable progress.'

'Then it is due entirely to the rigid discipline and sound moral training received here, sir.'

Joshua continued persistently, 'Mistress Randall is to take charge of a school to be built in the three hamlets.'

'A mistake!' declared Littlepage sourly. 'It will only make the children ape their betters, with no hope of achieving distinction. A man should be satisfied, sir, to remain in that situation to which God has seen fit to call him.'

'Then there would be no purpose in giving us free will, or intelligence. A man would not strive to better himself. A pauper would always remain a pauper.'

'Quite so,' declared Littlepage. 'But to my business . . .'

'You recall Elwyn Morris, I believe, sir?' asked Joshua, not to be deflected.

'Of course,' said Littlepage irritably, 'a difficult, abrasive fellow, for ever meddling in the affairs of others, demanding equality, fairness . . . People are not equal, sir, and the world is not fair!'

'The man is literate,' declared Joshua, 'and an honest, conscientious worker. He is now employed at the Port, upon the horse-drawn tramway as a haulier.'

'Then I pity them, Constable! He will provoke nothing but trouble and dissatisfaction. I tell you, sir, the man is a scoundrel, an agitator. He will be banding them into some unholy union to defeat authority and preserve their so-called rights, but I have neither time nor patience for misfits! To my business with you, if you please.'

'I understand,' said Joshua, 'that it is a matter of some delicacy, which you did not wish bruited abroad . . .?'

'Quite so,' said Littlepage.

Joshua waited expectantly.

'I am being harassed, sir! My . . . undergarments are being systematically cut up into holes, shredded . . .'

Joshua burst out laughing. 'You have called me here, sir, to discuss this . . . inconsequence?'

'It is no inconsequence. There have been threats to my well-being, my life even!' He produced a scrap of paper from a folder in his desk for Joshua's perusal. It stated, in poorly formed capitals: 'YU WILL BE NEX CUT'.

'A misspelt, uneducated hand!' declared Littlepage. 'The fellow's all but illiterate! Some ruffian, no doubt, resenting my position and influence.'

'Someone who takes exception to your use of them, certainly!' agreed Joshua. 'And to you.'

'Who, sir, could take exception to me?' demanded Littlepage, genuinely outraged. 'I try to do my honest best to give these people shelter . . . however dissolute, slothful, or undeserving they are.'

'No doubt,' said Joshua drily.

'They misunderstand me, sir,' cried Littlepage, in some agitation.

Joshua thought that, to the contrary, they understood him only too well. But remained silent.

'Well, Constable, what do you advise?' Littlepage insisted. 'What precautions would you take?'

'I would lock up my undergarments and nightshirts securely,' said Joshua, straightfaced. 'Meanwhile, if you will allow me to take this note as evidence, I shall study it most carefully.'

Littlepage nodded, handing it to him. 'You think, Constable, that I should arm myself?'

'Unwise,' declared Joshua, 'it might provoke violence, if the fellow is deranged. Better, perhaps, to be mild, placatory with all the paupers in your care, showing them more leniency than is usual, improving the quality and variety of their food. At least until the villain is apprehended.'

Littlepage nodded miserably. 'Meanwhile you will pursue your enquiries?'

'With all the effort it deserves, I promise you.'

'It is a sad world, Constable, when a man can be martyred for his good intentions.'

' 'Tis aptly said that the road to hell is oft paved with them,' agreed Joshua with commendable gravity, as he took himself to the door.

The nervous pauper who had presented himself with the message at Joshua's door was seated upon a bench at the Crown Inn. He had warmed himself well at the ingle-nook fire, drunk a pot full of ale and was now intent upon choosing a veal pie that he might smuggle it into the poorhouse for his good friend, Seth, who was becoming too ancient and infirm to venture beyond its walls. There would be no more lessons, no more words laboriously lettered, then copied, for the old man's eyes were failing, and his hands grew unsteady.

There were advantages in being a scholar, the pauper thought. It was a rare and wonderful gift to be so inspired. But he did not envy the old man. When a man, like himself, was known to be a fool, unable to read or write his own name, who could suspect him?

Chapter Twelve

If the unfortunate inmates of the poorhouse were puzzled by the insufferable Littlepage's softening of attitude, they accepted it unquestioningly. They had learnt to live for the day, and did not dwell upon whether his had been a true conversion or merely some passing mental aberration . . .

Rosa and Doonan had been equally surprised by the wave of genuine warmth and affection which had borne them triumphantly home from the justice's house. The villagers continued to bring small tributes to the invalid. Even the most poor and humble among them were anxious to show their concern and speed their hero's recovery. Each day they came to make their enquiries, bearing, perhaps, a single speckled egg warm from the hen; a basin of steaming 'cawl', the thick vegetable broth fortified with precious morsels of mutton, its surface gleaming with rings of golden fat and fragrant with herbs; one or two spiced cakes; or a pitcher of oatcakes crumbled into buttermilk – the unfortunately named 'shot'!

Rosa and Doonan received them, and such bounty, gracefully, relishing their concern and self-effacing courtesy. Occasionally, Joshua might call with an offering of bacon, or newly churned salt butter from the farm; or Jeremiah, with a fine crab or sea-bass, and would be persuaded to share in the culinary feast, after the statutory, polite demurring had been overcome. The meal was consumed with pleasure, for Rosa was an inspired cook, and Doonan as hungry for news and diversion as they for victuals.

The justice had, this very morning, sent a brace of pheasants from his estate, delivered by his gamekeeper, and often a fine hare or rabbit, perhaps less honestly come by, had been left discreetly upon the doorstep of the small cottage. Even Ezra the Box had been glimpsed surreptitiously leaving a rare offering of good French cognac – an event which would normally have had Rawlings the exciseman scurrying to his workshop, as upon many other occasions. However, it was the constable himself who had been witness to such uncharacteristic generosity. There were times, Joshua decided, when humanity took precedence over duty – a moral dilemma with which, no doubt, Robert Knight, as priest and justice, had often wrestled. Although Ezra was a mean, cantankerous little fellow, as crafty and sly as a fox, he was sometimes capable of acting unexpectedly, as now, as if to confound his critics and throw them into disarray. The pity was, thought Joshua, smiling, that the minute one began to warm towards him and rue one's misjudgement, he did something so unspeakably brash and outrageous that it needed all of one's self control not to clout some sense into his insensitive skull!

Joshua, like Rosa, was worried about Doonan. His wound was healing well, yet there was a restlessness about him; an irritability. His inactivity irked him and, despite Rosa's devotion, he missed his work at the quarry face and the earthy banter and comradeship of the men. There had never been an idle bone in the big Irishman's body, and he revelled in the physical satisfaction of his labours, forcing himself to the knife-edge of effort until he was painfully aware of the demands upon his hard muscled body and every nerve and sinew ached, mingled sweat and stone dust flaying his skin. He knew, although Rosa tried to keep it from him, that, despite the gifts from their friends and Rosa's frugal ways, their small savings had dwindled alarmingly. Rosa's mother would willingly have helped, but her lodging house was small, and the few shillings earned from occasional summer visitors had to sustain her through the lean winter months. Rebecca, Joshua knew, would willingly have made them a gift or loan, to see them through the bleak aftermath of the shooting, but was sensitive enough to know that Doonan's pride would have been wounded as cruelly as his flesh by the highwayman's bullet.

Joshua, seeing the Irishman's listlessness and air of defeat, prevailed upon Dr Burrell to allow the invalid a brief visit to the Crown Inn. So, to Doonan's delight, and Rosa's relief, Jeremiah had arrived with the cob and cart to transport him to the hostelry.

Cavan, onion-layered in warm winter clothing against the chill despite his mutinous protests, was finally ensconced upon the fish cart to Rosa's satisfaction. Jeremiah was sternly adjured to see to it that the invalid supped 'no more than half a jug of the local brew', remained 'no more than half an hour', became 'embroiled in no silly argument or wager', and 'did not exert himself with some overenthusiastic tale of his clash with the highwayman'. Jeremiah accepted with good grace, if little optimism.

Rosa waved the humble equipage upon its way. The fat pony panted and strained, its breath spilling little detached clouds upon the frosty air, amidst the drifting smells of horse sweat, leather and shellfish, for although

Jeremiah had ceremoniously scrubbed the cart, the stench of them permeated its very wood. Rosa watched until it was out of sight, torn between laughter and pain to see Cavan's joyful eagerness as he sat palely upright upon a stout wooden box, legs wrapped in clean sacking, Charity's head resting proudly upon his knees. Rosa saw Jeremiah smilingly turn to say something, and her husband's broad hand reach out to touch the dog's head as it gazed up at him. She turned away, her eyes surprisingly filling with tears which she brushed away roughly with her palms, not knowing if her feeling of loss sprang from weakness, or the knowledge that Cavan's need of her grew less, and they could never again share that same closeness.

Berating herself for a stupid, selfish girl, she turned briskly to her household tasks, first starting upon the laundering of those clothes shamefully neglected in her need to always be ready to comfort or amuse the invalid. Her moodiness dissipated as she beat the clothing with the wooden dolly-stick in the trough in the yard with quite ferocious enthusiasm, before hanging the lye-bleached garments upon the line, where they tossed and billowed in the wind, full-bellied as ships under sail. So absorbed was she that she heard neither the click of the latch, nor the creaking of the wicket gate into the yard. Yet, she was uneasily aware of some presence behind her, of being furtively watched. She would have swung around, but a man's voice commanded warningly, 'No! Do not turn, mistress! Stay! I would not have you see my face.'

Rosa knew, with a chill of certainty, that it was the highwayman who spoke. His voice was quiet, unemotional, even, and more menacing for being so. Rosa felt herself trembling so violently that it was with a real effort of will that she was able to form the words, 'What do you want of me?' Her voice was barely audible, for her throat was constricted with fear and her tongue seemed swollen, cleaving drily to the roof of her mouth.

'Why, mistress,' his tone grew mocking, amused, 'I come for you . . . to take you, as I promised.'

She heard the scraping of his boot soles on the cobbled yard and stood frozen with fear, waiting for the grip of his fingers upon the flesh of her shoulders. He had paused for a moment, and now his voice filled with a strange excitement. 'I am near enough to touch you. I have but to stretch out a hand . . .'

She closed her eyes, fancying she felt the foetid warmth of his breath upon her cold cheek, seeing again those remorseless eyes behind the mask, as she cradled Cavan's bloodied flesh.

'You will never be free of me.'

Rosa could hear a piteous, ugly sound, as of some animal trapped in pain, but was unaware that it came from her own throat. Sickness burned in her mouth as his fingers fastened upon her neck. With a scream she wrenched herself from his grasp, stumbling, half-crazed, over the cobbled yard as she fled to the haven of the cottage, nails raking the door's surface as she clawed blindly at the latch, desperate for escape . . . Her fingers, awkward and clumsy in her terror, seemed numbed as her mind, yet she forced herself within, half fainting as she slammed the back door, and scraped the bolt home. Then, face pressed hard against its surface, she slid down its length to the floor where she crouched, weeping helplessly. There she stayed, arms clasped protectively about her head, as if to ward off the menace of his blows . . . not knowing if it were the wind which moaned, or herself, or the mocking echo of his laughter.

* * *

It was thus that Jeremiah and Doonan found her upon their return. Charity ran to her at once, covering her face with anxious licks, before Doonan, regardless of his wound, swept her into his arms, carrying her to a couch where she clung to him piteously, weeping and trembling, too distraught to make explanation.

When Ezra's brandy had warmed and steadied her, she haltingly told them, to a roar of rage from Doonan so fierce that it seemed the rafters must crack. Charity ran wildly 'neath the shelter of the table, cowering, eyes closed, to make himself invisible.

Jeremiah, bidding Doonan care for Rosa, rushed outside to the cob and cart, forgetting to summon the dog in his haste, but Charity ran stoically behind him barking, claws slithering upon the cobbles in a fury to keep up with him. It was only when Jeremiah and the cart halted outside the constable's house that the cur was able to leap aboard and lie, panting but triumphant, head lolling, mouth agape to gulp at the air, rib cage shuddering like Ben Clatworthy's old bellows.

Jeremiah, after stammering out his news to Joshua, urged the cob towards the Warren and Pickett's Lease, the cart bumping and rattling along the rough track alarmingly, with the exhausted Charity floundering upon its boards, yet bouncing involuntarily with every rut.

Joshua ran urgently to the Crown to apprise Tom Butler and his men, and to raise a search party. Within minutes, Ossie, white-faced and grimly efficient, had saddled Joshua's grey, and the constable had taken the track past the Ancient Briton, the landlord rallying more men as the constable paused to make brief explanation of Rosa's plight. Within the time it took to saddle a mare, it seemed that every way that led from the village was being scoured by searchers, old and young, remorselessly intent upon their task. They rode for the most part in silence, unwilling to waste words or time. The viciousness and audacity of the man in returning to terrorise his victim chilled them beyond reason. It was abnormal, corrupt . . . With such a creature at large, no woman was safe, no home inviolate. He must be caught, like a rat in a trap, and, like a rat, disposed of before he spread his filth and violence, contaminating all he touched.

But the highwayman was not trapped, nor even sighted. Possessed, perhaps, of a rodent's cunning and self-preservation, he had concealed himself, or hurried away as stealthily as he had come, and Joshua and the searchers returned, baffled and disconsolate, to admit their defeat.

Joshua wondered afterwards if the highwayman had been watching, waiting to find Rosa alone, or if he had discounted Doonan's presence, knowing the severity of his wound. Or had he been perhaps armed and ready to shoot the Irishman should need arise?

In any event, it showed a streak of sadism and recklessness which appalled him. Joshua, disregarding the justice's explicit instructions, armed Doonan with a reliable pistol, begging him to keep it by his bedside at night, and somewhere safely accessible by day. He felt sure that Rosa's tormentor would return. Crazed as he was, who could tell if it was her peace of mind he wished to destroy, or Rosa herself, and Doonan with her? Should Doonan kill the creature, it would, at worst, be a killing in self-defence, or to protect Rosa from violation. None would hold him culpable for such an action, save, perhaps, the justice, Robert Knight. As for Joshua's own part, it would merit instant dismissal and, very likely, a charge of being an accessory to follow. As it was, he would incur Robert Knight's wrath for 'allowing the highwayman to escape capture'. Well, the future must take care of itself! All that mattered now was Rosa's protection and safety, and be damned to the consequences! He wished he could feel more confident about both!

Doonan's friend Emrys, oddly wraith-like under his drifting of white stone dust, his pony and cart similarly powdered and veiled, was on his way from the quarries at Stormy Downs unaware of the drama in the village below. Emrys was lustily singing some bawdy ditty, the lewdness of whose words would undoubtedly send a gentlewoman swooning at her pianoforte had she but comprehended them. A circumstance which worried Emrys not at all, having acquaintance with neither pianoforte nor gentlewoman - nor, indeed, the polite arts, as he would cheerfully have admitted. Still, it was a fine day, dry, if nipped with frost, and he was set upon a pleasant errand. He was smiling broadly as he tethered the cob and cart at Doonan's gate and rapped upon the door, only to be greeted by the enraged Irishman, face like a thundercloud, eyes engorged and starting out of his face beneath his shock of red hair.

'I will not stop,' Emrys began, 'I bring a message . . .' His voice trailed off helplessly as Doonan wrenched him inside, explaining the circumstances, crashing his fist into his great palm as he did so.

Rosa, who was now feeling secure in Doonan's company and protection, had recovered some of her composure and begged Emrys to take some ale with Cavan, or perhaps a dish of tea, for after her ordeal, even so wild an extravagance seemed justified. Emrys would have declined but, warned by Doonan's nod, accepted with gratitude as Rosa, glad to be occupied, hurried into the small scullery.

'Well!' said Emrys grimly. 'It has come to a rare pass when a bride can be molested and threatened in her own home. I cannot believe that the wretch is of sound mind to behave in such a fashion. I swear that should he show his face at the quarries, he would not live long enough to regret it!'

Doonan nodded, admitting, 'I have been urging Dr Burrell to let me return, Emrys. Yet now I fancy I should have no peace of mind were Rosa alone. Even should she have the company of Emily, Hannah, or her mother, what would it serve? Save, perhaps, to set them in equal danger? He would not hesitate to assault, or even kill, as I know to my cost.'

Rosa came back bearing a tray with ale and cakes, and busied herself at the fire, unhooking the steaming kettle. Doonan gave Emrys a glance of warning.

'I had all but forgot my message,' declared Emrys. He pulled a leather pouch from his jacket and emptied a small mound of coins upon the table.

'Emrys? What does it mean?' demanded Rosa. 'I am at a loss . . .'

'Every man at the quarries has given you, freely and with respect, half a day's pay,' explained Emrys gruffly. 'It amounts to what Cavan would earn in a full week at the quarry face. They asked me to tell you that you need have no reservations, or fear for the future. You will receive it each week until you return –' He broke off uneasily, unable to read the expression upon the bellicose Irishman's face. 'They did not know of Rosa's ordeal, I swear,' blurted Emrys. 'It is done kindly and with no thought of charity, I beg you to believe.'

Doonan stared at him wordlessly, and shook his head. Tears welled into his eyes and spilled helplessly, and he cradled his huge head in his arms, and wept, as Rosa stretched out a gentle hand to touch his unruly red hair.

Joshua, riding the grey across the sandy wastes of Pickett's Lease to meet Peter Rawlings at the Ship Aground, was thinking wryly that the name of their meeting place was oddly prophetic. Yes, that described his own position perfectly. He was indeed the Ship Aground. In his search for the highwayman, he had somehow drifted dangerously off course, at the mercy of currents and undercurrents which he could neither chart nor control; bedevilled by hidden reefs and sudden storms – the most violent and recent erupting from Robert Knight. He had been left in no doubt of his superior's displeasure, as the justice surveyed the constable critically through his gold-rimmed lenses, brown eyes cold.

'Am I to understand, Stradling, that you actually had the creature within your grasp and allowed him to escape?' He had banged his fist so hard upon the desk that quill, ink, and even his own dark jowls had shuddered perceptibly, and Joshua had studied his boots uncomfortably, mumbling, 'I fear, sir, that he outwitted us again . . .'

'Us? Us, you say?' demanded the justice irascibly. 'There is no "us" about it, sir! I was not involved! You must take sole responsibility for this disaster, this fiasco!'

Joshua nodded miserably.

'As for outwitting you, sir, I am not surprised, since you appear to be totally devoid both of wits and actions!'

'I acted immediately, sir, raising a search party . . .'

'With what result?'

'None.'

'None! There you have it, Stradling! The sum total of

your achievements in this affair! It does you no credit. No credit at all!' His thick brows drew together ominously. 'You are a bungling incompetent, sir. I declare, Stradling, I am disappointed in you – greatly disappointed!'

'As I am, sir.'

'You are?' Robert Knight blustered, puzzlement diverting wrath. 'What right have you to be disappointed?' he asked sharply. 'Instead of such useless self-indulgence, you should be taking action. That is what you are paid for, to protect the people of the three hamlets, not to wallow in useless introspection. You are altogether too inclined, sir, to sit about contemplating your own navel!'

Joshua felt a smile tug at the corners of his mouth, and tried helplessly to suppress it.

'I see no occasion for childish levity, sir,' the justice rebuked coldly. 'Such puerile behaviour ill becomes a constable.' Then, belatedly realising his error, and that he was losing control of the situation, he offered magnanimously, ' I concede, Stradling, that present events might give you scant inclination for such bizarre activity.'

'No, sir,' agreed Joshua, sober-faced, 'nor is it the right climate.'

Robert Knight smiled in brief acknowledgement, before admonishing, 'I am not unmindful of your attempts at humour, Stradling, nor of its value as a tool to distract me. However, it would be a pity if levity disguised the gravity of the situation. I am sure that Mistress Doonan did not find the episode in the least amusing! You have arranged some sort of protection for her?'

'There are those in the hamlets who are prepared to keep guard on her by night and day. There is no paucity of volunteers. Indeed, there is not a man or youth who would not imperil his own life to defend her.'

'As I would expect,' approved the justice. 'No doubt they see in the fellow's madness a threat to their own womenfolk. I believe Burrell was right when he said that the most chilling aspect is that the creature relishes the risk, the excitement, even, of bloodshed. It satisfies some evil, perverted urge within him.' He shook his head sadly. 'I fear that his encounters with Rebecca and Rosa bode ill. He must be caught, Stradling, and soon!'

'There is no word, sir, from the prisoners at Pyle? No confession as to who was behind the attack upon you, and the church? They were, after all, in possession of the chestnut mare.'

'I need no reminding, Constable, that you so mishandled the affair that the evidence is missing.' Joshua coloured guiltily as the justice resumed. 'They appear before me at the court-house at noon today to plead their case, such as it is. It is to be hoped that they will be persuaded to confess all.'

They could hardly deny the assault upon him, Joshua thought drily, since his eye was as blotched with colour as a skewbald's backside!

'I foresee no difficulties,' the justice was saying, as if in response. 'It is an open and shut case! Anyone with even half an eye could see it.'

'It is to be hoped that they will at least see the error of their ways! That they will get their just deserts . . .'

The justice looked at him keenly, 'I have no doubt of it. None at all. It is a hope we might all reflect upon with profit, Stradling.'

'Yes, sir,' agreed Joshua innocently, 'especially the highwayman.'

'I cannot decide, sir, whether you are deliberately obtuse or genuinely fail to garner the gist of my remarks,' Knight said irritably. 'You have developed evasiveness into a fine art! You had best be about your work.'

'Thank you, sir!' exclaimed Joshua, gratefully taking his leave.

And Robert Knight was left wondering what exactly it was that the young constable had thanked him for.

Joshua's meeting with Rawlings at the Ship Aground was barely more consoling, save for the local brew which they consumed with relish, while thawing their bones beside the roaring fire in the ingle-nook.

'So!' exclaimed the exciseman, draining his tankard of ale and signalling to the landlord to bring another. 'Robert Knight flayed you within an inch of your life. Surely you are no stranger to the whiplash of his tongue? I swear he has castigated me so often, Joshua, that I have the hide of an elephant.'

'And an appetite to match!' rejoined Joshua, watching incredulously as his companion downed more ale and a platter of bread, rough cheese and pickled eggs. 'I declare, sir, I don't know where you put it all!'

'Hollow legs!' Rawlings was unoffended. 'Did you not know that is where I store the contraband I seize?'

'Then I had best search the breeches and boots of all upon the docks,' observed Joshua gloomily, 'for I confess I have nothing else to suggest! The thieves must swallow their haul, like you. I tell you, in all honesty, Peter, that between that damned highwayman, the justice's wrath, and my own incompetence, I am all but ground into the dust.'

'And, like the dust, will rise again,' jested Rawlings, laughing at his friend's woebegone expression. 'I fancy, Joshua, it is an affair of the heart which makes you speak so. I cannot believe that the justice's choler could affect you thus: it is a hazard of our occupations. As natural and inevitable as a gale, and as quickly spent. As for the highwayman, he is that and nothing more. A man. He has no supernatural powers . . .'

'Save to render himself invisible,' said Joshua with the barest hint of a smile.

'Then we had best do the same,' advised Rawlings, 'and materialise at the court-house to witness the justice's performance. It will be a fine melodrama, I warrant! There need be no wagering upon who will play the hero . . .'

'Or that the villains will be routed,' agreed Joshua, tossing some coins upon the tray and inclining his head towards the landlord who thanked them for their custom, and bade them a civil good-day.

'I sometimes think,' mused Rawlings, as they walked towards the stables of the tavern to retrieve their mounts, 'that the justice has missed his true vocation. He should have been a strolling player. He has the flair for it, the theatricality, the presence . . . The pulpit and court-room are too small a setting, altogether too confined. He demands a wider stage.'

'To accommodate his ego,' suggested Joshua tartly.

'Come, Joshua,' chaffed Rawlings in amusement, 'jaundiced as you are, you must admit he has a way with words.'

'Exactly! He has no need to borrow other men's words. I can testify, he has more than enough of his own!'

When they had taken their seats in the small court-house at Pyle, and the full panoply of the law was set impressively in action, the performance began. There was no doubting the justice's role as leading thespian, for he managed always to dominate the centre stage, relegating all others, even the defendants, to minor subservient parts . . .

Joshua was called upon to provide evidence, as, it

seemed, was almost the entire male population of Newton village, including Ossie and Tom Butler. Although clad in their best clothes, and scrubbed within an inch of their lives, they seemed more awkward and ill at ease than the prisoners. Certainly, with their scowling faces, grubby and unshaven, and their clothing all too obviously slept in, there was no doubting who were the villains of the piece.

There appeared to be but one item of new evidence, yet it had Joshua gripping the edges of his bench and leaning forward to hear the better. It seemed that, despite the searches of the prisoners at the Crown Inn and in the cells at Pyle, the gaoler had, upon the information of another, discovered that one of the accused had secreted something behind a loose stone in the wall of his cell, although both men had strenuously denied all knowledge of it. The exhibit, produced and duly noted, was a pocket watch which Dr Burrell identified as being his own, opening it to read aloud the inscription: 'To John Burrell, From patients and friends'.

As to how they acquired it, where, and from whom, the prisoners remained stubbornly and defiantly mute. When asked how they pleaded to each of the charges, the accused declared, 'Not Guilty', entering a plea of mistaken identity.

'Mistaken identity?' Robert Knight had thundered, outraged.

Rawlings had nudged Joshua with the toe of his boot, keeping his face carefully expressionless, as the justice's face grew ever more crimson. A vein throbbed at his temple, a blue thread under the skin. His thick neck and chest swelled and grew thicker with rage as he repeated, incredulously, '*Mistaken identity*, you say?'

A hush had fallen upon the court-house, and even the

defendants, hitherto truculent and hostile, had paled, looking uncertain.

The justice's expression and whole demeanour changed, adding to their confusion, as he demanded with icy contempt, 'Am I to understand that you are witless, sirs, as well as liars and degenerates?

The prisoners shifted uncomfortably. Robert Knight paused, looking around the courtroom in mute appeal, before dropping his voice to admit, with feeling, 'I can scarce believe my ears!'

All eyes were turned accusingly upon the two men as he addressed them, seemingly in sorrow rather than anger. 'It was I whom you so brutally set upon while innocently at prayer. *My* church you desecrated with your blasphemy and thieving ways.' He shook his head, then, voice rising dramatically, he declared, with ringing conviction, 'No! It is not my church, but God's, and yours. It belongs to every man here today, even the basest and most degraded. Yes, even these pitiful wretches who sought only to violate and despoil, for none who confesses is beyond redemption.'

One of the prisoners, visibly affected, was snivelling, eyes downcast, but the other stared back with insolent malice. It was of him that the justice demanded, contemptuously, 'Mistaken identity, you say? When my body still bears the wounds of your savagery.'

Joshua tried desperately not to look at the justice's bruised eye, or at Rawlings.

'Do you think I am blind?' the justice was asking angrily. 'Deranged? An incompetent fool?'

Wisely the prisoners remained mute.

'Mistaken identity! When you were actually seized in the act. When you manhandled, and were identified by me, your victim, the constable, and every able-bodied man of Newton village?' He stopped speaking to gaze implacably at the bolder of the accused men, who stared insolently back at him, aggressive and seemingly unaffected, although it was he who first dropped his gaze.

'I find the accused guilty as charged,' declared Robert Knight. 'Accordingly, they will be taken to a house of correction, there to serve a month upon the treadmill, during which time they may reflect upon their violence and rapacity, and endeavour to purge their wickedness by confessing how they came into possession of the chestnut mare used by the highwayman, and the watch which he misappropriated under threats of violence. Thereafter, they will be transported to Botany Bay penal colony, there to remain for the period of their natural lives . . .'

There was a gasp in court at the severity of the sentence. One of the prisoners collapsed weeping and had to be assisted, but the more aggressive spat in the justice's direction, defiantly mouthing an obscene oath.

'In addition,' said the justice quietly, rising to his feet, 'you will be publicly whipped to deter others from foul blasphemy. Remove the prisoners,' he commanded the gaolers.

'I'll see you rot in hell,' screamed the offender as they secured him, struggling, with his chastened accomplice.

'Unlikely,' said Robert Knight, with no change of expression. 'I am as confident of God's good judgement as my own. You can but hope, sir, that the Devil takes care of his own.'

'Well?' demanded Rawlings, as they reclaimed their horses. 'Did I not tell you it would be a rare melodrama? What do you think of our thespian's performance?'

'Worthy of the bard himself,' declared Joshua,

smiling. 'A model of controlled emotion, contempt, and vitriol, exquisitively expressed, almost as impressive as the rehearsal with me.'

'I dare you to congratulate him,' said Rawlings, as he swung himself into the saddle and, laughing, urged his mare away.

Chapter Thirteen

During Rebecca's brief sojourn as guest of Robert Knight at Tythegston, and her affectionate reunion with Rosa and the wounded Doonan and, by singular good fortune, Joshua, life at Southerndown Court had progressed with its usual ordered serenity.

Sir Matthew's time was much taken up with the affairs of his estate and tenantry and his responsibilities as justice. That he missed Rebecca's affectionate nonsense was undeniable, but it was a loss agreeably softened by the astringent conversation of his friend, Dr Peate, and the gentler presence of Elizabeth and the redoubtable Mrs Crandle.

Rebecca, had she but known it, was not alone in her distrust of Humphrey Edmonds. During her enforced absence, Dr Peate and Elizabeth had made the drawing master's acquaintance. Dr Peate, despite a disposition to be charitable, as befitted a clergyman, was irritated beyond measure by young Edmonds, whom he found crass and self-opinionated. Sir Matthew, in passing the open door of the schoolroom, was an inadvertent eavesdropper upon one of their exchanges.

'You are fortunate, indeed, Dr Peate,' Edmonds was observing patronisingly, 'that Sir Matthew seems to regard you, a mere country vicar, as almost an equal.'

Dr Peate, face unnaturally flushed beneath the fall of

white hair, raised himself from his habitual stoop, to reply coldly, 'It is an impertinence, sir, and a calumny to suppose that Sir Matthew judges a man by anything other than his true worth. I am privileged to count him an old and valued friend. His estimate of your worth will be equally valid, of that I have no doubt.'

'Indeed,' drawled Edmonds languidly, 'you may be assured, sir, that I have no reservations upon that score. I am a gentleman and, as such, know my position.'

Sir Matthew could have sworn that he heard Dr Peate mutter, 'Hmmm, horizontal!' But thought he must have been mistaken.

'Come, Dr Peate,' insisted Edmonds brashly, 'have you no comment? No aphorism to edify me? You are invariably a fount of such uplifting quotations and platitudes!'

'No,' returned Dr Peate innocently, 'save that it is better to keep your mouth shut, sir, and let people think that you are a fool, rather than open your mouth and prove it.'

Sir Matthew moved away swiftly lest a chuckle betray him, reflecting that an experienced old dog could always be trusted to teach an insolent young pup his manners.

Later that morning, as the two old friends refreshed themselves with Madeira in the library, Sir Matthew ventured mildly, 'And what is your opinion of the new drawing master, Dr Peate? I trust you have an opinion.'

Dr Peate coloured before replying stiffly, 'That he is a conceited, arrogant, addle-pated little coxcomb!'

'Really?' said Sir Matthew, amused. 'How strange! On the contrary, I find him to be obsequious, self-effacing, servile, even.'

'Then it seems that he is all things to all men!' said Dr Peate drily. 'A very chameleon of a creature, imitating the colour of his surroundings. I find that a morbid trait, for it argues that he has a need to hide his true nature.'

'I have rarely heard you speak so impassionedly, my friend, and with such venom,' smiled Sir Matthew. 'It ill behoves a man of the cloth.'

'I hope, sir, that I castigate Lucifer with equal vehemence, else I would not justify my living.'

'Well said, sir,' applauded Sir Matthew. 'I can only give thanks that I am not a fallen angel, for I confess that I would sadly miss both my Madeira and your company.'

'I note,' said Dr Peate laughingly, 'the order of precedence.'

Elizabeth, too, had found the young tutor's company uncongenial, and his manner strange. When first alone with him, for he had come across her unexpectedly at her studies in the schoolroom, he had taken her portfolio of water-colours and charcoal sketches, studying them in silence for a while, before declaring in his cold expressionless voice, 'Very pretty, ma'am, and just what I would have expected. I declare that they are sensitively chosen, and executed with care.'

Damning with faint praise, thought Elizabeth, amused rather than resentful, as she continued to regard him with her customary attentive gravity, saying, 'I have no pretensions to talent, sir. I record only what I see, simply and for my own pleasure. If that is what you expected, then I have not disappointed you. Since to draw and paint is the necessary accomplishment of a gentlewoman, I require only that you refine my technique, not perform miracles.'

Edmonds had flushed, protesting stiffly, 'I did not say you were *without* talent, Miss Crandle, or that your drawings lacked merit. I find in some of them a misty, subtle quality, such as one sees in Japanese water-colours, the wash blurred and shadowed, with an almost dream-like quality, as if you have deliberately softened a landscape too harsh to accept.'

Elizabeth made no response.

'I know of your past, Miss Crandle.' He moved closer to her, importunately laying a hand upon her arm. Elizabeth drew away determinedly, slamming her portfolio shut, and tying it with deliberation to end the matter.

Edmonds, not to be diverted, persisted rudely, 'It is no reflection upon you, ma'am, that your father's weakness of character led him to gaol, or that your dead brother was a confessed murderer. I mean, their disgrace casts no discredit upon you. I am charitable enough to think no less of you for it.'

'I was not aware, sir, that you were qualified, or invited, to pass judgement upon me, or my family. Nor would I give it more credence than your crude interpretation of my sketching. I will not call it art, for that would lend it a distinction which it does not deserve. Now, if you will excuse me.'

Edmonds, sensible of his mistake, coloured, blurting grudgingly, 'If I put it clumsily, Miss Crandle, I beg you will dismiss it from your mind.'

Elizabeth paused, undecided, as he lifted Rebecca's portfolio from its wooden stand and unfastened its tapes, pretending absorption in the task. Yet, as he leafed through its contents, his expression became intent, excited, and he declared with real enthusiasm, 'Why, Rebecca is a natural artist, gifted and unusual. There is a boldness about her work, an originality and self-confidence, an arrogance almost. The pictures reflect her character well, would you not say so?'

'It is not for me, sir, or for you, to discuss or to comment upon Miss de Breos,' she reproved coldly. 'As for your assessment of her work, then it would be more fitting if you discussed it with her.' Elizabeth's voice was calm, and she retained her outward composure although inwardly seething at Edmonds' presumption and insensitivity.

'But you are in Rebecca's confidence,' he declared, unabashed, still studying the portfolio. 'You must know more of her true self than anyone, her feelings, her aspirations. From what I have gleaned, it seems she does not regard you as a servant. You are privileged indeed that she has chosen to allow you to live here, despite your unfortunate background. Few others would be so generous to their inferiors.'

Elizabeth's calm was replaced by an icy fury as she declared contemptuously, 'Inferiority is not dependent upon birth or breeding, sir. Nor is it governed by the misfortunes of others, or their inadequacies. It is a personal deficiency, as you must well know, sir. I beg you, step aside, that I may pass!'

Edmonds, humiliated but wishing to gain Elizabeth as an ally, mumbled his apology, regretting that he had so much forgotten himself as to offend her.

Elizabeth nodded dismissively, saying, 'If you will kindly step aside, sir. I must attend Dr Peate, my tutor, who will be awaiting me. I would not insult him with unpunctuality. As a gentleman, he observes the rules of proper behaviour and would never, knowingly or unknowingly, cause offence. Besides, I would be loath to sacrifice one moment of his company.'

'Hoity-toity, ma'am!' muttered Edmonds savagely beneath his breath as she left. 'Then go, and be damned to you! When the time comes, we shall see how far your pretty speeches take you . . . and who has the upper hand.' He slammed the portfolio shut and replaced it upon the stand.

If Dr Peate noticed Elizabeth's flushed cheeks, or the telltale trembling of her hands, he said nothing, greeting her pleasantly, then turning at once to their lesson, but later, Sir Matthew called her to him, saying, 'Elizabeth, my dear, a word about your painting lessons. In Rebecca's absence, I think it would be in order for your mother to be present, to act as chaperone. I have put this proposal to her and she agrees entirely. Mr Edmonds, unlike Dr Peate and your pianoforte tutor, is a young, unattached gentleman, and to be left alone together would invite comment and misunderstanding. You understand?'

'Perfectly, sir.'

Elizabeth's curtsey and bowed head could not entirely mask her smile of relief at such unexpected good fortune. Sir Matthew, who knew more of what transpired in his household than people suspected, was not slow to note it.

Rebecca, having greeted her grandfather upon her return, washed away the grime of travel and changed into a pretty day dress of pale silk, its surface subtly veined through with delicate colour as the petals of a rose, and pinning Jeremiah's brooch at its neck, ran downstairs to relate her adventures to Elizabeth. Elizabeth had missed her sorely, and there was a happy warmth and excitement in their reunion, with many impulsive hugs and kisses, and much feminine chatter. The names of Joshua and Devereaux were, not unexpectedly, prominent, for the two girls traded confidences freely, each secure in the discretion of the other. There was no constraint between them, despite the circumstances of their changed fortunes: Elizabeth's downfall from riches to penury, and Rebecca's elevation from poverty to the rank and privilege of a gentlewoman. Perhaps their shared knowledge of deprivation and betrayal by those whose protection they needed most, brought them closer in spirit. Certainly, neither envied nor resented the other, simply appreciating their present good fortune.

Sir Matthew, in his growing affection for the two girls, rejoiced at each new facet of their distinct and unfolding characters. So fresh and unspoilt were they in their burgeoning prettiness that he sometimes thought of them as gently opening blossoms. Rebecca was the more immediately arresting: vivid, colourful, with an unusual exotic beauty which drew the eye. Elizabeth's was the quieter, less flamboyant loveliness, gentle and appealing. She reminded him more of the little wild pansies which grew at wayside or ploughed field. The heart's-ease, seemingly modest and unprepossessing, yet with an unexpected loveliness which becomes apparent when you gaze into its heart. He suspected, and hoped, that young Roland Devereaux found it so, too, and might one day provide Elizabeth with the love and security that had been denied her since her father's disgrace.

As Rebecca related the adventures which had befallen her, Elizabeth exclaimed with the most gratifying horror at mention of the highwayman's callousness, and afterwards demanded news of Doonan and Rosa, Illtyd, Jeremiah and Emily, and all the good folk of the three hamlets. At Rebecca's mention of the Reverend Robert Knight's nephew and his companions, and their loutish behaviour, and her aversion to Humphrey Edmonds, Elizabeth, striving to be fair, had asked simply, 'Are you sure that your dislike of their brashness and drunken ways has not prejudiced you unfairly against him?'

'You actually like the creature, Elizabeth?' Rebecca demanded incredulously.

Elizabeth considered. 'I think that he is . . . adequate at his work,' she said carefully. 'I neither like nor dislike him, for he reveals nothing of his real self. Indeed, he appears to be so absurdly featureless that he scarcely makes any impression at all.' She smiled. 'I admit, Rebecca, that he treats me with such detachment, and his presence is so unobtrusive, that I half expect to turn and find that he has vanished altogether.'

'I wish it were so!' declared Rebecca. 'For I know my suspicions are foolish and ill-founded, yet I cannot dismiss them.'

Elizabeth nodded. She would not fuel the fires of Rebecca's dislike by confiding that she, too, disliked him, but without real cause. Elizabeth had early learnt, through her father's disgrace and her brother's violence, the folly of believing that people were all that they seemed upon the surface.

'I think, Rebecca,' she said after some consideration, 'that the wisest course would be to keep any doubts unspoken, for one cannot damn a man and seek to disgrace or ruin him on the strength of his manners, or lack of them, or because of the boorishness of his friends.'

'Yes, that is true,' admitted Rebecca doubtfully.

'Besides,' added Elizabeth smiling, 'it would undoubtedly be construed as a whim and mere female capriciousness. No, it is better that we treat him with reserve rather than contempt, for I fancy he is a young man who would prefer to provoke any emotion, even scorn, rather than be ignored.'

'But we must at least be sure that neither of us is ever

alone in his presence,' insisted Rebecca, 'for he is conceited enough, and stupid enough, to misinterpret reserve as modesty, or yearning even! I would not encourage him in his insufferable arrogance!'

Elizabeth laughed with her, satisfied that Rebecca now regarded their drawing master with amusement rather than fear. Rebecca knew that she must pursue the subject of Edmonds no longer. Elizabeth was right. It would be churlish and ungrateful, she felt, to spurn her grandfather's goodwill in employing Edmonds to instruct them. His family, the Nicholls, were known to both Sir Matthew and Robert Knight and, should the tutor be summarily dismissed, the relationship between the three families might be sorely strained and she would be guiltily aware of it, and that she alone was the cause. She could not confess, even to Elizabeth, that the thought of the highwayman abroad filled her with less terror than the reality of Edmonds within her own home.

Sir Matthew, with his usual thoroughness, had anticipated Rebecca's disquiet and his friend Dr Peate's misgivings by deciding that he would check more carefully upon Humphrey Edmonds, his background and antecedents. He had no personal mistrust of, or antipathy for, the young man, although he found him irritatingly unctuous and self-effacing. The tutor's testimonials appeared impeccable, and his referees, the Nicholls, above reproach; indeed, Mr Nicholl was a fellow magistrate and held in the highest esteem within the community. Nevertheless, he would summon the coach to convey him to Merthyr Mawr House, under the pretext of seeking information of a judicial nature, and take the opportunity to make discreet enquiries of Nicholl concerning his young kinsman. In this resolve he was forestalled by a letter from his friend, the Reverend Robert Knight, who confided that he had, with the aid of the gunsmiths concerned, and their records, traced the highwayman's pistol to its commissioning by the de Clare family, and thence, by copious letter writing, and not a little effort, traced its known provenance to the present owners, the Nicholls of Merthyr Mawr. It appeared that Mrs Nicholl was a descendant of the original owners upon the distaff side, and the pistols (for they were indeed a pair) were hers by virtue of inheritance.

Upon learning of this, Robert Knight had, he confessed, ridden out at once to Merthyr Mawr to make enquiries of the lady concerned, with whom he was well acquainted since her marriage, for he and her husband had been friends since childhood. 'Alas,' wrote Robert Knight, 'my enquiries came to naught. The entire family is absent upon that fashionable excursion, "The Grand Tour", and not expected back for ten days or more, only the servants remaining. I did not think it proper to make enquiries of the household staff in their absence.' The letter continued: 'This leaves the vexed question of how the highwayman came into possession of the pistol unanswered. Was it stolen, sold, or otherwise disposed of by Mrs Nicholl? Until she returns, the matter must lie in abeyance, and our one real clue to the highwayman's identity valueless.'

Sir Matthew returned disconsolately to a study of the letter which he had received from Joshua by the same mail-coach. The knowledge of Rebecca's clash with the highwayman had disturbed him deeply. He was more than ever convinced that the man's action in holding up the de Breos' coach was not accidental. He had addressed Rebecca by name and, were it not for the loyalty and presence of mind of Hughes and the bailiff, the consequences might have proved disastrous. No, it was more likely that the wretch had in mind the de Breos' jewels, and would have taken her hostage. The man, by his shooting of Doonan, had proved to be vicious and cold-blooded, and his persecution of Rosa displayed a cruelty and delight in inflicting pain which spoke of insanity. If Rebecca should fall into his hands . . . Sir Matthew dare not contemplate the consequences, for the child was dearer to him now than his own life. He had made elaborate and strict plans to ensure her safety, both at Southerndown Court and when venturing abroad in any of the carriages. He knew that the restrictions he placed upon her would be irksome and that she would chafe at them but obey dutifully. She had proved her courage often in the past, but he prayed that it would not again be put to the test.

In the light of the threat posed to her by the highwayman, his concern about Edmond's qualifications and suitability as a drawing master seemed absurdly trivial and unimportant. He was, Sir Matthew chided himself, in danger of losing his sense of proportion in his fierceness to protect her. Certainly young Edmonds was not the most prepossessing of his species. His sole sin, if it could be called such, was that in so desperately trying to ingratiate himself he, instead, alienated all those he sought to cultivate. If he nursed some secret, then it was probably that he could lay no legitimate claim to being a gentleman. God knows! there were enough by-blows of royalty among the aristocracy; indeed, that was how many lines began. Still, it would do no harm to have surreptitious enquiries made at the village in which he lodged and discover his habits, companions and pursuits. They were doubtless as innocuous and as colourless as he. Certainly he had carried out his duties as drawing tutor to Elizabeth quite admirably during Rebecca's absence. He smiled involuntarily. Who, indeed, could dare to do otherwise when chaperoned by the august and fastidiously correct Mrs Louisa Crandle?

It was doubtful if even the highwayman would have flouted Mrs Crandle's rigid protocol by so rudely addressing Rebecca, and terrorising poor little Rosa Doonan. He would most certainly have been rebuked sternly, and commanded to 'Mind your manners, sir!'. No, Edmonds was flesh and blood, and known, whatever his weaknesses and deficiencies. The danger to Rebecca, Elizabeth and others lay in the highwayman's anonymity. It paid to know one's enemies.

In the small cottage overlooking the village green, Joshua had eased off his knee boots and was sprawled inelegantly in a wheel-backed chair, wool-stockinged feet thrust towards the blazing fire of driftwood. He had abandoned his coat and his neckerchief and, agreeably sated with victuals and ale, was reading a letter from Rebecca. As the soles of his feet luxuriated in the heat of the flames, his toes curled and uncurled with sheer physical pleasure; a pleasure enhanced by Rebecca's most brazen and indecorous avowal of her need for him. The words, evocative and vivid, served an answering need in him and he longed to have Rebecca here with him, all warm flesh and vitality. At some of the more outrageously bizarre descriptions of life at Southerndown, entwined with wickedly accurate sketches, his mouth curled in amusement and he found himself laughing aloud. No, he thought, try as she might, Mrs Crandle would never mould Rebecca into a pallid wax doll of a lady, colourless, smooth featured, a tired replica of all others of her kind. Rebecca was an original. Others might be deceived by the cultivated aloofness of her manners and appearance, but not he who knew the wild Rebecca of old. That rebel, filled with passion and pity.

A hurried knocking upon the door broke his pleasurable mood. Swiftly, he pulled on his boots and jacket, fastening his shirt and neckerchief as he went, still flushed from the heat of the fire and ale.

Upon the doorstep, 'neath the light of the door lantern, was reflected the pinched, sallow face of Walter Bevan, the relieving officer to the poor. Joshua invited him within, but the man's demeanour seemed nervous, distracted, as he said, so quietly that Joshua had to bend his tall frame to hear him, 'No, I beg you ask no questions. There is someone at my house who would speak to you, on a matter of some urgency, but is unable to come to you openly. Pray, do not look about you, for we might be observed by others. I ask only that you come with me, making your manner casual, unhurried, as if our meeting is of little import.'

Joshua, pausing only to secure the door of the cottage and take a lantern, went with him, chatting inconsequentially upon the way, but aware of Bevan's ill-suppressed nervousness, for his responses were jerky and self-conscious, as were his movements. Bevan ventured but one remark unbidden. 'It seems you have wrought some great conversion upon the workmaster, Constable.'

'I?' asked Joshua in mock astonishment. 'I fear it would demand more clout than I possess! A thunderbolt upon his head, at least . . .!'

'Which is what it appears to have been.' Bevan's earnest, sallow face, pale in the lantern light, relaxed into a smile. 'I have it upon the very best authority . . .'

'Littlepage's own?'

'No. I am not a disciple of his cult of self-worship!'

said Bevan, with unusual asperity. 'I called, by chance, to see an out pauper but recently admitted to the workhouse, an old man, now bedridden, who had long been in my care. There was some rambling, confused tale of teaching an inmate to write; that same inmate who called upon you with a message, it seems . . . The old man showed me a copy of the note – a strange, ill-spelt missive, barely comprehensible . . . until his pupil explained all to me!'

'And your advice to the offenders in this blackmail, to which I am an innocent accessory?'

'To burn the evidence,' said Bevan,' and enjoy the blaze, for there will be a return to a colder, crueller climate, of that I have no doubt!'

Joshua nodded. 'Immoral, but practical, not unlike the workmaster himself,' he approved, and, smiling broadly, turned into the gateway of Bevan's darkened cottage. Bevan put his lantern upon the doorstep, then fumbled awkwardly with the key in the lock, his shadow looming tall and sharp-angled in the light. Joshua, following him within and along the darkness of the narrow passage, was aware of an unease born, perhaps, of his companion's nervousness and ignorance of what, and who, awaited him. Bevan preceded him hesitantly into the small, dank kitchen at the back of the cottage, its single deep-set window invisible from the road. Even before he lit the fish-oil cruse lamp upon the scrubbed table, Joshua could see by the light of their lanterns that they were alone in the sparsely furnished room. Bevan raised a thin cautionary hand to silence the question that sprang to Joshua's lips, then lifted the latch to the tiny larder. The constable took a step forward involuntarily, his lantern held above his head. He did not know what it was he expected to see in the thin truckle of its beams, but it was certainly not the crouched figure and the wan, upturned face of the ex-pauper Elwyn Morris, the whites of his eyes unnaturally luminous against skin still blackened with the coal dust of his day's toil.

'Morris . . .?'

Elwyn Morris struggled awkwardly to his feet, shielding his eyes against the hurt of the light, trying to identify the blurred shapes beyond. He was plainly terrified. 'Constable Stradling . . .?'

'Yes, I have come . . .' Joshua stretched out a hand to him as Morris released his grip from the stone shelf upon which he had levered himself upright.

'I was afraid they had . . .' Morris broke off, disdaining Joshua's proffered hand with the mumbled apology. 'I fear I am filthy and sweat-stained from my work, sir. I would not have come so if it were not urgent.'

Bevan led him to a wooden chair where he sat gratefully, grimacing and stretching his cramped limbs.

'Now,' said Joshua, placing his lantern upon the table,' you shall tell me what has occurred to set you in such a flux.'

Bevan moved silently to the door and felt his way blindly into the darkness of the passageway to keep vigil, unseen, at the window of the small parlour which overlooked the street, leaving Joshua and Morris alone.

'It is the trouble at the Port, sir. I have learnt who is responsible for the thieving.'

'You are sure?' asked Joshua.

Morris nodded and moistened his lips. In the lamplight, the curve of them showed pink, with the full softness of a child's, lending them a curious innocence. 'I was asked to join them . . . well, threatened.'

'Them?'

'Oh, it is well organised, sir! No haphazard, impulsive

affair. There is a Cornishman, a foreman upon the horse-drawn tramroad: a crude, foul-mouthed bully of a man, quick to profane and strike out at a man or beast.'

'And those who work with him are part of this affair?'

'They have little option, sir. It is true that he has brought in one or two of his own men, outsiders like himself. He appoints them in place of those who fail to reach their targets in loading the coal, or meet with injury upon the long way to the pitheads.'

'There are many such accidents?' asked Joshua sharply.

'Too many!' Morris's eyes were contemptuous under the raw-edged lids. 'If he cannot crush a man's spirit by setting him ever greater and more squalid tasks, he breaks his bones. There are many accidents carefully arranged for those who will not yield to pressure.'

Joshua nodded his understanding. 'There is no check upon him by the Duffryn-Llynfi Company? No enquiries into these accidents?'

'He is a law unto himself; he has power to hire or dismiss men like me. Ex-paupers, who have known degradation and poverty, will work until they drop . . . and if they do, they are expendable, like those poor beasts upon the tramway. Indeed, since the company is interested only in profit, we have less value than the horses, being more cheaply replaced.' There was no bitterness in his voice, he was stating an incontrovertible fact.

'You will join in this desperate game, Morris?'

'If it will serve some purpose for you, sir.'

'You know it is a dangerous game, and I cannot promise to protect you?'

Morris said quietly, 'I am not a brave man, Constable Stradling, I make no bones about it, for it is the honest truth. But it is for my daughter, Haulwen, I most fear.

She is all of my life, sir! Without me, she would be destitute and sent to the poorhouse orphanage. If I were hurt, unfitted to work, she would be taken away. Even should I recover, she would remain a pauper for six years before I could reclaim her. That is the rule . . .'

Hell and damnation to the rules, thought Joshua angrily, and the self-satisfied fools who make them. Aloud, he promised, 'I shall see that she is cared for. I beg you, have no fear upon that score.'

Morris looked at him long and keenly, then nodded, satisfied. 'I know that you are a man of your word, sir, and will honour your bargain.'

'As you, sir,' returned Joshua quietly, adding, 'you do not know how this . . . den of thieves operates?'

'Only that there are those at work in the cargo holds and upon the quay-side employed to steal. The goods are hidden in the trams of pit props and iron ore loaded by the labourers upon the dockside. These are sent upon the return journeys to the mines and iron works. Yet, upon the way, they are halted by others in the pay of the Cornishman.'

'His name?' asked Joshua.

'Penbraze, Saul Penbraze. I am to meet him tomorrow at the Port to give him my answer, although he can have little doubt of what that will be,' Morris said bitterly. 'I may choose to lose either my work, or my ability to work – through crippling, or blindness even – either way, he must win!' He shook his head ruefully. 'And pray, do not remind me, Mr Stradling, that I once boasted that I had always kept my self-respect. Had I not believed you would care for Haulwen, I would have sold it, and myself, knowing that a child with neither home nor father would feel their loss more deeply than some ideal she could not even comprehend.'

'Yes,' said Joshua gently, 'I understand, and I might make the same choice . . . but I thank you for coming here, and for your trust in me.' He held out his hand to Morris who, after hesitating and glancing at his own coal-grained one, took Joshua's as the constable's other hand closed warmly over it. Then, at a signal from Bevan, his visitor slipped out into the night, to be swallowed by darkness.

Joshua had returned but half an hour from the relieving officer's house, and was about to set out for a jug of ale and some congenial company at the Crown Inn, when there was an urgent rattling upon his door. He opened it with some regret upon the pinched, anxious figure of Ezra the Box, his little ferret face twitching nervously.

'Constable Stradling, sir, a terrible thing has happened . . .' he blurted, voice high and thin with panic.

'What now?' demanded Joshua unsympathetically. 'Has some client found fault with his coffin, or one of your smuggler friends put cold tea in your cognac?'

Ezra's face remained set and strained, and Joshua regretted his facetiousness, knowing that something serious was indeed amiss, for the undertaker always gave as good as he got, slyly relishing a good argument.

'Come within,' Joshua invited more kindly, but Ezra merely exclaimed, 'No. I cannot. I must return to my workshop. If you will come with me, sir, in your own good time.'

'What is it you wish me to see?' asked Joshua, puzzled.

'Not what, sir, who! I was driving my cart upon business across the wasteland which borders Pickett's Lease, when I saw a group of men ahead with lanterns. They did not see me, sir, for I stopped, not wishing to be seen . . . my business is my own,' he said defensively.

'Well, go on, man!' prompted Joshua.

'They seemed to be chasing at something with sticks. Bando players, perhaps, I thought, but from some other place, for I knew none of them, and I know every man hereabouts.'

Joshua stifled an urge to shake him, saying patiently, 'And then?'

'I saw this sack, a bundle of rags, I thought, upon the ground, and would have passed by had not the pony reared up and refused to budge. It was not a sack, sir, but a man, God help him! All but dead of a beating, blood-stained and scarce recognisable as the pauper, Elwyn Morris.'

'Where is he now?'

'In my workshop, sir, for I loaded him upon my cart, fearing he might die if left. Indeed, he may already be dead, for he uttered but two words to me, then grew too weak to speak more: "Stradling" and "Fetch" were all I could understand.'

'I will come at once,' said Joshua,' and I thank you for what you have done.'

Evans looked uncomfortable, then, 'You had best send word to Dr Mansel,' he said, 'for I cannot pay for his services.'

As Joshua nodded, Ezra added quickly, 'Although, I fancy it were better saved to pay for my own!'

Chapter Fourteen

Joshua climbed aboard Ezra's funeral cart, reflecting as he did so that few who made the journey with him returned. He directed his unlikely charioteer to let him alight at the Crown Inn, that Ossie might get a message to Dr Mansel, stressing the urgency and the need for discretion. He also bade him apprise Emily Randall of Morris's plight, and to beg her to care for Haulwen, for he feared for her safety in the lodgings at Port. Ossie needed no second bidding, but dispatched a reliable groom, at once, to the doctor's house upon Clevis Hill, promising that he would first seek Emily, then go himself to collect the child, for he was fond of her, and she would accompany him without demur, since she was ever pleased to see that absurdly cosseted, moth-eaten donkey of hers, which Ossie kept in his care, with so many other outcasts and ill-favoured beasts.

Joshua had bidden Ezra return at once to the wounded man, lest he be in need of care, promising to follow on foot as soon as he was able. Ezra had left the back door into his yard unlatched and Joshua, bearing a lantern from the stables of the Crown, slipped in surreptitiously, stepping cautiously in the darkness through the piled timbers and logs, the lantern beams casting strange shadows amidst their looming shapes, and circles of haloed light upon their richly textured grains.

Ezra was at the door of the house to lead him within, grimy finger to his lips, the only sound the soft rasping of the pony's breath and the shifting of its hooves upon the bed straw of its stall nearby. Ezra led Joshua through the cluttered paraphernalia of his rush-lit kitchen, with its mingled smells of old clothing, food and stale tobacco, overlaid with a persistent aroma of cats, and into a poky bedroom where Elwyn Morris lay upon a trestle, covered with none-too-clean sacking and a variety of old coats. Joshua was surprised and touched to see that Ezra had made some attempt to clean the coal dust from the injured man's face. In the flickering light of the tallow candles, smoking and smelling of burnt mutton fat, Morris's skin in the small blurred crescents which Ezra had exposed, gleamed with the bluish-white of raw bone. His hair was matted with congealed blood and there were grazes and lacerations upon his face, and the hand which lay limply across his chest was swollen and misshapen. The coal dust was spread with crusted blood, as if he had sought to cover his head from the frenzy of his assailants' blows.

'Dear God,' exclaimed Joshua, 'how could he survive such a beating? Those who attacked him are brutes . . . animals!'

Ezra nodded unhappily, 'I ask myself "Why", Constable? He is a poor man, recently a pauper. His clothes are shabby and he is covered with the grime of his labour. This is not the work of a footpad or a casual thief. They would look for richer pickings! Besides, everyone knows him to be an honest man, striving to make a life for himself and the child. No! this is the work of some well-organised band of ruffians and cut-throats, as I saw, and done for some ungodly purpose! A warning, do you think?'

Joshua hesitated, then, making up his mind, admitted, 'Yes, Mr Evans, you are right. I cannot explain exactly why he has been so cruelly ill treated, although I believe that I know the culprits.'

'You need say no more, sir. I understand, and will be as silent as the grave!' promised Ezra with unconscious irony. 'If Morris is in danger, then you may leave him here in safety. Neither your visits, nor the doctor's, will arouse comment, since there is often business to be discussed. Besides,' a wry smile revealed the pointed ferret teeth, 'I am not noted hereabouts for my lavish and ready hospitality . . .' Joshua made some vague sounds of dissent. 'No, 'tis true!' insisted Ezra, 'and well I know it and use it to my advantage. If you have the reputation for being a mean-minded, sly, cantankerous little toad, few will impose upon you, and you are free to go about your business unobserved and unhindered.' Joshua smiled at him with genuine warmth as he continued, 'Unlike you, Constable Stradling, or those in lesser crafts or trades, I have no fear of offending my clients . . .' He broke off as the man in the bed stirred and moaned, and Joshua bent over him anxiously.

'I had best unfasten the door to the street,' said Ezra quickly, 'for Dr Mansel will surely come that way, and I will need to hurry him inside, unseen, through my workshop.'

Joshua nodded, saying, 'Was it not there that you told me you had taken Morris?'

'Yes,' said Ezra awkwardly.

'It was kind of you to give him your bed.'

Ezra fidgeted in embarrassment, declaring gruffly, 'It is warmer for me by the kitchen fire . . . the bed is hard. Besides,' he confessed with a hint of his old truculence, 'the only place to lay him was in a coffin upon the trestles.

I tried to make him comfortable, do you see? I tidied him as best I could: got some water and a rag to clean his face. He awoke for a moment, and looked at me, crying, "They have done for me, then." '

Joshua, despite his concern for Morris, could not make reply, lest laughter betray him.

'So I took him to my bed . . .' said Ezra defensively. 'If some busybody outside had seen him start out of the box with a scream, it would have done my reputation no good.'

'Or them!' said Joshua.

'No! And, contrary to what you think, I do not need to drum up extra custom by frightening people to death. I have business enough!'

'Legal and illegal,' agreed Joshua, and Ezra nodded, grateful that their comfortable hostility was restored.

There came a soft knocking at the door, and Ezra hesitantly opened it.

To Joshua's surprise, it was not the plump figure of Dr Mansel whom Ezra led through the workshop with its smell of resin, oils and wood, but Dr Burrell. He saluted Joshua briefly, seeming not to see the undoubted squalor of the small room. All his attention was upon the pitiful figure on the bed.

'What can you tell me?' he asked abruptly. 'Footpads? An accident?'

'He was set upon by villains,' said Joshua, unwilling to explain too much before Ezra. 'Mr Evans saw it happen, and brought him here upon his cart.'

Burrell bent over the still figure on the bed, and said, 'It is as well that he did!' Then he demanded of Ezra, 'Bring hot water, if you please, and some clean rags . . . and have you no better light than these candles? Another lantern, perhaps, or oil lamp?'

He bade Joshua lift his own lantern to illumine the bed, while Ezra went upon his way, grumbling beneath his breath. Joshua caught the phrases, 'Not made of money, like some!' and 'Oil lamp, indeed!' and a muttered, 'Do a good turn . . . get no credit'.

Dr Burrell's glance met Joshua's in the light of the lantern, and he smiled, saying, 'Now that our most gracious host has been diverted, perhaps you will tell me the real story.' He went on deftly examining Morris, stripping back the old coats which covered him, probing and assessing, commanding Joshua as to where to direct the light, yet listening to his explanation without comment. 'The wound on his head is severe, and will need cleansing and stitching,' he said finally. 'I hope it is that which renders him insensible, and not some graver, internal injuries. The surface lacerations and contusions, I can treat, but he must be removed to a hospital. This company he works for . . .?'

'The Duffryn-Llynfi Tramroad Company.'

'They will pay for his treatment there?' Burrell demanded.

'I think not, for he has worked for them but a short time, and this was outside his duties. Even if they should, there would be more danger in removing him there. His attackers would learn of it, and his life would be forfeit . . . They left him for dead. They would not have run the risk of his recovering to inform upon them.'

Burrell's lean saturnine face was grave as he declared, 'It is evident that he cannot remain here, sir. You will be occupied with tracking these villains, and not in the position of affording him the protection he needs. The undertaker, Evans, will be unable to give him the constant care he deserves. He is a carpenter, too, is he not?'

Joshua inclined his head.

'Then he will need to be about his business,' continued Burrell. 'People will be coming here, seeking him out. He will be as much at risk as Morris. My own constant comings and goings will not go unremarked by those responsible for the assault. What is needed is a safe place, where he can be nursed in secrecy, with the solitude he needs.'

'Then there is no difficulty,' exclaimed Ezra from the doorway as he entered bearing a bowl of steaming water and some moderately clean rags. 'He can be taken where I was taken to escape the wreckers who sought me . . . to my friend, Rowden the miller, in the windmill upon Stormy Downs.' Joshua and Burrell exchanged startled, incredulous glances as Ezra continued placidly, 'Of course, he will need ample payment and extra help to nurse his visitor . . . as will I, to transport him there, and persuade Rowden to agree. I believe that he will do it for me, for he holds me in great respect.' He placed the bowl upon the cluttered rickety table beside Burrell. 'Yes,' he declared with smug complacency, 'I pride myself that Rowden knows my true worth. He all but wept when I left him.'

'With relief, perhaps?' parried Joshua, and Ezra regarded him coldly, unamused. 'You are right, Mr Evans,' offered the constable by way of apology, 'it is a splendid idea, and I congratulate you for your perspicacity. You are as ingenious as you are modest.'

'He is all of that,' agreed Burrell ambiguously, trying not to meet Joshua's eye.

'I will go and prepare the horse and cart, for there is no time to lose,' said Ezra.

'I will ride with you,' declared Joshua immediately, offering him his lantern. 'If you will halt at my cottage upon the way, I will collect my pistols, for we might have need of protection.'

When Ezra had gone, and Dr Burrell's ministrations completed, Joshua asked, awkwardly, 'And you, sir? How will you find your way to the windmill upon the downs tomorrow? Would you have me show you the way? I shall do so gladly.'

Burrell said gently, 'Have you forgotten, Joshua, that the same solace was granted to me? No, I am well acquainted with Stormy Downs.'

Joshua said, 'I do not know how your services will be rewarded, sir. Morris was, until recently, a pauper.'

'And dependent, as I, upon the charity of those who would care, asking no reward.' There was a silence between them, with Joshua aware of the rebuke, and Burrell fearing he had spoken too sharply.

'The child, Haulwen. She is safe?' asked Dr Burrell, seeking to redeem himself.

'Oh, yes. I have arranged that she be taken into the care of Miss Emily Randall, at the Crown Inn, who loves her as if she were her own child . . .'

'Then Morris and the girl are fortunate indeed,' said Burrell, and Joshua wondered at the flatness of his tone, and the pain in his eyes, before his face grew shadowed and unreadable in the spluttering candlelight.

After a restless night in which his dreams were haunted by images of spectres with bando sticks pursuing him relentlessly upon horse-drawn trams, and being nailed down in a coffin by a grinning Ezra, Joshua awakened gratefully to thin winter sunlight. A crusting of frost lichened the high window, and the water jug upon the bedside table bore a wafer of ice which he had to crack in his fingers before filling the bowl and splashing himself into painful awareness.

He had still not decided how best to tackle the Cornishman, Saul Penbraze, and his band of thieves at the Port. Their callousness in attacking Elwyn Morris angered him, and he hoped devoutly that a charge of murder would not be added to the list of crimes. He would ride out to the windmill on his way to the justice's house to see if there had been any improvement in Morris's condition . . . and, later, visit Emily at the coach house to see that the child was safe, and that they wanted for nothing. Unlike Ezra, Emily would be grieved and offended by any mention of payment for her services, but Joshua would ensure that gifts of food from the farm were offered, for such luxuries might be gratefully accepted as the tributes of a friend, incurring no obligation.

It was as well that Morris was safely housed in the windmill upon Stormy Downs, and that Dr Burrell would attend him there. It was strange how the strands of his own life, Burrell's and Rebecca's were interwoven . . . like threads in some unfinished tapestry, the colours subtly and almost imperceptibly blending, each stitch separate, yet needing the others to make the pattern complete. Ezra, too, was a detail on the canvas – although, Joshua thought, amused, more like a wicked caricature: a drawing by some political satirist, perhaps! He certainly drove a hard bargain! The fees for his services, and those of the miller and Rowden's sister, who would nurse the invalid, were little short of extortion! Still, Ezra had sworn that she was a competent nurse and the very soul of discretion, a childless widow who had nursed her husband tenderly until he died, and would tend Morris as devotedly. Joshua foresaw storms ahead when he told the justice of the cost of Elwyn Morris's rescue, which later must be approved and borne by the frugal-minded vestrymen. Yet, if it led to the capture of Penbraze and his henchmen, it would be a small price to pay.

Joshua dressed and partook of a hurried cold breakfast before setting out for the Crown Inn to fetch his mare, which Ossie swiftly saddled for him. A few reassuring words were exchanged with the ostler about Haulwen's safety, and her father's, and Joshua was riding under the archway of the Crown and over Clevis Hill to Tythegston Court for his meeting with the justice. A smile tugged the corners of his mouth as he remembered his meeting of the previous night with Rowden the miller. With Ezra driving the funeral cart, and Joshua ensconced on the open boards beside the inert figure of Morris, swathed in a plethora of sacks and old coats, they had made their halting way across the desolate heights of Stormy Downs. The night was sharp with frost, and a thin sliver of moon and a few high stars coruscated in the dark sky, but showed no light, almost, Joshua thought, as if through pinpricks in a black shroud illumined by a candle.

Rowden, on being aroused from his bed by the urgent knocking, had stared in stupefaction at the strange equipage, scratching his broad head then his ribs, blinking the sleep from his eyes, as if to rid himself of a bad dream.

'We have come seeking your help, as in the past,' explained Joshua, leaping from the cart. 'If we might leave this wounded man to your care. For, otherwise, his life is forfeit . . .'

Rowden had knuckled more sleep from his eyes, and shaken himself alert, like a dog from water, bidding them enter. Then, still in his vast nightshirt which, Joshua suspected, was fashioned from bleached flour sacks, he had padded out to the cart, lifting Morris as easily as a babe in his brawny arms, carrying him indoors to lay him tenderly upon his own bed. He had turned to Joshua, his eyes gleaming wickedly in the plump, dark-jowled face, to exclaim fervently, 'Thanks be to God, Constable Stradling; I was afeared you were returning Ezra!'

And Ezra had sniffed, face pinched and unamused, as the miller had clapped a hand, hirsute as a bear's paw, upon the undertaker's stiff back, generous flesh setting his nightshirt trembling with unholy mirth.

Joshua's expression was infinitely less sanguine as he rode through the impressive griffon-topped pillars of the gateway, and into the forecourt of the justice's house. He was quickly relieved of his mare by a respectful groom, who seemed to materialise silently from the shadows.

Leyshon welcomed the young constable with a smile, briefly exposing the ruins of his teeth. He took Joshua's helmet, placing it upon a hall chair, saying, with a pertinent glance towards where the justice awaited, 'A wintry day, sir, seasonal, but frosty, likely to find a chill in the air . . .'

'As one would expect,' returned Joshua civilly, answering the old man's conspiratorial smile with a nod, to show that the message had not eluded him. He followed the servant's hunched figure to the library door, where Leyshon announced his presence, and ushered him in.

'Well, Stradling,' demanded Robert Knight, replacing a letter upon his desk with obvious irritation, 'to what am I indebted for this unsolicited visit? Another catastrophe, I have no doubt? Murder? Mayhem? Or has the entire population of the three hamlets been spirited away by the elusive highwayman?'

Joshua looked at him steadily, and the prominent brown eyes faltered behind their lenses. Then Robert

Knight dropped his gaze, confessing sheepishly, 'I beg your pardon, Stradling, for rudely and unjustly venting my spleen upon you. It should rightly be expended upon that shiftless nephew of mine. He absents himself still from his home, with no word as to his whereabouts or fortune. My sister grieves his absence. Yet, if he were here, sir, I would make him grieve louder and longer, and to more effect! But that is not your problem.' His eyes twinkled. 'I am sure that your conduct causes your mother neither anxiety nor distress . . .' It was, from the justice, a most handsome apology. He continued more brusquely, 'But, to what brings you here . . .'

'A development in the affair at the Port.' Joshua related the events of the previous night as Robert Knight listened with growing distress.

'Morris? Elwyn Morris?' His brow creased in perplexity. 'Is he not the ex-pauper who gave evidence against the wreckers, at great danger to his own life?'

'The same.'

'You are quite sure, Stradling, that he is safe? That he will receive the best of medical attention?' His plump, loose-jowled face was ugly with concern.

Joshua told him of the arrangements which had been made with Rowden and his sister, adding that, although Dr Burrell refused all payment for his services, the cost would, nevertheless, be prodigious.

'Money! Money!' was the testy reply. 'A man's life is in the balance, sir. How can you weigh it against such a paltry consideration? I am surprised at you, Stradling, deeply surprised.'

Joshua murmured apology.

'There is any improvement in Morris's condition today?'

'I called at the windmill upon the Downs, sir, and he

was conscious and able to tell me a few words about his attackers. But he is very weak and in considerable pain from his injuries.'

'This Cornishman of whom you spoke . . .?'

'Penbraze, sir.'

'How do you intend to tackle him? There seems little purpose in challenging him directly, since we have no proof, save the word of Morris, who is too sick to give evidence, and might well die of his injuries.'

'I am to meet Peter Rawlings, the exciseman, today, sir. He is concerned in this, since brandy, tobacco and other dutiable goods are involved. He has infiltrated one of his men into service upon the tramroad, but I do not know, as yet, with what result.'

The justice considered. 'You mean, perhaps, to trap them in the act of stealing the cargo? Risky, and impractical. You would need many informants to keep watch upon all the ships and unloading bays.'

'Yes, I had considered that, sir. I hope to obtain information from Rawlings' man about where upon the tramroad the trams will be halted, and the stolen goods taken off by the Cornishman's gang.'

'Yet you will not capture him, for you say he works only upon the docks, supervising the loading and unloading . . .'

'If we can capture and detain the lesser fry, sir, I believe that they will implicate him. Many of them are involved against their will, fearing Penbraze, for he has the authority to hire or dismiss them, at will.'

The justice looked grave. 'You will need extra men, Stradling, in addition to those whom Rawlings can muster. Make any arrangements you think necessary. The vestrymen will sanction the expense without quibbling. You have my word upon it.'

Joshua thanked him, wishing ruefully that he had the brawny fists and fighting skills of Doonan to depend upon.

'When you learn the identities of those involved,' promised the justice, 'I will write you out warrants to search their premises, to see what can be recovered, and to produce fresh evidence. You have my authority to arm yourself for protection, but it is understood that you will use firearms only as a last resort, should it prove necessary.'

'Yes, sir, it is understood.'

'You will see that I am kept informed.'

'Of course, sir.'

Robert Knight nodded dismissal, rising ponderously and tugging at the bell pull beside his desk to summon Leyshon to show Joshua out, then turned to ask disconcertingly, 'Who was it who thought of hiding Morris in the windmill?'

'The undertaker, Evans, sir,' confessed Joshua.

'Evans the Box?' demanded the justice, to Joshua's surprise. 'I'll warrant that he did not act from philanthropic charity.' There was grudging admiration in his tone. 'Had we but half a dozen vestrymen with his acumen, industry and deviousness, then . . .' he recalled himself abruptly, 'then it would be a sad day indeed for the three hamlets,' he amended triumphantly.

'I have to say, sir, in Ezra's favour, that he rescued Morris when he had been left for dead by his attackers.'

The justice's shaggy eyebrows lifted in unspoken question.

'No, sir, he was aware that Morris was alive. He even made an attempt to wash and care for him.'

'I do him a grave injustice,' said Robert Knight, 'by my suspicion and lack of charity. Yet, I must declare him to be a most unlikely good Samaritan. Still, God moves in most mysterious ways and often chooses the most bizarre of instruments!'

Joshua was regarding him with unnerving innocence, as Leyshon entered to hear the young constable observe, 'The curate's egg, sir.'

'The curate's egg?' demanded Robert Knight.

'Yes, sir. Evans. Good in parts . . .'

'Leyshon, show Constable Stradling out,' instructed the justice, suppressing the barest flicker of a smile. 'Oh, and Leyshon . . .'

'Yes, sir?' The old servant halted, enquiringly.

Robert Knight appeared to be gazing intently out of the window as he said, blandly, 'The weather seems to be taking a turn for the better, less frost and a steady thaw. Milder altogether!'

Joshua reluctantly declined Leyshon's pleas to refresh himself with tea and bakestone cakes in the kitchens, because of the urgency of his duties, remarking as the groom delivered his mount to him upon the carriageway where he and the old manservant stood, 'It behoves me to leave when the barometer is set fair, Leyshon, for the climate can be notoriously changeable.'

Then he swung himself from stirrup to saddle and, with a swift salute, turned the mare towards Clevis Hill and Newton. First, he visited Emily Randall at the Crown, giving her news of Elwyn Morris and making sure that his daughter, Haulwen, was safe. He did not believe that Penbraze's men would be reckless enough to harm the child, thinking Morris to be dead. Yet, if they learnt that he had survived, might they not abduct her, believing that she might know where he was hidden, or use her as a means to blackmail others into giving information as to his whereabouts? He confided all to Ossie, sure of his discretion, and the ostler promised to remain watchful, and alert for strangers. Joshua knew that if it proved necessary, he would defend her with his life . . . To Tom Butler he mentioned merely that he had fears for Haulwen's safety and the landlord, posing no questions, had offered to set a sweeping boy to brush the cobbles upon the highway outside the archway to the stable yard, and to bring news of any altercation. Upon hearing Joshua's thanks, he had claimed, with a smile, that his customers 'were ever eager for a real eyeball to eyeball knockabout rout'. Besides, the pleasure of shove ha'penny and skittles were apt to distract men from the serious business of imbibing, whereas a scrap sharpened the thirst! Should a fight be offered, the constable would be doing him a favour!

Joshua's next business was to secure the services of men who would be free to follow him upon an instant. He considered that he would need at least five strong and belligerent helpers: men upon whose courage and obedience to command he could rely. Doonan was still too sick from his wound to help; Emrys unable to leave his work at the quarries. Jeremiah and Illtyd would certainly come; as would Daniel the wheelwright and Clatworthy the blacksmith, who had apprentices upon whom they could depend in their absence. The fifth? Tom Butler, he decided, would be best left to rally his men, should need arise. The landlord of the Ancient Briton, then? A massive, jovial fellow, not unlike Doonan in build, and used to heaving barrels and dealing with belligerent and drunken men . . . Yes, he would feel confident with Eli Proudfoot at hand. So, with this resolution in mind, Joshua rode out to ask him for his aid and, having received his firm assurance, continued to Jeremiah's cottage. The fisherman greeted him warmly, declaring that he would belabour Morris's attackers with the mercilessness they deserved, and bade Joshua ride on to make arrangements at the Port, for he would ride out upon the cob and cart to find Illtyd upon the common lands, and thence to Nottage to inform Daniel and the blacksmith of Joshua's need of them. There could be no doubt of their readiness to respond.

Thus relieved of one duty, the constable set out upon another. At the Port, the sailing ships lay upon the tide, serene and full plumed as swans asleep, seemingly unruffled by the noise and agitated movement upon the shore. Joshua loved the sights and sounds of the Port, its evocative scents, and the bustle and colour of the scene. Its diversity. The cargoes and passengers, sailors and labourers, trams and horses, intermingled in strange fellowship amidst the unplanned sprawl and clutter of chandlers' and carpenters' shops, rope-makers and fishwives. Over all towered the gleaming mountains of coal amidst foothills of ore and limestone, and the shifting rolling pitprops, redolent of pine resin, starkly pathetic, denuded of their shadowed-green branches . . .

Joshua went at once to seek out Rawlings at the exciseman's office, conscious of the curious glances and occasional greetings of the labourers upon the quays. Together they walked to a secluded vantage point, ostensibly conversing as they went, and pausing to study the sailing ships awaiting the tide . . . They moved without urgency to the harbour master's office, where Captain Ayde-Buchan greeted them with his usual good-natured ebullience. Joshua somehow felt, in the ex-naval officer's company, as if he were a junior naval rating, facing some minor disciplinary charge and trying, vainly, to ingratiate himself. When he had confided this to Rawlings he confessed that he, in turn, felt a shameful urge to answer Captain Ayde-Buchan with a brisk 'Aye-aye, Sir' and a rousing salute, before climbing the rigging to the crow's nest.

Ayde-Buchan's fine-honed face was intent now as the situation was explained to him, palely intelligent eyes alert as he considered the plan of action outlined. He nodded curtly. 'I anticipate no difficulties here,' he said confidently. 'None at all. Should some unexpected complication arise, then I will deal with it . . .'

Joshua could not doubt it for a moment.

'This man, Penbraze – a shifty, unreliable fellow. I have watched him at his work. Idle, and a bully, treating men and horses with contempt. I have seen too many like him on the lower deck, using others for their own ends. All blast and fury against authority, yet empty and useless as a pig's bladder when challenged. I have his measure, believe me, and would know how to deal with him!'

Joshua stifled a smile as Rawlings whispered, straight-faced, 'Hang him from the yard arm! Order him thirty lashes . . .'

'Flogging is too good for them, sir!' declared Ayde-Buchan as if he had heard. He held out a lean hand to Joshua, handshake firm, weathered face resolute, saying confidently, 'Have no fear, Constable. I will play my part. There can only be one outcome.'

'Well, two at most . . .' amended Rawlings, after Joshua followed him out into the salt-smelling air. 'Come, Stradling. Heave to, man. Let us splice the mainbrace at the Ship Aground!'

'As long as we don't perish with all hands!' replied Joshua, with more humour than he felt.

Chapter Fifteen

Emily Randall had left Haulwen in Ossie's care, to the obvious delight of both ostler and child. There was a rare and touching affinity between the two: that natural bond which takes no account of disparity in age or circumstance. So engrossed were they in their admiration of the aged donkey which had borne Elwyn Morris and Haulwen to safety from the wild hilltop farm, that Emily's words of farewell had gone unanswered. She was sure that they did not even notice her departure.

'Ossie', Haulwen had called the mangy, emaciated beast, its rib cage gaunt through its moth-eaten hide. Its skin had seemed altogether too large for it, like a carelessly thrown rug; its delicate legs too elegant for so grotesque and misshapen a body. Only its eyes had seemed alive, patient, watchful, all of suffering and survival reflected in their soft brown depths, an expression mirrored in the eyes of the child upon the crudely fashioned cart at its rump. As the child had leapt down, belligerent and protective, to stand at its head, exhaustion and fear in every line of her body, Ossie had come forward to take charge of them both. The taut young body had relaxed, and the tears had come as Haulwen had recognised the healing compassion in Ossie's eyes. Like so many sad and bewildered animals before and since, she had surrendered herself trustingly to his care.

It was a pity, Emily thought, as she crossed the green to the churchyard, that we lose that clear, unclouded eye of childhood . . . Haulwen had not seen a little bowed ostler, awkward-boned and ill-at-ease, outside the stable yard. She had seen Ossie as he truly was: a good and loving man, warm with pity. So, she had paid him the greatest compliment she knew, and called her poor, bedraggled donkey after him. Ossie had been amused and pleased, aware of the honour she did him. Emily smiled, reflecting that, to Haulwen's mind, both of her 'Ossies' were perfect, and who was to say that she was wrong. Certainly the donkey's burgeoning under the ostler's care had been little short of a miracle. Now it was plumply contented: cropped-close fur grown thickly lush as crushed velvet, hooves burnished to tortoise-shell.

Dr Burrell, skirting the village green on his return from a visit to a patient in Newton, saw the smile upon Emily's lips and the graceful turn of her head as she walked towards the churchyard gate, and instinctively slowed the horse to observe her the better. He had been debating whether to call upon her at the coach loft, to enquire about the child, that he might take news of her to Elwyn Morris in the windmill upon the Downs. Yet, he was aware that his concern for Haulwen, his patient, although real, was a secondary consideration . . . Upon his visit to the stable loft, following Haulwen's ordeal in the icy waters of the pool, he had found Emily's calmness restful, and her conversation intelligent and perceptive. He owed her a personal debt for writing Jeremiah's letters to him, and had found himself looking forward to them eagerly, as a small green refuge or haven of peacefulness in the aridness of his work among the cholera sufferers . . . It seemed from what Joshua had let fall, unthinkingly, that her life and affections were already bound up with Elwyn Morris and his child.

He hesitated for a moment, stroking the mare's neck, and watching as Emily walked slowly towards the gate, bending gracefully to lift the latch and enter the tree-stained churchyard. Then, upon an impulse, he rode across the green to secure his mount at the wooden barrier outside the gate and followed her within.

It was a cold crisp day, the January air clean, and smelling of bruised grass and damp earth and melting frost, the salt breeze from the sea clotted with the sharpness of seaweed and wet sand. Everything was washed with greyness, as if some painter, grown weary of colour, had brushed a sameness over all, blurring and obscuring detail, so that only a muted impression of stone walls, sky and silver-black branches remained. A dream landscape.

Emily was seated upon a stone near a grave still covered with turf, her dove-grey skirts spread out about her. She held a book in her hands, resting the spine of it against her knees, smooth bare head bent forward, so rapt in study of it that she did not hear his approach. Burrell, removing his silk hat, stood watching her unobserved as Emily began reading aloud quietly, intimately, as if in deep conversation with a friend. Yet the words of John Donne came to him clearly, and with a piercing sadness.

'*No man is an island*
Secure unto himself . . .'

'Perceptive words, ma'am,' he said, looking down at her with an expression which she could not fathom. 'Yet wasted, perhaps, upon so remote and unresponsive an audience . . .?'

'But not, sir, I trust, upon you,' she replied, smiling. 'Perhaps it is the quality of the listening that the poet would appreciate, rather than the quantity . . .'

She began to rise to her feet, but composedly, with no awkwardness, as Burrell put out a hand to help her. She hesitated only briefly, then put her hand into his. They stood, looking at each other for a moment, unspeaking. Burrell's eyes, deep-set and restless in the deeply grooved face, grew shadowed before he released her fingers, saying, with deliberate lightness, 'Is this where you escape for solace, ma'am?'

'No. But there were times in the poorhouse when silence and solitude would have served me well. And you, sir? You have some secret place?'

'No, ma'am.' His tone was abrupt. 'I knew too much solitude, too much silence. I was not my own best company.'

'Then you must have been grateful, as I, for other men's thoughts, sir, to fill your mind, and bring you ease . . .'

Burrell did not reply.

'I come here, Dr Burrell, to the graveside of one whom I loved dearly, her life scarcely beginning when she was most cruelly murdered . . .' Emily broke off in confusion, recalling with anguish the parallel with his own life. She seemed about to make apology, but continued carefully, 'I believe that Mary is here, in spirit, in this tranquil place, and bring her what solace I may. You will think it a stupid, morbid fancy, no doubt.'

'I think it is . . . kind, ma'am,' he said, 'and hope it brings you the comfort you would offer to her.' He stood there awkwardly, as if to take his leave, instead saying surprisingly, 'Memory can be a salve, or a corrosive, Mistress Randall . . .'

She looked at him compassionately, wondering which it had proved to be for him in his lonely incarceration. 'It is all we have of them,' she said gently.

'No, not of them,' he replied tonelessly. 'It is all we have left of ourselves, of what we once were . . .'

'True. But are they not, for good or ill, part of what we were, sir? Our lives are fashioned by all that has touched them, everyone we have ever known.' She glanced towards the simple, grass-covered plot at their feet, its only ornament a cross of plain wood, and continued earnestly, 'I do not believe that Mary, the child I knew, lies here, life ended, beneath that harsh soil, or that all she ever was must perish with her flesh.' She put out a hand to touch his shoulder gently. 'It is right that we should mourn these we have lost, Dr Burrell, but not that we should bury ourselves with them . . .'

'You have finished, ma'am?'

She flushed at the rebuke, hand dropping lifelessly to her side. 'Life, and we, must go on, Dr Burrell. And you, sir, have so much to offer, so much to give . . .' She faltered in confusion at her temerity, continuing more firmly, 'There are those who admire you, sir, for what you have accomplished, withstood . . .'

Burrell stared at her searchingly, dark eyes unreadable, before saying with sincerity, 'Elwyn Morris and his child are indeed fortunate, ma'am . . .'

'Elwyn Morris? You cannot think, sir, that it is fortunate to be beaten near to death, to be workless, the threat of paupery ever near to you?'

'I meant, ma'am, that with you at his side . . .' Burrell's face was bleak with hurt, disappointment.

Emily did not pretend to misunderstand. 'I shared with Elwyn Morris the horror of paupery, as I shared with all others so deprived. It is a bond not easily broken, nor should it be. My concern for him is that, and nothing more . . .'

Burrell stood there silently, but there was no mistaking

the sudden warmth that softened the corners of his mouth, or the realisation in his eyes, as Emily moved towards him and kissed him gently upon the curve of his jaw. Then, silk hat flung upon the grass, he took her into his arms and kissed her with a hunger and passion which he had thought dead. When he released her, Emily, whose book had fallen unnoticed to the ground, made no effort to retrieve it, or to rearrange the disorder of her hair and dress. She looked at him calmly, saying in her soft well-modulated tones, 'I never thought that my first abandonment to passion would be in a graveyard, sir, and that I should be the instigator!'

'And now you feel shame, ma'am? Regret?' he asked, amused.

'Not one jot or tittle!' she said comfortably, dissolving into laughter so infectious that Burrell laughed with her.

'I feared that your passion for poetry might have given you an over-romanticised view of such carnal delights. Left you unprepared . . .'

'Oh, I have been prepared, sir, from our very first meeting,' she declared unblushing. 'Yet you are right. The poets did not do my feelings justice. It is so very much better than I expected!' She bent to retrieve her book, and gathered his silk hat, handing it to him solemnly. He replaced it upon his head, then raised it most eloquently to declare, with mock gravity, 'I believe, ma'am, that in view of our . . . acquaintanceship, it might be considered quite proper for you to call me John.'

'I am delighted to learn your name, sir,' she said, with a deep curtsey. 'Yet, I hope our relationship will never be "quite proper". Indeed, not proper at all!' So saying, she took his arm primly as, with a pleasure which eased the tiredness and hurt from his face, he escorted her to the churchyard gate.

Joshua, riding out under the archway to the Crown Inn, dressed, as Ossie slyly observed, 'in full fig' and 'gaudier than a peacock's courting', did not see John Burrell and Emily crossing the village green. His thoughts might well have been upon the delectable prospect of his reunion with Rebecca, for it was thence that he was bound. Yet, even the image of her bright eyes and softly yielding mouth could not entirely banish thought of tomorrow's rout with Penbraze and his men, or that accursed highwayman. Burrell had given him the disturbing news of an interloper having used the abandoned shepherd's hut upon Stormy Downs, as refuge. The doctor had gone there upon an impulse, after visiting one of the outlying farms, prompted, he admitted, by curiosity and nostalgia. The ashes of a fire had still been warm, and there were the remains of a meal and a rough bed of dried ferns and grass. A vagrant, perhaps, or some passing drover? Joshua could not be sure. He had searched to no avail, returning often, and begging Illtyd to keep watch circumspectly and with a care for his own safety during his duties as haywarden upon the downs. Nothing more had come to light, and yet Joshua remained troubled. True, it had been searched after the highwayman's threats upon Rosa, but Burrell himself had lived there, undiscovered, for many weeks, in the full hue and cry of a murder chase . . .

Joshua, breasting the hill that led on its other slope past Tythegston Court, urged the mare onwards lest she turn, from force of habit, through its wide gateway. He felt a ridiculous sense of guilt as he neared the house: childish and quite unwarranted. His duties as constable absorbed him utterly, and he gave them all his time and devotion; not even taking those hours of leisure which were his by right. Why, then, should he ride by stealthily?

There was a sound of swift, clattering hooves, as the justice emerged through the griffon-topped opening and out on to the highway, plump body aquiver. He passed by so swiftly that Joshua was aware only of an impression of scowling disapproval. As he instinctively doffed his hat, Robert Knight's voice floated back, harassed and clear, 'I am glad, sir, that your duties press so lightly upon you. Mine press hard! I bid you good-day.'

Damnation to the man! thought Joshua in vexation, *he* is the one who is omniscient, omnipotent and omnipresent! Then he began to smile and, giving the mare her head, galloped towards the turnpike, and thence to Southerndown, and Rebecca.

The lanes and byways were winter-bleak, beyond them a blurred landscape of dark-brown furrows, damp fields and flowing hillsides, their dying ferns brown as foxes. There was a feeling of coldness and desolation in the scene. The trees, starkly bare of leaves, showed forlornly against the January sky; the hedges a tangle of blackthorn with only the dark, spiked leaves of holly and its few remaining crimson berries to give them life. Here and there, upon the way, sere strings of old man's beard looped vivid colour in beads of yellow, green and orange, garish and unexpected above bleached, dead grasses.

Joshua, remembering the lush greenness of that shining summer day when he had first taken Rebecca to his father's farm, thought how like the changing seasons were their own lives. Not only in the slow inevitable progression from birth to death, but in the swiftly changing patterns of light to shade; bleakness to warmth; poverty to abundance . . . Now, he supposed, was the springtime of their lives, the rising of the sap, the burgeoning of leaf and tree, the breaking of blossom. Then, the ripening of corn, the rich autumn harvest. He would not dwell upon bleak wintertime, there was coldness enough in the January air and the forsaken landscape . . .

The path rose high above the Ewenny River and the grey's hooves rang sharply upon the frosted winter air. Glancing back, Joshua glimpsed the snaking curve of the water and the giant wheel of the mill; its slow monotonous tread churning the waters into splashing foam. As the mare cantered past the bleak and ruined walls of Ogmore Castle, Joshua felt an indescribable melancholy, an ache of regret for the decay and passing of all mighty and splendid things, whether of stone or flesh. When the castle fell, as prize to the Norman knight, William de Londres, had he believed that it would stand for ever, proud, invincible as he? Joshua wondered. A perpetual memorial to his greatness? Yet now it lay as useless and forgotten as those who had laboured upon its mighty walls. And some there are who have perished as though they had never been . . . the words sprang unbidden to his mind, and he shivered involuntarily, his hand leaving the reins to tighten his coat about him. Strange that all that remained intact were the monstrous, rough-hewn stepping stones, surfaces worn and pitted by the ravages of weather, and the river's excoriating flow: the relics of everyday usage, as anonymous and grey as the men who had fashioned and borne them.

His sense of humour and reality returned when he saw below the antics of some venturesome wild ducks which had sought the shelter of the river mouth. The surface of the water bore a skin of opalescent ice upon which the ungainly creatures slithered and jostled, for all the world like mischievous children upon a slide, each demanding its turn, while, all about, the gulls and delicate-legged waders watched disdainfully.

He found himself smiling with genuine amusement, and the sight and cries of a skein of geese veering above the green mudflats of the estuary in graceful flight, further lifted his spirits. He heard the rhythmic beating of their wings and their strangely plaintive cries as clearly as if he flew with them, effortless and free.

Life went on, comic or tragic, filled with beauty or pain. It was life itself which survived, and for this small moment in eternity, he and Rebecca were privileged to be a part of it. Even as he thought of her, the wide sweep of gravel crunched beneath the mare's feet and he rode past rolling lawns and shrubbery to the porte-cochere of Southerndown Court. Almost before he dismounted, a groom was at his side to take the grey. The door was opened by a young footman, while the butler came forward to greet him with deference, and another footman relieved him of his hat and cloak.

Rebecca, unaware of his coming, was incarcerated with Mrs Crandle, discussing arrangements for the planned betrothal party for the three hamlets, but Joshua had no doubt that news of his arrival would see her rushing impulsively, dark hair flying, to his side. He begged that Sir Matthew, who was closeted in the library with his estate manager, should not be disturbed, and made his way to the little schoolroom, which Rebecca so loved, to wait for her there.

It was not Rebecca who entered when he glanced up, expectantly, but Humphrey Edmonds, bearing a portfolio – seemingly so engrossed in his thoughts that for a time he was unaware that he was not alone. When he saw Joshua, his pale composure slipped for a moment, and he hesitated awkwardly, unsure of what he should do. Joshua had a brief, startling insight into Edmonds' real feelings, as surprise, fury and contempt chased swift as shadows across the normally expressionless face, to be replaced by a careful smile. Joshua Stradling, gentleman and prospective owner of Southerndown Court, was altogether a different prospect from Stradling, low constable, the butt of his companion's ill humour, and his own, at Tythegston.

'Edmonds.' Joshua's nod was curt to the point of formality.

'Mr Stradling,' returned Edmonds with a bow. 'I was not informed of your coming.'

'Nor was there any reason why you should be, sir,' returned Joshua. Then, taking the sting from his words enquired, 'You are well, I trust, and happy in your employment?'

Edmonds flushed at the implied thrust about their relative positions, saying coldly, 'Sir Matthew is a most considerate man, sir. The type of gentleman I have long been used to mixing with . . .'

'Then you are fortunate indeed,' said Joshua without rancour, for he had intended no snub. 'Long may it continue, sir.'

Edmonds nodded, and turned to leave, but Joshua halted him with the enquiry, 'And your two companions, sir? Their stay in Ireland proved productive? Congenial?'

The simple question threw Edmonds into such fierce confusion that Joshua felt almost sorry for him. The tutor's sallow skin grew flushed, and his garbled words of explanation almost incomprehensible as he finished, '. . . so I know nothing of their plans, sir, or their whereabouts, not being considered worthy of their confidence, as, unlike them, I must work for a living!'

'As I, sir,' replied Joshua easily, adding, 'I believe your . . . family, the Nicholls of Merthyr Mawr House, are at present upon the Grand Tour?'

'That is so,' replied Edmonds stonily. 'They are fortunate in being able to indulge their preferences.'

'And they return when, sir?'

'I am not privy to their comings and goings,' said Edmonds brusquely. 'You had best enquire of their servants, sir, as of all other domestic matters.'

'You do not communicate with them?' persisted Joshua pleasantly. 'I should have thought . . .'

'They are not callow travellers, sir, to whom voyaging is a novelty and a luxury. They are people of refinement and taste, sophisticated and cosmopolitan, bred to such things. They would not feel the need to chart their progress so crudely. If you will excuse me, Stradling.' He bowed fractionally, and left.

Touché, thought Joshua, smiling against his will. Poor Edmonds, abandoned by friends and family alike . . . Yet, it should surely give him no surprise, for he is a most crass, disagreeable fellow, superior only in his own judgement.

Even as Joshua thought it, Rebecca entered, rushing to him, then flinging her arms about him, kissing him with quite unseemly enthusiasm, and Joshua, in abandoning himself to her embrace, willingly abandoned, too, all other thoughts. This pleasing interlude was interrupted, after a little discreet coughing and doorknob rattling, by Mrs Louisa Crandle, that good lady's observance of the social niceties being every bit as rigid and restricting as her newly adopted corsets. There followed a recital for Joshua's benefit of the arrangements planned for the party for the cottagers of the three hamlets, with his advice being sought upon matters of the liquid refreshment and victuals most suited to their tastes and appetites. Mrs Crandle admitted truthfully, and to Joshua's and Rebecca's open amusement, that although it had been her good fortune to supervise many delightful and memorable entertainments, she knew nothing of the habits of the rough hoi polloi.

Joshua, straight-faced, remarked that apart from greater quantities of ale and more substantial fare, such as meat pies for those men of sturdier appetite, she should provide the usual fare.

'It must be an event they will long remember,' he stressed, 'and they will not be looking only for those victuals they might eat at the local taverns. Besides, the ladies must be catered for, as ladies should, with delicacies and sweetmeats, and the tables decorated with fruit and flowers, silver and crystal, and garlanded with swags of greenery, as upon their official betrothal party. If such refinements were a tribute to one's guests, then Mrs Crandle must seek to excel herself in demanding them. There would never be guests at Southerndown Court more deserving of tribute, or more deeply loved, than their friends of the three hamlets.

So instructed, Mrs Crandle declared that all should be arranged, with the provision of fiddlers and other amusements, although she, regrettably, would be absent in London, and so miss the festivities. Sir Matthew, she confided, had suggested that she might visit the London house, for there were certain small commissions he wished her to undertake on his behalf, for which she was uniquely fitted. Although he regretted that it was not during 'the season', she might return, with Rebecca and Elizabeth, at a more salubrious time. Meanwhile, there were friends she could visit, and expeditions to the theatre, dressmakers and shops.

Joshua, realising that Sir Matthew had sought to extricate Elizabeth's mother from the obligation of meeting those who knew of her husband's disgrace, and her son's violent death, and to spare her humiliation, said gently, 'I shall regret your absence, ma'am, for your presence lends grace and pleasure to every occasion. Yet your delicacy of touch and sense of style will make the evening memorable, I am sure, through all your preparations. I thank you, ma'am, for the gracefulness with which you have listened to my few poor suggestions . . .'

Mrs Crandle, pleasure lending colour and prettiness to the pale skin 'neath the faded red hair, curtseyed low, requesting them to follow her into the drawing-room, where Sir Matthew awaited them to conduct them in to luncheon.

'Prettily done, sir,' said Rebecca, dropping a kiss upon Joshua's cheek when Louisa Crandle was safely outside the door. 'Why do you not make such pretty speeches to me?'

'Because,' he replied, sweeping her into his arms and kissing her noisily and deliberately, and with quite unnerving passion, 'my mouth, and senses, are better employed so . . .'

Rebecca drew away, laughing at the absurdity, declaring loudly enough for Mrs Crandle to hear, 'Unhand me, sir! Pray control yourself! A lady should not be treated thus . . .'

As Mrs Crandle's scurrying footsteps were heard returning, Joshua slapped Rebecca across her bustle, hard, and hurriedly composed his features to say, in bewilderment, 'I but offered you my arm, Miss de Breos. I find your absurd sense of humour offensive, ma'am, rather than droll, and ill befitting your status as a gentlewoman. Such flights of fancy need to be curbed, ma'am, else they will lead to trouble. I fear Mrs Crandle would not be pleased.' He glowered at her accusingly.

'You are quite right, Mr Stradling,' said Mrs Crandle

severely. 'I have tried, in vain, to curb such unladylike excesses. I can only hope, sir, that Rebecca will learn from your words and example.'

Luncheon was a fine, leisurely meal, with the good humour of the company adding spice to the excellence of the board. To compound Joshua's pleasure, Sir Matthew had invited Elizabeth and her mother and his former tutor, Dr Peate, who kept them vastly amused with his anecdotes and wicked impersonations of dignitaries whom he had found pompous and condescending. By tacit agreement, there was no talk of the highwayman, or Joshua's searches, although news was eagerly demanded of those in the three hamlets, and Joshua's family, who were to attend the betrothal party. Joshua noticed Dr Peate fidgeting impatiently during this exchange, as if preparing himself to speak, and yet, he said nothing, turning aside merely to murmur some pleasantry to Mrs Crandle.

The conversation turned to Devereaux, and their news of him, at which Elizabeth's usual serene composure temporarily deserted her, and she grew unnaturally flustered and ill-at-ease, an occurrence which went unnoticed neither by her mother nor Sir Matthew, who declared him to be, 'an excellent young man in every particular: sound, cultivated and well able to command the ship upon which he sailed, and his own affairs'. A tribute which heightened Elizabeth's colour perceptibly, but with which she evidently found no argument.

Dr Peate deflected attention from her by mention of a book which, he declared, had particularly taken his fancy, and the conversation, to Elizabeth's relief, turned to more erudite and impersonal matters. When the ladies had retired, and Joshua, Sir Matthew and Dr Peate were alone, indulging in masculine banter, and refreshment, Dr Peate confessed, 'I declare that I am in a quandary, Joshua, and do not best know how to approach a matter which has been causing me some distress . . .'

'Indeed, sir?' Joshua replied in some concern. 'I may hope that it is not my behaviour which has been the unwitting cause, for I would not offend you.'

Dr Peate smiled, waving the idea aside, and declaring, 'It is your brother, Aled, sir, who causes my concern. I have spoken to him sharply upon the matter, but to no effect. I am not one to listen to idle gossip and rumour, sir . . .' he broke off awkwardly.

'Pray continue, Dr Peate,' said Joshua,' for I know that you have only Aled's interests at heart, as, indeed, those of all your pupils, present and past.'

'It is a delicate matter, sir, concerning a young woman, an actress lately come from Ireland. A person, by all accounts, of low morals and reputation . . .' Seeing Joshua's involuntary smile, he continued, 'No, sir, this is no mere peccadillo, a schoolboy's kicking over the traces! It seems she has embroiled him in gaming for high stakes, and he mixes with dangerous company at her house, men of but low tastes, idle and degenerate, and women who were best avoided, for reasons which I need not specify . . .'

'You think I might have some influence upon him, sir?' demanded Joshua. 'Then I shall speak to him as soon as I am able. Yet I cannot swear as to the result, for he is above age, and responsible, in law, if not in fact, for his own conduct.'

Dr Peate nodded, observing sadly, 'I do not wish to alarm your parents unnecessarily, Joshua, yet, in all conscience, I feel that it is my moral obligation to tell them of this affair before it is too late to extricate him without lasting harm. Aled is a warm, generous-minded fellow, but impressionable, impulsive, too easily led. He has neither your stability nor your sense of commitment or duty.'

Joshua put a reassuring hand upon Dr Peate's frail arm, promising, 'Have no fear, sir, I shall do whatever is necessary. Aled respects you, as do I, and all who have come under your influence and care.'

Sir Matthew, seeing that Dr Peate was unusually grieved and disturbed by the whole episode, replenished his friend's glass, deftly turning the conversation to talk of wine, and its undoubted benefits. Thence, he questioned its value in literature, a subject upon which Dr Peate was persuaded to discourse with wit and authority, his agitation lessening as he grew progressively more eloquent.

There was but time for a brief discussion about the highwayman, Joshua's task at the Port, and the affairs of the Vale, before Sir Matthew bade him, 'Seek Rebecca's youthful company, rather than desiccated antiquities such as we, for you will wish to be away before dark.'

Dr Peate slyly and with an expression of extreme innocence declared that there was a question of etiquette which would occupy Mrs Crandle's attention, and his own, for some considerable time, and that he must seek her out that very minute, for it would not wait. So, courteously taking his leave of Sir Matthew, Joshua sought out Rebecca.

When she was dressed warmly in a pretty hooded cape of softest jade-coloured wool to keep out the chill, and he elegantly cloaked and hatted, they walked some distance from the house to a small gazebo which, in summer, bore a dark waterfall of Reine des Violettes roses. Now it seemed bleak and wintry as the grey rocks and foaming sea below. Rebecca let fall the hood of her cape, her dark hair a cloud about her delicately boned face, eyes wide 'neath the thick-fringed lashes.

'You had best take advantage of me now, sir!' she advised, smiling mischievously, 'for I fancy even Dr Peate's wiles and eloquence will not long detain Mrs Crandle!'

Joshua needed little urging to take her into his arms and kiss her eyelids, cheeks, and the soft, warm mouth, eager and responsive to his own. There were no thoughts of the morrow now, only an exquisite sweetness of feeling.

There would come a time, he thought, when they would truly be one, joined in flesh and spirit, a consummation inevitable and rhythmic as the ebb and flow of the tide . . . For now, he was content to breathe the fragrance of her skin and hair, that warm, indefinable smell of womanhood, and the promise of love. It was enough. He would gladly wait.

Chapter Sixteen

Riding home through the softly falling dusk, Joshua was grateful for the lanthorn which Rebecca pressed him to take, declaring that it would be dark ere he reached his cottage, and she would not have a wink of sleep, fearful for his safety.

As he breasted the final stage of Three Steps Hill, there came one of those glorious, unexpected winter sunsets: that last consuming burst of fiery colour before night extinguishes the sun. The sky, westward, was streaked with saffron, purple and rose, the sun a circle of flame, alive and translucent as a hand held against a candle. It lit upon the horizon in a bar of molten gold, cutting pathways of colour through the grey sea. So strange and moving was it, in its beauty, that Joshua halted the mare to watch until the last arc of crimson sank below the tide, as if extinguished in its deep waters. Then, upon an impulse, he turned the mare towards Stormy Downs, and the shepherd's long-forsaken hut.

He had taken the precaution of arming himself with a small pistol, with a mother-of-pearl grip, more suitable, he thought wryly, for a lady to defend her virtue! Yet, he had not wanted to travel to Southerndown Court unarmed; nor had he wished to alarm Rebecca, Elizabeth and Mrs Crandle by making his fears, and the gun, too plainly visible. Now he felt it, small and delicate, in his palm as he climbed quietly from the saddle, laying his lanthorn upon the ground to fasten the mare to the trunk of a tree abutting a dry-stone wall. Then, taking the lighted lanthorn in his hand, he crept forward stealthily towards the stone hut, his boots making no sound upon the grassy verge bordering the crudely hacked drainage ditch.

The hut was little more than four high stone walls under a roof of slatted timber and ancient slates, broken and decrepit. There was no window, merely a blank hole covered with raw sacking and Joshua, creeping forward, saw against it the flickering glow of a candle's light. Surprise was in his favour, and the swiftness of attack as, with his mouth dry and pulses leaping, he forced himself forward to kick open the rotting wooden door.

He could not be sure what it was that hurled itself at him, yelling, snarling, as a huge cudgel swept past his head, taking his silk hat with it, before cracking itself with a bone-breaking thud against the wall of the hut. So confused was he that he let the pistol fall to the floor, raising the lanthorn to see a shape hurling itself towards him, face distorted, all flailing arms, and legs viciously kicking.

'Emrys!' Joshua cried, 'for God's sake stop, man! It is I, Joshua . . .' But Emrys had wrestled him fiercely to the ground, and it was an unconscionable time before his cry was heard and his assailant allowed him to wrench himself free of his grasp, breathless and dishevelled.

'Oh, Joshua . . .' mumbled Emrys, scarlet and shamefaced in the light of the lanthorn which he had retrieved and handed back, one pane of its glass broken into ragged slivers, candle guttering.

'Perhaps you had better explain, sir!' Joshua picked up his pistol and thrust it savagely into his pocket.

'It was Illtyd,' said Emrys, shuffling awkwardly in his quarryman's boots. 'He told me of the highwayman, do you see . . .? I could not help with tomorrow's outing at the docks, fearing to lose my work at the quarries. So I resolved to stay at the quarry-floor shed, where we store the detonators and equipment. Then, when it was dark, I hid the pony and cart, and settled myself here. Be damned if I did not take you for the highwayman, Joshua, you being done up like a proper gentleman!'

'Well, I thank you for that thought,' said Joshua, smiling involuntarily, 'and for your actions, despite the fact that you all but took my head off with that blow . . .'

Emrys had appropriated Joshua's lantern, and was poking about in the ditch with his cudgel, to emerge with Joshua's silk hat, slimed, bedraggled, and smelling foully of stagnant filth.

' 'Tis lucky it was your hat and not your head . . .' He began to laugh, and soon Joshua was laughing unrestrainedly with him, tossing the hat deftly back whence it came.

'You had best be gone, Joshua, and I will fetch my cob and cart,' said Emrys, 'for with all this commotion, our bird will surely have flown, not to return . . .'

Joshua nodded. 'I have a hard day ahead of me tomorrow, Emrys, and after that almighty blow you struck, I swear that if I cannot have you at my side, then I thank God that I do not have you against me!'

Upon his return from Southerndown Court, and his abortive assault upon the shepherd's hut at Stormy Downs, Joshua rode straight to the Port. Rawlings had taken a small cottage there, reasoning that his unconventional life style and nocturnal hours would defeat even the most tolerant of lodging-house keepers.

He greeted Joshua with pleasure, and an offer of ale

which was gratefully accepted, and Joshua explained his dishevelment with an account of Emrys's assault upon him. Rawlings was vastly amused, ribbing Joshua unmercifully and claiming that he had been too polite to mention the disorder of his dress, assuming, quite naturally, that the constable had been caught in flagrante delicto by some irate husband, and was come seeking sanctuary. Then, with a few well-chosen phrases about the inadvisability of telling the justice of the farce enacted at the shepherd's hut, he replenished Joshua's ale, and talked of the affair at the Port.

The information gleaned by the exciseman who had been smuggled in to work as a haulier upon the horse-drawn tramroad, was that the bounty would be secreted in the first wave of wagons to leave. There were five loads, following in rapid succession, all of Scandinavian pitprops, and all to be delivered to the same colliery at Maesteg. There were two men to each team of horses and tram, and the informant did not know which were Penbraze's henchmen, and which of those employees of the company were drawn unwillingly into the intrigue, as Morris had been. The plan was simple. There was a disused forge and smithy some four miles inland from the Port, in remote countryside: ill-populated now, and not easily accessible because of marsh and scrubland. Here the wagons would be halted, briefly, and the stolen property unloaded and stored. After the reloading, when the horses and men had continued their journey, a band of Penbraze's hired roughnecks would ride in to retrieve the spoils and take them to a safe place, to be shared out, or set aside to be sold to the highest bidder. There were, it seemed, many outwardly respectable tradesmen who did not enquire too deeply into the source of such profitable merchandise . . .

'And the expected time of this unholy convoy?' asked Joshua.

Rawlings jabbed a finger at the map spread before them. 'It arrives at this spot, the old blacksmith's shop, between ten o' the clock and the half hour, unless some untoward incident occurs, a derailing, or the slipping of a load . . .'

'Then we will need to leave early, to find the best vantage point to hide ourselves, before Penbraze's men ride in to recover the goods.'

Rawlings nodded. 'Hutchings, my informant, does not know whether they will ride in, or already be installed and waiting to help with the unloading. Their presence would not be observed and remarked upon in such an isolated spot. The cottagers and smith are long gone, and few go to the place, even to gather rushes to make rushlights, for the ground is grown boggy and treacherous.'

'Then we had best have a care for our horses and ourselves,' said Joshua, smiling and rising.

'And for our silk hats!' agreed Rawlings slyly. 'For some of us cannot afford to be profligate and toss them into the mire should they become lightly soiled.'

'The justice would wish not only our hats in the mire, but our heads, should we fail,' Joshua reminded him, not wholly in jest.

Upon leaving Rawlings at the Port, Joshua turned the mare towards Nottage, to apprise Illtyd and Clatworthy the blacksmith of the plan for the morrow, and the time and place of their departure. Clatworthy readily offered to guide Joshua's party, 'knowing', as he said with pride, 'every stick and stone upon the way, even blindfold, for I was an apprentice at that very forge, until the old smith died and the hamlet grew deserted'.

Joshua, resisting all Sophie's and Illtyd's warm pleas

to take refreshment at their cottage aside the forge, rode thence to Jeremiah's house to give news of Rebecca and Elizabeth, first halting at the Ancient Briton to see Proudfoot, the landlord. Joshua bade him take charge of the attack, should need arise, for Rawlings and he would be intent upon secretly following the wagons along the horse-drawn tramway, lest any of the hauliers, finding that all was discovered, sought to flee to the Port to warn Penbraze. This being agreed, and Jeremiah also told, Joshua returned his grey to the stables at the Crown, delivering her into the willing hands of a stablelad, then mounted the stone staircase to Emily's coach loft to gain news of Morris, before returning for rest to his cottage.

Ossie and Emily were there, seated, leaping to their feet with confused and almost incomprehensible stories of the day's events. So voluble were they in their eagerness that Joshua had to bid them speak one at a time, and quietly, for the sake of his sanity and the child sleeping in the curtained-off alcove. Whereupon, Ossie politely deferred to Emily, and she to him; the silence stretching so long that he had to beg someone to say something ere daylight come!

'Yes, Elwyn Morris is much improved,' Emily answered his original query. 'John, Dr Burrell, is convinced that there are no internal injuries, although the beating had been severe, and he is still in much distress. But, oh, Joshua, such a day we have had of it! Dafydd paid a visit here, upon the farm cart, with James Ploughman who was delivering potatoes here at the Crown, to Tom Butler . . . Haulwen, knowing full well that the boy had but half an hour to wait while James Ploughman unloaded the sacks and refreshed himself within, begged that he be allowed to see the donkey . . .' She paused expectantly.

'So?' demanded Joshua, bewildered.

'So, sir, despite my stern warnings and entreaties that

she remain within the courtyard and not venture without, she took the donkey to graze upon the green, with that poor boy following unwillingly and trying, vainly, to dissuade her, yet fearful to inform me lest she be punished for her wilfullness.'

'She was not harmed in any way?' Joshua's voice was sharp with anxiety.

'No, but no thanks to her!' blurted Ossie, unable to restrain himself a moment longer. 'For no sooner were they settled upon the green than a stranger approached, taking her by the the arm, and demanding if she were Elwyn Morris's child. When she did not reply, he shook her most roughly, and tried to drag her away, to abduct her, but she kept firm grip of the donkey's halter, screaming, and refusing to loosen her hold . . .'

'What then?' asked Joshua, alarmed.

'The boy, Dafydd, went to her aid, laying about the man with a stick which he had picked up from the grass, clouting him about the head and shoulders until the ruffian, incensed, turned upon him instead. He wrenched the stick away and would have leathered the boy cruelly but, after a few blows had fallen, the donkey went to his aid, kicking the villain near senseless, and all but over the churchyard wall . . .' Ossie began to cackle, appreciatively, adding, 'It was lucky that Tom Butler had set that sweeping boy upon watch, who ran, at once, into the Crown. Within minutes the green erupted with furious ale drinkers from the inn, and the culprit was beaten and manhandled within an inch of his worthless life! He was fortunate to escape with his skull unbroken . . .'

'Where is he now?'

'Awaiting your pleasure, sir, in the cell next door, watched over while Tom Butler mobilises the gaol-coach. I knew you would be delighted, and told him so!'

'Indeed,' agreed Joshua, trying to stifle his tiredness, 'it is an excursion I would not miss for the world. I had best make myself ready to ride escort.'

'One other thing,' cautioned Ossie, 'Ezra drove here in as foul a temper as can be imagined, demanding to see you at once, to lodge a complaint, and insisting upon recompense.'

'He has been injured?' asked Joshua.

'No. Only his pride! It seems he set out in his funeral cart to visit the windmill upon the Downs. As he rode up Dan-y-Graig hill, he saw that he was being followed by two ill-natured villains upon horseback. Fearful that they would learn of Elwyn Morris's whereabouts, he drove all the way to Bridgend, pausing only to pay his toll at the turnpike, arriving with them still in fierce pursuit.'

'What did he do then?' demanded Joshua, concerned.

'Drove to the market, thinking to avoid them, but the knaves left their mounts, and followed him within, hot upon his heels. In desperation, he ran to the shelter of a stall, and bought eggs and butter and some salt codfish, spending every farthing he could lay his hands upon . . .'

'He managed to evade them, then?'

'Indeed not!' said Ossie, 'for when he emerged, they were there beside him, and he was so afeared, he dropped the eggs and was about to flee, or scream for aid, when the fellows stepped behind the stall, thanking him most courteously for his custom . . .'

There was a burst of laughter from Ossie which Joshua and Emily joined in, so wholeheartedly that it aroused Haulwen from her makeshift bed. She pulled aside the curtain, dishevelled in her nightgown, rubbing eyes heavy with sleep, to declare solemnly, 'My donkey is a hero, Constable Stradling, sir. He kicked a wicked man up into the air, but Ossie says that had *he* been there, he would have kicked his backside from here to Nottage . . .'

'I don't doubt it,' said Joshua, with commendable gravity, 'Ossie is a very remarkable man.'

Upon the morrow, when the sunrise was streaking the heathery sky with colour, Joshua arose too. He had returned from the gaol-house at Pyle, his truculent and uncommunicative prisoner safely behind bars, to snatch a few hours of sleep. Even that had proved restless and shallow, thoughts of the day's events, and the adventure to come, dragging him remorselessly to the surface . . .

He washed at the well in the yard, needing the coldness of the air and the iciness of the water to shock him into wakefulness. Then, returning to the kitchen of the cottage, he stirred the fire into life and made a hearty breakfast of cold fat bacon, oat bread and salted butter and strong ale. It was a ritual he was careful to observe, not knowing when he might next eat. Dr Peate might have deemed it some primitive atavistic instinct, Joshua thought, amused: an animal urge to equip himself for battle and survival. 'And the condemned man ate a hearty meal', he quoted aloud as he pulled on his knee boots and jacket, and prudently banked the fire with turf. Then, donning his helmet and seeing all was safely secured, he walked to the Crown Inn for his grey.

Rawlings and he had agreed to meet at one of the large stone barns at Nottage, where they could obtain shelter and keep watch unobserved through one of the arrow slits in its thick walls. There was no mistaking the sound of the first six-horse team approaching, with the rattling clang of the tram wheels and chains upon the iron rails, the cries of the men, and the snorting and straining of the passing beasts, their hooves clopping in steady rhythm.

They waited patiently until the fifth and last team had

passed, then stealthily followed, keeping a safe distance. The land through which the tramroad had been driven was lush and fertile, mostly pasture, with plump Jacob sheep and herds of drowsy cattle which looked up enquiringly as they passed by, their sleep already disturbed by the pine-laden wagons.

Soon, the flanks of Stormy Downs were distanced to the right, lightly veiled and softened with winter mist, while on their left loomed the shadowy blur of Margam hills, the ancient abbey lost in purple-green woodlands; and, far beyond, the distant, brooding shapes of the Maesteg mountains. It was to these gaunt and stony risings, their lower slopes and valleys scarred with long streets of dark pithouses, and darker pits, that the cargo was bound . . .

Now, the countryside was changing as they rode, the pastures giving way to winter ferns, grown brown and sapless, tangled bracken and stretches of marshland, fed by underground rivers and bristled with clumps of rushes where the horses' hooves sank and oozed mud.

'Here!' called Rawlings. 'Be prepared . . .'

But there was no need for his shouted warning: the noise and confusion of pitched battle clotted the cold air as they rode forward with pistols raised.

The tramroad was a chaos of terrified horses, and more terrified hauliers battling to control them as, with pitprops strewn dangerously all around, the beasts tried to flee the noise and confusion. Their handlers clung desperately to the leaders' chains knowing that, light of load, the crazed animals would bolt and overturn the wagons, injuring themselves and all in their way.

In every direction there were horses running wildly, their riders having been flung to the ground, or too engaged in the unloading of the spoils to see them safely tethered. There was a fiendish battle raging, on horseback and on foot, with the clashing of staves, the crack of wood upon flesh and bone, and the triumphant yells of the attackers amid the shouts of the injured. Added to the fury of sound and sights were the mingled smells of animal sweat and excreta, the dankness of marsh and the clean, astringent sharpness of pine resin.

Joshua halted the grey, briefly, undecided as to whether to ride into the fray, or to make for the forge and smithy, where the stolen goods had been thrown but, even as he hesitated, Rawlings was away on his black gelding, and making for the open entrance of hewn stone.

Joshua, glancing about for his own small group, identified Jeremiah, straight and forbidding, on a high-spirited mare from Ossie's stables. He was laying about him with a stave as he rode, eyes wild and restless as the mare's, his grey hair and beard streaming free as her mane . . . Like an Old Testament prophet, wreaking vengeance, thought Joshua, amused, as Jeremiah unseated another victim with a single blow, to ride on, triumphant . . .

Clatworthy was fighting, stave to stave, with a fellow nearly as massive as he and, even as Joshua watched, the enemy's stick was sent flying to the marshy ground, which oozed and sucked beneath their feet. A mighty blow of Clatworthy's fist and its owner lay beside his weapon, only to be hauled back from the oozing turf, dripping black slime, then lifted bodily into the air, and hurled aside . . .

Illtyd was darting to and fro into the midst of the action, swift and untouchable, delivering a sharp blow here, a kick there, as he rode by upon his miniature piebald, until unseated and held squirming by a giant of a man, with fists like raw hams. When Proudfoot, seeing his plight, thwacked the attacker in the small of the back with a crack of his staff that all but broke the offender's spine, Illtyd scrambled up, muddy but unharmed, to leap upon the piebald, and away into action again.

Daniel the wheelwright was there, too, although there had been doubt about his fitness after a vicious bout of the shivering ague. It had left him, Hannah, his wife, had confided, weak and listless. There was no sign of it now as he traded blow for blow with a glowering giant of a man, their fists thudding like sledgehammers upon each other's flesh as they staggered, but stoically held their ground. Just when it seemed that the battle was so even that they must both fall exhausted into the mire, Illtyd rode past sweeping his staff down the bend of the enemy's knees. The villain fell with an oath and a groan, to lie upon the spongy turf, relieved, perhaps, to have found escape . . . Effective, if unsporting, Joshua thought smiling, as Illtyd saw him and saluted with his pole before rejoining the fight.

Bloodied and bruised, unseated but game, Joshua's survivors refused to be beaten.

Joshua raised his pistol high, and fired a shot. There was a moment of stunned silence as all action ceased, and Rawlings rode to his side. 'My man, Hutchings, knows you all,' Rawlings cried loudly, 'and will vouch for those of you who have been coerced into this crime against your will . . . If you would fight on the side of the law, step forward now!'

There was some agitated shuffling and awkwardness as six of those hauliers employed upon the tramroad stepped forward, still clutching the horses' chains to calm them. Rawlings bade Hutchings identify them without delay, and having testified to their veracity and reluctance to be a part of the affair, the hauliers were told to wait where they stood, for instruction. Joshua then bade his men bring forward their prisoners and secure their wrists with the cords they had brought. All others were to remain standing, and to surrender themselves. If they chose to try and escape, he declared firmly, then they would fall to the exciseman's bullets, or his own . . .

As swiftly as it had begun, the fracas was ended. Penbraze's four stalwarts, upon the trams, showed neither spirit nor resistance, and those who had ridden in to recover the stolen merchandise showed as little will.

With the nine prisoners securely bound, and Hutchings, the exciseman, who had identified them as troublemakers, standing guard over them implacably with a pistol, the task of reorganisation began.

The six remaining hauliers who had been bullied and intimidated into Penbraze's service were desperately eager to make amends, and with the minimum of fuss and the maximum of speed uncoupled the teams of horses, reharnessing them to face the direction from which they had travelled. This accomplished, Joshua and Rawlings' men, under Joshua's direction, emptied the first and second wagons entirely of pitprops, leaving them piled aside the tramroad. It was hard and dirty work, for the pit-props were heavy and awkward to handle, and it was executed after much sweat and effort, and to an accompaniment of jeers and profanities from the prisoners, which did nothing to improve their tempers. However, when they were then instructed to load the captives into the first wagon, it was done with a zeal and enthusiasm which did them credit. If Joshua noted their new-found vigour, he wisely did not comment upon it.

This agreeable duty completed, Rawlings, leaving Hutchings on guard, turned his attention to retrieving the stolen goods from the defunct smithy, marshalling his men into transferring the booty of spirits, tobacco, victuals, cloth and personal treasures stolen from the passengers into the remaining empty wagon. Joshua's band meanwhile had, with some difficulty, captured the five horses set running by Penbraze's horsemen and, leading one apiece, had stationed themselves alongside the horse-drawn tramway, with Rawlings' men mounted upon the other side of the rails. So, at a signal, the bizarre little caravan moved off, with Joshua and Rawlings at its head.

One of the excisemen had early been dispatched to the colliery at Maesteg to give news of the capture and the fate of their pitprops, for none could ride back from there, to the Port, in time to alarm Penbraze. The strange procession of horses and captives, cargo and riders, was halted near Nottage, safely apart from the village. Then, with Hutchings as guard, the prisoners still protesting feebly about the roughness of the ride, and their bonds and bruises, Joshua chose one of the hauliers to ride with him to confront Penbraze. The rest, he knew, would be occupied in controlling their teams, but would be eager and willing to give evidence against the Cornishman when need arose. Illtyd was then dispatched upon his piebald to inform Tom Butler at the Crown that the gaol-coach would be needed, and any other conveyance which could be found, to transport the villains to Pyle. Ossie was to send all the stableboys he could spare to fetch their five mounts, and give them feed and stabling; and a messenger was to ride, at once, to the justice with news of events. When all was arranged to their satisfaction, Rawlings dispatched his excisemen to the Port, bidding them enter singly, and from different directions, so as not to cause comment and suspicion, and afterwards to mingle unobtrusively with the workmen upon the quays, but to be ready to act upon the command. Joshua's men were ordered to await the arrival of the stableboys and, when relieved of the spare horses, to follow circumspectly to the docks, to render whatever aid might be needed.

The confrontation with Penbraze had been planned to the finest detail. The harbour master was to summon him to his office, upon some pretext relating to the loading of coal for the Duffryn-Llynfi Company, which employed him. While he was thus engrossed, Joshua would enter, armed, and confront him. Rawlings, meanwhile, would escort Preedy the haulier about the port to identify Penbraze's known lieutenants, that the excisemen might take them unawares.

Joshua strode purposefully to his mission, pausing outside the harbour master's office to take out his pistol, then fling open the door. Penbraze was known to be a swaggering bully of a man, vicious and unpredictable, yet, even he, Joshua was certain, would never dare to use firearms upon Ayde-Buchan and in such a dangerous place. Were he so reckless, Penbraze could not hope to escape capture, and death . . .

As he kicked open the door, Joshua felt the churning of his stomach, and fear quickening his pulses, so that he fancied that they beat aloud within his head. He stepped back, expecting the Cornishman to hurl him to the ground, or crash forward to beat away his gun. There was no sound from within. Stealthily, fearing some devilish trick to unnerve or cripple him, Joshua crept forward, pistol held tight, despite the treacherous shaking of his hands upon its grip . . .

Penbraze, gagged and expertly bound, was lying helpless as a trussed fowl upon the floor beside the harbour-master's desk, eyes almost starting from his head with fury; face and neck crimson and engorged. Captain Ayde-Buchan, with a well-polished boot at Penbraze's chest, turned to face Joshua with equanimity, greeting the constable courteously, and explaining in apology, 'I regret, Mr Stradling, that I was forced to abandon our agreed plan. This miserable, snivelling creature attempted to come at me with that axe, sir, which you see embedded in the architrave. He made the mistake of attempting to remove it, to strike again, when I struck him a blow with that brass replica of a ship's cannon which I keep as a paperweight.' He smiled. 'I fear that it has suffered some damage, but it is not beyond repair.'

Joshua, stifling his enjoyment of the scene, demanded, 'You are not harmed, sir? By the axe blows?'

'Not a hair.' And, indeed, he did appear to be as unruffled, and as much in command of the situation, and of himself, as ever. 'I think, Constable, that you will have no trouble with his escaping, for, although self-praise is small recommendation, I assure you that my knots were ever a credit to me, and I practise them constantly.'

Begging the harbour master to keep watch over Penbraze until the rest of his work was completed, Joshua went out to the dockside to look for Rawlings and his men. Even as he turned towards the sound of clattering hooves, as Proudfoot and his band rode in, Joshua heard a hoarse cry, and involuntarily stepped back as a spade clanged fiercely down, striking sparks from the cobbles where he had lately been standing. Clatworthy had not paused for thought, riding furiously down upon Joshua's assailant, his great fist crashing the blackguard into the mountain of coal he had lately been shovelling. The rogue lay there, dazed, unable even to stagger to his feet to escape the avalanche of hewn coal descending about him.

When he, Penbraze, and all the other miscreants, had been herded together into a sorry, bloodstained group, Joshua and Rawlings supervised their removal to Pyle upon the gaol-coach, driven by a beaming Ossie, whose generous gap-toothed smile cheered Joshua almost as much as the success of his mission. Two of the excisemen rode with the ostler upon the box, to act as armed guards over the new batch of prisoners, while the second coach, which was Tom Butler's own and sportingly driven by him, had already been dispatched to Nottage. There the captives from the horse-drawn tram were rudely decanted, and also driven off to Pyle gaol with Preedy as overseer, and two of Tom Butler's brawniest customers, armed with stout clubs, secure upon the 'attic' lest their strength be needed. With nine stout men, trussed, and packed inside, tighter than pickles in a jar, Joshua doubted there would be much resistance . . .

'Indeed,' as he confided to Rawlings, 'their new means of transport offered scant improvement over the old, and a gaol-cell would seem a very Paradise on earth, should they survive to sample it!'

At this, Rawlings, with admirable acumen, suggested that all who remained of the fighting troops, both Joshua's and his own, should adjourn to the Ship Aground for well-earned refreshment. A premise which met with no contradiction.

Once ensconced there in comfort, Captain Ayde-Buchan rose to his feet, making an agreeably terse and witty speech about flagships and ships' companies, and the virtues of command, which left some of his audience confused as to detail, but aware of the heroic tenor of his address . . . There was no confusion, whatsoever, over his closing declaration, 'That all assembled were men he was proud to serve with and, following custom, he would see that they were rewarded with victuals and spirits'. There was a burst of cheering which the landlord led, as the harbour master bade them 'Splice the mainbrace, lads!'.

It was with genuine reluctance that Joshua later excused himself from the celebrations, declaring that it was incumbent upon him to make report to the justice.

He tethered his mare at the iron ring outside his cottage, going within only to make himself presentable for the interview and to snatch a hurried meal, seeing, with gratitude, that his cleaning woman had not only restored order, but prepared him a collation of cold mutton and pickles, and set out the ale, corn bread and a plate of freshly made bakestone cakes. He sat down gratefully only to be summoned by the furious screech of carriage and horses drawing up before his door.

'Hell's teeth!' he muttered with unaccustomed fury. 'What now?'

He opened the door upon the justice's coach, driven by one of the grooms, who leapt down agilely to pull down the steps for the occupant to alight. To his utter confusion, it was Leyshon who stepped out, clutching a strangely shaped parcel, his smile of delight wide over the ruined teeth . . .

'A message, sir, from the justice, within the box.'

Joshua opened it suspiciously, to reveal first, a note in Robert Knight's own hand, reading: 'Stradling, I congratulate you – should this prove too small, I will remedy it!'

Laughing now, Joshua lifted out the new and elegantly appointed high silk hat.

Chapter Seventeen

Hughes, negotiating the small de Breos' coach around the familiar curve of the highway which heralded the approaches to Southerndown Court, sighed despairingly. The young footman, seated beside him upon the box, glanced at him in concern.

The old man is breaking, he thought. This wind is chill for his bones. He cannot much longer endure such work. He stretched out a hand to touch the stout box which housed the pistols and blunderbuss, as if seeking reassurance that his own flesh and blood was still young, unlike the desiccated, misshapen claws which held the reins. He could not imagine what it must be like to be so ancient: body shrunken, hair sparse, deprived of joy and vigour in living . . . 'Twas no wonder the old man sighed! But Hughes's concern was not for himself, but for Miss Elizabeth within the coach. He knew how deeply these visits to her father moved and distressed her. Yet always she emerged composed, head held determinedly high, face a pale concealing mask. Hughes could not but admire her courage. But today the mask had slipped and there had been tears blurring the dark eyes, and still raw upon her skin. He had taken her hand to steady her upon the steps of the carriage, unable to tell her of his pity and affection for her, even by the pressure of his fingers upon her own, or a word. Yet she must have read it in his eyes, for she smiled gently at him as if he had spoken aloud, and touched his shoulder in understanding.

Oh, it was wrong! he thought. Wickedly wrong, that one so young should bear so much responsibility and hurt . . . It was not his place to judge his betters. That power was God's alone. But Mrs Crandle had a great deal to answer for on the day of judgement. It was as well that God was forgiving . . .

Hughes had eased the horses skilfully across the driveway and brought them to rest under the porte-cochere, and was about to leap down from the box, before the footman recovered his wits, when he was arrested by the sound of a lone rider approaching, his mount's hooves scattering the gravel beneath. The footman had already reached for his blunderbuss when the horseman came into view, and Hughes laid a restraining hand upon his arm, recognising the visitor, and raising his tricorn in greeting. The rider dismounted and, nodding acknowledgement, strode to open the door of the coach and help Elizabeth to climb down.

'Miss Crandle, at your service, ma'am,' he doffed his silk hat, and bowed gallantly.

'Captain Devereaux, sir.' Elizabeth smiled with genuine warmth and pleasure. 'I am surprised to see you, sir. I confess that I had thought you already upon your ship, the *Pride of Glamorgan*, and bound for Valparaiso.'

'No, ma'am.' His smile was as delighted as her own. 'I could not immediately take up my command. Her sailing is postponed for a week or more. I hold myself ready to embark upon the instant.'

'Then I am sorry, sir, that you have been disappointed.'

'Not disappointed, ma'am,' Captain Devereaux protested with sincerity, 'for my pleasure at seeing you provides the greatest compensation.'

Elizabeth flushed, and inclined her head gracefully at the pretty compliment, saying hurriedly to hide her confusion, 'I confess, sir, that, at first, I mistook you for a stranger.'

'But not an unwelcome one, I hope, ma'am?' Then, recalling the presence of the servants, he continued formally, 'I am here, ma'am, at the invitation of Sir Matthew . . .'

'Then we had best go indoors and find him,' suggested Elizabeth agreeably, 'else you will be frozen to the marrow, and unable to utter a sensible word!' She thanked Hughes civilly, and released him to the coach house as a groom came forward to take Devereaux's mount.

Once within, and relieved of his outerwear by a footman, Devereaux said gently, when they were alone, 'You have been crying, Elizabeth. I cannot bear to think of you being unhappy. I should want to make you happy for every day of your life.' He touched her cold cheeks with his fingertips, wiping away the traces of tears tenderly, and as if it were the most natural thing in the world, and Elizabeth looked at him steadily, not drawing away.

'I have been to visit my father, sir.' Her voice was low. 'I have been weeping not because he failed to recognise me, for he has long been in a world of his own, isolated, secure, with no remembrance of the past. Yet, today, for the first time, he recognised me, saying, "Elizabeth, my love, you have come to take me home, I know. How pretty you are, and how gentle. You were always my special joy".' Her eyes clouded with tears and they ran unchecked down her cheeks, splashing off her mouth and chin, as Devereaux stared, helpless, and pained by her distress.

'I did not know how to tell him it was but a visit,' she continued, 'that he must remain there always, without hope of comfort or release. Then he said, so low that I could scarce hear the words, "I shall be glad to go away, to some other place. Here there is a cloud upon my mind, a cloud upon the moon. Yet, when the light comes, it is too painful, and too terrible to bear, you understand, Elizabeth?".'

'You think he is beginning to recall the past?' asked Devereaux compassionately.

'I fear so. And when remembrance comes, I do not know if he will have the strength to bear the truth of it.' She bent her head, touching the cuff of Devereaux's sleeve as if to gain support from his presence. 'I only thank God that he does not recall the vileness and degradation of that prison cell, the stench of human filth, and vermin. Oh, but he is so pitiful, sir. Shrunken and bewildered, like a lost child. He who was always so strong, and supported me against all the imagined fears and hurts of childhood. It is as though he is now the child, and I his comforter. "You are the strong one, Elizabeth," he said to me. "You will bend and never break. A tree in the wind, surviving the storms because your roots run deep. Your mother is weak, my dear. All upon the surface, pretty blossoms caught by the wind, too fragile to survive. They wither and loose their hold." He spoke in images, his mind feverish.'

'And yet you understood,' said Devereaux gently.

'Yes, I understood. Oh, but he was wrong! I am not strong! My heart is breaking within me, and will never mend. I cannot tell you how pitiable he seemed, that monstrous red disfigurement upon his face, absurd and terrible . . .' She could not go on, and buried her face upon Devereaux's chest, and he held her to him, making helpless sounds of comfort. Finally, when she looked up, he said hesitantly, 'Elizabeth, my dear, I am not a man for fine speeches, for I am much alone, or with other men, and have not learnt the art. Believe me, I love you with all my flesh and mind, and beg that you will not doubt it. I left my ship but yesterday, and sent word to Sir Matthew that I would speak to him upon a subject dear to us both. He bade me come at once. You understand . . .?'

Elizabeth, bewildered and unable to follow his halting discourse, shook her head.

'You are the source and reason for my visit. I wished to first address myself to Sir Matthew, and to your mother, to ask permission, of course. If you will have me, ma'am? Marriage, I mean. Damnation, Elizabeth, will you give me no help? You have me confused. I ask you to marry me.'

'Then, damnation, sir! I accept.' Elizabeth, her face still bearing the traces of tears, smiled radiantly at him, saying, 'I dare say, Roland, that you have not made the most elegant proposal ever uttered, but I vow that I would not have altered a word of it.'

He took her in his arms and kissed her most satisfactorily, afterwards saying gravely, 'I swear, Elizabeth, upon my life and honour, that when we are wed, if there is a possibility of having your father released, then I will spare no effort in bringing him home. If that is what you truly want, my dear . . .'

As she reached up to kiss his cheek, too filled with love and tears to speak, he said, 'Upon receiving word from Sir Matthew, I took the mail-coach to Cowbridge, and there hired a mare from the livery stables, my trunks and other baggage being taken by carrier to my rooms at the Crown. But I have brought one personal gift which I beg that you will accept. It is but a small thing, yet it comes to you with a love which is limitless, I swear.' He removed from his pocket a soft pigskin pouch, and from it took a delicately fashioned gold heart upon a slender chain, fastening it carefully about her throat. Then, after kissing her gently upon the nape of her neck, was gone . . .

Elizabeth traced the outline of it with her finger, discovering that it opened upon a tiny clasp. Inside were the engraved letters: E.C. and R.D. And opposite, the words: 'In your keeping'.

So he had been as sure as she.

Captain Devereaux had left Southerndown Court, driving himself in a gig, at Sir Matthew's insistence leaving his mare to be returned to the livery stables at Cowbridge by a willing groom. His reception by Sir Matthew had been more than ordinarily civil, although the old gentleman had asked questions of him which were uncommonly acute and perceptive, before pronouncing himself agreeable to the courtship.

'Elizabeth,' he declared firmly, 'is as dear to me as a grandchild, and I have grown to think of her as such, sir. I stand in loco parentis, because of the tragic circumstances of her father's detention.' He broke off, then continued compassionately, 'But I have no need to remind you, sir, of that, since the tragedy was also your own.'

'Yes, Sir Matthew, that is true,' replied Devereaux gravely.

'Yet, Captain Devereaux, it is my unhappy duty to speak of it, to press the point, in spite of my reluctance to do so and the anguish it must cause you.'

Devereaux nodded assent.

'Elizabeth's brother, Creighton, murdered your sister. I regret I must speak so bluntly and incisively, it is better thus. There is no way to phrase it more gently, to spare you pain, sir.'

'I understand.'

'Knowing it will cruelly fuel your burden of loss, I must, nevertheless, demand of you whether, at some future time, it might cause you to . . . to turn against Elizabeth, to revile her with the memory of it. No, Captain Devereaux,' he held up a quietening hand, 'do not grow angry at my presumption, nor reply in haste. Think most carefully, sir, then give me your assurance that it will never cause anguish between you, or guilt . . .'

After due consideration, Devereaux said truthfully, 'I feel neither anger, sir, nor resentment, that you should tax me thus. I am only grateful that your affection for Elizabeth and concern for her future are so deep. I can only say that I know Elizabeth's grief for Mary to be as real as my own, and that she offered her the only friendship and kindness that she knew in her brief life. No, Sir Matthew, you may be assured that although the shadow of the past must always lie over us, for such sorrow is inescapable, it will never come between us . . .'

Sir Matthew, taking Devereaux's hand, and placing an arm upon his shoulders, said, 'Then I have no fears in relinquishing Elizabeth's care to you, sir. Indeed, I am grateful that she has the protection of one who will share with her the weight of a burden she has too long borne alone. I need not question you about your love for her, because it is apparent in all you have said and written to me.' He paused before continuing awkwardly, 'I must beg that you will allow me the privilege of settling a suitable property and annuity upon her, as is a grandparent's right. It would afford me honour and pleasure to provide the security her father would have offered had his circumstances remained unaltered.' He smiled. 'Self-indulgence is my only reason, Captain Devereaux. I do not doubt your ability to provide her with all that she requires in life, both materially and emotionally.'

Devereaux thanked him handsomely, with obvious warmth and sincerity, and the two men, relieved of the necessity of any further catechism, relaxed with a bottle of Madeira, to mark the occasion. Dr Peate, who had been hovering near enough to be called, should occasion for celebration arise, was delighted to propose a toast, declaring, 'It is a marriage which will afford me more pleasure than a maturing of the finest vintage. A rare privilege . . .'

To which Sir Matthew replied drily, 'Then I will have no need, sir, to raid my cellar for the nuptial celebrations, since you will be intoxicated enough with the occasion.'

'True,' said Dr Peate, laughing. 'But since you have done me the honour of asking me to dine with Captain Devereaux and Elizabeth, it will not offend me to seek my advice upon the subject. No sacrifice is too great in the search for perfection.'

'Agreed,' said Devereaux gallantly, 'and in Elizabeth, sir, I am pleased to admit I have found it.'

When Captain Devereaux had driven to his rooms at Newton, and the ladies were eagerly discussing plans for Elizabeth's official betrothal party in the early spring, should the captain's voyages permit it, Sir Matthew and Dr Peate adjourned to the library. Once settled, Sir Matthew summoned both Hughes, the coachman, and Rhys, his water bailiff, to enquire of them if there had been any progress in their surreptitious checking into the drawing tutor's movements and associates. It seemed a propitious time to discuss the matter, for Edmonds was absent from the Court, having begged permission to take one of the carriages to Cardiff to purchase supplies of oil paints and other artists' materials for use by his two pupils. It appeared that the young man led a life of frugality, abstemiousness and chastity, which Dr Peate observed tartly afterwards, would have done credit to a Trappist monk . . . There was no hint of scandal attached to his name; no dubious acquaintances. Strangely, no acquaintances at all.

Rhys had volunteered that his brother-in-law, who worked as 'boots' at the inn where Edmonds lodged, believed, although he had no factual proof of it, that the gentleman was too fastidious by far. His was the demeanour of a man overcareful not to be judged and found wanting! Since, as 'bootblack', he was in the rare position of observing the activities of the guests by night, after they had ostensibly retired to bed, leaving their footwear outside their rooms for his attention, he would increase his watch . . . Who was to say that the young man's nocturnal adventures beyond the inn were as blameless as his daily life? With that vague promise of help, Sir Matthew and Dr Peate had to be content for, within the hour, young Edmonds had returned to the house with his purchases, the groom who had accompanied him upon every inch of the expedition declaring unequivocally, that he had made no other purchases, visited no other establishments, and met no one, either by accident or design. Humphrey Edmonds was, indubitably, what he seemed.

Joshua, meanwhile, after a most cordial reception by the justice, Robert Knight, determined that he would ride to the cattle market at Bridgend, where his brother, Aled, was travelling to purchase a much vaunted bull, to renew the herd. The information had been conveyed to him, innocently, in a letter from their mother, who confided that Aled was dispatched there at the whim of their father, who declared that he did not know 'what devil had taken possession of the boy! He is ill-tempered, insolent and slothful! Indeed, he is grown altogether too big for his boots, ma'am, and will soon be cut down to size!'. It seemed, then, that his parents were unaware of Aled's gambling . . .

Joshua, enquiring of the landlord at the coaching inn, was shown through to the private parlour where, to Joshua's displeasure and concern, his brother was entertaining a bunch of drunken, over-loud revellers and, apparently, from the landlord's deference, meeting the bill for their excesses. He arose to greet Joshua, surprised and shamefaced, but acting with exaggerated assurance to hide his discomfiture.

'So, Joshua,' he walked unsteadily towards him, flinging an arm expansively about Joshua's broad shoulders, 'you have bearded the lion in his den . . .?'

There was a burst of drunken laughter and inanities from his companions.

Joshua nodded briefly, but made no answer, looking about him pointedly.

'Damn it!' exclaimed Aled defensively. 'Cannot a fellow have a little innocent amusement without bringing the world crashing about his ears? You have a face sour as an old crab apple, Joshua!' He clapped him hard upon the back, taking his arm persuasively. 'Come, let me buy a measure . . .'

'No, I thank you. My time is brief and my business is with you, alone, sir.'

Before Aled could make reply, a woman who had been seated with him arose to stand beside them, putting a proprietary hand upon Aled's arm, saying mockingly, 'Will you not introduce me to this splendidly dressed . . .

gentleman, Aled?' Her derisive glance took in Joshua's uniform and the splendid helmet he held stiffly to his chest as he stood, a head taller and straighter than any in the room. 'I am afraid, sir, that I do not recognise the regiment!' Her tone was maliciously amused. 'You attend some local fair, perhaps? A fancy dress ball?'

'No, ma'am,' replied Joshua evenly. 'I have not the honour of serving in one of Her Majesty's regiments. I keep the peace as best I can.' He turned abruptly to Aled, but the woman was not to be put off, pouting, tugging at Joshua's helmet, then putting it atop her busily arranged curls, overpainted mouth at first prim then wide with laughter at his discomfiture.

'Caroline . . .' began Aled, fidgeting, then awkwardly retrieving Joshua's headgear, 'I have the honour to present my brother, Joshua.'

Her eyebrows rose expressively. 'Ah,' she cried, sweeping a low curtsey, and extending her hand languidly in answer to Joshua's brief bow. 'So you are a farmer like Aled?' She raised her voice, enunciating with deliberate theatricality, that all might hear, 'We have here a farmer who likes dressing up. A labourer with Thespian pretensions . . .'

'No. *I* have no pretensions, ma'am.'

There was a burst of stifled laughter, at which she turned scarlet, saying scathingly, 'Perhaps you are more at home, sir, in the company of hogs, and muck . . .'

'Indeed, ma'am, I find them a modest preparation for the realities of life . . .' He bowed with exaggerated courtesy and, taking Aled's arm, squired him firmly and unresistingly without.

'Damnation, Aled!' he declared, shaking him roughly. 'Have you taken leave of your senses? What possesses you to seek the company of such idle louts? They are nothing but parasites, blood-sucking leeches! They will bleed you dry, man!'

Aled pulled away furiously. 'What business is it of yours! You damned interfering fool!' His face was contorted with venom. 'This is my life! Keep out of it! I will brook no interference, I warn you! These are my friends . . .'

'Friends? And for how long? Until your money runs out? And that painted doxy, sir? With her posturing and stagey ways, a failed actress! Must you flaunt her publicly to humiliate your family? You are the talk of the Vale, sir!'

'Am I indeed? Then I will give them something better to talk about . . . for I intend to marry her, directly!' He was still unsteady upon his feet, but there was no hesitancy in his speech, no wavering. He turned and started back towards the parlour.

Joshua hurried after him, placing a pacifying hand upon his arm, saying quietly, 'I speak, Aled, because you are my brother, and from affection for you . . . Are you not here on a mission for Father?'

Aled pulled roughly from his grasp, crying, 'Let go my arm! You are not my keeper. Let the farm and my father, and that confounded bull, go to Hell, for all I care! I have slaved long enough. I have better use for the money!'

Yet, even under the heat of the words, Joshua, who knew him so well, recognised the pain and bewilderment, the childhood cry for help. And he knew he was unable to give it.

As he rode back to Newton, disconsolately, upon the grey, cursing his ineptitude, Joshua was disturbed more by the remembrance of his brother's female companion than Aled's gaming debts. There had been about her a brittleness, a feverish, unnatural gaiety which spoke to him of laudanum. He had seen its effects upon Dr Mansel's wife: its decay and bitter corruption. He prayed God that Aled's stupidity and infatuation would not drive him to that.

As he descended the Clevis Hill and rode towards the Crown, he saw Jeremiah's cob and cart, with Charity triumphantly ensconced upon it, driving past the church and towards Pickett's Lease and the sea. The dog, standing firmly on his four splayed legs to survive pothole and rut, lifted his wedge of a head to bark a welcome as Jeremiah raised a hand in greeting, calling back importantly, 'Tonight at the Crown then, Joshua! You have not forgotten, I hope?'

'I would not miss it for the world!' he shouted back, remembering, with remorse, that tomorrow was Jeremiah's and Sophie's wedding day, and tonight, Jeremiah's modest celebration, a fact he had forgotten, so immersed was he in his brother's problems. He knew that Devereaux had brought the gift of an earthenware dinner service from Rebecca, in Sir Matthew's gig. She had wept upon Joshua's shoulder on his last visit declaring that, small informal wedding or not, she *would* attend, despite Jeremiah's earnest pleas that she remain at the Court for her own safety. Only Joshua's stern rebuke that concern for her would cast gloom over the happiness of the day finally persuaded her.

'Yet, highwayman or not, nothing will prevent me from being there in thought and spirit!' she declared, and it was this message that Joshua conveyed to Jeremiah and Sophie, only to be treated to more tears from the tender-hearted bride-to-be.

'I'll be hanged for a lunatic,' exclaimed Jeremiah feelingly, 'if women don't shed more tears at a wedding than a funeral! It is enough to put terror into the stoutest-hearted bridegroom!'

Yet Joshua saw how tenderly he wiped the tears from Sophie's eyes.

The rigours of his bachelor celebrations notwithstanding, Jeremiah arose early on his wedding morn to catch the tide, for a change in life style was no argument for sloth. Then, his preparations for the day completed, he washed at the well in the yard, spurning the shelter of the outhouse or the comfort of heated water, dressed and set out for the church. As he walked, his mind was filled with a thousand memories, long hidden, built up as a coral reef, fragment upon fragment, washed, and revealed fleetingly by the changing tide. The girl he had loved so briefly and taken as his bride . . . unreal now, yet for ever young and unchanging. The child who died . . . Rebecca's coming and the changes she had made. Sophie and Illtyd . . . a new life, a new responsibility. A new adventure. He squared his shoulders resolutely, and walked through the gateway and into the churchyard of the small stone church, then from his buttonhole he took the sprig of rosemary he had culled from the garden of the cottage, and placed it gently upon the turf-covered grave with the smaller grassed spot beside.

'Rosemary for remembrance, my love . . .' he said the words within his mind, but the tears in his eyes were real and, for a moment, the stark branches of the sheltering tree trembled and blurred as mistily as the past, as if a soft breeze stirred them. Then, filled with pity and love, he went upon his way.

When Jeremiah rose from the front pew of the church, with Joshua beside him as supporter, he was dimly aware of the echoing emptiness of the church, the soaring timbers of its saddle-back roof, and its grey stone walls. He felt its cold emptiness echoing the bleakness within himself, in the absence of friends and well-wishers. Yet, it was he who had insisted that it be so: a quiet wedding for propriety's sake, for they were no longer young, and he and Sophie had been wed before . . . Now he wondered if he had been too harsh, although Sophie had listened quietly to all he had said, not seeking to dissuade him from his stubborn way. As the Reverend Robert Knight gravely called them to him at the altar, Jeremiah half turned before mounting the steps to see Sophie, with Illtyd beside her, hunched and awkward in his new clothes, yet with such radiant joy and pride upon his face, that Jeremiah felt his throat tighten with tears. Then, Jeremiah's eyes met Sophie's, and her love and serenity were unmistakable as she gazed steadfastly back. It was at that moment that he knew that whether there were four people present, or four hundred, it made no matter. In spirit they were already joined, making their vows before God, and neither circumstance nor man could again put them asunder.

Outside the church door the rector told them of his pleasure at the union, saying that he must fetch his mount from the stables at the Crown and bidding them first allow him the honour of drinking a toast to the newlyweds' happiness. The four of them accepted with surprised pleasure, and followed him within.

Tom Butler came forward eagerly, and with evident warmth, to conduct them to his small private parlour where, at once, there was a wild explosion of noise and excitement as their closest friends of the three hamlets descended upon them with kisses, a babble of congratulations, tears and hugging. The trestle table was groaning with fare and prettily decorated with silk flowers and streamers which, Jeremiah declared, 'Would not disgrace a May Queen, or my beloved Sophie, who is the prettiest and gentlest of maids ever born.'

The rector spent a considerable time polishing his lenses, which had become quite ridiculously misted over at the happy well-prepared scene of affection and good-will. His toast to the bride and groom was simple and sincere: 'May you always be as surrounded by loving friends as you are today, and may your love for each other grow and deepen . . .'

Jeremiah thought if he loved Sophie any more his heart would break with the joyous hurt of it.

Chapter Eighteen

When the revelry at the Crown was finally ended, late into the night, Jeremiah and Sophie prepared to walk home to the cottage beside the dunes through the wintry moonlight. Joshua and Illtyd, with a much improved Doonan, Rosa and their many friends, crowded cheerfully to the door of the inn.

There, to the newlyweds' astonishment, was Tom Butler's coach, horses and carriage bedecked and ribboned as a Mabsant birch, and Ossie upon the box, spruced up to match.

They left in a hail of good wishes, Ossie first descending regally to press upon them a polished horseshoe to hang above their doorway.

'No luck is needed in a house where there is love,' he declared solemnly, adding, 'still, it is a commodity one cannot have too much of . . . Be sure to hang it the right way up, now, else all the luck will fall out!' His well-rehearsed speech delivered, Ossie ushered them into the carriage with due ceremony, and drove away to resounding cheers which made the horses fidget nervously and prick up their ears, while Sophie grew quite pink and goose-pimpled with pleasure.

When Ossie had left, Jeremiah opened the door and carried Sophie, laughing and protesting at such foolishness, over the threshold, to the frenzied excitement of Charity, who leapt and barked and altogether showed off quite alarmingly, before feasting upon a wedding treat of his own which Tom Butler had thoughtfully packed into a basket. Then he fell to sleeping, gratefully, beside the fading fire.

'We had best follow Charity's example,' said Jeremiah, smiling, yet feeling an awkwardness that things might not be right between them. Jeremiah's small bedroom was cold and unwelcoming, with no covering upon the bare boards, and for the first time he was aware of its inadequacies as the pale moonlight illumined its bleakness.

'You must do what you choose, my dear, to alter it,' he said, and Sophie nodded. She was already abed. She had brushed her dark hair by the light of the candle, and dressed herself in a voluminous nightgown, while he, eyes carefully averted, was divesting himself of his wedding clothes in the darkest corner of the room, nervousness making his hands clumsy and uncertain . . .

Suddenly he stopped, saying, with agitation in his voice and manner, 'Sophie, there are things I must say . . . explain to you . . .'

'My dear,' she said gently. 'What is there to explain? Or excuse? The past has made you what you are, and it is the man you are now I love, and married, Jeremiah. I do not begrudge that poor, dead girl your youth, Jeremiah, nor your love, for it was all that was good in her brief life . . .'

'You are a fine woman, Sophie, and kind,' he said, much moved.

She shook her head. 'No, Jeremiah, I just see things as they are. My husband was a good man. He accepted Illtyd, and never made complaint, or railed against him for what he was . . . and was not. We were never in want. Yet I cannot pretend that I loved him deeply, as with a woman's passion for a lover, for he was a just man, but without joyousness . . .'

Jeremiah in turn nodded his understanding, saying earnestly, 'Sophie, my dear, I have little to offer you, I fear, save my work, and my affection for you and Illtyd, which you cannot doubt. I am not a young man. I have few possessions, save this roof over our heads, and the cob and cart, but I will work for you, and try to make a good life for us all. For Illtyd is as much to me as the son I lost, and will never be aught but my own flesh and blood . . .'

There was a long silence before Sophie said, her voice unsteady, 'I have never doubted it. As for Illtyd, I have never once, despite his frailty, wished him anything but my own dear son, and rejoiced in his living, although I have wept sometimes for his sake, and the harsh resentment of others.'

'You will never be in want again, Sophie, nor Illtyd, I promise.'

'No, and I am glad of that, my dear. But do you not see what I am trying to say to you? Perhaps I put it badly. I mean, Jeremiah, that it is not freedom from poverty I cherish in you, but the freedom to love . . . You are all of my heart, and for the first time in my life, I know the true depth of passion and yearning for the touch and the flesh of another . . . I say it without shame, for it is the simple truth, and I thank God that He has shown me what love can be . . .'

Jeremiah stood there, naked, but filled with such a joy and stirring of love he could not speak, simply taking up a garment to cover himself for decency . . . but Sophie had slipped off her nightgown, and was sitting there, the moonbeams falling upon the white skin of her body, and touching the soft contours of her breasts with light. Yet the light in her eyes was brighter, more luminous, as she said gently, 'No. Do not dress, Jeremiah . . . You need feel no shame or reserve before me. Your flesh is beautiful in my sight. Let there never be anything but joy and openness in our loving, my dear . . .'

And as he moved to the bed, and took her in his arms, burying his face in the sweet softness of her breasts, her dark hair falling about him, the tears were wet upon his cheeks . . . In Sophie, he knew, was forgiveness and comfort for all that was past.

Illtyd had spent the night as the guest of his friend, Roland Devereaux, at the Crown Inn. It was an invitation he had accepted eagerly, partly out of deference to the newlyweds, and partly because he and Devereaux were the best of friends. Joshua had remained with them for a time, as Devereaux spoke of the voyage, tracing the perils and uncertainties of the route, with its sudden unexpected excitements. He did not disguise the deprivation and boredom of shipboard life, yet his enthusiasm for the sea, and the places he visited, re-creating their colour and strangeness, their sights, sounds, and even, Illtyd could swear, the smell in the air . . . Devereaux's news about his courtship of Elizabeth was listened to no less avidly, and with equal delight, and the three of them toasted the proposed union with such enthusiasm that, after Joshua had left, Illtyd swore that he had no need to voyage under sail, the floor of the Crown offered peril enough, rolling more violently than a ship in a storm . . .

Upon the morrow, Devereaux was to return to Southerndown Court, to dine at the lodge with

Mrs Crandle and Elizabeth, who had dispatched, by his hand, written invitations to Illtyd and to Emily Randall, to join them in the celebration. They would travel in the gig upon Sir Matthew's insistence, Devereaux returning it upon some future occasion, when convenient, for he was expected to be a frequent visitor at the Court until his next sailing . . .

The trio set out in some style the next morning, with Captain Devereaux at the reins, the two gentlemen looking, as Ossie unfeelingly remarked, 'frog-eyed and frog-coloured' after their celebrations. Emily was, as always, graceful and serene, in a gown of silvery-green, like the downy newness of horse-chestnut leaves. Ossie bowed to her gravely, and complimented her upon her elegance while bemoaning the inadequacy of her escorts. Then, tongue in cheek, he declared, 'Pray, ma'am, have no fears for Haulwen's safety while in Rosa's and Doonan's care. They will spoil her outrageously. Should Dr Burrell come nigh, I will inform him, at once, of the child's whereabouts, for it has not escaped me how devoted he is to the child's care . . .'

Emily, with high colour, and equal gravity, thanked him as he left with a flourish, chuckling extravagantly at the joke, to Illtyd's and Devereaux's complete mystification as Emily strove to hide a smile.

While the gig continued its elegant journey to Southerndown Court, Rawlings and Joshua were set upon a less salubrious journey, to the court at Pyle. It was the day of the hearings before the justice of the rogue who had tried to abduct Haulwen from the village green, and of Penbraze and his cronies at the docks and upon the horse-drawn tramroad. To Joshua's unalloyed pleasure, the directors of the Duffryn-Llynfi Company had decreed publicly that they would take no action against those poor wretches who had been bullied and blackmailed into helping the Cornishman to commit his crimes. Their concern was with the hard core of confirmed thieves, whose actions had sullied the good name of the tramroad, and of the shipping lines and docks. In addition, the justice announced, beaming delightedly at all save the defendants, there would be an official presentation to Elwyn Morris, when he was recovered, for his public-spirited actions, and to the harbour master, Captain Ayde-Buchan, RN, retired. The constable and excisemen, of course, had merely been undertaking their duties, but were, none the less, to be congratulated upon the efficient manner in which they were executed. Joshua was smiling broadly at the way in which the justice had expressed it, until Rawlings kicked him in warning, when he assumed an expression of suitable gravity and authority, as Robert Knight's gaze alighted upon them both.

'Dear heavens, Joshua!' said Rawlings admiringly when they were safely delivered of their horses, and riding away, 'the justice excelled himself today, in invective and rhetoric. I have never heard him in finer form! What was it he called Penbraze? A debased scoundrel; a spineless degenerate; a worthless husk of a creature, with neither morals nor compassion. No wonder Penbraze wriggled and twisted like a worm upon a hook!'

'I'll wager he twisted more violently at the sentence,' said Joshua. 'Five years' hard labour for the assault upon Morris, and three years for the thefts, with, first, a spell upon the treadmill at a house of correction, to give him pause for reflection . . .'

'Not much chance to pause,' exclaimed Rawlings drily, 'judging by that goose upon the treadmill at the Crown! Although, I agree, 'tis much on a par with

Penbraze for viciousness of disposition and brain power!'

'Perhaps,' suggested Joshua, smiling, 'his strength lies in his legs, like the goose and young Haulwen's donkey! I confess I could scarce keep a straight face when the justice declared that the ass was the only one involved with sense and discrimination . . .'

There was a rattle of wheels upon the highway, and the pounding of hooves, with jangling harness, as Robert Knight approached them, driving a pretty, open gig. 'Gentlemen,' he said, slowing and raising his silk hat expansively, 'I bid you good-day, and a happy issue out of all your afflictions. You will be pleased to learn that the largest shareholder in the Duffryn-Llynfi Company will personally honour Morris and the harbour master.' He passed by cheerfully, chins atremble, only to call back, 'No less than Mr Benjamin Disraeli, himself!'

'Pleased!' declared Joshua, outraged. 'Think of the protection the man will need, and I, the only constable! It will be a madhouse, sir! With Robert Knight clucking and fussing everywhere, like a broody hen!'

'Then,' said Rawlings, urging on his horse as Joshua turned into Tythegston Court behind the justice's gig, 'I hope it will not be you, my friend, who lays the egg!

'I regret, Stradling, that I have received a most distressing communication. One which affords me the greatest disappointment,' declared the justice, frowning.

'Indeed, sir?'

'It seems that Mr Disraeli will not, after all, be able to officiate at the presentation ceremony. Time and pressure of duties preclude it . . .'

'That is indeed a grief and disappointment!'

'Yes, I knew you would judge it so, Stradling.'

'And his replacement, sir?' asked Joshua apprehensively.

'I have been honoured with that privilege, sir . . .'

Joshua beamed quite fatuously, unable to hide his relief. 'Then it will please all honest men, sir. I declare that I am delighted at the prospect!'

Robert Knight, recognising Joshua's evident sincerity, rang for Leyshon, and ordered him to bring a bottle of his finest brandy. He would be pleased to tell Sir Matthew, at Joshua's betrothal party, that the boy was showing distinct promise. Yes. Distinct promise.

In the long white-washed farmhouse set in the rich pasture lands of the Vale of Glamorgan, the talk, as in the hamlets, was of the betrothal party of Joshua and Rebecca. Joshua's father was seated upon the edge of the brocaded half-tester bed pulling on his breeches and looking strangely out of place amidst the feminine frills and delicate furniture. He was stolid, a little below average height, and with that sallow, almost swarthy, complexion which sometimes goes with unusually dark hair. Now, it was made high-coloured with choler, as he declared irritably, 'I tell you, Charlotte, I have a mind to stay at home. I am sick to death with the whole idea of it! Who listens to me? No one! I am ignored. Of less influence upon you all than . . . than a beast of the field!'

His wife, pretty and elegant as her surroundings, smiled from her pillow, for he did, indeed, resemble nothing so much as a fierce, flat-headed bull, snorting and unpredictable.

'I do not know how my sons came by such obtuseness! Joshua, thwarting all my plans to send him to Jesus College, in order to become a low constable, if you please! As for Aled, I swear I do not understand him! He seems to have taken leave of what little sense he had! Absent for three days with those effeminate, posturing friends of his while the farm goes to rack and ruin about me, and, now, the auctioneer tells me, he did not even present himself to bid for that bull! I tell you, Charlotte, I do not know what has taken possession of the boy! He has become unhinged!'

'Perhaps he has developed some romantic attachment, my dear. He is of an age . . .' she suggested mildly. 'You have always encouraged him to make a good alliance.'

'Yes, a good alliance, ma'am! From the rumours I hear, he has taken up with some painted Jezebel, a failed actress, vulgar and penniless, no better than a common slut, ma'am, if you will pardon the expression. Why could he not have found a woman of intelligence and sensibility, like Rebecca?'

'Do you not recall, my dear, that you were inordinately rude to her when first you met?'

'Rude to her! *I*, Charlotte . . .? I fear your memory must be playing you tricks. It is some other young lady of Joshua's you have in mind. You know I am devoted to her.'

'Then you will be pleased to attend the party, sir, for her sake.'

He hesitated. 'Well, I shall wear my ordinary, everyday clothing. I will not be ribboned and bowed like some ageing milksop, so there's an end to it!' he declared, busily fastening his waistcoat.

'Ageing, my dear? I fancied I must have misheard you. Why, you are a fine figure of a man, in your prime, Philip. You have the bearing and authority to set off fine clothes perfectly. I grieve that Joshua and Aled do not possess that . . . quiet distinction. Yet it cannot be acquired, my dear, it is inborn, and what I first noticed in you . . .'

He regarded her doubtfully, saying, 'Joshua tells me

that Dr Mansel is invited. Were you not a . . . close friend of his, Charlotte? Was there not some understanding between you, before we met?'

'He was an acquaintance only, Philip,' she corrected him steadily, 'a young house-surgeon at my father's hospital, and one of many I knew . . .'

Philip Stradling nodded, unconvinced. He would never know why she had chosen him to marry from all the worldly and elegant gentlemen who sought her love. She was the most exquisite and fragile thing he had seen in all his life, and so she had remained. As elusive and decorative as a butterfly, he sometimes thought, but fearful always that his rough, intrusive touch would rub the life and colour from her, as cruelly as the torn membrane stills an insect's wings. Charlotte, who loved him dearly, and knew of his self-doubts, knelt upon the bed and placed her slender arms about his neck, kissing his cheek gently, to his acute pleasure and embarrassment, and declaring, 'I have not seen Obadiah Mansel these many years, but Joshua swears he is grown bald as a bladder of lard, save for a few unsightly wisps of hair, and that he is plumper than a mole, my love. Indeed, not unlike one, it seems, since he fills his skin more tightly, and has the tiniest, most ridiculous legs . . .' She felt a pang of remorse, which she quickly stifled, to continue, 'While you, Philip, have the most elegant of legs, and a figure any man half your age would envy. I declare that you have scarce changed since the day we met, save to grow more handsome and authoritative.'

'Nonsense, my dear!' He disentangled her arms firmly from about his neck. 'You do not have to go to such devious and exaggerated lengths to persuade me. I shall wear the confounded clothes you have purchased for me, since it gives you pleasure, even though I feel like a turkey cock parading his tail and wattles.' He grew suddenly serious, asking abruptly, awkwardly, 'Have you been happy all these years, Charlotte, really happy? I do not mean contented.'

She took his hands in hers and looked steadfastly into his eyes, saying, 'I would never have been as happy with any other man living, I vow. I married you, my dear, knowing you to be a strong, reliable man, severe but just, and someone I could learn to love. You were so different from all those mincing and posturing gentlemen I knew, with no thought in mind save their own pretty faces, fashion and gaming. I thank you, my dear, for teaching me to truly love you, for you are a fine, generous man, and a loyal husband.' She smiled. 'And a good father, whatever your present misgivings . . .' As he made to protest, she placed her fingers upon his lips, saying, 'No, you have asked me, sir, so I will answer honestly! You have given me so much love and faithfulness, a fine home, two wonderful sons . . . You are my rock, Philip, but more than that, my joy. Without you, I would have nothing, for all would be dross and ashes.'

'Charlotte,' he said, bewildered. 'I cannot believe, understand . . . How . . .?' he broke off helplessly.

'There is more, Philip, if you will but listen . . . I am alive only when I lie, protected, in your arms, my body and spirit one with yours. You have taught me that there is a joy in giving. I confess that such joy as I feel in my two strong sons is only exceeded by the ecstasy that went into their making . . .'

'Charlotte!' he admonished, truly scandalised. 'I had never believed you capable of such wantonness. Yours is not the attitude of a lady, ma'am, for ladies neither think nor speak of such basely . . . secular things!' His face grew scarlet with mortification. 'We are not animals, ma'am.'

'Are we not, Philip?' she replied equably. 'Then, I confess, I have been labouring under a misapprehension.' She dimpled prettily. 'I shall try, in future, I promise, to endure rather than enjoy, although, I declare, it will prove a long, hard battle . . .' She laughed aloud, adding wickedly, 'For I cannot look upon you, sir, without reliving the delicious warmth of our coupling, and looking to future distraction.'

'I shall try to forget, Charlotte, that you have spoken so,' he said stiffly, 'even in the intimacy and privacy of the bedroom. I shall go now, my dear, to my duties, hoping that when I return, you will have recovered from this . . . aberration, and that I will hear no more of such talk.'

But he could not forget. Her pretty, intelligent, mocking face came between him and all he did, rendering him confused and absent-minded.

Damn it! he thought. One should not think of one's wife with the same carnal yearning as for a wanton; a street woman, versed in the lubricious needs of coarse male flesh . . .! He glared towards the window of the bedroom he had so recently quitted, seeing her in his mind, brushing her loosened fair hair . . . But she was standing there, still in her nightgown and she waved to him gaily without reserve . . .

She saw him smile, against his will, then his shoulders lifting with uncontrollable laughter as, shaking his head, he turned his attention upon the puzzled farm bailiff. Satisfied, she turned aside.

At Southerndown Court, the three guests from Newton were received with the utmost civility by Mrs Crandle, and with unfeigned delight by Elizabeth, who had hugged her growing love for Devereaux so tightly within herself that it was a release and excitement to share the news with friends she trusted. She had the greatest respect for Emily, and knew that, despite her brother, Creighton's, involvement in the death of the child she loved, Emily would bear her no malice and rejoice in their happiness. As for Illtyd, he was a true friend who, through his own suffering, had understood her own, and helped her to survive it. It was not merely gratitudc, but love, Elizabeth felt for him: the love she would gladly have given to her own brother, had he shown the need, and worth. It seemed to Devereaux's perceptive mind that Mrs Crandle had made some effort to adjust herself to meeting those friends of Elizabeth's whom she considered to be of the servant class. Strangely, it was Emily she treated with the conscious charity of a Lady Bountiful: the great lady dispensing a few scraps of comfort to the deserving poor. A role which Emily accepted with quiet amusement, maintaining her usual serenity. After her initial scrutiny of Illtyd, which took in every detail of his deformities, and which he received with no embarrassment whatsoever, Mrs Crandle accepted him unconditionally. There seemed to be a genuine rapport between these unlikely associates. Since Elizabeth was so pleased, Devereaux would have liked to believe in its honesty; but knowledge of Mrs Crandle's character persuaded him otherwise. It was, he supposed, more the reaction of one presented with a strange creature of unknown habits as a pet who is relieved to find that it does not bite, and is house-trained. Devereaux could not forget Mrs Crandle's rejection of her poor wretch of a husband, nor forgive her selfish abdication of her responsibilities to Elizabeth. In her relief at finding a suitor for her daughter, whom she considered socially acceptable, she gave no thought to the past, nor, he was sure, to Elizabeth's happiness. Her only concern was to forget the scandal. She would have welcomed anyone who offered such escape. No, he was not sorry that her 'duties' took her to London. He liked the plain, honest folk of the three hamlets who had accepted him so readily into their midst, and he would not have had them treated with contempt, or condescension.

Rebecca, as Elizabeth, was pleased to see her favourites, and held a special admiration and affection for the little hayward. At Sir Matthew's strong insistence, reinforced by Rebecca's earnest pleas, they remained to dine at the Court, and the old gentleman was warmed by the laughter and unaffected enjoyment they brought to his table, and to Rebecca, whom he loved.

Yet, it was to Illtyd that he, too, was inevitably drawn, feeling in his presence, as did so many others, the sheer courage and goodness of him. It was a positive warmth and radiance of spirit which seemed to flow from him; a happiness which could not be dimmed by his deformity or circumstance. Sir Matthew had taken Devereaux and Illtyd to his library, offering them refreshment after the meal, while the ladies talked of the plans for the party, and Elizabeth's concerns, and Mrs Crandle's visit to London. Sir Matthew, who had been surprised by Illtyd's quickness of intelligence and wit at the dinner table, had been even more impressed by Emily's proud claim that he was the finest pupil she had ever had, and a most voracious reader.

'And where, sir, do you acquire your books?' he asked pleasantly.

'Oh, I have none of my own, sir, save a child's primer, which Mistress Randall gave to me. Yet, I am fortunate, because Joshua will allow me to borrow his, and Roland, also, although, I confess, I have read them all now cover to cover, and might repeat them backwards!' he smiled.

'It would give me great pleasure if you would treat these volumes as your own, sir. You may come and go here freely, without disturbance. If you wish, I will furnish a small reading-room for you, nearby, where you may have warmth and privacy.'

Illtyd was so overcome with pleasure and gratitude that, for a moment, he could not reply, but his expressive eyes spoke word enough before he finally stammered, 'I cannot thank you enough, sir. I will not disturb you should I come, nor take unfair advantage.'

Sir Matthew put a hand upon Illtyd's ill-shaped shoulder, saying gently but with conviction, 'I hope, sir, that you will not come too quietly, or in secret, but will make your presence known to me. I think of my books as companions, and well-loved friends, who will divert and amuse me. I should like to think of you as such, if you will afford an elderly gentleman such opportunity.'

Illtyd assured him that it would give him the keenest of pleasure, and Devereaux felt the rare, vicarious satisfaction of knowing one's friends are in perfect accord, with that deeper, personal satisfaction of a man in love.

Chapter Nineteen

Sir Matthew de Breos had repaired to the the monastic calm and orderliness of his library at Southerndown Court, accompanied by a willing Dr Handel Peate. The grounds and great hall were a scene of such bustle and frenzy, in preparation for the morrow's betrothal party, that Dr Peate declared that it defied description! Yet, if pressed, he confessed smiling, he might have likened it to 'the labours of Hercules, performed in the Tower of Babel'. An observation with which Sir Matthew could not but agree.

Rebecca and Elizabeth had seen Mrs Crandle upon the carriage to Cowbridge, where she was to alight at the Bear Inn and take an inside seat upon the mail-coach to London, where a chaise was at her disposal for any expedition she might choose to make. Rebecca did not doubt that there would be many, for Mrs Crandle had taken so many gowns and shawls, and so much baggage, that Hughes the coachman declared to the footman who accompanied them, 'As like as not, she will need two mail-coaches, sir: one to carry her and her toiletries; and one for her trunks, alone, and even then, it will take three changes of horses, else they will drop in harness!'

In fact, she left without disaster, although the coachman and guard were doubtful if the restraining net behind the coach would hold firm, should any of her luggage fall adrift. A half sovereign apiece remarkably lightened their pessimism and ill humour, although such honoraria were strictly against the company's rule. To Hughes's secret delight, and Mrs Crandle's extreme displeasure, she found herself seated next to an elderly lady (and she could not doubt that she was a lady, because of her eccentricity), carrying an ear trumpet, a plethora of jewels hanging about her person, and resting upon her bony knees a live parrot in a cage.

'Judging by its vocabulary,' ventured the footman, as they drove back in the carriage to Southerndown Court, 'it was once the property of a sailor, and one of coarse disposition! I swear I have never heard so many oaths and curses, some of them quite new to me!'

'They say that travel broadens the mind!' observed Hughes complacently.

'Indeed!' agreed the footman, laughing. 'But by the time the good lady has reached Gloucester, her mind will be so broad that they will need to lift off the door of the carriage in order that she might step down for refreshment!'

'I am only glad that the coaches and carriages are all needed for Miss Rebecca's party,' said Hughes with feeling. 'I do not think I could have long survived a journey to London and back with Mrs Crandle!'

'No,' said the footman, as they took the drive to the stables, 'nor would I wager much upon the parrot's chances . . .'

Rebecca and Elizabeth were delighted with the arrangements for the morrow, and had no misgivings about the party's success, for Mrs Crandle had spared no effort to see that all was perfect. There were to be lanthorns upon poles edging the widely curving driveway to mark the route of the departing revellers, and those hung in the trees were to have coloured glass, that they might glow in the darkness, bright and delicate as fireflies or dragon-flies upon the wing. Trestles had been set up in the great hall and covered with cloths of snowy damask, to be arrayed with victuals and drinks, and garlands of fresh flowers, and fruits. And there were seats where the elderly and infirm might pause, while others found entertainment in dancing or conversation, amidst the plants and ferns of the great domed conservatory. There would be a small but elegant orchestra of a dozen musicians to entertain the visitors, and to accompany the dancing. Nor were their more mundane needs neglected, for Mrs Crandle, following custom, had set aside an anteroom to receive cloaks and overcoats, and an adjourning-room, furnished with gilded mirrors, console tables and chairs, exclusively for the pleasure of the ladies. This was thoughtfully provided with toiletries and indispensables, such as pins, and needles and thread, that the ladies might not only refresh themselves, but repair the hazards of the journey, or of a clumsy dancing partner upon a hem.

Upon arrival, the guests would be warmly welcomed with bowls of hot, nourishing soup fortified with a negus of wine, sweetened with spice and lemon, for the night air would be chill, and the travel tedious and uncomfortable. Rebecca, scanning the copious lists of directions about everything from the disposition of the household staff to the removal of ice for the desserts from the ice house in the grounds, and the provision of sal volatile or the services of a physician should it, unhappily, prove necessary, was forced to admit that Mrs Crandle had done the people of the three hamlets proud . . .

Sir Matthew, now safely cocooned from the holocaust outside, and relaxing with his companion, Dr Peate, in the masculine austerity of his library, had earlier had an uncomfortable interview with the young drawing master, Humphrey Edmonds, whom he had summoned to attend him.

'I hope, sir,' Edmonds had begun with ingratiating unctuousness, 'that my instruction of the young ladies meets with your unqualified approval. I attempt, at all times, to foster their undoubted talents for art . . .'

'Yes, yes, sir . . .' interrupted Sir Matthew, waving the tutor's carefully rehearsed speech aside, brusquely, 'I have no complaints as to your ability or conduct, sir . . .' Edmonds relaxed visibly. 'I thank you, Sir Matthew, for your confidence, which I shall hope, always, to earn and deserve.'

Sir Matthew fought down a rising sense of irritation at the young man's obsequiousness, feeling guilt at his inability to like him. Because of it, he said, with unusual warmth, 'Indeed, Edmonds, your tuition of your pupils does you credit. However, I have called you here on another domestic matter . . .'

Edmonds looked puzzled, alarm showing in the usually controlled face, as Sir Matthew continued, 'As you know, there is to be a party here, for the people of the three hamlets.'

'And you wish me to attend, sir?'

'No, that is not necessary, and no part of your duties, sir!'

Edmonds' expression did not change, but heat surged beneath his skin, leaving his sallow face mottled with redness, as if he had been struck a blow.

Sir Matthew affected not to have observed, continuing, 'I merely wished to suggest, sir, that you attend your duties as is usual, in the early morning. Thereafter, you may make whatever arrangements you choose to fill your leisure.'

'I see,' said Edmonds stiffly. 'I am obliged to you, sir.'

'I understand that Miss Elizabeth wishes to sketch the church at Ewenny Priory, and I have received permission for her to do so.' Sir Matthew hurried on. 'I am sure that the architecture will be of unusual interest to you, sir, since the south transept is almost entirely preserved, the tower reached by a beautifully arcaded gallery. Its armorial tiles and sepulchral slabs I found extraordinarily interesting. One of Maurice de Londres, who began the building, dates from 1149. Another, a canopied effigy of a knight in chain armour with sword and shield, is thought to be Gilbert de Turberville, Lord of Coity, who . . .' Sir Matthew's enthusiasm faded in the face of Edmonds' cool lack of interest. The tutor had, unsuccessfully, attempted to stifle a yawn, causing his employer to remark coldly, 'I fear I bore you, sir. I forget that sometimes my listeners lack the interest and erudition of my friend, Dr Peate. You will forgive me. Perhaps you are finding your duties too onerous, sir?'

'Indeed, no!' exclaimed Edmonds, discomfited. 'It is I who should beg your pardon, most humbly, Sir Matthew,' he smiled deprecatingly, 'I fear that I do not sleep well at night . . .'

'A sign of a guilty conscience, sir, or too rich a diet,' said Sir Matthew, dismissively, 'but irrelevant to the matter under discussion. You will accompany the two ladies to Ewenny upon the coach tomorrow, since that is their wish, returning early that they may make preparations for the betrothal party. I suggest, sir, that if you are sleepless tonight, you might edify your mind with study of a history of Ewenny Priory.'

Edmonds had the grace to blush at the reprimand.

'Upon the following morning, Miss de Breos, with suitable armed protection, will be visiting the cottagers early, with gifts of food and drink remaining from the celebrations, as is the custom. So you may delay your morning lessons until eleven o' the clock, since you seem to be in sore need of rest.'

Edmonds bowed formally and, with his face carefully expressionless, although inwardly he was seething with humiliation and fury, withdrew. How dare Sir Matthew treat him as a damned servant! He was an arrogant, ridiculous old fool, who recognised neither true breeding, nor intelligence. Well, he would soon learn the folly of underestimating a man! As Edmonds walked angrily towards the schoolroom, a thought came to him. Perhaps, after all, I was not invited because Sir Matthew considered these people my inferiors, vulgar and low-born, members of the despised labouring classes, without my social advantages. They would be awkward and ill-at-ease with their betters. I doubt if Sir Matthew himself will attend!

Edmonds was a young man with an unquenchable flair for self-deception!

As Sir Matthew dwelt upon the encounter, telling Dr Peate of the proposed outing to Ewenny Priory, the footman delivered a message from Rhys, the bailiff, saying that he would speak with him upon a matter of importance. Sir Matthew bade the servant admit him at once, thinking his urgency to be concerned with the running of the estate.

'It is about the investigation, sir. My brother-in-law at the inn. The bootblack, you recall . . .?'

'He has discovered something?' asked Sir Matthew with interest.

'Yes. It appears that . . . the person of whom you enquire leaves the inn each night after midnight to meet someone nearby, who brings a mount for him. They ride off together, never returning until a little before dawn.'

'You are sure of this?' Sir Matthew's voice was sharp.

'There is no mistake, sir. Yet, because of his duties, and the lack of a horse, my informant was unable to pursue them. However, should you wish me to, I will gladly follow them tonight, for I am adept at following poachers and interlopers without being seen, as you will perhaps testify.'

'Indeed,' agreed Sir Matthew, smiling. 'You are a master at your craft, else I fear my game larder and the ice house would be deprived of their offerings, as would my table.'

He hesitated only briefly before urging, 'Yes, Rhys, follow if you can, but go circumspectly, and armed. You have my authority as justice.'

'Well, Dr Peate?' demanded Sir Matthew, when Rhys had excused himself from their presence. 'And what do you make of that?'

'I, sir?' asked Dr Peate innocently. 'Nothing . . . save that it occurs to me, in passing, that young Mr Edmonds would not conduct a courtship in so secretive and bizarre a fashion! I remarked to you, once, that the gentleman, for that is what he so strenuously claims to be, is all things to all men! Exactly what he is to his nocturnal companion, it will be interesting to discover . . .'

'Come, my friend,' adjured Sir Matthew, 'is it so difficult to fathom? Could it not be that young Edmonds, for all his foppishness and affected airs, has red blood in his veins? A secret assignation each night, riding out in darkness, keeping scrupulous silence? Is not that the known behaviour of many another of his age and gender? I willingly confess, sir, that it offends me less than his confoundedly servile and obsequious ways. I daresay that his attentions are set towards some married woman of good yeoman stock whose spouse is obligingly absent, or some willing village girl, a servant with whom he is reluctant to be seen.'

Dr Peate looked unconvinced.

'Such behaviour is execrable, no doubt,' continued Sir Matthew, 'and to be deplored, but not in itself a sin.'

'Adultery,' declared Dr Peate stiffly, 'is most certainly a sin, sir.'

'Yes, yes,' agreed Sir Matthew dismissively, 'and if I find substance in such allegations, then I will see that Edmonds is dismissed upon the instant! He would be morally unfitted to act as tutor to Rebecca and Elizabeth; although, I fancy they would grieve such a loss as little as you, sir.'

'I freely admit that I dislike the man,' Dr Peate acknowledged, adding generously 'however, like you, I would not see him victimised unfairly.'

'No,' declared Sir Matthew, as if thinking aloud, 'my sole fear is of some threat from the highwayman. Yet, with an armed guard to face, as once before, I cannot think that he would easily risk his worthless neck. He fled, you recall, when challenged by the gamekeeper's pistol, his only thought to escape and nurse his wound. Such men are cowards, sir. They attack only those whom they believe to be defenceless, unwary. No, I fear he is more likely to attack when we have lowered our guard, lulled into a sense of false security.'

'Perhaps,' admitted Dr Peate, 'or perhaps he has ridden elsewhere, where none suspect him and robbing is easy, and without the hazard of powder and shot.'

'But you are not convinced?'

'I am convinced of only one thing.'

'And that, sir?'

'That Edmonds would be mortally offended that you

suspect him of being red-blooded.' He smiled, saying in answer to Sir Matthew's unspoken question, 'He would most vehemently claim it to be blue!'

Early upon the morrow, Hughes brought the smaller de Breos' coach to rest beneath the porte-cochere; upon Sir Matthew's instruction an armed guard was seated upon the box beside him. It was a cold, clear morning with a nip of frost which reddened and dampened the flesh of Hughes's nose and pinched colour into his ear tips under the straggling hair that escaped his tricorn. His gnarled hands upon the reins ached incessantly, the joints of his fingers and knuckle bones grotesquely misshapen, yet there was still, he thought with satisfaction, a delicacy and sensitivity in his touch which none of the other coachmen could match. It was as though every thought from his mind flowed unhindered through hand and reins into the animals he controlled, bringing instinctive response.

His thoughts were interrupted by the arrival of Miss Elizabeth and Miss Rebecca, accompanied by their drawing tutor, Edmonds, and Miss Rebecca's silly little maid, Effie, who, Hughes thought indulgently, was as flighty as a partridge, and neither ornament nor use. Still, the child was good-natured enough, if prone to flights of fancy. Yet, given her background in paupery, who would not try to escape it?

The journey to Ewenny Priory was brief and uneventful, the horses snorting and eager in the icy air, their breath rising in mist from their nostrils, as the mist rose from the frozen dampness of the fields upon the way.

Upon arrival, Hughes and the guard had the good fortune to be invited into the kitchens of the house, and he thawed his bones gratefully at the fireside, glad of the ale, heated with a mulling iron, which brought a painful tingle to his flesh through coursing blood . . . It appeared there were gypsies camped nearby, beside a small stream; their arrival causing mixed feelings among the household servants. There was an extra guard put upon flocks, and water bailiffs grew more vigilant.

'Why, then, are they not sent upon their way?' asked Hughes.

'They come upon a pilgrimage,' explained the cook, a plump, red-faced old woman with awkward feet, pain giving her otherwise pleasant face a look of patient disapproval. 'There is an ancient gypsy "king" buried within the churchyard, or so they claim. It would be a foolishness to deny them a right to visit their own. Besides, there are curses and blights enough upon noble families, as well as the poor, and none would risk their vengeance.' There was an awkward silence in the conversation, with the normal clatter of sound and work strangely magnified.

'It is right to let people mourn the dead, even their ancients,' said Hughes finally, 'the church holds no law against that. Yet curses and such it holds as witchcraft . . . superstition!' He gathered up his tricorn as the footman came to warn him of his passengers' return, thanking the cook warmly for her hospitality.

'Church, or not,' she said, wiping her hands upon her snowily starched apron, 'there are things beyond sense and understanding, good and evil, both. They should not be meddled with, but neither can they be ignored.' She appealed to Hughes directly, 'Do you not agree, sir?'

'I am an old man,' said Hughes simply. 'If I have learnt anything, it is the wisdom of letting sleeping dogs lie . . . for, aroused, they may prove their savagery and resentment, even when they have seemed harmless.'

Upon the homeward journey, a young child, barefooted and filthy, ran heedlessly across the path of the coach, intent only upon reaching the lean cur awaiting her upon the bank. She would have fallen beneath the pounding hooves or been crushed by its wheels, had not Hughes, with the instinct born of long experience, anticipated her flight and reined in the horses to a shuddering stand, where they stood, sweating and wild-eyed, trembling uncontrollably, yet not, perhaps, as terrified as those within the coach.

At once the footman had leapt down, but clutching his pistol still, wary of some trap, as Edmonds flung open the carriage door, dishevelled, voice high and tremulous, to command Hughes, 'Drive on, sir! 'Tis but a gypsy child, and worthless. If she had been trampled beneath their hooves, it would be no matter. Drive on, I say! It is an order!'

Even as he spoke, Rebecca had brushed past him angrily to take the girl in her arms and wipe away the frightened tears, unmindful of the child's filth and matted hair, or of the ill-fed dog, teeth bared into a snarl.

Within seconds, it seemed, there were a dozen gypsies upon the scene, jostling, surly, surrounding both Rebecca and the footman at her side. Yet their enmity seemed directed not at them, but at Edmonds, who, with unseemly haste, was attempting to struggle inelegantly back into the coach, terror lending awkwardness to his flight.

A brawny-armed man, with a shock of grey hair, had appeared, his presence, and the silence which fell upon them, marking him as their leader. The dog was curbed at his command, and the child restored to its mother, a young black-haired woman, clad, like the infant, in ill-assorted rags of clothing, yet strangely impressive, with her arrogant bearing and fine eyes.

'I believe, ma'am,' said Rebecca gently, 'that she is mercifully unharmed, thanks to the quickness of my coachman. She ran, unthinking, to what called her attention, as children will . . .'

The woman nodded, cradling the child closer to her.

Rebecca opened the reticule which hung from her wrist, and took out a gold coin, saying, earnestly, 'I beg you accept this token, ma'am, not as payment of any kind, but in simple gratitude for the child's safety, for had she been harmed, my grief and sadness would have equalled yours . . .'

The gypsy woman's eyes travelled from the coin to the grey-headed man, who nodded almost imperceptibly, and she came forward to take the coin, giving it into the child's hand. At a signal from him, the group fell away, leaving a pathway through their midst for Rebecca and the footman to return to their travelling places. She heard his expelled sigh of relief as, pistol gripped tightly, he used his one free hand to clamber on to the box beside Hughes.

'Well,' said Edmonds petulantly, as the carriage drove off, 'it is as well that is over! Such people are verminous savages, rough and unpredictable!' He shuddered fastidiously. 'You were foolish, ma'am, to place yourself in such a perilous position.'

'In the absence of a gentleman to defend us, sir,' exclaimed Elizabeth coldly, 'was there an option?'

Upon their return to Southerndown Court, the two young ladies were swiftly drawn into the preparations for the day's revelling.

'Fluttering as restlessly as moths at a candle flame,' declared Hughes to the footman, shaking his head in affectionate amusement, 'and to as little purpose. It is to be hoped they will not fall exhausted ere evening comes . . .' Of Edmonds, he said nothing, watching him expressionlessly from his perch upon the coach, as the young man strode with conscious arrogance along the gravel drive to the pillared gateway. A pretty cock pheasant! thought Hughes contemptuously. Too concerned with his own appearance to want his fine feathers ruffled, I'll be bound! But have a care, my beauty . . . lest you find yourself plucked and put into a pot. And with that in mind, he abandoned the horses to be uncoupled by the grooms, while he made report of the gypsies to Sir Matthew.

Only a short time before, that venerable gentleman had been closeted with Rhys, receiving news of the night's surveillance upon Humphrey Edmonds.

'I followed him, sir, as you bade,' offered Rhys, 'hiding my mare and myself in a place where I might observe, but not be observed by others.'

'And his destination?'

'A great house, set in its own parkland, upon the fringes of Cowbridge, sir.'

'To what purpose did he visit?' demanded Sir Matthew, frowning in puzzlement.

'I enquired that, discreetly, this morning, sir, for there were none about last night, at that ungodly hour, save those entering and leaving the house, whose suspicions I dare not arouse. It seems it is some sort of gaming house, ill run, and of low reputation. There is a woman involved.'

'A woman?'

'Yes, Sir Matthew, a coarse, vulgar, young creature, by all accounts, who encourages the young gentlemen to spend profligately upon cards and wagering. It is rumoured she is not averse to selling herself, should the stakes be high enough . . .'

'Indeed!' exclaimed Sir Matthew drily. 'I congratulate

you upon the thoroughness of your intelligence, and will see that your informant is suitably rewarded for his aid.'

The bailiff thanked him, adding hesitantly, 'If you will forgive the impertinence, sir, from what I have gleaned of the . . . person concerned and his activities, it would appear to be the gaming tables which attract him, since his predilection is rumoured to be towards his own sex, rather than young ladies . . .' The bailiff flushed, fidgeting awkwardly.

Sir Matthew merely nodded, with no perceptible change of expression, thanking Rhys civilly, before dismissing him to his duties.

Was Rhys correct in his assumption? Sir Matthew wondered. Perhaps not, for often young men who were ill-at-ease in the company of women of their own station, were drawn towards those who demanded nothing of them save payment for their flesh, in bawdy houses. Yet, Edmonds was so fastidious and correct in manner and dress. Who was to judge? Whether he dissipated himself with women, or with gambling, such secretly indulged vices made him vulnerable to blackmail, or the temptation of theft . . . In either event, he was unfitted for his role as tutor to Rebecca and Elizabeth. Damn it! Why had he told the fellow he might fill his leisure as he chose today, and need not return to the Court before eleven o' the clock on the morrow? Edmonds had best make good explanation when he came! For the moment, his own thoughts were better directed to Rebecca's and Joshua's celebration for those of the three hamlets. Nothing must serve to spoil their pleasure in it. Smiling, expectantly, he went to prepare himself for the arrival of their friends.

Was there ever a party, he was to think afterwards, which started with such pleasure and rare good humour, and ended so unexpectedly?

* * *

There could never have been seen a more motley and ill-assorted caravan than that which set out from the Crown Inn to Southerndown Court; nor one in better spirits. There was not a carriage to be hired for miles around, nor a hack, be it ever so broken-down or winded, left in a livery stables. Even the vestry's gaol-coach was pressed into action, for none could be so ill-humoured as to commit a felony upon so auspicious a day, and were a man so crass as to try, then there was none to take him in charge. Ossie's horses had been begged and borrowed; Haulwen's donkey forced into unwilling service; and every delivery-cart, farm-waggon and funeral-cart was awash with cheerful voyagers. Dr Mansel, seated comfortably in his small curricle beside his colleague, Dr Burrell, was heard to say in affectionate amusement, 'Well, sir? What price your Grand Tour? I'll wager there has not been such an exodus since Moses led the flight into the promised land!'

'Let us hope,' replied his companion, 'that there is not a plague of the great miasma in our absence, for I'll be damned if I will gallop back to treat it! They will have to await my return!'

At a signal from Hughes upon the larger de Breos' coach, with a footman at his side, and Sophie, Hannah, Emily, Rosa and Doonan the invalid, and Mrs Howarth inside, the ungainly procession moved off. There were few children about, and these overawed by the magnificence of the spectacle, or subdued, and inclined to grizzle in the care of strangers. Haulwen had been earlier sent to Dafydd's farm, for the Widow Crocutt was loath to leave her young brood, and Haulwen's excitement was comical to see, for she was to pay a visit to her father, upon the way, at the windmill. Emily declared that Elwyn Morris would be flattered, indeed, to know that his daughter ranked him next in precedence to the Tamworth pigs!

It was Jeremiah who guarded the rear of the carnival, travelling upon his ancient fish cart, with Charity at his side, at Rebecca's express command. It was not until they arrived under the porte-cochere, to barks and cavorting from Charity, who recognised Sophie and the others descending from the coach, that the reason was made known. Jeremiah was conducted to the stables, only to find Joshua and Rebecca already there, dressed in their party finery, before them, a strange, canvas-covered bundle. He was asked to unveil it, to shrieks of ill-suppressed excitement and anticipation from Rebecca, who was almost beside herself with glee. Revealed was a prettily painted cart, and writ large upon its side, the elegant words:

JEREMIAH FLEET AND SON
PURVEYORS OF CRUSTACEANS
TO THE GENTRY

Jeremiah's face was a picture of mingled incredulity and confusion as he asked, 'What does it mean?'

'It is a gift for you, Jeremiah,' cried Rebecca, hugging him tight in her eagerness and anxiety that he be pleased.

'But what do the words mean?' he asked gently, 'for I am not able to read, do you see?'

There was a moment of stillness, before Rebecca explained quietly, 'When first we met upon the seashore, when Mary Devereaux was drowned, they are the grand words I told you I had thought to have painted upon my old fish cart, and they made you laugh, Jeremiah, you recall?'

'Yes,' he said, smiling broadly now, 'I do recall, and I

shall be proud to drive so fine a carriage, my dear.' He turned to Joshua. 'And is my own name truly writ upon its side?'

'And more,' said Joshua, as Jeremiah traced the brightly painted words. He guided the fisherman's fingers to his own name. 'For it reads, "Jeremiah Fleet . . . and son".'

Jeremiah stood very still. 'Such happiness is almost too much to bear,' he said, his eyes uncommonly bright. 'In such a short space of time, to have acquired a loving wife, a most splendid carriage, and a son.' His eyes wandered to the doorway of the stable where Illtyd stood. 'A son,' he declared proudly, 'who can read!'

Never had there been such appreciative guests, nor so much spontaneous joy and unrestrained laughter at the Court. Everything was declared to be perfect, from the welcoming lanterns set about the drive's trees to the warming soup and the great hall bedecked with greenery and with fresh flowers from the fine conservatory. The ladies prinked and preened before the mirrors, sampling the toiletries and scents like the attar of roses as to the manner born, congratulating each other upon the elegance of their dress, and their fine complexions. Even Effie, who had been dispatched from Rebecca's dressing-room to assist the household maids, so much forgot herself as to smile at the womenfolk, and enjoy herself, although never entirely forgetting that she was in the service of a truly great lady, and behaving with dignity as befitted her exalted situation. The tables were declared to be 'finer than anything the dear queen could expect'.

'It was a pity,' said Hannah, 'to disturb their symmetry by eating so much as a bite!'

Indeed, with the elegant swags of greenery and ribbons,

and the epergnes filled with flowers, fruit and delicious sweetmeats of Carlsbad plums, Turkish delight, sugared almonds, and chestnuts in the sort of syrup which Emily declared to be French, and incredibly sophisticated . . . they were, at first, quite overcome. Yet, soon, they had forgotten the intimidating presence of the flunkeys in their livery and powdered wigs, the silver and the crystal, and set about the serious business of eating. There were hams and brawn, capons and ducks, geese, crabs and lobsters, and even a small sucking pig, from which some of the ladies reluctantly hung back, as Ezra declared it looked 'not unlike a small boiled infant!'. There were custards, jellies, plumb-cakes, cheesecakes, pies and tarts of every description. Indeed, so bewildering and prodigal was the feast that Doonan, who had boasted that he would sample a taste of everything upon the board, had to admit defeat, and retire, with barely one hundredth of the offerings attempted. Yet all, without exception, tasted the ice cream, in a variety of colours and flavours, for it had never been seen, or even heard of, before, by any present.

'It was,' exclaimed Rosa delightedly, 'like supping from rose petals . . .'

Leyshon, who was there upon Joshua's express wish, swore it set his teeth on edge more than a tooth-puller's pincers! Yet, wincing, and sucking painfully, he carried off a plate in triumph to an arbour, where none might hear his groans . . .

Such dancing and stepping out there was, with every one tripping a measure most elegantly, and Sir Matthew the most attentive and generous of hosts. As he led Sophie, pretty and pinkly dimpled, in a new gown of softest clover colour, into a waltz, he declared, 'I have long wished to make your acquaintance, ma'am, for Rebecca has spoken much to me of your kindness and warmth to her. You have a most intelligent and remarkable son, Mrs Fleet, and now, I believe, a husband of merit and distinction . . .' His eyes twinkled. 'Yet, I declare, ma'am, it is they who have cause to rejoice in their good fortune.'

Sophie was so pleased and fussed that she missed a step and coloured in confusion. Yet it was a compliment she would long treasure.

'Handsome is as handsome does,' she told Jeremiah afterwards, 'and the old gentleman is almost as handsome as you, my dear . . .'

The orchestra played with grace and vitality, for they could not but be drawn into the enjoyment of such a happy, carefree throng, accustomed as they were to the familiar boredom of the rich and privileged. Emily seemed to dance a great deal with Dr Burrell, Ossie noticed, pleased, although to Emily herself it seemed the briefest of excursions in his arms. Sir Matthew had soon squired Illtyd into the company of Dr Peate, and they were quickly engrossed in lively conversation, for Sir Matthew had determined that, somehow, he would persuade his friend to take upon himself the tutorship of the boy.

Joshua danced frequently with Rebecca, guiding her expertly from the ballroom and into the domed conservatory where he was able to kiss her most satisfactorily behind the potted palms and orchids, to the delight of several ancients who were resting their bones, but not their eyes and ears . . . which they had feasted, but recently, upon Elizabeth and Captain Devereaux.

Rawlings, looking sartorially splendid, was engaged in amorous dalliance with a farmer's daughter from Nottage. Daniel and Emrys were arguing companionably about the merits of pork or veal hot water crust pies, and

Joshua's father was loosening his high-frilled collar with a finger, and smiling expansively upon Dr Mansel, when there was a sudden hiatus. A quietness that was palpable . . .

Charlotte Stradling, pretty in a dress of kingfisher-blue silk, gauzy and iridescent, paled and grew still. Her husband, following her gaze, froze in speech, his face incredulous then taut, with pain and anger.

Rebecca moved forward gracefully to meet her late-arriving guests: Aled, pale-faced and composed; at his side a woman with a dress deep-cut, indiscreetly low to show the curve of her full breasts, its colour and style of the utmost vulgarity. Above it, her face was painted and rouged absurdly, and she swayed slightly as she approached. To Joshua, who was at Rebecca's elbow, she appeared to be unmistakably drunk, a belief confirmed by the aroma of spirits. Joshua's fury with his brother was contained beneath an icy calm, as he greeted them briefly but courteously, to overloud and gushing exclamations from Aled's companion. There was an awkward silence as the four moved from the entrance of the great hall and towards the curious onlookers.

It was barely a moment before Robert Knight, who had been standing at Sir Matthew's side, moved purposefully forward, saying, with ill-concealed anger, 'If you will follow me into the library, sir, and you, ma'am, I would have a word . . .'

Once they were within, Joshua, Rebecca and Sir Matthew standing, bewildered, beside them, he made explanation, saying, 'I see, ma'am, that you wear a string of most distinctive pearls, and a citrine and diamond brooch which I believe to be the property of my sister . . . Perhaps you will be so good as to explain how you came by them?'

'Caroline?' Aled's face was confused, ashen, as he said, 'Will you please tell the justice, Mr Robert Knight . . .'

'Why sir,' she said, eyes glazed and swaying slightly, 'there is no mystery! It seems we are related, de Courcy is but my stage-name. I am, in law, Mrs Charles Dodderidge. They were a present from your esteemed nephew.'

Chapter Twenty

Joshua did not know whether Robert Knight or Aled was the more astonished by the young woman's announcement; certainly the justice was the more outraged, by her claim to kinship.

'I must hope, ma'am,' he said with icy civility, 'that this is merely some ludicrous jest, which you and my nephew have planned to embarrass me before my friends and parishioners. It bears the stamp of his vicious ill-humour . . .'

'No jest, sir.' She came forward, fumbling awkwardly within her reticule and steadying herself upon the justice's arm. 'If you wish, you may see the papers . . .' She began to laugh stupidly. 'I cannot seem to find them, they move about so . . .' She gazed about her, eyes unfocusing, inviting the company to share her amusement.

The justice disengaged her arm firmly; colour had suffused his skin and a vein had risen to throb at his temple, yet there was about him a certain dignity, despite the absurdity of the situation. 'It is my nephew, ma'am, I wish to see, if you will furnish me with his whereabouts. No, I do not doubt that he has married you!' he added bitterly.

'Come, Aled!' the woman commanded as if the justice had not spoken. 'I grow bored already. There is music and refreshment without. Let us join the revelry, for, I swear, this company is colder and more unwelcoming than the grave!'

Aled gazed about him anxiously, allowing her to take his arm, but looking strained and indecisive.

It was Joshua who spoke. 'You will go nowhere, sir! You will remain until this matter is settled. As for you, ma'am, it were better that you returned to your house and husband.' He glanced towards Sir Matthew, who nodded decisively and pulled at a bell rope.

'A servant will accompany you to your carriage, ma'am, and return you whence you came . . .'

A footman entered in response to the summons and, after a few words of murmured instructions from Sir Matthew, led the young woman out by a private way, making but little protest, the two elder gentlemen in attendance. When Joshua, Aled and Rebecca remained, Joshua turned upon his brother furiously, demanding, 'And are you now satisfied, sir, that you have all but ruined our celebrations? You have humiliated Rebecca publicly, before her friends, and tarnished what was to have been, for many of them, the most memorable event of their lives . . . You have brought embarrassment to me, and shame and disgrace to our parents! I tell you, sir, if it would not compound your infamy, I would take a horsewhip to you!'

Aled was so pale and distraught that Rebecca was alarmed lest he fall to the ground, for he seemed about to faint. He scarce raised his head, making no reply.

'A chair, sir,' Rebecca said, taking him gently by the arm.

'No! Let him stand up, like a man!' commanded Joshua harshly. 'For he has behaved like a stupid irresponsible child, with no thought for the consequences!

But, believe me, should my father have access to him, he would long rue his folly!'

'I did not know she was married, and to the justice's nephew, I swear . . .'

'And does that excuse you, sir, for your drunken, public philandering? Married, or not, the woman is not fitted to mix with decent society, and if you dare to suggest that my people of the three hamlets do not merit the description, then I shall box your confounded ears until they . . . sting!'

Rebecca, distressed as she was, could not but smile.

'Now, sir, some apology and explanation is needed,' Joshua ordered harshly.

Aled said, colour flaring raggedly beneath his skin, 'I have been a fool, and worse . . . and I regret it most bitterly.' He turned to Rebecca. 'I beg that you will forgive me, and believe that it was a silly, mindless joke . . . foolish bravado, never meant to injure or offend.' His lip trembled, and he dashed a hand across his eyes, confessing, 'At first, I was amused by Caroline, thinking myself a fine blade to have caught her attention, and to mingle with the careless, sophisticated crowd always about her. Then . . .' he paused, shamefaced and embarrassed, 'her demands for gifts, money, grew ever more pressing. I wagered more to satisfy them and, as my debts grew, so did her hold upon me, with her finally declaring that she was intent upon marrying me, and nothing less would do. I have been half-crazed with worry and fear, not knowing how best to act!' He buried his face despairingly in his hands.

'How much do you owe?' Joshua's voice was brusque, pitiless.

'Well . . . I gambled the money for Father's bull.'

'You damned idiot!' Joshua took him roughly by the

shoulders, and was in danger of shaking him insensible in his rage, had not Rebecca intervened.

'How much do you owe?' she repeated Joshua's question.

'I was on a winning streak . . . I could scarce believe it . . . Nothing I did could go wrong . . .'

'You damnable fool!' cried Joshua, exasperated and clutching him by the neckerchief. 'Answer! How much do you owe?'

'Ten pounds only,' said Aled as he was released, flushed and dishevelled. 'Did I not tell you I was winning? If you will but lend me that, Joshua, Father need never know about the gaming.'

'The Devil take you!' cried Joshua. 'Not a penny will I give you! You shall account for your own villainy! If you so much as set foot in a gaming house again, sir, I will, personally, strip the hide from you!'

It was upon this scene of acrimony that Sir Matthew and Robert Knight re-entered, the justice declaring, 'Sir Matthew has convinced me that it were better to seek my nephew in the morning, lest my absence be noted, and lend fuel to the fires of rumour. I regret, Rebecca, my dear, that I was forced to act as I did upon so rare and special an occasion. You have my deepest apologies . . .' He bowed formally, his face pained and distressed.

'I am only grateful, sir, that you agreed to remain for, without you, our party would have been incomplete, and we would all have felt the loss of your company.' She curtseyed gracefully.

'But we will feel no loss at *your* departure, sir!' Joshua said, coldly, turning to Aled. 'I suggest that you leave at once by the swiftest and least obtrusive route, for my patience is at an end, and I will not be held responsible for my actions!'

Aled bowed shamefacedly to Rebecca, then made stiff acknowledgement to Sir Matthew, the justice and Joshua and, with evident relief, quitted the room.

'Shall we return to the festivities, my dear?' suggested Sir Matthew gently. 'For it would not do to discommode Joshua's parents and your many friends.'

Rebecca nodded, and smiling, and with head held high, placed her hand upon Joshua's outstretched arm, and joined her dancing, chattering friends.

When Joshua was engaged in reassuring his parents about the cause of Aled's absence, persuading them to remain, Rebecca called Leyshon to her side, knowing he was discreet and trustworthy. Without explanation, he accompanied her, as bidden, to the coach house, where the chaise Aled had hired for the occasion remained. He had dismissed the groom and was about to drive off, his face set with exhaustion.

'Aled?'

He turned, scarce seeing her for a moment, so deep was he in thought. She passed ten gold sovereigns in a pouch into his hand, prising it from the reins to do so.

'You were kind to me once . . . a long time ago, when I had no friend at your father's house. I have not forgotten, sir. I offer not charity, but a long-owed debt . . .' She smiled. 'You see, you are not the only one who recognises his obligations.'

Aled gestured helplessly, unable to find words.

'There is but one condition, sir . . . that you speak of this to no one. No one at all!'

He nodded, bending down from the carriage to kiss her cheek, then urging the horses onwards, moved off through the lanthorn-starred dark.

Within the great house the sounds of music and merriment continued, the revellers unmindful now of the drama which had been played out, festive and carefree. The justice unbent enough to request Rebecca to 'step a measure' with him, which he did with a grace and lightness which confounded his size. That his nephew's greed and deviousness depressed him, she had no doubt, yet he concealed it admirably, requesting the honour of a waltz from Sophie, the new bride, and from Rosa, whom he had grown to admire and respect during her sojourn at his house. He smiled and conversed with ease and animation, knowing every parishioner in the three hamlets, their cares and sorrows, joys and deprivations, taking all such burdens upon himself . . . Yet, with none, thought Rebecca compassionately, to take on his . . . save God! she amended silently, wondering if Robert Knight was sometimes wishful for a human hand to slip shyly and reassuringly into his own.

'Daydreaming?' asked Joshua affectionately, coming to stand at her side.

'Nightdreaming,' she corrected, smiling. 'It is near midnight, and soon all will depart, and there will be silence here, and tonight will pass as if it had never been . . .'

There was a sudden flurry of excitement as Sir Matthew, standing smilingly upon the curved sweeping staircase, held up his hand for silence, the whispers and fidgeting dying away as he declared, 'If my granddaughter, Rebecca, and her fiancé, Mr Joshua Stradling, will come forward, there is a pleasant duty to be performed . . .'

A space was miraculously cleared in the centre of the great hall, the folk of the three hamlets surrounding it, their faces pleased, self-consciously nursing a shared secret. Rebecca and Joshua did as they were bidden, their mystified expressions adding to the crowd's mirth and good humour. It was Ezra the Box who came forward, pinched ferret face twitching with nervousness, sweat beading his upper lip as he stood clutching a box covered in brown Bristol paper, and tied, incongruously, with a bow of red ribbon . . . He thrust it unceremoniously into Rebecca's hands, gabbling as he did so, 'From the people of the three hamlets . . . may . . . may . . .' his face crimsoned unbecomingly, then he triumphantly dredged up the words, 'your future be prosperous and long.' His face relaxed into a smile of relief, exposing his little sharp teeth, as he slipped gratefully into his place in the crowd, only to creep out and whisper, 'I made it! Every bit, save the mount . . .'

Rebecca, smiling, opened the package to reveal the most exquisite loving cup of carved wood, its surface smooth and polished as jade, its tracery as delicately wrought! It was set within a base and rim of chased silver, yet it was the unbelievable intricacy of their entwined names, and the carved patterns in the wood, which took her breath away. That it was a labour of the deepest, most affectionate kind, she could not doubt, recognising, too, the effort and deprivation it must have cost to find the money for its setting by the silversmith. They were looking at her expectantly, awaiting a verdict . . .

'Oh, my friends . . .' she cried, her eyes filled with the happiest, loving tears. 'My dear, dear friends . . . I shall treasure and keep it all of my life, as a true measure of your kindness and love . . .' She broke from Joshua's side, running to where Ezra stood, sullen-faced to hide his pride in his workmanship. Impulsively, Rebecca took him by the hand and dropped a kiss upon his cheek, to the spontaneous cheers of all who watched, and even Joshua and Rawlings, smiling, applauded.

When, replete with hot toddy, the visitors reluctantly took their leave, the caravan moved away with Joshua at its head upon the grey. The ladies were once more settled beside Doonan in the de Breos' coach, but driven, now, by a younger coachman, because of the late hour and the coldness of the night. Rebecca and Elizabeth stood upon the steps beneath the porte-cochere, Sir Matthew and Dr Peate at their side.

There was humour, yet pathos and sadness, in the passing of the strange cavalcade. Jeremiah left last upon his shining new cart, a lanthorn hanging at its rear, Charity asleep beside him, dined and fussed as gratefully as he, but on a hambone in the kitchens. Rebecca watched until the last vestige of his lanthorn's glow was swallowed up in darkness, and only the firefly glimmer of the lights in the trees and edging the carriageway remained, dancing and blurring before her eyes. How could she have thought that tonight would be over and dead? Gone without recall. She remembered Sophie's words to her, when she had first left the three hamlets to dwell at Southerndown Court. 'You will still be with us, my dear, in spirit and remembrance . . . for God gave us memory, that we might have roses in December . . .'

Upon the morrow, there was many an aching head and blurred eye in the three hamlets, but none, save the infirm and ancient, could afford to lie abed. The justice was the earliest of risers, for he had spent a sleepless, troubled night, not through overindulgence, but in dwelling upon the duplicity of his nephew, Charles, and the sorrow it would cause the boy's already wretched and overburdened mother.

Without delay, and forgoing the comfort of breakfast, he bade Leyshon summon the coach, and set off towards the great house near Cowbridge, where his nephew and . . . that insufferable creature (he would not, even now, admit to kinship) ran their gaming house. It was a truism that squires and clergy often indulged in wagering upon cock-fighting, bull-baiting, bull-terrier matching, and other insalubrious gaming. In fact, many were their known instigators, but not Robert Knight. He considered such 'sports' to be barbarism: cruelty of the most vicious kind. Nor would he countenance bare-knuckled pugilism for gain, although he was sorely tempted to wreak such violence upon his erring kinsman! The gain, he thought sourly, would be to his own poor spirits! So it was with apprehension and not a little shame that the Reverend Robert Knight bade the coachman drive to Charles Doddridge's gaming house and, if rumour were founded, whorehouse, too . . .

The coachman set down the steps of the carriage to allow his master to dismount then, seeing the unusual hesitancy and nervousness, offered an arm to support him. Robert Knight's eyes were firmly upon the door to the house. He would take the young rapscallion to task, whatever the consequences, and retrieve the jewellery stolen from his sister, Clara. That painted Jezebel should wear it no longer! Had he to tear the pearls forcibly from about her neck, then he would do so, regardless of paid henchmen and bully-boys. Let them do their worst! If he died in the attempt, well, so be it!

He lifted the knocker and thundered it against the stoutness of the door, righteousness giving him strength. It echoed bleakly through the empty hall, the deserted rooms . . . Robert Knight, in fury and disbelief, tried the locked door, running from window to window. There was no mistake, the place was empty. Bare of life. The birds had flown.

On the silent journey back to Tythegston Court, he begged God to forgive him for the murderous feelings within his breast. How zealously and oft he had preached that stern commandment, 'Thou shalt not kill', or wrought fearful judgement upon those poor failed wretches who stood before him in the courts. Yet, now, had he Charles Doddridge within his grasp he would have torn him, cheerfully, limb from limb!

It was the last he would see of his nephew, he had no doubt. Even he would not be so crass and foolish as to return! So, he had failed again. Robert Knight bent his head in anguish, burying his face in his broad hands. Was there not some relief, he wondered, under his apparent rage? He tried to be honest with himself. As justice, he should have brought the young man to trial for theft. As priest, he knew the canons of the moral law, 'Thou shalt not steal'. As brother, could he have borne the burden of Clara's reproachful tears and pain? A severing of the love that had always been between them? He wished he knew, and was glad that he did not know.

At Southerndown Court the servants had been abroad early, and the detritus and disorder of the night removed. Effie had taken Rebecca's tray from the housemaid and awakened her sleeping mistress, opening the window draperies upon a cold and uninviting morn, demanding which gown and travelling coat she should set out for Rebecca's visits to the cottagers.

'None!' declared Rebecca lazily, from the comforting depth of her bed. 'Leave my morning-gown, for I shall rest awhile and pay my respects when I am fully awake. And you shall accompany me. Before luncheon, perhaps, for they will greet their victuals and refreshments with greater appetite, and will be eager to see me gone!'

Effie did as she was bid and left, reflecting upon the indolence of the rich, and the industry of the poor, but cheered by the prospect of an outing in the de Breos' coach.

Elizabeth, who had awakened early in her room at the Court, for Sir Matthew would not countenance her being alone in the Lodge in her mother's absence in London, descended the stairs and made an early breakfast. It was but eight o' the clock, and three hours before her drawing lesson. After visiting the priory at Ewenny, she had recollected leaving her paints and sketch book behind a pillar in the arcaded hall. Yet, even as she had become aware of it, the gypsy child had run on to the highway before the coach, causing so much consternation and alarm, that she had felt constrained from mentioning it. She would ask one of the coachmen to take her there, now, to retrieve it. It would not have been of account, for the objects themselves were of little value and no great loss, but she had drawn upon her sketchbook a likeness of Devereaux which she wished to have framed for herself, and would not have Edmonds see it. It was too personal a view, and too revealing of herself.

Effie was leaving the coach house as Elizabeth approached, having told Hughes of Rebecca's change of plan, but Elizabeth bade her remain. Hughes was doubtful about the wisdom of undertaking such a journey, but Elizabeth seemed so perturbed and so adamant, that he dare not do more than murmur a warning about the darkness of the morn and the gypsies upon the way. She brushed aside his fears, saying that they would be gone but an hour or so, and be back before the rest of the household was stirring. So, taking a strong young footman as guard upon the box, he ushered Miss Elizabeth and Effie within and, setting his tricorn upon his thinning hair, took up the reins and set out, the frail light of the whale-oil carriage lamps falling bleakly upon the burned-out lanterns that marked the way.

The horses had settled into a steady, comfortable rhythm, with the grey light over the sea paling to silver as the sun streaked the sky to crimson, rose and saffron. Hughes motioned towards it, loosing a hand from the reins as the footman turned his gaze seawards. There was a violent shouting and urging from the rocky bank above as two horsemen scrambled fiercely down the grassy surface, one firing a pistol, its noise shattering the air and making the carriage-horses rear and plunge, whinnying in terror . . . Hughes would have driven onwards, sure of his mastery of the leaders and wheelers but, in loosing the reins, he had lost control. The young footman had taken up a blunderbuss from the box which housed the arms but, even as he raised it, the highwayman's pistol shot rang out, shattering his flesh as, face surprised and disbelieving, he slumped hard against Hughes's shoulder, blunderbuss falling from his hands aside the coach wheels . . . Hughes, fighting to control the horses which still reared and pulled alarmingly, felt as if his arms would be dragged from their sockets and he from the box to be trampled 'neath the flailing hooves, but still he struggled to control them, fearful that should he fail, the coach and its occupants would be dragged headlong by the panic-stricken beasts, to end upon the rocks below . . .

The masked riders both had their pistols pointed upon him now as he sweated and strained to bring the horses and coach under control, the horses finally trembling to a halt, with Effie's hysterical screams rending the air, and his head.

'You are mistaken, sirs,' Hughes began, 'if you think I carry aught of value to you, but you are welcome to the few pence I own . . .'

One of the men kept his pistol levelled at the coachman's head, the other wrenching open the door of the carriage and dragging Elizabeth, furious and struggling, to stand beside it. Then he bundled out Effie beside her and, with an oath, slapped her hard across the mouth to still her screaming, before throwing her, dazed but mercifully silent, within again.

Elizabeth had quietened, now, in the face of the highwayman's abuse of Effie, saying contemptuously, but with scarce a tremor in her voice, 'You need not vent your spleen upon a harmless servant, sir! You may take what little money I have, and be gone. I have nothing else of value to offer . . .' But, even as she spoke, her hand moved instinctively to hide the pearls which Sir Matthew had given her and Devereaux's gold locket at her throat.

The man's eyes above the kerchief which covered his nose and mouth gave the only indication that he smiled as he replied, 'You do yourself an injustice, Mistress de Breos. You are of more value than you know!'

'I am not Miss De Breos! You are mistaken, sir!'

Elizabeth's denial was so swift and vehement that for a second the highwayman seemed in doubt, until his companion, pistol still upon Hughes, said evenly, 'A pretty act, Mistress de Breos, and one which deserves credit for its impudence! I cannot but applaud your spirit, but know how painfully, and with what ease it can be broken . . .'

He motioned to Elizabeth with the tip of his pistol, and the man who stood beside her seized her about the waist and, despite her kicking and scratching at his hands, set her across the horse's neck, leaping upon the saddle behind her.

Hughes, cursing his helplessness, would have torn a pistol from the open arms-box, but knew, from the man slumped at his side, that his fingers were neither swift nor steady enough. They would surely kill him, and the child within the coach, wanting no witnesses to their crime. Swiftly, and with scarce a thought, save to get away and give alarm of the abduction, he reined on the horses, the coach rattling upon its way before they had realised his intent. There was a wide passing place not far upon the way, where he might turn safely, if not with ease, and then he would urge the horses back and to the Court, ere they realised his ploy, or came in search of him. As he turned, he saw the villain who had fired at the footman mounted at the wayside, pistol primed and cocked in readiness. With all the force and strength he could muster, he drove the horses on, knowing the risk he took. As he swerved the coach to set the gunman at disadvantage, the pistol shot exploded and with it, the pain, searing his thigh, near blinding him with shock and the burning fury of torn flesh . . .

Yet, he would not halt now, could not. With a shout and a cut of the whip at Elizabeth's guard, which sent the pistol flying from the man's upraised hand, he was upon his way, shouting at the wheelers, forcing them on with the habit of long practice, although pain made him all but senseless to time and place.

As he rounded the carriageway to the porte-cochere, eyes blurring with unshed tears, and Effie's screams ringing out, wild and disordered, the air was filled with the sounds of cries and running feet . . . It was Sir Matthew, himself, who took his hand, then cradled his head, as the servants set him down gently upon the grass.

'Miss Elizabeth,' he said despairingly, 'they have captured her. I could not stop them . . .' The tears were pouring unrestrained from his eyes, falling upon his outstretched hands and the bloodied mess of flesh and blood at his thigh.

'The footman?' he asked. 'The footman, sir?'

But before Sir Matthew answered, Hughes knew that the lad was dead.

It was a murderer, and abductor, they sought now.

Chapter Twenty-One

Sir Matthew had taken swift and decisive action to seek out the highwaymen and in summoning aid for Hughes, whose age and frailty made the flesh-wound in his thigh a matter of gravest concern. Now the victim was safely abed, with a doctor's nurse in constant attendance, and Sir Matthew frequently at his bedside. Effie had been surrendered into the reassuring care of the housekeeper and revived with sal volatile, and now, with a stone hot-water jar at her feet, was lying in bed in the servants' quarters. The face she raised to Rebecca was pitiful in its pinched ugliness, her nose more raw and moistly fleshed now than ever, in her shock. Yet, there was no doubting that a small part of her relished the attention and notoriety she was exciting from all about. The footman-guard, who was scarcely more than a lad, had been removed to the undertaker's house and his parents apprised of his courage; although it had done little to stem their immediate grief. His body was to be returned to the private chapel at Southerndown Court to await burial, and Sir Matthew's provision for the bereaved family had been unhesitating and generous. The boy's mother had begged that a sin-eater be allowed within, with salt, that the lad be buried in a state of grace. It was a custom which filled Sir Matthew with dismay, yet he could not find it in his heart to deny the request, although he knew that Dr Peate would deem it savage and pagan. As a compromise, Sir Matthew bade the family 'do all that was necessary for the peace of their minds', saying that he would take upon himself all payments, in gratitude for the boy's courage.

'We have travelled a long road together, my friend,' he thought as he sat watchfully at Hughes's bedside, seeing the thin bloodless face beneath the wisps of white hair, skin translucent as parchment and showing the blue of veins beneath. The hands upon the coverlet were gnarled and deformed, like the boled and leafless tree without the window. Should Hughes recover, Sir Matthew promised himself as he quietly rose and crossed the room, he would see that a cottage was furnished for him upon the estate and a pension paid.

The voice from the bed was faint, and spoke with difficulty, but Sir Matthew, turning from the window, went to him at once, bidding him not to speak, for it would use his energy and weaken him.

Hughes shook his head impatiently, 'They did not know it was Miss Elizabeth . . .'

Sir Matthew, thinking his mind to be wandering uselessly, said gently, 'Sleep, now, that you may conserve your strength, I beg of you . . .'

'No!' Hughes would not be gainsaid. 'They did not know Miss Elizabeth, you understand, for they called her Mistress de Breos . . .'

Dear God, thought Sir Matthew, the significance of the old coachman's words dawning on him, and when they discover their muddle, Elizabeth might very well die!

He sent every man he could spare from the estate to hunt the abductors, and a messenger from his household to alert the justice at Tythegston, begging him send word at once to Joshua and Devereaux that all from the three hamlets might join the pursuit. 'For now,' he declared, 'murder and abduction are added to their crimes. A hue and cry has been called, and the penalty for the offenders must be death!' The little knowledge of the men which had been gleaned from Hughes and Rebecca's hysterical little maid, he imparted to the justice, deploring its paucity.

Thus it was that Joshua, returning to his cottage from a tedious mission to Cowbridge gaol, found the justice's groom awaiting him at his doorstep. The message from Robert Knight was terse but uninformative, and there was no doubting its urgency.

'Come immediately, Stradling. Brook no delay. Leave all else.'

With grave misgivings, Joshua remounted his mare and rode out to Tythegston Court.

He was not prepared for the justice's exhausted face and air of helpless defeat, as he broke the terrible news of Elizabeth's abduction. Joshua could only think of Devereaux, and what it would mean to him, and of the joyful innocence of their meeting last eve. If Devereaux should lose her now, as cruelly as he had lost Mary, Joshua doubted whether he would find the will to survive.

The justice was regarding him compassionately. 'Your news of the prisoners at the gaol-house, Stradling?' he prompted gently.

'As you thought, sir. The men who assaulted you at the church were in the pay of others. "Men of quality", they said "gentlemen who gave them the chestnut mare in payment for some service they dare not specify".'

'The names of these men?'

'They could not say. Nor were their descriptions any

more helpful than those given by the passengers upon Doonan's coach. They swore that their theft of the church plate was of their own volition, and not instigated by the highwaymen . . .'

'Highway*men*?' echoed Robert Knight. 'You mean that they also saw two of them?'

'Not two, sir, but three masked men, with whom they claim they conducted their business. A ruse, perhaps, to hide the identity of the true assailant.'

'You believe the prisoners?' Knight's voice was unusually sharp.

'Yes, sir. They are already serving their sentence, and what would it profit them to lie?'

The justice's face was suddenly more careworn, as he declared, 'I thank God that wretched irresponsible nephew of mine has fled, and that woman with him!' He ran his hand tiredly across his face. 'I confess to you, Stradling, I had fleetingly thought that he, and that young tutor of Rebecca's and Antrobus might have been involved . . . It would have killed my sister, of that I am sure, for he has already caused her too much grief and heartache.' He gathered himself with a visible effort, saying with contrition, 'How selfish and cruel of me to be dwelling upon my own small trials when Elizabeth's life is at stake, and Captain Devereaux stands to lose all that is of worth to him. Marshal whomsoever you will, Stradling, to assist in the hue and cry, paying no heed to the cost, for I will hold myself personally responsible . . .' Then, summoning his coach, he set out, at once, for Southerndown Court.

Sir Matthew de Breos had rarely felt such despair and helplessness as he awaited news from Elizabeth's searchers. The death of the young footman lay heavily upon him, and concern for Hughes, who had been in service to the family since he and the old coachman were little more than children . . . But heaviest of all was the burden of not knowing Elizabeth's fate, or the whereabouts of her abductors. There had been no demand from them for ransom money for her release, and he feared that, upon finding out their mistake as to her identity, they would be ruthless enough to kill her . . .

With Rebecca and Robert Knight beside him in the library, he sat, restless and ill-at-ease, unable to turn his thoughts to anything but the terrible events of the morning. Then, seeing Rebecca's stricken face, and realising that the child felt that her tardiness had been in some way responsible for all that had occurred, he said gently, 'My dear, it is best that you continue with your lessons, although, I know, you will have little heart for them. Life must go on as normally as possible, for all our sakes. Dr Peate will soon be here, and I believe Mr Edmonds will be awaiting you.'

Rebecca rose obediently and settled a kiss upon his cheek, a gentle arm about his bowed shoulders, before dropping a curtsey to him and the justice.

Scarce had they begun discussing their plans about the disposition of the men available for the search, a map outspread before them, than Rebecca came rushing back, breathless and visibly distressed.

'Oh, Grandfather . . .' she could scarce speak the words for her agitation, 'it is Mr Edmonds! He has not come here today, and they have sent word from the inn that he was absent all night, and his room cleared of all his possessions.'

The justice, who had risen anxiously at her words, face flushed, was now slumped in a chair, face drained of all colour, hands trembling. He seemed to find difficulty in breathing, his skin unnaturally damp. Rebecca ran to his side to support him while Sir Matthew poured brandy, thrusting the glass to his mouth and prising it through the stiff lips from which a trickle of saliva ran.

'You are ill, sir! I will summon the doctor,' Sir Matthew said.

The justice, who had partly recovered his composure, but still remained pale and shaking, said, 'No, I beg of you, it would be to no purpose . . . It is because I feel sure that I know who is responsible for this infamy . . . Yet, I pray to God that I may be wrong!'

Elizabeth's fury at being dragged so unceremoniously from the coach, and the assault upon Effie, had abated now and had turned to anguish and coldness of heart at her predicament. She was, mercifully, unaware of the young footman's death, for all had occurred so swiftly, and with such drama, that she had scarce been aware of anything but her own anger and contempt for their attackers. She was grateful for Hughes's presence of mind and courage in seeking to turn the carriage and fetch help, not realising that the old coachman had been wounded, for he had driven on without pause . . . Soon, she knew, someone must come in search of her . . . for Sir Matthew would set up a hue and cry, and Devereaux and Joshua and her friends would spare no effort. Now, with hands securely tied and a kerchief about her eyes, she lay upon a rough trestle-bed in some unknown place, wondering what the outcome would be.

She tried to retrace the route and sounds upon the journey there, but her mind was confused still with shock, and she could scarce think clearly. She knew that a carriage had been awaiting nearby, for her journey upon the highwayman's mount had been desperately uncomfortable but brief, and flung across the saddle, face downwards to earth, she had been too frightened and ill-at-ease to raise her head and take in her surroundings. Before entering the coach, she had been roughly blindfolded. She had glimpsed upon the box, she remembered, some shadowy figure, cloaked and masked, she suspected, like the other men. Yet she could not be sure. Once within, she had heard an urgent whispering from her two abductors, and one had apparently climbed aboard as her gaoler, while the other took his companion's horse, for she heard the clatter of hooves at times, above the rattle of carriage wheels and the sound of harness . . . Then, this cold unfriendly place into which she had stumbled, numbed and unresisting, thinking it best to reserve her strength for escape, should opportunity come. To her surprise, there had also been a woman's voice, harsh-toned and distinctive, as if, Elizabeth thought, she played out a part, listening carefully to her own performance, assessing her own voice as she spoke, finding it pleasing . . .

'So . . .' she had exclaimed, amused, 'the little pigeon has flown into our snare, quite unsuspecting. I welcome you, Miss de Breos, and the bounty your capture will bring . . .'

'It is not Miss de Breos.' The voice was of the man who had held the pistol upon the coachman's guard.

'Not? Then you have bungled the affair, you stupid fool!' There was stinging contempt in her tone.

'No! Not so stupid, my dear . . .'

Elizabeth fancied from the sounds that he had crossed the floor and had taken the woman by the wrists, hearing her struggle to be free of him. He must have hurt her consciously, for she recognised the pained cry as the woman wrenched away.

'Do not call me stupid, ma'am!' the man's voice gave

cold warning. 'I swear Antrobus did not recognise our mistake, for she was cloaked and hooded, and when we saw our intended victim at my uncle's house, he was ever in his cups! Too fuddled with wine and ale. So I kept up the pretence that I believed her to be the de Breos' heiress . . .'

'But why?' the unknown woman demanded, bewildered.

The voice of the man who had dragged Elizabeth from the carriage intervened, amused and triumphant, 'Because he clearly recognised the virtue of pretending she was unknown to us, ma'am, lest our involvement be deduced.'

'Then this woman is worthless to us!'

'Not so, ma'am, for if you recollect, that . . . cloddish oaf of a farmer who was so besotted by your undoubted charms and escorted you last eve, let slip that Sir Matthew has a ward whom he loves as dearly as his own grandchild.'

Upon these words, Elizabeth was rudely hurried away into her narrow, airless room, and flung awkwardly across the bed. She felt a tug at her throat as the chain of Devereaux's locket snapped, and the woman's fingers fumbling greedily at her nape as the pearls were removed from about her neck.

'You will not be needing these, my dear,' the woman's voice was ugly with cupidity and implied menace. 'No, I doubt that you will be needing them again!'

Her mocking laughter seemed to echo all about as Elizabeth tried to struggle upright, hampered by her blindness and bound wrists, until the door slammed shut, the key rasping with harsh finality in the lock.

To those who searched for Elizabeth, riding selflessly from every small hamlet and dwelling, the winter dusk came too early, and they rode on by lantern light, sometimes in groups, but often alone, scouring every track and woodland they knew, every ruined building or empty hut . . . Yet no sign of her or her abductors was found. Like foxes, gone to earth, they were buried in some safe, inaccessible place, prepared to lie low until their predators tired, and gave up the chase.

Yet Devereaux, Joshua thought with compassion, seemed to burn with some feverish, awful intensity, a fierce energy that would not let him pause or sleep. Sir Matthew had bidden them both stay at the Court, setting apart rooms for them and providing comfort and refreshment for them and all who searched. Devereaux rarely returned, save for some new directions, or to exchange those who rode with him for fresh and willing helpers. As dawn broke, he returned briefly, distraught, unshaven, refusing all offers of food and drink with courtesy, but with a firmness which brooked no argument. Joshua, whose search party had returned but a few moments before and was intent upon discussion with the justice, excused himself and went to Devereaux's side, putting a comforting hand upon his arm, for there were no words that could speak of the depths of his pity and feeling. Devereaux nodded, then turning aside, called together another group of waiting riders and, with a few brief words to Robert Knight, exchanged his mount for a freshly saddled one and rode away at their head. Joshua, seeing the lines of tiredness and despair, and the bruised exhaustion about his eyes, would have bidden him rest, but the justice shook his head in warning.

'He rides because he must,' he said compassionately, 'to still the devils of fear and revenge within him . . . and to curb thought. He is a man possessed, and until Elizabeth is found, will remain so.'

Rebecca, who had snatched a few hours of restless,

troubled sleep, had returned to be with them. Sir Matthew having fallen asleep, head bowed upon the desk, had remained there throughout the long night until Rebecca touched his shoulder gently to arouse him, and lead him, unwilling, to his bed . . . 'Elizabeth?' he cried out as he woke with a start.

Robert Knight shook his head. 'The search goes on, sir.'

Sir Matthew's eyes, tired and still heavy with sleep, mirrored them all as he rose unsteadily, cramped from the awkwardness of his uneasy sleep. 'May God give her courage,' he said quietly, 'and strength of spirit, for my own is sorely tried . . .' and, taking Rebecca's outstretched arm and willing shoulder for support, walked with painful slowness to his bed.

Elizabeth resolved to keep track of the hours and time of day, for she did not know how long she would remain there, imprisoned, alone. She had been given some coarse rye bread to eat with a basin of oatmeal soaked in buttermilk. The tray had been banged down heavily upon a small table of some sort, beside the bed, and for a moment she had hoped, wildly, that they might untie her hands and blindfold, that she might feed herself, but she was quickly disabused.

It was the woman who came, for Elizabeth had identified her step and the rustling of her gown and petticoats. Without a word, she had pulled her prisoner upright upon the bed, surprise and blindness making Elizabeth move awkwardly and cry out in alarm.

'Here, ma'am, since you are helpless and stupid as a newborn babe, then I must feed you as one!' The spoon rattled against her clamped teeth, the woman jerking her head back roughly by the nape to make her open her mouth, and forcing the mixture between her lips. Elizabeth struggled to resist, fearful that it might contain laudanum or some compound to drug her and render her insensible, but her gaoler persisted, time after time, until she was scarce able to breathe, suffocating and nauseous, feeling it run from the corners of her mouth and dripping from her chin . . . 'No more!' with a furious effort she raised her bound hands sufficiently to lash out blindly, sending bowl and contents flying, presumably upon the woman's gown, for she scrambled from the chair or stool where she had been seated, sending it crashing, with an oath . . . A furious dabbing and brushing with hands, then silence, before Elizabeth felt a stinging blow across her cheek, with something raking her cheekbone painfully, then a warm trickle of blood . . . She did not know what might have happened had not the door been rudely flung open, and a man's footsteps crossed the room . . . She knew only that it was neither the man called Antrobus, who had dragged her from the coach, nor the other who had pretended he thought her Rebecca.

'Miss Crandle, your humble servant, ma'am.'

Elizabeth said stupidly, and with such relief that she felt the tears burning her eyes beneath her hateful blindfold, 'Mr Edmonds! Oh, I thank God you have found me, sir . . . You have come to take me away from this accursed place, I know, and to my home. Untie my blindfold, sir, I beg of you.'

'No, ma'am,' the voice was amused, mocking. 'I fear you are in error. It is I who have brought you here. I have long planned such an adventure . . .'

The pain in Elizabeth's breast, and the anguish of her disappointment, made her close to screaming aloud for some relief from the darkness and bitter hurt of it. She had to fight hard to stop herself from running blindly past her captors and out into whatever danger lay beyond . . . When she spoke, it was with a control and iciness which surprised her. 'Mr Edmonds,' her voice was contemptuous, 'how stupid of me to have expected you to behave like the gentleman you aspire to be, sir, when it is obvious that neither birth nor breeding allows it . . .'

'Damn you,' he said viciously, 'how dare you condescend to me, you arrogant bitch! You are nothing! The whelp of a lunatic and criminal; sister of a murdering drunkard, and living upon charity!'

'Yes,' said Elizabeth with quiet amusement, to provoke him the more, 'but, then, sir, I know both my background, and my father . . .'

There was a silence in the room, oppressive and malign, the worse for Elizabeth's blindness, but shattered by the woman's coarse, insensitive laughter. Elizabeth expected retribution, but none came . . . She heard the rustling of the woman's gown in her swift leaving, perhaps at some signal, or furious look from Edmonds, for her laughter had swiftly grown subdued and died away . . .

'Well, ma'am,' said Edmonds, 'it seems you are prepared to fight. We shall see how long your defiance lasts. We shall need your signature upon a ransom note to Sir Matthew. Believe that I shall find a way to guide your hand. Dead or alive, it will make no matter. You will be delivered to him, as promised.' His voice was once more correct and expressionless. He might have been speaking of colour and line, or shading and perspective, in some schoolroom lesson at the Court. He withdrew silently and without hurry, carefully locking the door. Elizabeth concentrated upon replacing the image of his pallid, self-satisfied hypocrisy with a picture of Devereaux. She did not question that he would find her, only what he might find.

By noon, the relentless hunt for Elizabeth's captors and the murderer of the young footman had spread farther afield, embracing woodland and copses, the ruins of long-abandoned tunnels and bell mines, as far as the sea shore. It was while Joshua was searching the thick groves of trees which flanked the highway from Merthyr Mawr, where the highwayman had first emerged to shoot at Doonan, that he heard the familiar rattle of swift-moving wheels and the rumbling of a coach upon the way. Bidding his search party bar its way, and force it to halt, he waited. Then, with pistol raised, rode out from the grove to question the occupants. The coachman was at first alarmed and suspicious, suspecting a trick by some rogue highwayman but, upon learning the nature of Joshua's search, swiftly opened the carriage door upon the apprehensive members of the Nicholl family, returning unheralded from their Grand Tour. Mrs Nicholl's distress at the news of the murder, and abduction of Sir Matthew's ward, was echoed by the whole family, and an offer of help was immediately given.

'I beg you convey my condolences upon this sad affair to the gentleman, and assure him that I, my household staff and tenants are at his disposal, sir.'

As Joshua thanked him and made to ride away, Mr Nicholl called out, 'You have no knowledge of whom these villainous wretches are?'

'It is feared, sir, that one might be the nephew of Mr Robert Knight, and another a kinsman of yours, Mr Humphrey Edmonds . . .'

'Edmonds?' The surprise and consternation upon

Nicholl's face would have been comical, but for the circumstances of the encounter. 'He is no kinsman of mine, sir, although he was lately in my employ as drawing master. He was the natural son of my housekeeper, now dead, and, to my unfailing regret, I allowed him to be educated with my own sons. A mistake, sir. A grievous mistake!'

'Yet you wrote him a testimonial, sir, for Sir Matthew engaged him solely upon your recommendation,' declared Joshua, puzzled.

'Indeed, I did not!' Mr Nicholl's tanned, firm-fleshed countenance reddened with the vehemence of his denial. 'He is a thief and a villain, sir, for that is how he repaid my indulgence, stealing all manner of valued mementoes and small family treasures in my absence. I have it upon the authority of my eldest son, who wrote to me of his suspicions. The letter awaited me in our London house, where we rested overnight upon our return. It seems that as soon as he taxed Edmonds with it, the villain denied all knowledge, yet fled, it is believed, to Ireland.'

'Do your losses, perchance, include a pair of fine antique pistols?'

'They do, sir, with the crest of my wife's family, the de Clares, engraved upon them. You have recovered them then, sir?' he asked eagerly.

'No, I suspect that they have lately been used for violence and murder, sir.'

Nicholl said soberly, 'I regret it, bitterly, and will ride to Southerndown Court within the hour with all the riders I can muster.' He called to his coachman, bidding him drive on. 'Edmonds will end upon the gallows! I wish to God I had never laid eyes upon him. Thief, forger, and now it seems, murderer! It appears he had an accomplice in one of my grooms, a stupid, loutish fellow, who furnished him with mares from my stables, in my absence, a foolishness which took him to gaol.'

As the carriage drew away, Joshua wondered whether he should return to Southerndown at once, or ride on to the three hamlets to see what news awaited him there. Deciding upon the latter course, he called first at the disused shepherd's hut upon the downs to no effect, and then continued to his cottage. Upon the doorstep lay a small bundle, wrapped in coloured rags, which he opened with some hesitation and misgiving, fearing what it might contain. There was no note, nothing save a perfect replica of the half-dyed chestnut mare.

Without pausing to enter the house, he turned the grey and urged her towards the gypsy encampment near the priory at Ewenny, arriving there with the mare in a lather of sweat and foam, and his own heart beating wildly and uncontrolled. He knew from the quiet deference of their greeting that his arrival had been expected, and that he came at the behest of their leader, and must abide by their laws. He had once allowed a small favour, to the fury of the justice, Robert Knight. Now he would claim its return.

With excitement and apprehension surging through his veins, Joshua urged the grey upon the short distance to Southerndown Court. It was a strange irony that Humphrey Edmonds, by his callousness towards a gypsy child, had made himself a powerful enemy among those he affected to most despise. It might well prove his ruin.

In his absence, a ransom note had been delivered, by messenger from the mail-coach. There was no doubting its authenticity, for it bore Elizabeth's signature. The demand was for ten thousand pounds . . .

Devereaux had lately returned to the Court, his pallor

and gaunt young face bleak testimony to his frustration at failing to gain news of Elizabeth. Joshua approached him gently with the news that her whereabouts were known to him, and that a trap had already been set. The gypsies, certain of their terrain and craft, would secretly surround the hunting lodge, set deep into the woods of the Nicholl estate and await their coming. There was a pathway close by, known only to the family and to Edmonds, it would seem, wide enough to take a small coach, for that is how Elizabeth had been transported there. Upon Devereaux's wild, triumphant cry, Sir Matthew and Robert Knight came hurrying, fearful that it was grave news he had learnt, and in his pitiful, anxious state, unable to bear the truth of it.

Within minutes, their routes and actions had been planned, and they were setting out upon their mission. Devereaux's men were to travel by the single footpath which led from the estate to the hunting lodge, and to wait within the trees at a place to be indicated to them by the gypsies. Joshua's force was to ride along the coach-path, where they would be halted and taken on foot to where Elizabeth was held . . . Under no circumstances was any man to take action of his own, whatever the provocation, or to make his presence known, until the gypsies had entered silently and taken their captives, lest Elizabeth's life be forfeit.

Elizabeth knew, without doubt, with Edmonds's coming, what at first she had only suspected: that the three men were those of whom Rebecca had spoken, the justice's nephew, Antrobus and Edmonds. One of them was indubitably the highwayman who had shot Doonan, a man of violence, with a callous disregard for causing hurt or death. She had moved tentatively and quietly about the confines of her small cell, feeling with shoulders or feet the walls and sparse furnishings, so that, should opportunity come, she might run with more sureness to the door to escape.

Which of the men was to be most feared, she did not know . . . Antrobus, whose affected, languid air could be dropped at will? Charles Doddridge, who had fired at Hughes and the footman deliberately to wound or kill? Edmonds, whose dislike of her could make him cold and pitiless, and whose hatred she had so foolishly fed with her contempt? Or was there not one highwayman, as thought, but three, all murderous and depraved enough to kill for gain? Once again, the sound came, as it had done so often before from somewhere high upon the wall, a grating, perhaps, or fault in the bricks that made up the inner wall . . . She would not listen! It was done to curb and demoralise her . . . That strange whispering voice, so close at hand that she feared, in her blindness, that its owner actually stood near enough to reach out and touch her . . . As he had touched and terrified Rosa.

'You will never escape me. I will be watching, waiting. You will never be free.'

She burrowed her head into the harsh pillow of the bed, trying to shut out the sound of it. Repeating in her mind the poems Dr Peate had taught her, the names of her friends, flowers, animals, plants . . . anything to fill her thoughts and keep her sanity, for it haunted her hour by hour, coming to her even in the shallow haven of sleep. She would not let it destroy her! Soon they would come for her and release her, and her terror would be over.

Soon . . . Very soon.

When all were assembled outside, Joshua and Devereaux armed and ready to fire should any of the highwaymen escape, the gypsies moved upon the hunting lodge, silent and sure-footed as the forest animals in their common habitat. The justice had come to stand beside Joshua; with him, upon the coach, Rebecca and Dr Burrell, whose hand Joshua had shaken with the first real warmth he had ever shown him when Burrell declared simply that he would stay, and for as long as need arise, for Elizabeth and others might be in sore want of his ministrations.

To the watchers without, screened by the darkness of the woods, their wait seemed endless, unaware, as they were, of the drama and conflict within the hunting lodge . . .

To Elizabeth, it scarce seemed a moment from the time the gypsy woman was laughingly admitted with her basket of wares to the terrifying noise of battle and confusion; then the swift grinding of the key in the lock, and gentle, sympathetic hands untying her chafed wrists and the blindfold from her eyes. At first, the sudden pain and the radiance of the light kept her blind, until blurred shapes and colour took life and form, and she rested her head upon the gypsy woman's breast, grateful for the warmth of living flesh . . . cradled to her as the child who had so miraculously escaped the carriage wheels.

She scarce cast a glance at the four who stood in sorry dejection in the outer room, sullen and unspeaking. Edmonds, it seemed, had been the worst hurt, resistance, or memory of his callousness to the gypsy child, leaving him bloodied and with a knife-cut to his cheek, his clothes torn and disordered . . .

Once without the lodge, Elizabeth stood hesitantly upon the step, shading her eyes against the brightness of the day, conscious only of warm, smiling faces and her own filthy, dishevelled state . . . Yet, when she saw

Devereaux, she ran to him at once, notwithstanding his pistols and, forsaking her courage, wept upon his chest for sheer, loving joy.

Even as she ran, Caroline Doddridge had passed her husband the pistol hidden in her sleeve. Remorselessly, Charles Doddridge levelled it at Elizabeth to take aim, but the justice had raised his own pistol and fired. Doddridge stared at him in surprise and disbelief for a long moment, then staggered and fell where he had stood . . . his pistol dropping uselessly where he lay. The justice ran to him, hurling his pistol away wildly as if it burned in his palm. He lifted his nephew's head, seeing the redness of blood burgeoning in ragged petals across his breast . . .

Charles Doddridge's eyes were brightly mocking as he said, 'Your aim does you credit, sir . . .' A bubble of blood escaped the corner of his mouth to trickle to his jaw. His grip upon the justice's arm grew hard as Doddridge's eyes opened wide and terrified at some private recognition. 'Uncle . . . please . . .' Robert Knight bent his head low to listen to the thin frightened voice, once again that of the heedless boy he had so dearly loved. 'Uncle, I beg you . . . pray for me now . . .' the voice was raw with hurt. Robert Knight cradled him gently in his arms, hugging him like a child, as he murmured his words of comfort.

Then he closed the cold unseeing eyes, and made the sign of the cross upon his brow. He stumbled to his feet gazing about him helplessly, his face etched in such pain that all about were stilled.

Caroline Doddridge made no attempt to go to her dead husband, nor did she shed a tear . . .

But Rebecca broke away from Joshua's restraining hand to run to Robert Knight, putting her arms about him, drawing him to her, stroking the poor, bewildered head, crying, 'Oh, but it is kinder so . . .' Then, 'It will be all right,' she promised helplessly. 'It will be all right . . .'

Robert Knight lifted a grief-stricken face to hers, 'Yes . . .' he said quietly. 'Yes . . .'

But he knew with the cold certainty of death that it could never be all right for him again.

Now read the following extracts from the fourth in this series of Welsh village life

A Seagull Crying

by

Cynthia S. Roberts

Spring came unexpectedly to the shores of Wales. The sun grew suddenly warm. Throughout the long winter it had been pale and without heat, as if it, too, had been cased in ice; with rivers, ponds and frozen earth.

Now, with the melting of the snows, came a resurgence of life; a quickening of blood and sap. Trees were downy with buds, as softly furred as the animals which stirred within their hollow depths. In the high branches, nesting birds scolded with shrill voices, or sang with such fragile sweetness that the spun-glass notes seemed to quiver and splinter upon the air.

Joe Priday, pierced by some shard of memory, paused in his labours at the anvil of his small forge, the steady clanging of iron upon iron slowly dying. Hearing the thrush's fluid song, so haunting in its purity, he felt such a violence of pain for what was over and lost that, for a moment, he was unable to continue. Tasting the saltiness of sweat crusting his lips, he wiped a leathery palm across his mouth.

It was just such a spring when his wife had first come to him, and now, all that remained of that warm and loving flesh he had shared was his daughter Ruth. Seventeen years on, and it seemed but yesterday. Priday's dark eyes grew blurred from the sweat which ran down the springing black curls at his hairline, splashing in droplets from nose and jaw. He sniffed, shaking his head irritably to rid himself of them, hearing them hiss and spit upon the white-hot metal he worked.

Glancing out from the small stone smithy with its roof of turf, its open front screened by the gates of scrolled iron he had fashioned, he saw his daughter Ruth passing upon the narrow, dusty way, and his face softened to tenderness. He could hardly, even now, believe that this child was truly his, and not some changeling, so gentle and ethereal was her beauty.

She set him in mind of lambs and wild daffodils, and the soft yellow downiness of newly hatched chicks. Oh, but she was such a sweet and gentle thing, filled with compassion and tenderness, and loved by all. A glowing, golden girl . . . His throat was thickened with pride and love as he acknowledged the swift smile and wave of her hand as she led her small donkey to the great pool, fondling its soft ears, soothing and coaxing it over the rough stones of the track.

Oh, but his Ruth was more than a memory of what was past, he thought, she was a promise of happiness present, and to come . . . She was all of his life.

He turned abruptly to the apprentice, labouring at the anvil, his blows striking upon the metal with the clean resonant lightness of a bell.

'Well done, Tim, my boy!' he praised warmly. The boy's face, already polished red as a burn from heat and exertion, glowed brighter than the fire with happiness. It was spring. The sun shone. There was nothing in all the world he would have exchanged for that one rare moment in a perfect day.

Joshua Stradling, the young constable to the three small

hamlets of Newton, Nottage and the Port, was feeling equally euphoric as he rode his splendid grey mare from the courthouse at Pyle. Upon the justice's, Robert Knight's, instruction, he had been seeking information in that dusty crypt below the courthouse which held the brittle remains of long-dead cases. The work had proved tedious and unrewarding, and he had been glad to emerge from its depressing dullness into the clear sunlight of a spring day.

Joshua, despite his mere two and twenty years, possessed a quality of calm authority, reinforced by his strength and stature. He was a little over six feet three inches in height, strong-boned and broad-shouldered, most splendidly arrayed in his constable's uniform, and the singularly impressive helmet, designed by the parish vestrymen. His corn-coloured hair grew thickly beneath it, and his blue eyes were keenly observant in the clean-featured face, his fairness of skin stirred to warmth and colour by exposure to wind and weather.

There were many young gentlewomen within the three hamlets and, indeed, in the Vale of Glamorgan beyond, whose innocent dreams were invaded and made captive by his presence. Yet, if Joshua was aware of the yearnings of his admirers, he gave neither encouragement nor sign. His affection was for Rebecca de Breos of Southerndown Court, whom he had loved as cockle maid and, now, as heiress to Sir Matthew de Breos. She had always been to him a woman of quality, and would remain so, whatever her situation in life. It was of Rebecca, with her vivid, dark beauty and intelligent, blue eyes, that he was thinking now as he rode homewards towards his cottage in Newton village.

The cry that broke the silence was savage and wild,

more animal than human . . . Some creature caught in a trap, Joshua wondered uneasily, or the eerie call of the curlew, possessed by the restless soul of one drowned? The mare stumbled and would have halted, ears pricked back in terror, eyes wild, but Joshua, with a firm rein and reassuring word, steadied her. Again the cry came, desolate, and filled with such an agony of despair that Joshua felt the soft hairs at the nape of his neck prickling and rising in alarm as urgent as the mare's. Yet, at once, he set her resolutely upon the nearest track through the dunes and towards the sound. The going was hard and progress slow, for the mare's hooves could get no purchase upon the fine sand, sinking in its shifting grains, scarce able to breast its awkward slopes. Upon the peak of the highest dune, bounded by tufted spears of marram grass, Joshua gazed over ridge upon ridge of smaller dunes, and to the gullies and grassy plains between. It was then that he saw with concern a dwarfed, unrecognisable figure, struggling along a path through a cleft in the dunes. It stumbled and wove its way, seemingly without purpose or direction; someone sick, perhaps, or bearing some burden, Joshua could not be sure, for distance defeated him. He turned the grey towards the lone figure, feeling bewildered and strangely apprehensive. For a time other sandhills obscured it from view, and then, suddenly, unexpectedly, Joshua was on the pathway behind it, calling out urgently.

The figure stopped and turned, disturbed by his cry, and Joshua was, for a moment, unable to summon his senses to rein the mare forward, so strangely terrifying was the scene. The man's face was twisted with such anguish that it was scarce recognisable as human. There was a wild despair about him, a fury bordering upon madness, and although he had turned, Joshua could not be sure that he was aware of his presence . . . In his broad arms the man clutched an obscene bundle of bloodied rags, filthy and sand-smeared. It was only when Joshua had leapt from the saddle and stood face to face with him that he saw, with sickness and horror, that what the man held was the body of a girl . . .